P9-AFD-046

ABBOTT AND AVERY

Abbott and Avery

Robert W. Shaw

Viking

VIKING
Viking Penguin Inc., 40 West 23rd Street,
New York, New York 10010, U.S.A.
Penguin Books Ltd, Harmondsworth, Middlesex, England
Penguin Books Australia Ltd, Ringwood, Victoria, Australia
Penguin Books Canada Limited, 2801 John Street,
Markham, Ontario, Canada L3R 1B4
Penguin Books (N.Z.) Ltd, 182–190 Wairau Road,
Auckland 10 New Zealand

First published in 1987 by
Viking Penguin Inc.
Published simultaneously in Canada

LIBRARY OF CONGRESS CATALOGING IN PUBLICATION DATA
Shaw, Robert W.
Abbott and Avery.

I. Title.
PS3569.H3854A64 1987 813'.54 86-40492
ISBN 0-670-81624-8

Printed in the United States of America by
Arcata Graphics, Fairfield, Pennsylvania
Set in Garamond #3
Design by Ellen S. Levine

For

Barbara, Brian, Craig, and Warren

ABBOTT AND AVERY

1

The creature would not cooperate. A mere brain stem, it could not play along. By the book, it was supposed to sleep soundly through the night. Instead, lately, it bestirred itself with a scream at 2 or 3 A.M., and only a long ride in the car would calm it down.

It lay in a wicker basket wedged between the dashboard and the passenger seat of Abbott's car. Abbott drove a circuit of suburban streets, down Irene, up Eleanor, across Patricia, and out and back on a strip of fast-food shops.

To stay awake, Abbott grumbled. So deep was his fatigue that he needed a moment's mental groping to remember the creature's name. It was Avery.

"Avery. How'd we get into this?"

Avery slept now, heavily, but the screaming lingered as a vibration on Abbott's nerves. The cry of an infant—how accusing it is, a howl from the heart of the species over your ineptitude. No wonder infants get themselves abused.

Abbott glanced over and grumbled a wisecrack. "Hey! You want a punch in the fontanelle?"

Horrible thought. He was lightheaded from the week's interrupted sleep.

"You want boric acid in your bottle?"

Enough. He might be tempted.

On the strip, he pulled into the parking lot at the all-night Dunkin' Donuts. The light there was strong enough to read by. He'd be wise to make use of this quiet hour and review his notes—get a leg up on the forthcoming day's work. He put on his glasses and fished some papers from his side pocket. Random notes for editorials, some having to do with infants. One said the abortion rate in the city had increased. Abbott glanced over. "Avery, you lucked out."

There was no sigh of gratitude from the basket. No sound at all, not even the snoring that usually followed night cries. Abbott bent low and lifted the blanket from around the puckered face. He leaned closer, inclining an ear to listen for breathing. He recoiled from the spray of a wet cough.

Some new ailment? A cold?

Abbott drove directly home, skipping for tonight the order of coffee-to-go and raspberry doughnut that he had been instituting as a habit on these night rides. A new habit to tame a new kind of emergency. What's life but routinized emergencies?

At home, in the living room, he hoisted Avery over his head for a quick sniff of the crotch. No better way to check whether a diaper change was needed. Olfactory retrieval of the cowbarns of Abbott's boyhood, though lacking any grass-eater sweetness. Mouth-breathing, he wiped, scraped, scrubbed, dabbed, folded—Heath had taught him how to change a diaper. Heath was his daughter, and it had occurred to him that in all of her infancy he had never learned to change a diaper. Women's work.

Avery's cough sounded croupy. Only a few days ago—or a week ago in the blurring of time—the pediatrician had said, "Everything's going fine." Then, the examination over, the doctor had watched Abbott fumble with the legs of Avery's snap-button suit. With a professional smile as stark as a death's-head, the doctor said, "Will I be seeing the child's mother today?"

Remembering this now, Abbott knew what he should have said. He should have said "Fella, I *am* the child's mother."

And now the child was coughing despite mother's fussy care. A cold? Abbott pictured the result: There'd be snot on his lapels as well as vomit down his back, from burpings, and shit on his hands from the child's squirminess during changes. Oh yes, he *was* the child's mother. And failing at it.

He looked down. The child's eyes were puffed into slits. The child resembled, not Winston Churchill—that standard model—but the oldtime actor Edward G. Robinson in a gangster role, the wizened babyface scowling. The face was turned to the side, and the child's hands lay aloft and half-fisted, as if life were a stickup.

So young and already in the know.

Abbott considered staying home today. He'd be exhausted at work; meaning would drain from sentences as he wrote them. He'd grow wobbly-headed in the muddle of his thoughts while, across from him, his young assistant would set a fast and taunting pace.

Yes, he'd stay home; he'd call in sick again and keep Avery home from the babysitter's, and they would do something together, something . . . "nurturant." That was Heath's word. He'd go on jabbering to Avery, for maybe sound waves got across to the child and felt sort of chummy, like a friendly tickle or a poke in the ribs.

No, be honest: He'd go on jabbering because it was his own version of crying, his parallel monologue of gripes.

As Avery slept, Abbott leaned on the rail of the crib, chin on forearms, reflecting. In the popular sentiment, babies are a joy to their grandparents. Babies are supposed to be a symbol of hope. The life cycle triumphs—notions like that. But babies arrive at a story's end, not the beginning.

Abbott checked the baby's breathing for proof the story could continue. It was neurotic, he supposed, his fear that this little half-life might wink out unnoticed, but he had seen Heath checking, too, on weekends when she was home. She would settle her hand like a bird on Avery's back to feel the rise and fall of the narrow little sea.

"Hey," Abbott whispered. "You know about apnea?" He fished in his pockets for the statistics. "That's when your breathing stops."

Shirt pocket . . . no.

Inside coat pocket, left. Riffle, riffle . . . no. Some jottings on the city's tricentennial, and a few clippings on bills in the legislature.

Inside coat pocket, right . . . no. A page of figures ripped from an annual report. Why?

Never mind now. Reach and riffle. Coat, side, left . . . no. A shopping list, last week's. And a memo from his friend, Earl, confirming next week's get-together for sherry and chess.

Pants side pocket, right . . . here, amid wadded newsprint, was the clipping on abortion and one on child abuse, but still no stats on apnea.

Pants side pocket, left . . . no. Oh, so tiresome, the habits of a lifetime.

Pants back pocket, right . . . no. A tearsheet from a Vermont paper, a light editorial on pinball games that he'd plagiarize for a piece of his own.

Pants back pocket, left . . . no. Only his wallet.

Wallet, of course! The note was tucked among others in the money compartment, a roomy space containing little money.

"Eight thousand a year," he whispered to the sleeping infant. "That's nationally. Nine hundred in the state. I should write something. What do you think? I'll write something indignant, say: *This must stop.*"

Wait a minute. The figures sounded wrong, and alongside them he'd scrawled an ugly acronym, SIDS, whose meaning escaped him now. The hell with it. He threw the note into an ash tray.

He returned to the living room and lay down on the sofa to nap while Avery slept. Mother needed his sleep, every available minute.

. . .

In midmorning, when the baby's crying resumed, Abbott awoke instantly, surprised as ever by a keenness of mind that coexisted with his fatigue. In the moment of awakening, even before space-time bearings and the first grope for a cigarette, he recognized the special nature of the cry and felt his legs stirring in response. It was unlike the nighttime squall. And it was not fear or pain—those cries were sudden, as when he had dropped Avery in the sink during a bath last week—a blare followed by an airless, terrifying quiet before the rib cage reinflated with a series of gasps.

No, this cry had a slow buildup, had been building for some time in Abbott's consciousness, and now it was rhythmic. An outcry, then a whistle of sucked-in air. This cry had a meaning. It meant hunger.

Abbott heated a bottle of formula and shook a few drops on the back of his hand. Heath had taught him how to prepare formula. Heath, the daughter who was trying to teach her father how to be a father, for the first time. Or mother, rather. Whatever. On the living-room table, where Abbott now propped his feet as he held the feeding infant, were magazines and books that Heath had collected, a little library. Women's magazines with penciled articles; Dr. Spock's book, of course; books by experts Abbott had never heard of: Piaget, Erikson, White.

Freud, too.

Why Freud? Oh, a great poet, but outdated, surely, in baby lore. Abbott recalled reading in Freud years ago that being fed is the origin of love. Uh-uh. Woebegone Avery ate very well. In Abbott's arms, he sucked noisily on the bottle, pausing only to cough.

In a world of liars (including oneself), in a world of professional witnesses, why trust experts? He seemed to be learning Avery's signals all by himself. He had identified several cries, hadn't he? Award him his Red Cross babysitting pin.

No, be serious; this was a matter of survival for both of

them, the need to understand Avery's motive for the nights of sleepless misery, treatable only with rides in the car. Some mental link, adult to infant, might be found, if one dug for it. He and Avery were both *homo sapiens*, were they not?

Dig for it. Once, Abbott recalled, he had been a fair-to-middling reporter. Oh, *long* ago—the 1955 floods, the 1960 political conventions—but perhaps he could revive the old tricks of inquiry and guesswork and go straight to the source. Go in like the old hack that he was, with no degree, no credentials, no attaché case, just a wad of blank newsprint in a baggy pocket—pants side pocket, right—and a vestige of wonder under his skepticism and his ignorance. Barge in and try to get a feel of things and note it all down.

Avery coughed again, spilling formula.

"Breathe deep!" Abbott shouted.

Clouds of steam billowed around them, a man hugging an infant to his white-haired chest, the two figures naked, wet, amid the white swirls and the hiss of water. The clouds hid the contours of the shower stall, so they seemed to be enclosed in a stereotypical hell. But as hells go, this one was life-giving. The steam would clear Avery's croupy chest, Abbott thought. He himself breathed better here in this walk-in vaporizer.

"Everything's going fine," the pediatrician had said. Abbott's own doctor had been less encouraging in a recent appointment. Walk three miles a day. Lose thirty pounds. Quit smoking.

Quit smoking, for Christ's sake. Just like that—forsake your forty soul-kisses a day from Lady Nicotine. Live, live, the doctor had insisted, as if one's physiology, one's meat, were all by itself a state of grace.

As Abbott grumbled aloud, he noticed Avery scanning his face. The look was unsettling, a gawk showing no human recognition. The big eyes skittered over Abbott's features; and the head, that dome slicked once over lightly with brownish down, wavered as if Abbott were out of focus. It was already driven, this little creature, to process the strangeness around it, to make it—lotsa luck—intelligible, or at least consistent. The human brain, what else does it want but a settled life, a safe dependable beat like the dullard heart? If an object moves, you stare it into predictability. Meantime, you fear it, or delight in it. Delight. Abbott, though not given to pediatric play, found himself willing to strain a little his own dullard heart and to clown around a little in his and Avery's privacy.

He jiggled like an ape in the steam. Let's pretend. Let's go straight to the source. Life was arboreal once more, and he an ape with white fur on its chest, on its sagging pectorals. He emitted ape grunts and jigged faster, bobbing his head. And Avery, the ape's young, clung with a multipoint hold: toes curled, pudgy legs wide-scissored, belly pressed almost flat against Abbott's soapy chest.

Abbott slipped. It was a near fall. The infant skidded down Abbott's chest and out onto the slope of his paunch before the ape's long arms caught its young and secured it. Avery smiled after this ride.

Yes, a rare smile!

"Are you conning me, Avery?"

The smile: biology's biggest con. Only a wince at first, perhaps caused by gas pain, but the recipient of the smile feels flattered and pants for more. The smiler enjoys the show, the funnyfaces and peeks and belly squeezes, which come on cue. Then big natural smiles, promoting wilder antics, tie the knot.

But what the hell. Abbott chuckled at the smile—it was wide, stupid, and gummy—and gave Avery another ride.

After the shower, Abbott felt refreshed enough to face work. He'd drop Avery off at the babysitter's and put in an afternoon appearance.

After all, why break old habits? One lives by values, even if they're no longer fashionable or even realistic. Values like *Day's work for a day's pay* and *Keep your word.* His many sick calls of late had not been lies. He suffered from a social disease called "family problems." People approached, tremulous with sympathy, but retracted their hands. And he could hear the whispering around the social sickbed: "Poor Abbott. His wife took a walk and then his daughter got pregnant. He's stuck with an illegitimate kid."

In some eyes, like those of Mrs. Ouellette, there was censure. Her unasked query was: "Where is this kid's mother?"

Now, rather brusquely, Mrs. Ouellette took Avery out of Abbott's arms and placed the baby in a crib, one of several set lengthwise against the front-room wall of her flat. She was a caretaker of toddlers, as well—at least five or six gamboled around the rooms or lay on the bare floor in front of the television set.

Abbott shouted hello to Mrs. Ouellette over the TV din. "I think he has a cold today!"

She palmed Avery's forehead. "He's not hot!"

"He's been coughing!"

She said Oh, well, she'd check later and mash an aspirin if need be, but "maybe it's only the sniffles! I'll give him some honey and lemon juice! You leave it to me and don't worry!" She gripped Abbott's elbow and steered him toward the door. He looked down at her. A small woman, stout, in a housecoat. A "child care provider," according to her ads. Never say "babysitter," for that word provoked a flash in those dark eyes and a haughty recital of qualifications, including motherly love and CPR training. Abbott, as always, resisted asking whether she was licensed, and whether she knew that the legal limit in home day care was six kids, fewer if infants are taken in. At the door Abbott motioned her out into the hall, where he could speak without shouting. "One more thing. Carry Avery around now and then, if you don't mind. Around the room. He likes the touch, you know."

Mrs. Ouellette blinked at Abbott, who for the first time

noticed black saucers of fatigue around her eyes. He added, "When you get the chance."

She continued to stare. Flustered, he stated rather stiffly for Mrs. Ouellette his correction of Freud. "Love has its origin in touch."

Well, doesn't it? Why did this woman gape at him now, her head cocked? He had stated an obvious fact, long forgotten by him: the fact that mammals are programmed to touch, in fun as well as in the better-documented contacts of torment. Skin-to-skin fun, as in the shower with Avery.

Mrs. Ouellette remained blank. Agog. She seemed to be waiting for some emotion—hopefully a civil one—to swim up out of weariness and fill her vacancy of face.

Gaping back, Abbott rethought their conversation and had a sense of how he must appear to this woman: dry, yes; and obtuse, yes; neurotic, certainly; pompous, for sure.

Ah, the hell with her. The hell with them all.

2

Losing sleep, mixing formula, dealing with a rude babysitter—how had all this come about? How could a man old enough to fit the truisms of "life crisis" and "burnout" that you see in the Sunday features all at once become a mother?

Heath had called one night from college. "I've made a stupid mistake and I've got to talk to you about it. I really fucked up."

A child of her times. She could curse like a field first sergeant or spout jargon like an academic. Though he cringed from the language—either style—Abbott supposed he should feel lucky that he had a daughter willing to confide in him. What had he done to deserve this? Trying to remember Heath, her life, now that she faced trouble, he remembered a vague double of himself, a chauffeur driving a schoolgirl around a circuit of streets—down Irene, up Eleanor, across Patricia—to and from rehearsals, recitals, dances, whatnot. Mostly swim meets. She had been a titlist in the butterfly. He remembered long afternoons in the rain-forest air of pool sheds, where he was volunteered into service as a timekeeper, crouched at pool's edge with wet shoes, a stopwatch in hand and chlorine bubbling in his sinuses. He sniffed, trying to recall that taste, but a more vivid memory intervened. Heath at age twelve or thirteen, making some sort of glum appeal. It was winter. She was climbing into the car after a cello lesson, dragging the case over dirty snow piled at curbside. She said, "Oh, I'm so *sick* of it!"

Sick of what, precisely? The cello? Snow? He couldn't remember. Probably he hadn't asked. Probably his response was a pat on the head, some diverting joke, the ministrations of a wisecracking pal to whom you gripe and show tears but otherwise ignore because of his lack of moral force in your life. Now, facing an older Heath, Abbott decided he had no earned right to dictate any terms to her, or even to console. He could only assent. That would be easy because, even when tearful and in trouble, Heath had a take-charge manner.

"I will not have an abortion," she said, pacing in the living room. "Don't even *hint* at it."

Abbott, slumped in his armchair, paused before nodding agreement. Perhaps long pauses with eyes on the floor would be taken as intervals of thought, preludes to judgment.

She said, "And I won't give the baby up for adoption. That sounds stupid but I know I couldn't do it."

Long pause. Nod.

"The father wants to get married, but I don't know."

"Who is he?"

"You'll meet him. He insists on meeting you."

I'll kill him, Abbott thought.

"He's all gung ho about 'doing the right thing.' " Heath sneered over these words, apparently a quote from the young man. "But I don't know; I might go through it alone."

Heath stopped pacing and self-consciously touched her cheek. She looked stricken, mouth-breathing like the victim of a bad cold, and she squinted at Abbott as if his face might hold a clue for a reading of her own emotions. "Well? No one-liners?"

"This is no joking matter."

"Why not? It's *corny* enough."

"How do you feel?"

"Idiotic, how do you think? Why *me*?"

Peeking at her, Abbott discerned no swell of pregnancy. None would show until the final month. She was a big woman, burly like her mother—those swimmer's shoulders—and her bulk was accentuated by coveralls, that current item of fashion that made young women look like old railroadmen, with eye shadow instead of coal dust on their faces.

Those tearful eyes fixed him again, searching for advice, perhaps, or even a challenge. Receiving none, she turned away in a huff and resumed pacing.

"You can count on me," Abbott said.

She thanked him—"Thanks, Daddy"—in a low moan. Low expectations predictably had been met. She added: "How do you think Mother will take it?"

Long pause. Negative nod.

On the following weekend, Heath brought home the sire. Lew by name. A tall, stooped young man wearing an Army field jacket and a mustache, a bushy Pancho Villa model. He bore down on Abbott for a handshake, striding into Abbott's aura, sneakers impinging on Abbott's wingtips. Abbott looked up at a studied manliness of face, a fine-eyed gaze. The eyes acknowledged the strain of this meeting but at the same time signaled: No sweat, friend. We're cool.

"Glad to meet you, Wes."

Wes? Here, calling Abbott by his first name, at first meeting, was his son-in-law, or rather, his son-in-law-to-be, or rather, his son-in-law-maybe-to-be. Here, with *bandito* hair on his collegiate face, was an impression of stare-'em-down, toe-to-toe impulsiveness, held tenuously in check. The scoundrel who had wronged his daughter. The sonofabitch who had knocked her up.

Ah, well: cool it, as they say. Times change. Morals certainly had changed. More than two million youngsters like Heath and Lew currently were cohabitating, according to statistics probably already out of date. And not in decades had Abbott owned a shotgun.

No amount of cooling it, though, or coolness, could keep

the boy at bay. As weeks went on, he haunted the house and insisted on being friendly. After he had met Abbott's estranged wife, the boy strolled unbidden into the living room to talk about it.

Can of Budweiser in hand, Lew plunked himself on the couch. He stretched out his long legs and imparted a man-to-man observation. "Wes, I think your wife is a very attractive woman."

"Do you?" First my daughter, Abbott thought; now my wife?

Lew sipped beer and passed his hand across his mustache. "Yeah. For her age, I mean." His tone implied that only a fool would disagree that Claire was attractive. Claire was not. In the lengthening silence, Lew added: "She *does* have a lot of presence."

"All I've noticed this year is her absence."

Lew laughed with the ruefulness of a man who has lost his last chance for a graceful exit. "Can I feed you any more lines?"

"Go ahead," Abbott said, "tell me about it." Better the boy should talk than just sit there grinning or long-faced, antsy with good intentions.

"Well, she's so *tanned*, you know. She's all . . . *weathered*, from being out on the beach a lot. She collects those little stones she uses in her work now. You seen any of it? It's neat."

Abbott shook his head.

Little stones now? Before, it was paintings. Then ceramics and handpainted china. It was dried flowers and stained glass. It was lace and leather, prints and pewter, blown glassware and thrown pots . . .

"And she's *big*, man," Lew went on. "You see her and you think, wow, this is a *person*. But the impression I got was . . . well, here's this earth mother coming down on us, on Heath and me, and she's got all these stones gathered in her skirt, and she's coming down on *me*, and she's yelling, 'Kill! Kill!' "

Abbott smiled. There might be hope for this boy.

Claire telephoned once. Writhing over the soap-opera tone of their conversation, Abbott took Heath's side, perversely.

"She's wasting her life," Claire said. "Just throwing it away."

"Things are never that simple." Closing his eyes, Abbott tried to imagine Claire's face. He tried to recall their last meeting—her words, what she was wearing, the weather. No images surfaced. He must have been sleepwalking that day. Among other days.

"Okay, she's limiting her opportunities," Claire said. "Can't you get through to her? I can't. And that boy is a dolt."

"I think he's charming."

"Wes, you're going to have to *face* this."

"I thought we raised her to make her own decisions."

"Oh, you never cared." Claire's voice deepened, a teacher's throaty warning that could carry across a playground. "You never gave a *damn*."

The hell he didn't. He cared. Did she care? Months had passed since her walkout—rather, her mystifying refusal to come home from a vacation. She had remained alone on Cape Cod, a so-called liberated woman, allowing her life to imitate pop sociology.

He did care about Heath—enough to step forth and volunteer to be a good grandpa. He dissuaded Heath from a plan to keep the baby with her at the university, off campus. It would be easier and cheaper, he said, if he handled it at home until she finished school in a semester or two. She agreed that, at all costs, she must get her degree.

Oh, the good grandpa had his motives, obvious to him later. One was to atone for his noninvolvement in Heath's life. His offer so surprised her, in fact, that for a moment she screwed up her face as if to spot a catch. Another motive was downright nasty: to make the absconded Claire feel guilt. Family politics: nothing dirtier.

Aside from that, he thought an infant—such a novelty—would unspook his house, strange in Claire's absence. And infant care, as he remembered it dimly from Heath's own babyhood, was a breeze, was it not? He'd dabble in it and hire a woman for the heavy stuff. Simply another routine.

"It'll be tough," Heath said. "I'll have to double up on courses to finish quicker."

"No, you won't." Lew flathanded the air, a gesture signifying control of their future. "I'll get a job. You won't have to knock yourself out."

"I want my own job; I want the independence, Lew. Get that straight."

Lew scoffed. "An anthropology major who can type."

"Fuck you. I'll get something in computers."

This exchange, as Abbott recalled it, was part of a series of conferences the couple held in his living room as the months dragged on. Abbott felt remote from them, from that big chubby-cheeked girl there, and her gangly swain. Innocents, both of them, face to face, seated on the floor, an ashtray between them as they puffed cigarettes and bickered about their possible joint parenthood. They insisted on confiding in him, but what wisdom could he offer? Wisdom of the aging—what does it mean in a fast-changing world? The aged can offer perspective, based on a relaxed sense of time and import, but the young won't abide such irony—and damn well shouldn't. Sitting off to the side in his armchair, he was a dusty resource for them, to be tapped now and then for a reference, or a laughable opinion, or a horrible example. And he winced over the intimacies they aired, and their barracks language.

Half-listening, he drifted. He dictated to himself a paragraph, an entry for the obituary one composes in some moods.

". . . though reserved in manner and dress, Abbott was a democratic man approachable by all . . . and nowhere was his humanity more evident . . . than in his relationships with young people . . ."

Wait a minute. He tuned back in to the couple's talk. Heath had mentioned a fourth party, an "Avery." Apparently it was their name for the unborn baby. He inquired.

Heath patted her belly, which had rounded noticeably at last. "It's an androgyne."

"Androgyne?"

"It can go both ways."

"I'm not sure I . . ."

"Androgynous, Daddy. An-drah-gin-us."

Was she saying that her child would be born hermaphroditic, or—God knows, nowadays—reared as a bisexual? What obvious meaning had he missed?

Irritably, she laid it out for him. "There are boys named Avery, right? And there are girls named Avery. Got it? We can't go wrong."

"Hey, show Wes some respect!" Lew leaned sideways and patted Abbott's left knee. "If it wasn't for his help, all your bullshit independence would go right out the fucking window."

"I know that." Heath leaned sideways and patted Abbott's right knee. "Daddy, we owe you a lot."

Abbott twitched his upper body. This would be interpreted, he hoped, as jaunty good cheer. "What are grandfathers for?"

"Thanks to you," she said, "I'll finish quick and still have quality time with Avery."

What was "quality time"? Abbott dared not ask.

"And, thanks to you, Lew has time to do something adventurous."

With these words Heath struck a recurring theme: that Lew owed himself an extended fling, which, in her words, would "enrich us as a couple, for later." Whatever that meant. Lew, a senior, would finish school soon, months ahead of Heath. She said, "You can go work on the Alaska pipeline. Have fun and at the same time make us a bundle of money."

Lew laughed, a shriek of ridicule. "They finished it."

"They did?" She smirked at herself.

"Long ago. They went ahead without me." Lew turned to Abbott as if for joint crowing at this uninformed girl, but Abbott had lifted his eyes to the ceiling. He was adding to the paragraph for the obit. Make it: ". . . nowhere was his humanity more evident than in his relationships with young people, with whom he loved to converse—and to listen—with a twinkle in his eye."

There. Suitably trite.

Now, what were these idiots talking about? Heath had mentioned "nukes." They were talking about the nuclear plant in Seabrook, New Hampshire.

"You could go up there and protest," Heath said, "with the Clamshell people."

"Do people still do that?" Lew asked.

"I remember you said you wanted to do it for Avery's sake."

"That was only a whim, for Christ's sake!"

"Oh? What about the Appalachian Trail? You said you wanted to walk it alone and test your inner strength, your inner life. Right after graduation."

"Something has come up," Lew said, "in case you didn't notice."

"Test your inner life—a *terrific* idea. You'd be proud and I'd be proud."

"I said something came up." Lew pointed a finger at Heath's belly. "And I *am* proud."

"After Avery's born," she went on, "and you know we're both okay, then *do* it. Hit the trail, I'm not kidding."

Lew, dumbfounded, swung out his hands in wide arcs and slowly brought them down against his chest. "Look at me. You are looking at a father—remember? You are asking a fucking *father* to go take a walk in the woods."

"You're no *father*." Heath squiggled closer to Lew across the living-room rug. She placed an arm around him. "You're a confused guy being handed a kid out of the blue. Sweetie, I'm confused too. I don't know what the hell we're going to do. People tell me I'll feel different about things after Avery's born. I don't know." She looked around for understanding from the two somber male faces. She pinched Lew's chin and turned his face toward hers. "After you come home," she said, "we'll both have to work our asses off to save for a house. Because that's the only way to survive these days, for a family. Right, Daddy?"

Abbott, glad to provide an unassailable fact or two, said, "A hedge against inflation."

"Right," she said. "I don't know if I want that lifestyle. Do you, Lew? Really?"

Lew's gaze intensified. "For Avery's sake, yes."

"How can you be so sure?"

"I'm sure."

"Get out there and think about it," she said. "All I know is, a child needs a secure, stable life."

After recalling this talk of months ago, Abbott, leaning on the rail of Avery's crib, reflected on the subsequent events. An easy labor—so the doctor said; a healthy infant, and then a period of tranquility—tranquil for him because Heath and friends handled most of the feedings and the rest of it: the pacing, the singing, the rocking, the changing: chores that were simple, and even—some of them—pleasurable.

Then, struggle: Heath now back in school, struggling with extra work and stealing weekends at home; he himself struggling with the care of an infant who had turned troublesome; and Lew struggling along at two-and-a-half miles an hour with a pack on his back, at last report somewhere in the Carolinas. Abbott pictured that stooped, somewhat pigeon-toed stride out in a limbo of trees. And he brooded over a new anxiety in Heath. Now that Avery was real-life, she seemed to have developed second thoughts about Abbott's fitness as a childtender. Witness that library on the living-room table and her nagging about "nurturance."

To understand those young parents, to intuit their needs and the changing shape of his own involvement with them, Abbott would have to retrieve more of their talk and—for the first time—listen. But not now, not yet. The first motives to be plumbed were Avery's, whatever mindset existed behind that rumpled, ruddy, little-old-man face in the crib.

It was evening, and Avery had eaten. He cried, seeing Abbott leave the bedroom, but Abbott by now knew the language of the cries. This bray would soon let up. It would subside into melodic babbling as the infant stared at the mobile that Heath had rigged over the crib. Perhaps, tonight, there would be no bawling and no exhausting night ride.

In the living room, reading the day's *Call*, Abbott grew aware of another sound besides the burblebabble from the bedroom—snatches of his own voice. He was reading aloud to the infant even though he wanted it to shut up and fall asleep.

Ah, well. Self-contradictions were no surprise anymore. And if, by now, he was maintaining a one-sided dialogue without even knowing it, well, he'd keep it deft, organized, even grammatical, to befit his calling and Avery's potency as a rational being. Pretending that Avery could understand him, as his silent collaborator, maybe he'd illuminate some motives of his own.

As he went on reading, an ancient newsreel flashed to his mind: He saw the roly-poly figure of Mayor Fiorello LaGuardia, reading the Sunday comics to the children of New York over a radio mike, during a newspaper blackout in that city many, many years ago.

So many years. LaGuardia, the Little Flower, long dead, and Abbott—then a boy watching a newsreel in an eastern Connecticut movie house—now more than half a century old.

Much had changed, but not headlines. On the page he held, he saw *Urge*, *Hit*, *Deny*, the same old verbs twisting the arms of proper nouns. And, as always, the stories like all stories were full of holes, gaps at which the reader eavesdrops, waiting for clarity, waiting for another story, one's own or the race's story, to be told.

There was no further sound from the bedroom. Abbott tiptoed in. Was Avery breathing? Abbott bent low and heard the wet wind of deep sleep in the seashell. Some days before, the infant's cough had ceased.

Abbott closed the door and returned to the living room to think. It was time to become a reporter again, and go straight to a source.

3

He took off his suitcoat. And asked himself why in the hell, in the privacy of his own home with only a sleeping infant for company, did he still wear a suitcoat?

". . . Abbott, editor of the editorial page and dean of the staff, was reserved in manner and dress . . ."

He took off his shirt and examined its color in the light of the bridge lamp: black around the inside of the collar as in that well-known television commercial, and elsewhere off-white tending toward yellow, like the newsprint in his pocket.

He finished undressing. He held up his jockey shorts by two fingers: a rag half frayed away from its lifeless elastic waistband. No wonder his scrotum had been bounding painfully of late when he walked: no support.

He lay down on the floor, matching Avery's accustomed position for the feel of it. The rug smelled. He was a lousy housekeeper.

Had Claire left him to escape housekeeping? In his new bachelorhood he had discovered that the replacer of underwear and the vacuumer of rugs during all the years of his marriage had not been Wesley J. Abbott, just as Wesley J. Abbott had never been a babytender.

Why, really, had Claire skedaddled? Abbott tried once more to recall in detail the kiss-off—the weather on that day, what she was wearing. They were on vacation at the Cape. The weather was . . . clear and breezy, good for a ritual stroll on the Outer Beach. She wore a dress of some ice-cream color. Peach, was it? Raspberry? Her white cardigan sweater was hiked up in back, short. His sportcoat also hung short, for both Claire and he had grown slightly hump-backed in middle age. They were two S-curves of hump and paunch, side by side, plodding through the sand.

Claire hugged herself as though chilled from the wind off the waves. She was watching him, waiting for her words to register. She had said, "I've got good years left and I want them up here to myself, for my work."

Years? Work, did she say? Arts and crafts?

Abbott was flabbergasted. She said they had paid their dues to each other and, for the time being, to Heath.

Oh, a little solitude would have been allowable if she had wanted it; he'd have nodded okay. But what she asked was no less than a separation. What about public opinion? And his comforts? *Their* comforts, rather, their low-key consortium.

In the old days, he supposed, a husband would have grumbled, "Change of life." Nowadays a husband might grumble, "Women's Lib." But neither applied: Claire had been independent, more or less, with a job, her own friends, and her so-called work. Their Wellfleet cottage could not have been financed on his pay alone.

In the cottage she continued to hug herself, this big woman now oddly girlish, as if scared or self-surprised, or huddled protectively around her resolve. At the same time her eyes were wide with concern over whatever pain he might be feeling. "Try to understand. It's a last chance."

"Last chance for what?"

"It has to be done alone. You have to be alone to invent anything."

"Invent what?" Facts, give him facts, amid this madness. Did she mean a breakthrough in the arts, a success story at her age? No, Claire wasn't that simpleminded. Whatever the motive, she didn't know, or knew gutwise and couldn't say, or felt that words would only deflect off his obtuseness. She repeated words he'd heard before: "You don't need me, Wes; you haven't needed me in years." But all old marrieds feel that way, don't they?

"It's something you have to do," she said. "You try to feel unique, even though you know you're just routine."

"What's wrong with routine?"

"And you try to feel light even if you know you're only deadweight."

Deadweight, yes; stretched out deadweight tonight on the smelly living-room floor after a used-up marriage and another evening of young-mother tribulations.

Ah, forget it. He'd recall Claire and her nonsense later for another try at understanding.

He did a sudden push-up. Deadweight, was he? Then another. On the third, his upper arms began to tremble and his breath caught. Once upon a time—way back in GI days—he could do forty push-ups.

Abbott, get down there and gimme forty!

From where he lay, puffing now with his chin on the rug, he saw the old-style wooden legs of his furniture, some of the antiques that he and Claire had bought on trips. From this angle they looked thick and judgmental, the legs of a censorious public. This public was whispering:

"That's Wesley Abbott down there. He has 'family problems.' His boss wants him to write 'funny pieces' about it. Abbott's being funny right now, trying to imagine himself into the mind of an infant."

Imitating on Avery pose, Abbott huddled up, arms and legs tucked under his body and his rump in the air. Feeling foolish to the point of tears, he got up, turned out the lamp, and resumed his self-hug in the dark.

Now there was another interruption. Of all unlikely events, his sex woke up, semi-tumescent. But the cause was mere sensation, not sexual hunger. It was the feel of air flowing over his nakedness, a sense of physical well-being. Nakedness, or course, was the key to this assignment—air sensitizing his skin just as touch had reawakened his mind in the shower with Avery. And there was more: He felt half-alert for the first time in a long while, even half-excited, going into this madness.

He whispered to the imagined public to focus his thinking. "This is your correspondent, Wesley Abbott, reporting to you from the fetal position."

But how?

With a little bag of tricks—fantasy, empathy, whatever—he would try to divine an infant, a little bag of reflexes. Is there an infant consciousness? It has no ego, no I, no space-time, no sense of causes. It is a nowhere with phantoms—the adult caretakers—drifting in and out. It has no guides, such as Virgil in Hell. And no quips waft about in dialogue balloons, such as those of Eggbert the cartoon.

Heath, for sure, would have a quip for this experiment in regression. Looking down, squinting at the huddled Abbott, Heath might toss off some term—"Oh, a little role-playing," or "Psychodrama, hmm?"—with a now-I've-seen-it-all sneer, mouth bunched on one side of her face, her query to be followed by fault-finding: "What are you doing about his awful diaper rash?"

But, forget Heath. On with the assignment, this very subjective piece of reporting.

Naturally, he'd have to fake it. All reporters fudge. He'd have to pretend that raw sensations could scan themselves with understanding and produce a central I—an I with an old newspaperman's big vocabulary and random knowledge.

All right, a start. An impossible I.

Abbott froze. He had heard a noise from the bedroom. It had sounded like a hiccup. He waited. No repetitions.

All right, back to work. An impossible I, whispering to itself, incantatory. An old wordslinger's version of Avery's babble.

Okay, I am in my crib. I am cooing up at my mobile.

I wave my arms. I blow a saliva bubble. Blublubububu-bupup ppp.

No. Not enough. I need more sensations to make this work. I am in the shower. I'm wet. Warm. I'm slippery all over. I hear hissing. An enormous phantom is holding me, a ghost in the steam. He jounces me up and down. It's like being in the car. Yes, I am in the car. The phantom is taking me on a night ride, perhaps this very night (God forbid) to silence my need to cry. We move along. I sense . . .

Water and wind. The liquid sounds of traffic. A truck, a big rig, is gusting by like a long wave awash, whoooosh, a wave full of phosphorescence. We are driving along the fast-food strip and there are continuous waves and wind. Breezes are eddying through the side vents of the windows. I sense . . .

Rocking. A languid jostle as we drive. And I feel a throbbing, it's like a pulsing of myself, as we idle at the stop-lights. I'm cradled in this drive. I feel the padded creak-ings of the car. I sway in these cycles of stop-and-go. I see . . .

Light. Washes of pastel on the strip, and postlamp blobs of light on the other streets of our circuit. This circle, this rhythm of muffled noises—of liquid and wind and wet light—is my life. I am insulated within the flow of its forces. It is womblike.

Womb, of course!

I'm in a goddamn *womb.* No wonder I can sleep on these rides.

Liquid and wind—lifeblood is gushing to me through membrane. I hear the gurgles of a neighboring gut. I hear a distant creaking—it must be my mother's joints. I ride with her breathing and her heartbeat. Her voice reaches all the way down to the warm bath that encloses me; the sound is conducted by her bones.

This bliss can't last. My paradise begins to tighten; I'm being forced out of it in spasms, head first; my head is rubbed raw from the friction. I'm being corkscrewed down a tunnel toward a void, toward . . . blinding lights! And looming phantoms dressed in white. They have ear-splitting voices. "WELCOME TO OUR WORLD." They dangle me by a foot; they wrench my body lengthwise out of its accustomed curve. A chill pierces my chest and begins to pump itself in and out—breathing, they call it. They flop me onto a cold metal surface and proclaim my weight. All laugh. I've been yowling, arched in agony and panic. Now I huddle, resuming the posture of my life. I try to reclaim it, my life, with a long sleep.

I awaken. One arm inches out. It senses nothing.

I extend my legs, my other arm.

No waters, no sound. Nothing but rough fabric, in which I'm wrapped, and the stillness.

I've been abandoned, and I wail and thrash with loneliness for my life, for the liquid and the wind.

Loneliness.

As discoveries go, it was shamefully obvious.

It confirmed his earlier guess that Avery was lonely—that was all—and needed touch. Any mother could have told him, he supposed (excluding Mrs. Ouellette), or maybe some of Heath's academic tomes or women's magazines stacked on the living-room table.

Maybe he was wrong, or oversimplifying, but look at the results over the past week: less night bawling now and more smiles, conning him, as he increased his walkabouts with Avery and lulled the kid to sleep with bedtime stories, his cranky commentaries at cribside.

The night crying could have been caused by any early-life indisposition, now being outgrown. Nonetheless, why not give credit? Let all the wire services transmit a bulletin: ABBOTT HAS DONE SOMETHING RIGHT.

"Infants need it! The touch I told you about!"

He had to shout over the din of toddlers and television in Mrs. Ouellette's flat. There were at least seven small bodies today, not counting the babies in cribs along the front-room wall, although he may have counted one or two of the ambulatory ones more than once as they scurried in and out of the room.

He had new instructions for Mrs. Ouellette, that weary babysitter. He had asked her two weeks ago to carry Avery around now and then; today, he asked her to increase these brief attentions to, say, once an hour—"when you get the chance."

Mrs. Ouellette, in a housecoat, her hair disarrayed and her eyes puffy, snatched Avery out of Abbott's arms and placed him in a crib. Then she turned, gaping in that familiar way—a look of astonishment, or exasperation, the head cocked, the jaw adroop—sustained as if she were collecting the last of her energy for a response, hopefully civil. Finally, a response came, an uncivil smirk. She said, "Anything you say, Mr. Abbott."

Oh, come now. Was his request so unreasonable? He should say, "Where's your license, Mrs. Ouellette?" Or: "There are too many kids here. You're breaking the law."

No, don't. Have a heart. The fault was his, in having hired this woman, to whom his motherhood seemed to be a scandal or a joke. He had been indifferent to think that her zoo with its proliferating brats was a suitable place for Avery.

It wasn't, and the proof appeared several days later: a bruise that Abbott discovered during a shower, a purple blotch with a red center on Avery's thigh. Since he hadn't dropped Avery recently, and since he had quashed, so far, all impulses to swat him, the injury must have been inflicted at Mrs. Ouellette's, probably when she was out of the room for a john break or a fit of nerves. It was a pinch, delivered probably by one of the brats, maybe as the others gathered around to giggle at the screams. Mammals love to touch.

"I won't take you back there," Abbott said. He leaned on the rail of the crib and outlined his plans as part of the night's commentary.

"I'll make some polite excuse to her. We'll hire somebody new. More attentive. What do you think?"

Avery's head wobbled as—ever alert, ever uncomprehending—he made an anxious visual search of Abbott's face, as if tallying the features or trying to match pieces of a puzzle. Then, as Abbott held the bottle for Avery to drink, the gaze lidded over greedily and turned inward.

"I'll take the day off to look," Abbott said. "Maybe two days off. If I had the guts and any money, I'd quit and take the job myself."

A peculiar notion. After saying it, reflecting on it, Abbott recalled what his friend Earl had said on a recent night out—one of Abbott's precious weekly nights out for chess and conversation at Earl's apartment.

Earl had said, "Old loners like us can have dogs but not people."

Poor Earl. Morose, of late.

"You'll get too attached," Earl had added. "Somehow you'll exploit that kid."

4

Earl fondled the joints of his right middle finger. "Bone spur," he said. "Goddamn arthritis."

Abbott, oblivious, set up the chess pieces.

"Did you hear me?" Earl yanked at the finger as if a ring were stuck on the middle joint. "Sonofabitch hurts."

"Maybe it's the non-crippling kind."

"First my knees, now my finger."

"Can you still type?"

"Is that supposed to be a consolation?"

"Make your move," Abbott said.

Health complaints from Earl were rare. Age showed in his face but not in his body, the body of a scrappy runt quick in his movements. The sore finger straightened itself and prodded the white king's pawn two spaces forward. Abbott hunched over the board. For days he had awaited this moment—the opening of the weekly game. At home, during Avery's naps, he had practiced a variation of the Sicilian Defense, his latest weapon in a long effort to lift his average against Earl, a onetime club-level player.

Earl showed no surprise as Abbott won center control of the game in the opening. Glancing up, Abbott saw that his friend was studying, not the finger any longer, and not the game, but Abbott himself—Abbott's chest—with a look of sorrowing concern. "For Christ's sake," Earl said, "look at yourself."

Abbott peered down at his shirtfront. Had Avery spit up on him, unbeknownst?

Earl said, "You've got the shakes."

It was true. Though motionless now, Abbott caught a sense of his earlier tension: crossed leg jiggling, fingers plucking at his double chin, eyes strained to the point of headache. It was as though he were playing for his life in this casual game.

"Pathetic," Earl said. "You need some excitement in your life."

"I get enough excitement."

Earl sniggered. "Robbing the cradle." He added: "The infant mewling in its nurse's arms."

"Puking," Abbott said.

"That, too."

"No, you forgot 'puking.' I think the line is 'mewling and puking.' "

"You sure?" Earl tensed, and his voice thickened as in response to an insult. Abbott tried to neutralize his own expression in the face of this heat. Then Earl cooled off; he shrugged in calm acceptance of the correction. Normally, this old editor would have continued to bristle if second-guessed. He would have called for a bet, waggling his arm for the handshake; he would have scurried like a monkey to his reference books in the shelves along the wall. And, if proved right, he would gloat, retracting his upper lip from his teeth in the grimace he wore when savaging young reporters.

Earl poured his third sherry of the evening and resumed the game. Soon his indifferent moves ensured an easy and joyless checkmate for Abbott.

"You win; live it up." Earl lay down his king. "Did you read about Dunning?"

Dunning. Was that a wrinkle in chess, like castling?

Earl refreshed Abbott's memory. "Real-estate man. Killed in a crash."

"Ex-councilman."

"Right. Don't you read our own rag?"

"Not if I can help it. Sometimes I read it to my grandson."

Sourly, Earl said, "Cute," then: "It was a kamikaze crash."

"How do you know?"

"The cops know. And the insurance guys, but they'll have to pay anyway. You know the scenario."

"A one-car crash," Abbott said.

"Right. No passengers. It was classic."

"Into an abutment."

"On I-95. On a rainy night."

"No skid marks."

"None."

"It's too bad."

"What's bad about it? He did it right." Earl clutched an imaginary wheel in his hands and hunched over it. "You don't dare survive and be a vegetable. You've got to gun right in there full speed, full tilt." Earl loosened one hand from the wheel and waved himself on.

"Like an emperor on his horse," Abbott said. "Leading a charge."

"You *got* it. Take a bow."

"Or like a kid on the crest of his glands."

"Right! Or like a man on top of his job."

Now they were clicking: Abbott and Earl, the comedy team. Abbott imagined them—one stout, the other scrawny—in top hats, or clown ruffles, during such patter. They were good at it, provided the humor was black.

For instance, suicide. Was Earl, so morose of late, weighing that option? Maybe. An ex-family man, out of touch, alone, tired of his work. Dying is one's final obligation. If a friend, rational, opts like a good Roman for a quick and responsible exit rather than a slow death on his feet, well, what can you say?

Abbott said, "What the hell are you doing?"

Earl had stepped over to the television set and was fumbling with the videocassette recorder. They never watched television on their evenings except for major sports events that Earl taped. "Putting some excitement in your life," he said. "A few laughs, anyway."

He had put on a sex film. Abbott slouched in his chair. "I forgot my dirty raincoat."

"Shut up and watch the fucking movie."

Wasn't it enough that Earl patronized the massage parlors; must he also subject Abbott to pornography? Then again, what are friends for? Friends tolerate minor foibles.

Abbott watched, snorting along with Earl at the film's inadvertent humor, its artlessness. Two old hypocrites, Abbott thought, playing critic but at the same time priapic, and a bit squeamish about this, avoiding each other's eyes like strangers in a lavatory choosing urinals at a distance. For Abbott, the film's initial arousal soon gave way to boredom and that detachment of mind in which sex and the body appear absurd. In this mood, estranged, hardened as if to report an execution, he ceased laughing.

"Watch the bozo with the tattoos," Earl said. "He's a cattle boss."

A sharp observation. The actor, in putting a woman through a quick run-through of positions, cued her with little slaps on the flank. How many times had Earl screened this film?

Earl announced the finale was coming up. "It's too much."

Indeed. The flank-slapper approached two women on a bed who were enwrapped in a "69" position. He took the girl atop, anally, his testicles dangling over the forehead of the undergirl. The undergirl, tongue out, wagged her head in a show of passion like a wet dog shaking itself as the man withdrew to ejaculate on her face.

"Off!" Abbott yelled. "Turn the goddamn thing off!"

Earl, shrugging, stepped over to the set and turned it off.

First Amendment or no, Abbott thought, such footage

should be banned. "What's next?" he said. "To follow that act, you'd need a murder."

"Wrong," Earl said. "To follow that act, all you do is throw the kid a towel. You sound like Mary Worth."

Who in hell was Mary Worth? Abbott remembered: that matronly moralist of the comics.

"But you're right," Earl said. "These flicks are no good. You need a live one for real fantasy, and I'm not talking hookers."

Whatever that meant.

Earl returned to his chair and poured himself another sherry. A long interval of silence and glum drinking followed, in which Earl appeared to be framing an argument in his mind. His hands and lips moved; his eyes shifted about. At the same time, Abbott reflected on the ruins of this precious evening out. All he had wanted was a game of chess and some conversation. For himself and Earl, at their best, conversation was a joyride. No shoptalk, no personal soap operas, no despair over the day-to-day—true friends omit such dreck and revive whatever united them in the first place. This, for himself and Earl, was a shared heyday over which they could fly free, setting things to rights. During the Korean War, in which both had served, were MacArthur's objectives right or wrong? Which was the best of Adlai Stevenson's great speeches in the '52 campaign? Which was Faulkner's best novel? In what round of the rubber match did Tony Zale knock out Rocky Graziano?

Apart, he and Earl were solitary nobodies. Together, they were the two sides of a bright, if outdated, coin, like, say, that ancient medallion pairing Homer, the Great Cheerleader, with Archilochos, the Great Malcontent. They were political strategists, armchair generals, critics, sports archivists—freewheeling curators of a lively museum open once a week, only to them.

Now, across the room in his chair, Earl mumbled half-drunkenly. "What you need is a young girl. An avatar of the girlfriends of your youth. Do you know what I'm saying?"

Abbott knew only that it sounded sick.

"The same powerful feelings, but this time under control. A trip back home. Do you follow me?"

No, Abbott didn't follow, and if he was Mary Worth, then Earl was the quintessential dirty old man.

Earl's eyes blearily scanned Abbott's chest. "My live one will have a friend. I'll fix you up."

"No jailbait." A joke, this, but instead of topping it, Earl gave a prolonged, prudent nod, with his lips tight. His breathing had become slow and audible. Although his eyes remained open, now fixed midway to Abbott, he seemed to have fallen asleep.

Ah, well. Abbott tucked his chessboard under his arm and left for home.

Earl would sober up tomorrow. Maybe he had needed this lapse. Maybe he would shake off his gloom and snap back to his old playful-ornery self. Maybe he'd get a refund for his vile movie.

And next week, as always, at the appointed hour, he and Abbott would reopen the museum. Their civilized routine would prevail.

At home, everyone was asleep. Heath had come home for the night to spell Abbott off for his evening out. The only sound from Avery's bedroom was an occasional lone hiccup.

In the living room, Abbott lay his chessboard on the cluttered table, where its lacquered surface gathered light from the bridge lamp and caught his eye. He rubbed his fingers over nicks in the shine. For years he had lugged this board to and from Earl's each week. It was a handsome piece of work: walnut, almost two feet across, and each of the sixty-four squares was a separate inlay. It had been made by some forebear—who? Some checkers-loving great-uncle or second cousin who had stolen the time from chores. And this family heirloom, the only one Abbott knew of, had wended its way down to him, the last of his line along with his two older brothers. They, Dana and Keith, had gone to Maine long ago to jacklight deer and grow Christmas trees for a living. Abbott hadn't, in recent years, received a Christmas card.

He went to the bathroom, locked the door, and settled himself on the bowl. Though ugly, Earl's film had awakened a sleeping libido, an itch to be scratched. Abbott closed his eyes to find an image for this task, hopefully one from the start of the film, when the performers were still acceptable as fantasies, as facsimiles of the human. He saw a woman bestriding a man. Erotic—not the hobbyhorse bounding so much as the way she leaned back at the peak of it, her long hair a glinty horsetail spill down a spine beautifully arched, and the face tilted way back in laughter. Such high spirits had not been drug-induced in some sleaze factory; this image, he realized, came not from the film but from his memory, some long-ago girlfriend riding a carnival Whip or something. Sure. What was her name?

Never mind. A name search might dispel this loveliness. Hold on to it.

5

Abbott leaned over the rail of the crib. It was cribside news time. "We're going to see your old man soon—out on the trail. Aren't you thrilled?"

Avery's eyes searched. They skittered in what seemed to be alarm; then, finding Abbott's face, they warmed with recognition, and Avery smiled.

"Conning me?" Abbott reached down and tickled Avery's toes, which recoiled. "We've got new boots for him. He keeps wearing out boots—must be dragging his feet. We're his outfitters. We'll take food, too; freeze dried. Goddamn expensive."

Abbott lounged against the rail. This was a nightly pleasure, bringing Avery up to date on the outside world, what Abbott knew of it. "We'll take him some cold beer, too. The kid will like that."

Responding to Avery's grin, Abbott worked his own mouth, making clown faces. He clicked his upper dentures, then ran his tongue over them. Did funnyface have halitosis tonight? No; when he leaned down and breathed at the infant, there was no eloquent grimace; instead, a hiccuping chortle deep in Avery's throat, and a twitching as if the slug-shaped body were trying to spring upright for a hug.

"Relax." Abbott lay the weight of his hand on Avery's belly. "You see, his friends have been supplying him and now it's our turn. We're supposed to meet him at a crossroads in the Berkshires. Your mother drew us a map. Sure as hell, we'll get lost."

Excusing himself—"Don't go away"—Abbott went to the living room, picked up an apparatus of metal tubing and fabric from under the table, and returned to the crib. "See? This is a baby carrier. Ba-by car-ri-er. With this, I'll carry you on my back and we'll hike a little way with your father. Until I keel over."

Abbott adjusted the straps and shrugged the carrier into place on his shoulders. "One-size-fits-all. I found it in the closet." He squirmed out of the carrier and held it over Avery, dangling it from a finger as the baby haltingly reached up to fondle the fabric. "Your grandmother used to carry your mother around in it at the beach. Years ago."

Abbott returned the carrier to the closet and checked his watch. Although feeding time was near, Avery had not yet cried. In recent weeks he had cried less and less, a healthy sign: security amid one's habits.

Abbott warmed some milk. Returning to the crib, he saw Avery's eyes darting about, alerted by the footsteps. When Abbott reappeared over the crib rail, the eyes flashed again in recognition that was followed by a smile, a gurgling, a speed-up in the bicycling of the fat legs. Then Avery spotted the bottle and his body shuddered excitedly and both hands groped, rising in short jerks. Avery could hold a bottle unaided now, another advance in growth. Abbott felt an impulse to start taking notes on these developments.

"What do you really see?" he asked.

The baby's eyes drowsed, half-lidded. A blue vein beat in the large, domed, white brow.

"What do you feel?"

Avery's cheeks pulsed as he sucked on the bottle.

It was time for another assignment, another attempt to feel this creature's experience rather than simply make guesses from its behavior.

Abbott lay down on the living-room floor. This assignment would be easy—no need to strip down like the last time and do a fetal. All this job required was a field of vision.

Lying on his back, Abbott looked up at the ceiling. It was nubbly plaster, yellowish with nicotine stain in the corner over his armchair. He imagined the ceiling as a blank.

"Like a window," he said, reporting on this vision to Avery in the bedroom. "It's blurred a little on the sides, this window. The blurs are the shadows of my nose. I see them when I move my eyes—transparent shadows, like very faint smears on glass."

Now Abbott raised his hands and moved them slowly, jerkily, imitating Avery's hand movements, into the field of vision from the sides. He studied the inching progress of his right hand.

"It's an instrument, a pronged instrument, a sort of claw. Claw, yes. It's like the claw machines I used to play as a kid. For a penny. Or was it a nickel? I think a nickel. You work the levers, learning to grope; the claw snatches a gewgaw off the heap of prizes. But here the only levers are my eyes; they are nudging the claw along with their invisible power. Now the claw sees a prize. It swipes at this prize, it wants it. But it goes too far, it reverses, it cuffs at it. It's clumsy as hell. But now, finally, *gotcha*. And this prize—wonder of wonders—seems to be another claw. So it is. It has entered the field from the other side. And what I see is a miracle, one of those taken-for-granted, everyday miracles. I see my hand feeling my hand feeling my hand. This is the beginning. Now let intelligence begin."

Abbott dropped his hands to his chest and closed his eyes. "Enter the Impossible I. Remember him? Remember *it*, rather; it's sexless. We invented it weeks ago. We left it in a void in the last episode. It had just been born, and it was wailing for its lost life. It's you, of course.

"Now you're moving. Part of you is. Let's call it a head.

This head is composed of sensors on a weak stem, called a neck. This head is scanning for a sign, though it doesn't know why or what. It knows nothing, but it tracks. It is tracking soft sounds, voices. Footsteps.

"Anyway, that's what your mother told me, from her reading. Heath, mother of this I. She said at this early stage you were tracking moving points of light. And contours. Curves.

"And circles, especially, a circle with little circles inside it, like the human face. The human face orbits our Impossible I—you—like a satellite. And these orbits begin to mark the passage of time.

"You can't think or speak, of course, but if you could, you might be saying, 'I see Face again. Face was here before. It is here again. Now I can recognize it. I quake for it, making bubbly noises, sucking my fist.'

"No!"

Abruptly, Abbott sat up. He lit a cigarette in frustration. "It's not working," he called; "I'm talking like Baby Snooks. Do you have any ideas?"

There was no sound from the bedroom, no pre-sleep cooing or knockabout jingling of the bells on Avery's overhead mobile. Abbott got up, tiptoed into the room and slipped the empty bottle from the sleeping infant's hands. He went to the kitchen, washed the bottle and nipple and placed them in their plastic rack. He returned to the living room and sat down again on the floor, pondering the difficulty of his assignment.

"The problem," he said, lowering his voice, "is that, so far as anybody knows, there's nothing down here in this I of ours but blind need and a threshold for habit. So the word 'I' won't work at this early stage, even as a metaphor. But we've got no choice; I'll have to fake it."

Abbott rose up on one hip, scooted crabwise over to his armchair and used an ashtray there to stub out his cigarette. He lay down to resume the assignment.

"Here goes. We're giving you the impossible power to report to yourself about what's going on. And about me—Face."

Abbott folded his hands on his chest and closed his eyes.

Wait. He sat up, tensed over a noise from the bedroom. A brief gargling noise, like choking. No, chuckling. The infant had merely laughed in his sleep.

Or laughed at his grandfather's brainstorming.

Abbott stretched out again and lowered his voice to a slow, bedtime-story murmur.

"I see Face again. It materializes from me. I've seen it many times in the window of my gaze.

"I quake for it, bubbling and sucking a fist. I do this because Face brings warmth. Wholeness. Face re-creates my old life of liquid and wind whenever I'm lonely, or when I'm in pain. When Face recedes, I'm unhappy with myself. I'm diffuse with loudness and struggle.

"The orbits go on. Face arises, is absorbed into me, is reborn from me. I find pleasure in these reappearances. And peace. Now, in the intervals without Face, I make new discoveries that calm my crying. Crying itself becomes a discovery—it is a sound that I can modulate, a game to charm what someday I will call my 'ears.'

"Ditto for my 'fist.' It unfolds into nubs, which can wiggle independently. This fist-flower used to flit elusively in my view. Now I can rediscover it on command. It has a counterpart across the way, and the two find each other. They nestle in mutual feeling.

"The old life of rage and torpor is draining from me. A new life flows from the recurrences of Face and my discoveries. I find more enjoyment in myself, in the adventures of my eyes, hands, mouth—all the nameless powers. These were isolated but now they begin to join forces. They match their meager notes. In the magic of their hookup, they enrich and extend my repertoire. Each chance little action seems to make the next one possible.

"Look, grasp, listen. The 'mobile' overhead—if shaken, this thing, this part of me, makes a noise, rings bells.

"And stretch, feel, look: the act of arching shakes all of me pleasurably—'body,' 'crib,' 'walls,' all.

"Meantime, more enjoyment flows from Face—curiosity over what it does and changes in its patterns. Nothing is so compelling, so central, as Face. Nothing moves so much, or so unpredictably. It conjures up laughter, exciting all my powers at once.

"Look: Face has hands. Look: It is rubbing them together. It is rubbing them with such ferocity and such a cry that I would recoil in fright if not for the marvelous result of this rubbing: a shower of dancing, drifting points of white."

Ah, yes.

"Do you remember that day? Were you traumatized by it?"

Abbott remembered. Those drifting points of white were pieces of paper—rejected editorials that he was ripping up as Avery looked on in delight.

Avery, in fact, had inspired them—a spate of editorials on child and youth issues, written after the baby's arrival. The boss had bounced most of these pieces, sending them back in the interoffice mail with memos attached. Abbott had brought them home.

There was the editorial condemning child abuse, including corporal punishment:

MEMO: *Wes: Soften this one. Our readers don't spare the rod.*

And the piece on the city abortion rate, which Abbott remembered reading to Avery one night in the Dunkin' Donuts parking lot during a ride:

MEMO: *Wes: Unlocalize this. Makes the city sound like an extermination camp.*

All right, Abbott could concede that he'd oversentimentalized a bit on that one. What really angered him and provoked the paper-shredding act that thrilled Avery was a confidential memo, which came in a separate, sealed envelope.

WES: *Are things under control yet at home? See me soonest about possible column on child care.*

After reading this—the reminder about writing a kooky column that would rob him of the last of his dignity—Abbott screamed, "That sonofabitch!" And Avery, startled, popeyed, began to howl. Abbott apologized.

6

"So you took three days off to find a new babysitter."

Saying this, Denham looked pained, like the victim of a joke whose point has eluded him. But he leaned back behind his desk with a show of readiness to listen, and of sympathy, too, as if Abbott were a woman employee of the old days claiming the "curse" as an excuse. Day-care woes would be no less foreign to the boss's experience, Abbott thought.

"Takes time," he said. "Not many good ones. Few and far between." Breathless, he gulped air between these phrases. His anxiety puzzled him, for Denham was not a man you'd call intimidating. Rather, a mild grayhead like himself, with similarities: primness in jacket and tie, a complexion like library paste, a face deadpan, reserved.

There were differences, as well. Taking note of Denham's hair—barbered almost cadet short—Abbott pictured his own, curled like wood shavings over the tops of his ears and over ring-around-the-collar in back. Who at the *Call* except Denham could afford regular haircuts?

Abbott breathed deep to steady his voice. "I've gone through two already. The first one took in too many kids. The second took in too many men friends. That's no joke. I went over there one morning—"

Abbott stopped. The boss had lowered his eyelids and raised a palm, signaling that he needed no evidence of scandal to accept Abbott's excuse. He wagged his head like a dismayed parent. "Is there anything we can do to help?"

Abbott swallowed more air and said, "Sure. Drop by the house. Change a diaper." He awaited a complex reaction to this joshing.

Denham's mouth drooped at the corners, shaping a wicket of censure or hurt. But almost at once the wicket flipflopped into a thin smile, the happyface of a superior acknowledging your joke, poor as it might have been. "I'm glad to see you haven't lost your sense of humor, Wes. That's why I wanted to see you this morning."

Denham leaned forward, elbows on the desk, and Abbott tensed, flattening his feet on the carpet.

"The column," Denham said. "I've been waiting for samples."

"Yes. Well, I have a problem with the concept."

Again, fleetingly, Denham looked hurt—the look of a boy whose playmate has turned spoiler of the game.

"It's the gimmick," Abbott said. "Too slight. Like a one-issue campaign. It can't last."

"It'll last if *you* write it." One hand lifted off the desk and fidgeted, sketching in the air what might have been a fraternal pat on the shoulder. "You've got the touch to make it a heartwarmer."

Heartwarmer? This cliché warned Abbott that the aloof publisher he faced was about to undergo a change in persona. "You're one of the old pros," Denham said. "You and Earl. We don't have many of you fellas left." He stood up and removed his jacket. "Earl came to us from New York, didn't he? The Big Time."

This recollection was a cue, and Abbott followed the script. "The *World-Telegram.* He was an assistant managing editor."

Denham sat down and rolled back his cuffs. "The *Telly*. When did the *Telly* fold?"

"Way back. In '63, I think."

Denham pushed up his sleeves and looked down at his

forearms, studying them as if they bore old tattoos. He snuffed up a deep breath. "It was a great paper."

No, it was not, but Abbott kept his mouth shut in accord with this moment of silent prayer.

Now Denham yanked at his tie, loosening it. A touch of dishevelment, even of raffishness. Enter the Old Pro, an actor somewhat conflicted in his role. This Old Pro barked in soft tones. He did not eat cigarettes or quaff machine coffee as they do—so one hears—on the metropolitan dailies. He leaned way back and laced his fingers behind his head but refrained from propping his feet on the desk. He said, "The column will last, and it can't miss. A man your age"—he chortled, qualifying this thought—"*our* age, Wes, your age and mine, a man saddled with child care. How he fumbles his way through it. All the funny things that happen, told in your snappy prose."

Abbott looked away, smiling to himself over an insane whim: to lie down on the carpet, right here and now, and do a fetal in an effort to divine the depth of coldness in this man. How could any boss, even one so quirky, ask you to write cutesies, a sitcom, about your ruined domestic life?

"Think of all the angles," Denham said. "What you just told me—about missing three days of work because you couldn't find a babysitter. Why, that's hilarious! Sort of. And aren't there long hours involved? I understand children keep you up late. Mine are grown; I don't remember."

Abbott looked around the office. It was too neat, as news offices go. Lawbooks instead of old papers filled the floor-to-ceiling shelves. Denham, by training, was an estate lawyer, and the *Call* his inheritance, a sideline. A tax toy.

"A regular feature," he went on. "It could be funnier than Erma Bombeck—it's in that vein. It could be a . . . well . . ." Denham raised his brows as he withheld some term in his mind. The patrician in him seemed to squirm over the word, but the Old Pro finally gave it voice. "It could be a *biggie*."

Abbott gazed at a series of framed front pages on the

wall to the right of the lawbooks. The moon landing, D-Day—a progression of events leading in broad skips of time all the way back to the start of the *Call*'s one hundred and fifty-odd years of mediocrity.

"You can create your own title," Denham said. "But I have a suggestion. I think it's pretty good. It's"—he paused—" 'Grandfather Knows Best.' How does *that* grab you?"

Abbott blinked at the framed front pages. His eyes burned. He grubbed at them with his knuckles, an action that reminded him of Avery. He got up and walked to the office window, turning his back on the Old Pro in a risky but exhilarating snub.

"Well, what do you think? Annoyance had deepened the boss's voice. "My title flatters our older readers. And that's our audience, Wes, let's not kid ourselves. But your column could appeal to young folks, too, in the suburbs. That's the whole schmear."

Whole schmear? What was a schmear?

"The city is dying," Denham went on. "What's the percentage of elderly?"

Abbott nodded that he didn't know. No longer would he serve as the boss's personal computer. If asked, he'd spout the figures on *Call* circulation decline, but surely Denham knew those by heart. "What we need," Abbott said, briefly turning around, "is a consultant's study."

Consultants cost. "What we need," Denham said, sounding aggrieved now, "is for every staff member to work harder—work like the dickens doing what they do best. We've gotten fat and lazy."

Down at the curb a sanitation crew was picking up trash on its weekly rounds. Abbott watched as three or four men emptied cans into a slow-moving compactor truck. Often he had watched this crew from the window of his office down the hall, admiring those huskies. They could toss those cans around like beach balls. They could heft them two at a time, even in bad weather when the cans were heavy with rainwater or chunks of ice.

Abbott wondered: Can I do that?

Oh, perhaps. Back straight, lift with the legs. Grunt and brag. Years ago he had been a fieldhand. A lusty, bullworking boy—pick-'em-up-and-put-'em-down, all rhythm and revery—an able animal with an Old Gold, unfiltered, tucked behind his ear and a paperback book bent to the curve of his dungaree pocket. Brawn and brains. Where had they gone? At some moment—when he was writing, probably, shrouded in smoke and *Call* opinions—a long-term process had consummated itself, unmarked. In that instant his coronary arteries had narrowed a micromillimeter—whatever—too much. Later, a dip appeared in a routine EKG. They labeled it oxygen deficiency under stress. But this condition wasn't totally irreversible. At worst, all he ever felt was a kind of pressure-pain and a frog-jump irregularity of the ticker, cutting off wind. Like right now. But it wasn't absurd to think that, on a lark, he could bound down the stairs, leaving Denham in mid-spiel, and join that crew and live via his muscles again, savoring his salty armpits, mind free and mouth loose. Bullworker for a Day.

Too romantic a notion? Hell, yes. Abbott glimpsed a more likely future: Denham would insist on this column; Abbott would refuse to write it (his first refusal); Denham, insecure and unpredictable when opposed, would fire Abbott; Abbott, though scared to death, would rejoice on his way to the poorhouse.

For now, Abbott heeded the warning in Denham's voice; he returned to his chair. Denham leaned toward him with folded hands and squared shoulders. Irony and concern seemed to war in his eyes, as if Abbott's remoteness could prompt either curious laughter or a referral for counseling. "Your funny pieces always gave the *Call* some class. You used to be good for . . . how many? . . . four or five a week."

Abbott nodded wonderingly. Yes, he had been a workaholic. Nothing wrong with that, but your workaholic usually has something to show for his work. He had—count 'em—(1) a job gone sour; (2) a bank account not quite covering Heath's final tuition payment; (3) an old ark of a house, paid for but falling apart; (4) a summer cottage in Wellfleet that had been appropriated by his runaway wife; (5) a bastard grandchild to care for almost full time.

"Why, I can remember when you wrote a pretty good political column."

Only *pretty* good? Syndicated, it had run in a half-dozen papers around the state. But he'd grown tired of it, of the interchangeability of those lawyers and salesmen whose ambitions he had chronicled. And Denham, owner of a business with a vested interest in the rhetoric, hadn't cared at all that the column was dropped. He'd said, "Nobody wants to read a sentimental liberal in the 1970s, Wes." In other words, a new status quo to be wooed.

Abbott fumed, reliving these old gripes. He was angry. Angry at Denham, the would-be Lou Grant. Angry at the *Call*, this rag devoted to BUSINESS AS USUAL and owner whims, and angry, most of all, at himself for brooding and gnashing like the new Earl. Face it: nothing's more tiresome, more pathetic, than a malcontent over the age of fifty. You've been somewhere in your life but nothing solid was found, nothing solid was adequately sought, and now you have nowhere to go but home. And home was where, at that moment, he sat. Figuratively, on Denham's carpet.

"You seem to be having a problem with all this," Denham observed. "Is it personal? No problem, use a pen name. You're a pro—you know the tricks. The main point is that a man, not a woman, is doing the child care. So we'll get men readers as well as the gals. The world is changing, Wes."

Abbott was tempted to say, "I've noticed," but deeper gratification would lie in getting through the rest of this interview without speaking a word. Surliness, yes. Sulking through a confrontation—a peculiar tactic but nothing new. Acting like some crabbed old Yankee farmer.

"People are changing. Not to my liking, and obviously not to yours, Wes, but we've got to keep up. The family is dying as we know it. More and more men these days are getting involved in raising children. Single parents; house-husbands, whatever *that* is; young fellas asking for paternity leave"—Denham chuckled—"and they're actually *serious* about it. You've seen 'em—young fellas toting babies on their back, out in public."

Denham leaned back, smiling the happyface; he seemed to be waiting for Abbott to match it, sign of a subordinate's assent. When none came, the aggrieved boy reappeared in the lines of Denham's mouth, but only for an instant. The boy gave way to an adult, one too delicate to rant at an employee showing obvious emotional problems. "Well, I guess you get my point."

Abbott nodded.

"You've written editorials about child care, I know. I've cleared some of them."

Abbott nodded.

"Some were good. You know, the other day I was talking about all this with Mrs. Denham."

Abbott pictured the wife so formally referred to, the hostess at company shindigs he used to attend.

"She thinks it's an outgrowth of the women's movement. No doubt."

Scuttlebutt had it that many of Denham's ideas came from his wife, a shadow publisher. It wasn't paranoid to think that, apprised of Abbott's case, she might have suggested "Grandfather Knows Best" as a form of paternalistic therapy. *Dear, tell your writer to write his troubles away.*

Denham reached out to his desk calendar. "All right, I'm assigning a deadline. I want some samples."

The telephone rang, interrupting the selection of a date. Denham lifted the receiver, and with a testy wave of his free hand he signaled to Abbott that the interview was over. He palmed the mouthpiece long enough to say, "Write me something. Soonest."

One ordeal over, Abbott plodded on to another. In his office down the hall he faced, not a bogus old pro, but a genuine young one, his assistant.

Eddie had removed his shoes. He sat with stocking feet up on his desk, next to the screen of his video display terminal. He had the VDT keyboard balanced in his lap and was typing. The rapidity of his work belied the lounge-lizard pose. A Popsicle stick—a cigarette substitute—bobbed on his lip.

"Nice of you to drop in," he said.

"So nice to be here," said Abbott.

"Well, what happened?"

"We had a little chat."

"Are you on probation now?"

"I was given a bonus."

"Did he chew your ass?"

"That's not his style."

"Oh yeah? I've heard he actually fires people. Every twenty years he cleans out the deadwood."

Eddie has stressed "deadwood." Abbott stepped around behind the young man to see the screen of his terminal. "I've fired people myself," Abbott said. "Every six months I clean out the smartasses. What are you working on?"

Eddie faked a long yawn, drawling syllables: "The tri-cen-*tenn*-ni-al."

A yawn-maker, indeed. A digest of history to mark a municipal birthday. "You need the practice," Abbott said.

"Thanks."

A mere "thanks" as a retort? Abbott awaited sharper stuff, up to Eddie's standard. At the same time, he felt a wave of weariness over the tension between this young fellow and himself in their two-man cubicle. Eddie looked tired, his eyes squinty with VDT strain. And Abbott noticed a red blotch on the pocket of the boy's shirt; he had fallen victim again to the company's leaky ballpoint pens. Abbott said, "You've been wounded."

"I know." Eddie glanced down at the blotch and then rolled his eyes at the workplace. "Cheap outfit."

"Forget that piece," Abbott said.

"What?"

"I'll finish it—the tricentennial. I'll bat it out; I know it all by heart."

"You were there, huh?"

The sarcasm could be forgiven. Ever since Avery's arrival in the world, Eddie had been doing most of the office work, and he had covered up for Abbott's frequent absences—until this week. Looking down at Eddie, at his thinning blond hair and the red stain on his breast, Abbott said, "You need a break."

"How'd you guess?"

"You need a greater challenge. Do the statehouse file."

Eddie looked up in surprise, stilling for a moment the bobs of the Popsicle stick on his lip. The statehouse file had top priority: editorials giving the *Call's* views on pending legislation. In a tone both snide and eager beaver, Eddie said, "Hey, I've been promoted!"

"It's time you learned to be the publisher's PR man."

"I can live with that. For a while." Eddie studied Abbott. "You're serious?"

"*Dead* serious. I may be cutting my own throat."

"I don't know his slant on all those bills."

"I'll tell you," Abbott said. "I know how he feels about every damn one of them."

Abbott turned to the window. Gazing out, he riffled once more through his mental dossier on Denham. He knew all the man's public attitudes as well as his body language. What's more, he and Denham shared the same heritage. Yankees, both, though from different levels of that dwindling minority. Abbott, Swamp Yankee; Denham, scion of entrepreneurs. Portraits of earlier Denhams hung in the conference room and in alcoves of the oft-remodeled old red-brick building. Denham harked back to Victorian mansions atop this milltown's hills. By contrast, Abbott could trace his descent from a frame farmhouse with junked cars beside it and a NITE CRAWLERS FOR SALE sign amid the dandelions out front.

Exactly! The image of the house flooded Abbott's mind, erasing his awareness of Denham, the office, Eddie teething on a stick, the scene down in the street, the trash cans now empty and toppled at the curb. Abbott was home again, revisiting the scene of his earliest years, feeling it with all his senses. He shivered; he felt a stinging wash of tears behind his closed lids. Trying to blunder into Denham's existence, he had blundered into his own.

What on earth was happening in his head? Ancient memories had been erupting like starbursts out of fogs of mild amnesia. Was this fatigue? His dual life as worker and mother had exhausted him. But never mind. Enjoy it—enjoy these lost scenes, even the pang and the heartbreak of them. He saw . . . the yard, yes; the stacked cordwood; a child's swing—a truck tire on a rope, dangling from an apple branch over a sunlit patch of sand. He smelled . . .

. . . lilac! This memory must have been imprinted in early spring. Lilac and road tar, which he used to gouge from the roadbed for chewing gum. He heard, or thought he heard . . .

. . . a chirr of insects in weeds, and, off in a freight yard, the squeal and bash of boxcars coupling.

Where were the people? He strained to evoke them . . .

"Mr. Abbott! Hey, you all right?"

The trip back home ended like a dream. Hearing Eddie, the alarm in Eddie's voice, Abbott knew the boy had called to him more than once. Abbott awoke to find both his hands clenching the windowsill and his forehead pressed against the glass. His legs were wide apart—how long had he been standing this way? He must have staggered. He seemed poised for a somersault through the glass. He blinked his eyes dry and turned to face Eddie, who had risen from his chair with one arm out as if to prevent Abbott from collapsing. Eddie was open mouthed, the stick gone from his lip.

Abbott squared his shoulders. "I'm all right."

"You almost fell. Jesus!"

"Only a stroke. I shrugged it off."

"Man, don't *joke* like that!" Eddie's hand fell but only part way. "You sure you're okay?"

"Never better." Abbott unbuttoned his jacket to begin the day's work.

"You sure? You look terrible."

"Fit as a fiddle, to coin a phrase." He assumed it had been a dizzy spell, that was all. He sat down at his desk across from Eddie's and ruffled some papers like an anchorman at the end of the evening news. "But next time," he added, "you inherit my job."

Eddie's arm flew up again, now in anger. "I said don't *joke* like that! For God's sake, it's *sick*!"

Abbott raised a hand in truce. All right, he'd gone too far, being candid; he'd broken the limits of the banter by which he and the boy tried to soften their rivalry.

Eddie said, "You don't have to rush things. I can *wait*."

For how much longer? At thirty, that young pro there with his unloosened tie and rolled sleeves was overdue for graduation from the *Call*. He was waiting, not for Abbott's job—no prize—but for the title. "Editor of the editorial page" would outshine "editorial associate" on a résumé when Eddie made his move for work on a respectable paper. And Abbott knew, from his frayed but still viable ties to the grapevine, how Eddie described him to others at staff parties and in the watering hole: as a burnout, an advanced case blighted by family troubles and ill health, ripe to be fired or retired.

Still flustered, and still watching Abbott for signs of a seizure, Eddie tried to compose himself with the ritual of lighting his pipe. It was a curved briar. Striking matches, Eddie sucked flame into a bowl too tightly packed with a beginner's aromatic cavendish. The poor kid, Abbott thought. Strong enough to quit cigarettes but alternately forced to chew wood or make smoked ham of his tongue.

Having spoken frankly once, Abbott decided—what the hell—to do it again. "You've been overworked," he said, "and you haven't squawked about it. I want you to know I appreciate that."

Eddie's eyes flicked about in the pipesmoke. He seemed to be searching for a reply suitably flippant, befitting the rules, but after a moment he gave up and echoed Abbott's sincerity. "No sweat. I've learned a little here."

"You have?"

Eddie's solemn nod affirmed the incredible.

"Well, you'll need it," Abbott said, "because I'm going to loaf some more before the ax falls."

Eddie narrowed his eyes as if, amid mixed signals, a subtle deal were being offered. After some reflection, he said, "Tell me the slant on those bills. Before you go."

Fair enough. Starting today, Abbott would play coach, one who could be forgiven for sneaking off the field now and then.

A burnout, was he? Well, a man does tire of his work, first the content and then the techniques, but he can find a residual pleasure in teaching it, one on one.

In the late afternoon, Abbott loosened his tie and folded his cuffs and batted out some editorials in advance. These would buy time for days off and for his forthcoming trip to supply Lew on the Appalachian Trail.

First off, a "funny piece." With the baby-care column in abeyance—forever—he'd be wise to flood Denham with funnies. He'd play Scheherazade, spinning tales to save his neck.

He wrote about a rise in the price of pinball games up in Vermont, using a stolen "bright" item that, as he revised it, became a lament about inflation. Not very funny, really. He was losing his touch.

A burnout then, after all?

No! Even in his current slump, he was batting about .500 in getting his editorials past Denham's screenings and into print, though it had to be conceded that Denham, an avid vacationer, often wasn't around to screen, and Abbott was second in command over the content of his pages.

Abbott hit the SPIKE key on his terminal, sending his pinball whimsy into oblivion. He'd try something else. After all, didn't he know all the tricks?

All right, first off, a hard-hitting THIS MUST STOP editorial on highway fatalities. A good warmer-upper, Walter Winchell style. Hackety-hack-hack.

Abbott followed this up with a random scolding of city officials. Good filler anytime, hinting at such verities as rubber stamps, closed doors, and smoke-filled rooms.

Next, as a favor to ease Eddie's burden, a vigorous defense of a state sales-tax increase that Denham backed and that Abbott opposed. Flackety-flack-flack.

Next . . .

Next?

Oh, come on, come on—he tried to think, tried to dig some platitude out of his thoughts like toxic waste, to be lifted as if with tongs . . .

Ah, some flag-waving. A good WHERE'D THE GUMPTION GO editorial. The boss accepted these, some of the time.

" . . . It is time for every individual to buck up. It is time to put our frustrations into perspective, to restrengthen our will, flex our muscle, find new purpose, and strive for excellence in our daily lives . . ."

Nauseating but serviceable. Feeling a little bit relieved, Abbott sat back for some automatic writing. Like a fieldhand he'd lose himself in the rhythm of his work, clockety-clock-clock. His subconscious typed out a token glimpse of international affairs—clerkity-clerk—a rewrite of a *News-*

week report. And it spewed other staples—nostalgia, like old trains, toot toot; and nature comment, twitter twitter.

Oh, hundreds of words of clackery by a cluck, topped off with a few outrageous pieces meant only to show Denham that he hadn't lost his sense of humor—or his spunk. A plea for the licensing of parents. Stronger civil rights for children.

Abbott punched the log-off keys, emptying his screen except for the blinking green eye, then stared at it for a long time.

Leaving the *Call*, he paused in the newsroom to check his mailbox for messages. There was a note from Earl, placed there last night. Earl worked nightside, and this message was the first from him in weeks. He had broken their years-long string of weekly soirées.

"Dear Aunt Abigail," the note began.

Getting nastier, Earl.

"Drop by next week, regular time. I have a surprise for you."

Surprise, hell. Dancing girls in the museum?

7

The journey to the woods for the father-son reunion required a long checklist for Avery. Packing the car, Abbott checked off each item. Besides Pampers and the other supplies that he carried to and from the babysitter's each day, he packed:

A sun bonnet. Check.

The baby carrier. Check.

A pacifier. Check.

Bug spray. (Hellish deerflies out there in the Berkshire woods.) Check.

Lotion, powder, pre-moistened wipes . . .

All this and more, but his own checklist for the trip seemed longer than the baby's. Inderal for heart rhythm. Swallowed—gulp!—check. Isordil to open the arteries. Check. A bit of Valium—two and a half milligrams—for the long drive. A squirt of hemorrhoid cream to ensure peak performance lest he waddle in pain on the long-awaited hike with Avery on his back. A few deep belly breaths for the alveoli . . .

Oh, despite all this decrepitude it would be a whizbang day, with good moments for everyone—himself, Lew, Avery—good moments, those little plenitudes amid routine.

Avery fell asleep on the way, lulled by the auto womb. Following Heath's map, Abbott found the rendezvous point with no trouble. It was on a country road near the mouth of a wide path, probably a connector to the main trail. Abbott parked on the shoulder of the road, and, sooner than expected, a hiker appeared on the path. Tall, bent under his orange backpack, and gaunt. Abbott recognized the slightly pigeon-toed stride, and he waved. Here was the son-in-law-to-be, or possible son-in-law-to-be, who had trekked all the way from Stone Mountain, Georgia, since Abbott had seen him last. Now full-bearded, Lew looked fifteen years older, although he and Heath were very young in Abbott's view, hardly light years ahead of their offspring.

Abbott sprang from the car, opened the trunk, and took from the cooler one of the cans of beer he had brought for Lew. He held it aloft for Lew to see and to anticipate, and then opened it. The snap of the pop-top echoed like a weak shot in the woods. Abbott awaited a bellow of gratitude.

Trudging up, Lew said, "Shit, no," in a voice whispery from disuse; "I'd bloat." After a limp handshake, he unshouldered his pack and, moving as slowly as an arthritic, he climbed into the back seat of the car. "A soft place to sit," he whispered. "That's all I want." He sprawled out, groaning loud and long and plaintively with each unlimbering move. "All I've wanted for *days*." Then his eyes slid slowly over to the right and he saw Avery asleep in the car crib.

The long-awaited reunion. Abbott prayed that Avery would awaken, would smile in greeting and perform one of his winning numbers, a burble and a reach, the routines that enlivened Abbott's own days. But the infant slept on, eyes tight and lips a duckbill pout, even as Abbott lifted him out of the car crib and carried him around to the open door for the father's inspection.

Many weeks ago, Lew had been awkward with his son, jittery with mixed feelings; today he went slack as if those feelings were unmanageable in his present fatigue. His camp-begrimed hand moved out to stroke Avery's brow, but faltered.

"Go ahead," Abbott said. "Take him."

"Nah, he's asleep. Let him sleep."

"Take him! He slept all the way out here."

Lew accepted the infant, cushioning the bonneted head with his palm. He whispered, "His neck is still weak, right? You've got to watch out for their necks."

"It's strong now."

"Really?"

"He's growing."

"Yeah. I can see that. He's not so red."

"Seven pounds heavier than when you saw him."

"No shit!" Lew smiled slightly and peered down at the groggy face, which now twitched irritably. Lew flinched. "Here!" He extended the cradle of his arms.

"Hold him," Abbott said. "Get acquainted."

"No. Here!"

Abbott took the infant, this hot potato, and returned him to the car crib.

Lew slumped lower in the seat. His eyes closed; his mouth fell open; for a moment he appeared to have fallen asleep. Then he said, "This is ridiculous."

Abbott looked at Lew, at Avery, at the scene around them: hemlock trees glimmering with sunlight. Ridiculous?

"I should be with him," Lew said. He jerked a thumb at Avery, avoiding a further glance. "Not out here."

Abbott said nothing. The day's promise of good moments was fading. There was no need to hit the dirt and do a fetal to imagine how tired and guilty this young man felt. Abbott cursed himself for unintended cruelty. Instead of cheering Lew, he'd devastated the young man by dangling a son at him. There was an unadmitted wish, perhaps, to be relieved of the infant right here and now; let Lew pop it into the backpack like a carnival doll and be off with a wave and a thank you.

After another long pause resembling sleep, Lew said, "Papa takes a hike. My sisters wouldn't even *talk* to me. Heath said, hey, don't worry about people's opinions. Well, I worry. How do *you* feel, paying the freight?"

"Don't worry about that," Abbott said.

"Does she want to get married or not?" Lew opened his eyes long enough to take in Abbott's shrug.

"I don't think she knows what she wants," Abbott said.

"It's ridiculous."

Abbott turned up his palms. He wouldn't meddle or take sides. He'd only foul up further.

"She thinks I'm a fucking lightweight," Lew said. "Well, I'm no self-made man, like you, but I've done a *few* things."

"Finish the hike," Abbott said. "It's almost over."

"Over? Tell me about it."

"To tell you the truth," Abbott said, "I wish *I'd* had the opportunity."

"You aren't missing anything. It's a sidewalk out here. No bears, no crazy hillbillies, *nothing*." Lew gazed vacuously around at the woods. "Listen, all my life I'll know that kid is mine." He gestured again at Avery but did not look. "What am I supposed to do, forget it? Is that what she wants?"

Abbott shrugged. "Do you want a ride home?"

Lew's gaze settled on Abbott's chest before his eyelids rolled shut again. "No. Fuck it. I started this hike, I'll finish it."

"That's the spirit."

"That's the way I am. If I start something, I finish it."

"That's commendable."

"I'm saying I won't give up on that kid."

"I don't think anybody is asking you to."

"They'd better not."

Lew's head lay at rest on the back of the seat; presently, it slumped to one side, just as Avery's used to when the baby was only weeks old. In a moment Lew's slow breathing became audible, a soft snore.

The memorable day was over. Abbott found himself standing alone on the shoulder of a country road, a father and a son napping in his car.

. . .

Abbott walked over to the mouth of the path, squatted there in the ferns and sipped the can of Budweiser he'd opened for Lew.

Did Heath-Lew have any future? A vital question, this, because Abbott-Avery couldn't last much longer, given Abbott's age and condition and his job problems. On her visits home, Heath never spoke of plans, only of Lew's hike, this self-testing fling that he was supposed to be enjoying. Heath had followed his progress via messages from friends who had supplied him en route. "Now he's in Pennsylvania!" "He's in New York state now!" A child clapping hands over a race, or, perhaps more like a handclapping parent, like Abbott himself applauding Heath's butterfly stroke in the swim meets of the past.

He went to the car for another beer and returned to the path and lay down there. A restful spot. The ferns smelled spicy in the heat, and hemlocks overhead filtered the sunshine, paling it with their soft needles. He closed his eyes against this peace and imagined his living room, the strife and confusion there in the pre-Avery debates. Heath and Lew, face to face, seated on the floor. Lew, rangy, with a mustache. Yes, a mustache back then, a Pancho Villa. And Heath, broad-shouldered, with eyeglasses on a round but small-featured face. A big, babyfaced girl, pregnant, her child already named. And off to the side, Abbott himself, incidental to the goings-on, a period piece for comic relief or stray information, half the time unseen and much of the time mortified by the talk and the intimacies.

"Let's try something," Lew said. "You say you love me. How do you feel when you say that? Say it, and tell me what you're feeling."

Heath was skeptical. "What's this, Gestalt or something?"

"Just answer the question, okay?"

"Well, to begin with, there's a certain animal appeal."

Lew made a wry face. "Chest hairs."

"No, I mean it, Lew. That's important." Heath laughed despairingly. "We have a child on the way to prove it. And you do everything . . . *wholehog*, as Daddy would say." A flick of Heath's hand indicated Abbott, seated in his armchair. "But the real question here is knowing yourself."

Lew scoffed. "*Know thyself.*" He turned to Abbott. "Wes, you've got a lot of years on us. Do you know yourself?"

Abbott said, "If I were starving, would I eat human flesh? Who knows?"

Heath said, "Daddy, we're trying to be serious. Not . . . Socratic or whatever."

Yes, that's how it went, the talk. Abbott couldn't recount it verbatim, but he had listened at least half the time, and he had a newspaperman's good memory for quotes or at least for the shape of them. And therein lay clues, perhaps, to the real needs of these talkative children. Mentally, he began filling a notebook, the transcript of a meeting . . .

HEATH (*hand on her swollen belly*): When you say you love Avery, what do you really feel? And don't give me any father-love bullshit.

LEW (*after long reflection*): Tense and confused.

HEATH: Right. You're confused. So am I. Right now, we don't know our own selves very well, or each other.

LEW (*belligerent*): Oh yeah? Well, listen, you're hiding something and you don't even know it.

HEATH: Fire away.

LEW: You harp on little whims I had, like walking the trail and all that shit. What about your own dreams? Aren't they important?

HEATH (*after a long inward look, pensive*): I really don't have any. No. But Avery's changed all that. Avery's my dream. Her needs. Or his needs.

LEW (*tone of parody*): *A little child shall lead her.* Sweetie, that's bad. That's passive.

HEATH (*wide-eyed, as if startled by insight*): I know.

LEW: You needed me to lead you into things.

HEATH: It's true. All along. I still need you. I *love* you.

LEW: Then let's set the goddamn date. Now. I mean the wedding date.

HEATH: Go walk the trail. Then we'll decide. I really do love you.

If she really loved him, per Young Love, why in hell was he out here slogging through the forest, zomboid, with her blessing?

As that philosopher, Denham, had noted, people have changed.

LEW: All right, let's do it. We should've done it months ago.

HEATH: Is that your family talking, or you? (*to Abbott*) The asshole went and told his sisters I'm pregnant. Can you believe that?

LEW: You're stalling because of your mother.

HEATH: Shit. They're on your back. And they want it all—the white veil, for God's sake, the how-to sex book from some pastor; no thanks.

LEW: That's bullshit! They don't care about the ceremony, all they want is a party. Will it kill us to give them a little fun?

HEATH (*placating*): Oh, Lew, I love your family, and you know I love a party, but what we've got to do here is know our own minds.

LEW: You're stalling because of your mother. You won the big fight over having Avery, and now you dump me so she can save face.

HEATH (*after pondering*): No, I don't think so. I mean, that does sound plausible—I'll admit anything. But I really don't think it's true.

In this case, this reconstructed dialogue, Heath appeared to be right, and Lew wrong. Abbott could claim no insight into the snakepit of mother-daughter relations, but Claire had cut her losses by now with what seemed to be good grace. Claire had been close by during Heath's labor, a mother sweating it out offstage; and since then, Heath had visited her several times in Wellfleet, taking Avery along. And Claire—vital news, this—was knitting a crib quilt for Avery.

LEW: I know why you're afraid of marriage. Your parents. (*quick apologetic glance at Abbott in his armchair*) Look at 'em: married since the year one and now they're split.

HEATH: That's not fair. They're a special case.

ABBOTT (*snorting into full wakefulness*): Special case? I always thought of your mother and me as ordinary people.

HEATH (*arch*): What the hell does that mean—"ordinary people"? Mother wanted to be an artist, and that kind of person should never get married. She made a bad mistake, bad for everybody.

ABBOTT (*leaning forward in his chair, surprised by this partial truth*): Maybe so, but give her credit. She lived out the consequences.

HEATH: Exactly my point. Would Lew want to live out the consequences if he fucks up?

No good. These snippets of talk kept leading, not to the children's motives, but to himself and Claire. And in the context of this day—soft light in the trees, cold beer tang in the nostrils, the nearness of the Appalachian Trail, so open-ended—amid all these outdoor glories Abbott remembered a hike he had taken with Claire, a joy hike.

They were students then, together for a year at a teachers' college until the draft caught up with Abbott. Before the call came, they took a trip and ended up hiking the forearm of Cape Cod, the National Seashore.

A young couple, a couple of possible I's new to each other, frolicking ankle-deep for days along the Atlantic in rare perfect weather, their voices relinquished to the surf and wind. They strode mile after mile through the foam, surfbirds always ahead of them, ascending and alighting at a distance.

How did it start? An ordinary beach stroll until someone said, "Let's keep going till it ends."

Sure, why not? Let it never end, experiencing that pea-green vastness rolling up wedding lace at their feet. Back then, Young Love was grounds enough for marriage. They scrounged up a single sleeping bag, a canteen, a World War II surplus pup tent, and started out. Eastham, Wellfleet, Truro . . . the same thirty-mile route hiked a hundred years earlier by good old Henry Thoreau, God rest his soul. Thoreau, however, had had it easier: He did not have to camp in the bluffs to duck federal rangers on patrol for overnighters.

Who was it who had said, "Let's keep going . . ."? Abbott presumed it was Claire, who proved later to be more the adventurer in their lives.

Wait.

Was he falsifying his memories of this hike? Be careful. That's a trap for the aging. Stare everything in the face. When you think of Great Lovers, think of them lying open-mouthed on their backs for a snooze; when you think of Great Rivals, think of them sitting down to a friendly game of cards. Abbott recalled the cold night fog off the ocean, mosquitoes in the jackpines, and his apprehension over the rangers. He and Claire were discovered before reaching land's end. Flashlights with irate voices behind them flushed the couple out of a hollow among the dunes and waved them out of the park. They hiked across to Provincetown, losing their way in prickly dune forests, and slept, exhausted, under the P'town public wharf, along with other wanderlusters there, some of them drunk, drugged, or demented, on a hot morning that smelled of dead fish.

Abbott shook Lew awake. The kid had slept for an hour and would have to make up time, possibly hike at night by flashlight, to meet his other outfitters on the trail.

Hurriedly, Lew packed the supplies Abbott had brought, and he laced up his new boots for a break-in period. "Thanks for these," he said. "And thanks for taking care of Avery. Thanks for everything you're doing."

"I'm enjoying it," Abbott said.

"Sure." Lew smirked over this reply. "It'll end. Don't worry. Maybe I'll cheat a little. Use the thumb."

"Maybe that would be smart."

Lew, crouching to lace his boots, looked up quizzically for a second, and Abbott did a double-take over his own words. Earlier he had given this boy a coachlike pat on the back; now he'd encouraged him to dog it. Old Abbott, self-made man of principle.

Lew shrugged his packframe into place and, after final good-byes—none, conspicuously, for Avery—he trudged off on the path. "Katahdin next," he shouted, and vanished among the hemlocks.

Mount Katahdin! Trail's end in Maine. More glories. Abbott thought of Katahdin's waterfalls, and the screams of loons. He was tempted, as planned, to scoop Avery into the baby carrier, hoist the infant onto his back, and to hike a ways; he'd catch up with Lew. But Avery was still perversely asleep, and Lew had set a fast pace. Anyway, how far would he get, Abbott wondered, on that upgrade, before breathlessness and the onset of hemorrhoidal fire? Such pain could be laughed off, but how far would he get before feeling heart skitters and the pressure of a heavy man's foot against his breastbone? The critical dip in the EKG.

All right, hell, if his time happened to come out there

on that path, so be it. But Avery would be on his back. What would happen to Avery?

After sleeping all day in the car, Avery was wide awake tonight, over-alert, and Abbott gave up hope of any rest for himself. To relieve the infant's boredom, Abbott moved him around: jiggled him on a knee, placed him on the living-room floor. Changes of position for changes of sensation.

"Travel is broadening, Avery."

Avery, on his back, gave lunging kicks. Those stumpy legs in overalls seemed intent on flipping the baby upright.

Abbott decided to improvise a chair for him. The sitting position, still somewhat unfamiliar, held a calming fascination for Avery. Abbott went out to the car and brought in a spare tire, an old one without a wheel. He lay it flat on the living-room floor and sat the baby in the hole, tucking pillows around him so that he wouldn't wobble.

"There. That better? Bet you didn't know your grandfather was such an ingenious old bastard, did you?"

For a while Avery sat still, looking bemused.

"We'll just sit here and talk." Abbott settled himself in his armchair. "Talk all night, if you want. I'll take tomorrow off. It won't matter."

It wouldn't matter because Denham was away. The Denhams traveled often, trips whose expenses the boss wrote off by doing travel pieces or conference reports upon return. Meanwhile, Eddie was holding the fort in Abbott's office, filling the daily hole with Abbott's mediocre pieces and with bushytailed work of his own. Abbott pictured that young assistant speed-typing at his VDT and chewing a toothpick or something. Somehow Eddie found time to dig and write for the op-ed page. A series on housing, last month. Lately, a series on the lives of deinstitutionalized mental patients.

"A credit to the trade," Abbott said. "And I'm a goof-off *exploiting* him."

Restless again, overexcited by the day's breaks in routine, Avery beat his arms on the pillows and whined. Abbott lifted him out of the tire hole and placed him belly-down on the floor.

"Go ahead, cry. I'll cry, too."

Groaning along mockingly, Abbott watched the creature's movements. It raised its head. It straightened its front flippers, frog-kicked with the back ones, and stretched its neck as if to expand its field of vision. Abbott could feel the strain, the tension in that lumpish body and in that head, that swaying and slobbering bulb of sensors and receptors. Abbott could sense urges way down in that Impossible I to—heaven help us!—crawl.

Mobility: It was coming fast, and Abbott realized it would put new pressure on him. It would require new actions, a higher order of wakefulness and intuition. It would require more than mere nursing of a helpless being, and more than mere words, his whimsical communions. Abbott felt impelled to shout to the absentee parents.

Help! Settle your differences! Get together, and take your baby off my back.

Help, help! Fear of crawling!

8

Earl had promised a surprise. Not another sex film, Abbott hoped. Maybe Earl had purchased a fine bottle of sherry to celebrate the reopening of their museum after these weeks of silence. Or maybe he had obtained a record book that would settle definitively some longstanding debate or bet. For example, in what round of the rubber match did Sandy Saddler TKO Willie Pep . . .

No matter. Whatever the surprise, Earl must have dispelled his blues. Once more there would be good talk, old cues and props and mutual applause. Once more the curators would fly, wholly contained in their reminiscences, enjoying crony immortality. And their evening would begin with good chess. That afternoon, as Avery napped, Abbott brushed up on his variation of the Sicilian Defense; and at the appointed hour in the evening, his chessboard tucked under his arm, he knocked at Earl's apartment door.

"Dear Abby!" Earl crowed the welcome. "Come on in!"

Abbott opened the door and saw the surprise—the shock. A girl. Not a film image but a life-sized figure in the round, curled in the easychair.

Earl sprang up from the couch to make introductions. Abbott caught the name Sharon.

It was a doll, of course, had to be—one of those big inflatables that perverts or the hopelessly lonely buy, or that a jokester like Earl might buy on an occasion like this. But no, the eyes shone; there were perceptible tremors, the aura of a life. Furthermore, the doll was mobile; it had arisen and was advancing toward Abbott to shake his hand. Impressions dizzied him: a sunny grin, saying, "Hi, Mr. Abbott," a swishing of hips, nipples waggling at him like fingertips under a T-shirt. His sinuses billowed with the girl's scent, and his scalp bristled as she took hold of his half-raised hand, lifted it, and pumped it.

Through his daze he heard Earl's voice, hearty: "Call him Wes; we're all friends here!" Ah, his puckish little pal was savoring this scene. Abbott saw Earl's grave, comradely nod, and then felt Earl's arm slide around his shoulders and guide him with gentle pressure to the couch. He felt the chessboard being slipped from under his arm—"We won't be needing *this* tonight, Wes!" A drink was put in his hand.

Details. Notice the little details if you would survive an overwhelming world. Abbott tasted sherry. Same old stuff, museum house brand. Some things in life could be trusted.

To the girl, Earl said, "You wouldn't know it to look at him, but this old gent is a proud papa."

"You're a grandfather, right?" the girl asked. "I know Earl's only kidding."

Breathing evenly now, and at a safe, unresonant distance from the girl, Abbott took a longer peek. That T-shirt bore the letters TRACK BUM and a picture of colliding stock cars.

"I bet your grandson's adorable," she said. "What's his name? Dummy Earl doesn't even know."

Abbott muttered Avery's name.

"I like that. Tell me about him."

What to say? Her presence in the museum had shocked him, but even more shocking was his continuing fluster now, his shovel-handedness, like that of a teenaged boy exposed amid his fantasies.

Nevertheless, when in doubt, one talks.

"He's healthy. So the pediatrician tells us. And his disposition is pretty good. About half the time. He's developing on cue, I think. Maybe faster in what you call gross motor skills . . ." Abbott paused, feeling silly over this report. His listeners waited a moment longer, heads inclined, and then Earl said, "Thank you, Dr. Welby," and Sharon, with a wriggle in the easychair, said, "I bet he's a *doll.*"

Abbott studied her. Not very pretty. Then again, all young girls are attractive in one way or another, in manner if not in looks, and Sharon's manner was that of a high schooler sitting pretty at a first interview—knees joined, hands folded like gloves atop them. A girl both smiley and circumspect, her voice a little too musical. She said, "You're like a single parent, right? Sort of?"

"Sort of."

"How you holding up? That's really tough." She gave a pout of sympathy.

"Oh, it is, it is," Abbott said, warming. He'd ride this topic until Earl explained the mystery of the girl's presence. Runaway niece, trollop for the evening, or whatever.

"The toughest part is finding babysitters," Abbott said. "They're few and far between."

The girl squinted with interest. A good listener, far more attentive than Avery.

"I've gone through three already. The first one took in too many kids—babies lined up against a wall for older kids to pinch."

Sharon winced as if she herself felt the pain. "Kids can be mean."

"I've noticed that. At the next place, the woman had more men friends than kids. It's the truth," Abbott added over Earl's horselaugh. "Every morning, new faces, shaving or eating breakfast."

"Government grant givers," Earl joked. "Observers with Ph.D.'s."

"On some afternoons," Abbott said, "no one answered the phone."

"Weird!" Sharon piped.

"They were all out playing," said Earl.

"Earl, that's not funny! Go on, Wes." The girl leaned forward, jiggling in suspense. She surpassed even Heath as an audience for his day-care horror stories.

"Well, next I tried a big place downtown, the only one that takes infants. It's called 'Kentucky Fried Children.' "

Earl grunted over this joke—a steal from city social workers. Sharon looked mystified, then caught the joke or pretended to catch it, and she tittered.

"A jungle," Abbott said. "Over-enrolled and understaffed. Now he's with a woman who you know, Earl. Remember Ma Heaphy?"

Earl slapped his knee. "Cityside did a feature on her and I wrote the head." He rocked forward, tickling his brow to remember; then: "Get this: '300 CALL HER MOM.' "

Sharon gawked. "Three hundred?"

"Foster kids," Abbott explained. "Over the years."

"At about a hundred and eighty per kid per month," Earl asked. "Right?"

"Thereabouts. The other day I asked her to give Avery a little extra attention. Carry him around now and then, because . . . well, love—*attachment*, I should say—has its origin in that, you see, in touch." Abbott hesitated, once again seeing puzzlement in the girl's face and disgust in Earl's. Earl was tiring of this topic but Abbott pressed on. "Heaphy said, 'Don't spoil the baby, friend, just let him cry it out and go on about your business.' "

"The bitch!" This yell from Sharon cracked the girl's mind-your-manners facade. She glared first at Earl and then at Abbott as though daring these older and supposedly wiser people to disagree or to put her down. "A home like that should be full of love. Babies should be *smothered* with love."

Smiling over these sentiments, Abbott doubted that this

child knew much about children, but, as a street kid, she might have stories to tell about parental delinquency.

"Anyway, the whole thing is frustrating," he said. "Day care—it's a stepchild. There's too little control and a lot of abuse. I should write something about it." Saying this, he felt the energy of indignation, a surge that surprised him because it did not immediately begin to wane. He turned to Earl. "Don't you ever feel like working again? I mean, going out there and digging something up, saying something."

"Shit no," Earl said.

"I'm serious."

"I'm serious, too. I'll never hustle again."

"I'd like to get off my duff and go out there and do a series. Something might come of it, who knows? A bill to consolidate the control."

Earl smirked. "Denham would bury it in the women's pages."

"Lifestyle pages," Abbott corrected.

"New name, same old shit." Earl thrust his face at Abbott. Earl, too, seemed to have experienced a rush of indignation. "*Everything* is the same old shit. Wake up, look around! Same series, same bills, same jokes. Same cutesies about kiddies—no offense. And the same—"

Sharon groaned and went limp in her chair; presumably she'd heard all this before.

"—same votes. Same trends. Same half-assery, and the same murders and rapes. Need I go on?"

"I think I get the picture," Abbott said, but the litany continued as Earl leaned over with the bottle to refill Abbott's glass. "Same non-events. Same things owning you—same ropes and stakes. Same pointless holidays. Same anniversaries. For Christ's sake, they should be occasions for mourning."

"If things are so bad," Sharon said, reaching over and waggling her glass for a refill, "how come you haven't jumped off a bridge?"

"What's next might be worse. People cling to what they have. Look at Abbott here."

Abbott shrugged over this view of him as a stick-in-the-mud. The new Earl, like Claire and many other people, did not understand the function of routine in human life. An anniversary, for example—say a golden wedding anniversary—is a triumph of habit over pain, nothing more, nothing less. "You talk like a burnout," Abbott said. "That's my title. At the *Call*."

"The hell it is. It's mine!" Earl thumbed himself on the shirtfront. "And they know it. Next time anybody hands me some shit over there, I'm through."

"I may be through already," Abbott said, "in point of fact."

Sharon rolled up her eyes. "What a pair of go-getters!"

"Woodward and Bernstein," Abbott said. Did the girl have a sense of humor? If so, let her be given a gold star on her report card, and let her be forgiven for all that harem-girl makeup around her eyes.

"Number one malcontent," Earl persisted. "I'm the guy."

"Wrong. Do you have to have a long talk with yourself every day before you go in?"

"A long talk with myself every fucking *hour*!" Earl's hand slammed the coffee table.

"Do you call in sick half the time?"

"I *am* sick. Do you pray for a heart attack so you can retire early?" Earl stood up with hands fisted at his sides.

Abbott heard another groan from Sharon. "I don't believe you guys. I mean, you're fighting—you're actually almost having a *fight*—over who's the biggest deadhead."

Was the girl perceptive, more or less? If so, another gold star, Abbott thought, and let her be forgiven for that streak in her hair, as fleecy white as thistle seed. He turned to Earl, whose face showed a competitor's rage, the eyes hounded. "Are you really sick?"

Earl sat down. He said, "Nah, not really," then gruffly nodded, meaning yes-but-let's-not-talk-about-it, and at last he blurted: "Stomach. It went bad years ago in New York, over the tension; now it's going bad over the boredom." He laughed—the snarl of a man withstanding a good joke on himself. He folded his arms at the base of his rib cage as if his chest were a clumsy piece of armor, a cuirass a size too large for him, and his eyes went starkly unseeing as he forced a burp.

"You never told me," Abbott said.

"Are we to tell each other our little ailments, like some old married couple?"

"Lord, no," said Abbott.

"We're a comic pair, Abigail. Sharon's right."

"In any case, you win," Abbott said. "I concede. You're the number one sadsack at the *Call*."

"I told you so." Earl leaned back and swigged sherry.

The girl gave a mock cheer.

Abbott watched her as the conversation went on, fading now into the listless shoptalk of two journeymen, the voices slurred a little from drink. When was Denham expected back from Tahiti or wherever? Next year, would the Christmas bonus be pin money or, as usual, a gift certificate toward the price of a turkey? This dreary talk saddened Abbott; never before had it fouled the hallowed air of the museum. But it was Earl, not he, who had toppled the museum by introducing the girl into it.

She listened sharply, eyes flicking from face to face. And so bouncy! Sitting, only a second ago, with legs folded under her; now with one foot out, twitching. And now she scrunched forward with elbows on knees, her legs in a springing position, heels raised off the floor.

A mental connection occurred: Abbott realized that his own pose mirrored the girl's. On impulse, he sat back and crossed his legs. So did she. Dear God in heaven, a game of monkey-see, monkey-do; how long had it been going on?

Discovered, she smiled with tongue tip showing between her teeth. Then her teeth clamped her lower lip in a childlike expression of guilt.

Earl's urchin, Abbott realized, was flirting with him. Dear God in heaven!

Presently, she stood up, stretching, patting away a yawn. "You two dudes have got a lot to talk about—bitch about, I mean—but I gotta get some sleep." She looked at Abbott and giggled. "Actually, it was very nice meeting you, Wes." She advanced for a handshake, and once more her nearness caused a bristling of his hair and a ripple of gooseflesh. He felt pain in the hinges of his jaw, as from a tart taste. He gulped saliva. "If you ever need a good babysitter, call me," she said. "I'm not kidding."

She went down the hall to Earl's bedroom. Abbott expected to see her emerge in a moment with a coat and a handbag and to leave the apartment for her home—wherever the wanderling holed up. But she reappeared in a robe too large for her—Earl's—and crossed the hall to the bathroom. Soon Abbott heard the shower go on. His inner eye glimpsed soapsuds sliding down skin as soft and clear as Avery's.

"Well, what do you think?" Earl said. "My live one."

There were countless questions to be asked. Abbott picked at random.

"She's your niece?"

"Niece? Who's got a niece?"

"Is she living here?"

"If she wants to. Right now she wants to."

"How old is she?"

"Older than she looks. Schizophrenics have a way of looking young."

"Are you telling me this child is crazy?"

"It's a joke; ask her sometime. Why are you shaking your head?"

"I remembered something. You said old loners like us shouldn't have people; we'd exploit them."

"Right. I said we should have dogs." Earl snickered, remembering this line.

"I didn't happen to notice four legs on your stray."

"No, but my dog knows more tricks than your dog. You're jealous."

Jealousy—absurd but true. Abbott felt resentment toward that waif luring his crony astray. And it was safe to assume that Earl had likewise resented Avery as a new preoccupation in Abbott's life. "Earl, you're right. We're a comical pair."

"Like a pair of old queens."

"Worse. Two old maids."

"Even worse! All these years, boring each other with war stories and playing chess like geezers in a fucking hospital."

Those words hurt. "Earl, I was never bored."

"I know you weren't. You needed it, so I went along." Earl clapped a hand on Abbott's shoulder. "I'm not a total prick, you know. But it's time for a new life."

The noise of the shower flow had ceased. Abbott pictured Sharon toweling down. Sharon bending over, drying between her toes. These images grew salacious; to dispel them, Abbott rubbed hard at his eyes; they burned; he was tired. Bushed. Beside him on the couch, Earl quaffed sherry as if it were beer. "A new life," he said, "from scratch. No more Earl the copydesk gnome."

"Picking up a teen—that's a new life?"

"It's a start. I'm feeling my way."

"Post-fifty debauchery. Whoopee."

"Sneer all you want. I've got the guts to change. And you're welcome aboard, pal. Sharon has friends." Earl's eyes rolled upward—see-no-evil—as his arm made the piston-rod gesture signifying sex. "And if you like Sharon herself, it's okay with me if it's okay with her."

"I think I remember the term for that. Sloppy seconds."

Earl flinched. "Don't make me out to be *crude.* I'm trying to help you, for Christ's sake."

The bathroom door opened. Abbott opened his smarting eyes and saw Sharon, robed, crossing the hall to the bedroom. She paused to grin at him and deliver a bye-bye wave of the fingertips. Abbott's forearm jerked up in response.

"She does like you," Earl said. "You must have tickled her uterus with all that babytalk."

"Earl . . . this is sick."

"Sick, my ass. It feels good and nobody gets hurt. Don't get bourgeois on me."

"All right. What you're doing is corny."

"I never claimed to be chic."

"And it's dangerous."

"You're right. I *love* it."

If this ornery little man couldn't be shamed or scared, maybe he could be reasoned with. Abbott said, "Saviour complex."

"What?"

"You pick up a ragamuffin to redeem her. Akin to the Pygmalion complex, observed in men our age. You see, my daughter leaves her schoolbooks around the house and I browse . . ."

Earl placed forefinger on palm, ready to tally. "Shall I count for you the ways of redemption? The box lunches, the blowjobs . . ."

"Spare me," Abbott said. "Please."

"Have I killed your bullshit speculations?"

Abbott leaned forward and sank brow into palms. He heard: "Now listen to me," and felt Earl's hand kneading his shoulder; and in the silence he imagined Earl sagely nodding, marshalling words for a speech.

"Now tell me about your dreams, doctor. Do you dream of old girlfriends?"

Abbott swayed passively with the rhythm of Earl's kneading.

"Old girlfriends. From way back. Wa-ay, wa-ay back, when you were sixteen, seventeen."

Abbott wearily nodded no. Fingers snapped near his face.

"Come on, Wes, don't fade out on me now. We've come too far. Think!"

All right, of course he had such dreams; doesn't every man? He dreamed of long-forgotten beloveds in bobby sox and ponytails. Jeannine—whatever happened to Jeannine, the girl he had remembered as a rider on a carnival Whip? Buxom as the actress Jane Russell in *The Outlaw*.

Earl sighed. "Remember how sweet it was back then? So sweet and hot?"

True. The horniness of those years is unsurpassed. Young love. Loved ones with skin like Avery's, a natural smell as fresh, hugs as wholehearted.

"So sweet and hot," Earl chanted. "That time of life when love is never again so desperate, so *alive*."

True, all true. The dreams were unbearable, sometimes, in their poignancy. Ambushes from the past, leaving you stranded and wet-eyed as you awaken in the present, a veteran of, say, twenty thousand awakenings, arising to plant the markers and dig the grave of another day.

Abbott raised his head from his hands. "It's true." He thought of the female demons of myth. "Succubi."

"Yes," Earl said, "but also angels of mercy. Because they can superimpose themselves on a man's blah mate. Or occupy his empty bed."

"That's true. They uplift the marital beds."

"They transform the national chore into bliss!"

Ah yes. Here, in a surprise appearance, was the Abbott & Earl team, clicking as of old. Hand us our tophats and canes, and start the music, maestro.

"Those lost days," Earl intoned, bowing his head.

"The last true passions," said Abbott.

"The sweetness and heat."

"The innocent promises."

"The rapid-fire orgasms."

"The whole hearts."

Earl echoed, "Whole hearts," then cried, "Yes!" and Abbott's head wobbled as the hand that had been kneading his shoulder suddenly slapped his back. "I think you understand," Earl said. "There's hope for you." The comedy act had ended; Earl's pitch went on. "I'm not talking just sex. I'm not senile, Wes, not yet. I know how sex ends up—cold snot on your leg. What I'm talking about is energy and life." Earl's arms described a wide arc. "Recaptured in wisdom. A handle on it."

Abbott nodded along blearily, but felt rising doubts. As he sought words for these, he became aware that the spiel had ended. He looked over and saw that Earl had settled back on the couch, all animation gone. The sherry appeared to have caught up with him, to have stilled the bandwagon. His eyes, red, gazed inward, and he breathed so raggedly that Abbott wondered, again, whether Earl really was ill. Emphysema? He was a heavy smoker, like Abbott himself, and like Claire. Claire had emphysema. Abbott wondered what Claire was doing at that moment.

He shambled to the kitchen and splashed cold water on his face. He found his chessboard in the front room and went to the door. He looked back. Earl hadn't stirred; he sat sprawled. Earl had made his bed—a bed of old images; why wasn't the damn fool lying in it with his recycled girlfriend?

Good-bye, Abbott thought, and good luck. One learns something every day—or something is confirmed for one—and today's confirmation was that, by a certain age, men no longer have close friends. Maybe it's the ingrained rivalry under the buddy-buddy, or because, by a certain age, men see themselves as failures.

9

All right, friendship, work, marriage—all had crumbled. But one strong day-to-day tie remained, the temporary tie with Avery. It was pleasant—Abbott would admit it—to be greeted each day with total human warmth. It was gratifying to be recognized, to see eyes glow at the sight of you, and a body quiver as if to spring into your arms. A look once inhuman—seeing you as thing—now flooded with pure welcome for a fellow creature, Abbott: Face. It was nice to be applauded, even if the clapping hands were maladroit, often failing to connect. And it was good to be smiled at, to be thoroughly conned. No other adult, Abbott thought, not Heath and certainly not the babysitters, won such ear-to-ear grins. All in all, this association had its charms.

It also held an imperative like a shout in Abbott's ear: Stop shillyshallying, Abbott, get off your duff and get into shape lest this infant die in some fluke accident.

He shuddered over the possibilities. What if he should keel over and croak in the house? Avery would die of thirst before discovery. And what if he, Abbott, should slip and break a hip during one of their steambaths in the shower? The consequences were too horrible to think about, although old local newspapermen know such things happen.

In the first place, how had he ever allowed himself to slip into such dilapidation? A lazy death wish, maybe, or a wish for any kind of change, even illness. Some benign illness to swaddle him and say: Forget duty, Abbott, no longer put one foot in front of the other.

But now his steps multiplied. He went to the hall closet and dug out a pedometer, a relic from his Lew-like youth. At K-Mart, he bought a stroller for Avery, a deluxe model with a fringed sunshade and a storage space in back.

Months ago, the doctor had prescribed a three-mile daily walk. Now, within a week, Abbott reached the two-mile mark, pushing Avery a mile out, a mile back, down Irene Street, up Eleanor, across Patricia—afternoons full of hyperventilation and forced smiles at passersby and the click of the pedometer on his hip.

Soon the wind improved; the fungoid feet healed; the hemorrhoids withdrew. These results were encouraging, but, in addition to exercising, Abbott had cut down on cigarettes and food, and he was jittery and starved at a time when Avery himself was developing new frustrations.

Abbott tried to empathize. They were shopping today, and all around itself the Impossible I saw new parts of its existence to be touched. The little claw machine was going beserk, wanting to paw all its new prizes—the colors, shapes, and textures that Abbott placed next to it in the shopping cart.

And the Impossible I couldn't understand why Face should keep whisking these new things away. It couldn't understand why the hand that rocked the cradle should now pry open I's claws and steal these new worlds of self—"oleo," gone; "bread," gone—for eternity. There was no space-time in I's little head, but an urge to feel and mouth every object that passed before its eyes.

"Oh, I understand," Abbott muttered. "I understand." All around him, passing before his eyes, were attractive young mothers pushing their Averys in shopping carts.

He perused one in jeans as tight as Sharon's, bending over the frozen-foods bin. As she moved away, he was tempted to follow, to stalk her down the aisles to watch the dimple and bounce of those buttocks.

AGED SATYR AMOK IN SUPERMART. His health seemed to be reviving, at least in fantasy. This unseemly horniness evoked boyish guilt, which in turn projected ill will into the minds of the young women.

Look at that dirty old creep mumbling to the baby. Somebody call a cop.

But he knew that what the mothers noticed, if anything other than Avery's state of cleanliness (and the absence, maybe, of a designer label on his overalls), was only a sedate, somewhat seedy grandpa whose hand kept jerking toward his shirt pocket for a forbidden cigarette. Maybe they thought he was palsied.

Meanwhile, Avery, beet-faced, whined and flailed his arms. Abbott growled, "Shut up!" He handed Avery the bread to squeeze and crinkle. "I'm not legally obligated to take care of you. Keep that in mind."

He wanted a smoke; he wanted ice cream. He wanted a Dairy Queen sundae and a doughnut from Dunkin' Donuts. Avery gummed the wrapper and began to pulp the bread. Abbott wanted to pound on him, this infant, this miserable little bastard—a *certified* bastard—who would soon be mobile, and then one year old, then "terrible two." And later a stereotype: a pinched, aggressive little face shadowed by the peak of a baseball cap and half-hidden behind a balloon of bubble gum. Avery would be learning by then the ways of his elders, the scuffling and brute puzzlement, the world. By then, Abbott thought, he himself would be gone, with any luck.

He wheeled the cart around and hunted for the woman in the tight jeans. There she was, in household goods, spectacular—at each step, a double jounce of one buttock as its sister across the way began to gather and flex for its own impending galumph.

But this chase was absurd, and hardly the best of supermarket manners. Abbott turned his attention to the food prices, the equivalent of a cold shower. Some cans had a smudge of stamped, superimposed prices on them. "This place is all sex and high prices," he grumbled to Avery. "Both out of my reach."

He recalled something that Heath or Lew had said during their debates. "We've been raised to be consumers," one of those parents-to-be had said. Probably Heath, more the cultural critic. "Nothing much more is asked of us."

An old plaint, and a half-truth, but it was worth repeating—worth repeating in some form in the *Call*, sneaked in among his superficial opinions and the tributes to ribbon cuttings and Downtown Shopping Days.

His shopping done, Abbott went to the checkout line. His eye scanned the tabloids in the rack, the headlined fiction about Burt and Liz and Farrah and Liza, *et al.*; who were those people? Oh, he knew, sure, but who gives a diddlyshit about them? Receiving his change, he fumbled with it—somehow it didn't count out right—and he felt himself reddening under the glare of hurried customers in line. As a result of this mild paranoia and his craze for his 11 A.M. cigarette—only one minute away—it seemed that all the queued-up young mothers were judging him.

Look at the loser. A failure as a husband, a nonentity as a father, a mediocrity at his trade. In his late-middle years, a half-assed mother's helper . . .

The 11 A.M. nicotine—he lit up out on the curb—dispelling this whining. He sat down on the curb, out of the pedestrian flow, dizzied from the cigarette but also calmed by it, his mood revived and his thoughts beginning to clear. How silly, he thought, to have felt ashamed and angry over nothing more than the offense of growing old. With one hand he pushed the cart back and forth to lull Avery. As Avery continued to whimper, Abbott opened a box of chocolate cookies and placed one in the baby's fist. "*Bon appétit.* Mess yourself up." Abbott reminded himself to bring a bib on the next shopping trip.

This place, this far end of the curb in front of Finast, was as good a spot as any for another bedtime story. Why not? Other mothers, Abbott had noticed, talked in public to their infants—horses talking to their riders. The story would be another installment mumbled to the listening post—this infant now muddying itself with cookie drool—in the hope of illumination. Another assignment.

Why did Claire leave?

"Your grandmother," he said. "That big girl who ran away to the beach."

The story had a central question: Why did livable habit in the Land of Steady Habits turn into cabin fever? Searching his mind, he found that no answer had washed up, over these weeks, from the problem-solving preconscious.

"We never fought. We talked sometimes. We even made love, though rarely, I'll admit that. Nights when we went out to dinner and drank two bottles of wine. Then she'd look thirty years younger. Like the young Liz. Maybe I looked like Tyrone Power."

Abbott sucked a final, whistling drag from his stub of cigarette, looking, he supposed, like a teen curb-sitter inhaling marijuana. He paused to feel the wave of well-being, short-lived, in which he could organize his thoughts.

"A summary. Note this down.

"One. I didn't have enough vitality for her. So it seemed.

"Two. She was a dreamer who wouldn't quit.

"Three . . ."

Three? What was three? This enumeration brought no focus; maybe a narrative approach would be better.

"Okay. Not long after we were married, she had a one-woman show at the city library. I happened to be on the board of directors.

"Some years after that, she had a one-woman show at a bank downtown. I happened to know people at the bank.

"Are you getting the picture? Through all these years and more, she taught art at a junior high school. She had no teaching talent, either. She burned out before 'burnout' was coined. All those kids, fourteen-year-olds throwing spitballs of modeling clay.

"Meanwhile, I was climbing the job ladder. And doing public service. Busywork, a spasm of it. I was like you, an apprentice. The basic lessons: You learn to get out of your own way and put one thing down in order to pick up another. But I ask you, what's wrong with that? How else do people live? They live in the daze of doing the expected. Am I right? Livable habit. What did Claire want, for Christ's sake? All around us, our friends were outgrowing their dreams, more or less peaceably."

Abbott's hand darted to his shirt pocket, caught itself, and fell. He fluttered his lips with a long exhalation and shook his head to clear it of a returning languor.

"Dreams. Don't ask me what mine was. Let's say to be another Walter Lippmann. But, truth is, I wasn't unhappy writing about streets and sewers. And as to Claire's dream, well, I was like Eisenhower—I didn't know anything about art but I knew what I liked. I liked Claire's puritan dedication. We're good puritans."

Rambling again, rambling. This story needed more flesh, more anecdotes. An anecdotal approach.

"Okay. I'd come home from a hard day at the *Call*—there was a plane crash, say, with a rising toll, causing me no personal grief, of course, but a nightmare of updates and replates. I'd slump home and Claire would say, in this parade-ground voice that some teachers bring home from school, she'd say, 'What really happened today, Wes? Anything you'll remember in two weeks?'

"Later I'd get even. I'd go into her studio. She'd be lifting a tray of gimcracks out of the kiln, or painting motifs on china or something—she dabbled in everything after the painting flopped, and I do mean everything. Basketry, stained glass, hangings, macramé, you name it. Anyway, she'd be there, working; her face would be puckered around a cigarette and one eye closed in the smoke—pure concentration. I'd sidle up to the latest thingamajig and squeeze off a sniper shot: 'This just doesn't grab me.'

"But we didn't fight. We're civilized. She'd stand tall

with that wooden-Indian face of hers, and clam up. And so did I. I wanted peace. Lord, I'd worked hard for it. But peace to me was humdrum to her, I guess. Bland. Well, God bless humdrum. God bless bland."

Again, Abbott reached for a Camel. He remembered his vow and flapped his hand as though cooling it from a burn. How, he wondered, do nonsmokers concentrate? How did Eddie do it? He noticed that Avery's fist was chocolate-covered, and the infant was trying to swallow it. He handed over another cookie lest the baby strangle. Famished from dieting, he took a cookie and nibbled on it. He'd subtract one hundred and fifty calories from lunch.

"Now and then our feelings would get together, like relatives at a funeral. You'll find out some day. They all say, 'We should really get together more often.' Then they go home and lose the address."

Abbott looked up; a shopper had come his way from the flow down the curb and was eyeing him. A woman, fortyish, whose glance shifted from Abbott to the chocolate-smeared Avery and back again, narrowing, as she passed on toward K-Mart.

Abbott hunched up on one ham, raised his arms and heaved himself to his feet. "We better move," he muttered, "or I'll get arrested." With both hands he massaged his lower back, stiff from curb-sitting. He pushed the shopping cart to the parking lot, stowed the groceries, and strapped Avery in the child's car seat. He settled himself behind the wheel and lit a cigarette. The noon cigarette, way ahead of schedule, but necessary. He dragged deep and turned his attention inward. There, in the reviving lucidity of his mind, he'd remember more.

"More details every time I try. The weather, and what she was wearing. It was windy. She was wearing a white cardigan over a summer dress of some ice-cream color. Raspberry! It was raspberry. We were walking on the Outer Beach, two empty-nesters on their afternoon stroll. Plodding up-beach, in the dunebuggy tracks, rather than down in the breaker foam, where we had hiked years before. I've told you about that famous hike. Well, picture us now: plodding along, the two S-curves of hump and paunch. On this day I was feeling smug because we were in the clear at last, financially. Our house and the cottage were just about paid for. We were property owners where once we had been vagabonds. And pictures were beginning to flit through my head—Mount McKinley, glaciers—the first images of an idyll for retirement. We'd buy one of those silver Airstreams and roam the country. I saw myself at the picnic table of a site, a late bloomer typing up commentary as good as Lippmann's, and I saw Claire nearby at her easel, painting a late bloomer's masterpiece, happy at last. I was sure Claire would go for this idyll. I even thought I'd described it to her. After all those years of marriage, wasn't my inner voice audible to her? I was reading RV catalogues in the drugstore; hadn't she divined my intentions?

"She said, 'I'm not going back.' This remark had a breathlessness about it, as if getting it out winded her, but I paid no attention. I used to make 'em myself—end-of-vacation laments. 'To hell with the pension, I'm not going back.'

"She was in the chair, the wicker chair. She hugged herself, acted chilled. She even looked girlish. I mean that—girlish, this big impassive woman. She looked scared, or surprised at herself, huddled around some resolve that had taken her a long time to work up. She said I didn't need her, hadn't needed her in years. 'Oh, maybe you did at the beginning,' she said, 'you were a shy kind of fella.' I resented that. 'And I needed you,' she said, 'because you said you liked my work.' So much for the Young Love we'd had, broken down to its idiot simplicities. I sputtered for a while. She toughed it out, becoming the wooden Indian, and I drove home in a sulk.

"A week later I drove back, hopefully to bring her home. Back to joyless sanity, God bless it. C'mon, Claire, I wanted to say, come back to making the meals and cleaning house. What I said was, come back to the real independence you had. Your hobbies and the craft-fair circuit with your friends.

"But she'd dug in. She had taken a job teaching ceramics to retirees, and she was having the cottage winterized. I told her she'd get woods-queer and end up babbling to herself. She said, 'I've got the brains and discipline to handle this.' At home, I'd already begun babbling to myself.

"I asked if she wanted a divorce. It seemed the logical next step. But the question only amused her. She said, 'There's no lover in the picture, Wes,' laughing deep, Old Stoneface going soft, and I laughed, too—a shared guffaw—for neither one of us is what you'd call a romantic catch. I told her that, if divorced, we'd duck the marriage penalty on our taxes. She sobered and ask if a lawyer's fee wouldn't offset the saving. Picture it: two old Yankees, haggling."

"You have to be alone to invent anything," Claire said, "and it can take a lifetime."

"Invent what?"

"You know only what you know," she went on, "but there's joy in finding it out. Somebody said that. I don't know who."

Unused to speechmaking, she sat back in the wicker chair and shrugged. She looked up at Abbott through lowered eyes. Girlish again, he thought; and despite his resentment he felt a wave of tenderness over the renewal she appeared to be feeling after a week on her own. A glow, as they say. He nodded for her to continue.

"What you find out is a kind of truth. It outdoes reality. Reality's a mess—I'm quoting you on that." She smiled but he did not react to this little nudge of familiarity. She went on: "This truth saves you." She rolled her eyes ceilingward as if to imply that any sensible person would be scandalized by such claims. "Am I making any sense to you?"

Well, some, yes. He'd admit that. Truths are usually off-the-wall; they are incidental to intention. Answers to the deepest queries arise from a single shining paragraph in a bad book, say, and even from overheard conversations.

"Is it silly," she asked, "to think I might still have something to contribute?"

"I suppose not," he said, thinking: *Grow up and come home.*

Her voice had trailed off. Now it returned with calm confidence. "This truth, it's a mastery and a freedom. So far as I can tell, freedom is pretty simple. It's to call something something else and to act on that, stick with it."

"You're talking about madness," Abbott said.

"Freedom, too. Listen, God knows, I'm no thinker. Not much of a doer, either, but what I'm talking about is this intensity of your whole self, all of you, what you are. You *know* it—the world put right, or a life better lived. Maybe I should use the word 'now.' I don't mean 'Now Generation'—all that kid stuff—but 'now' as in '*Forever is composed of Nows.*' "

Claire spread her hands on her knees and waited for Abbott's reaction.

He was puzzled. Her speech was so abstract—college-kid talk. Esthetics? In matters of philosophy, all he ever thought about, if he thought it at all, was ethics, the problem of trying to be of use. A set of myopic actions, if you will, fumbling for a rough fix on the terrain.

He had been touched, though, by her closing line from Emily Dickinson. He recalled that, back in college, he and Claire were Dickinson fans. They would throw lines at each other out of context, to reflect their feelings and their situations. A little game they played. And Abbott recalled that he was hard to beat. Rote memory was one of his petty powers over Claire. So now he reflected for a while, trying to remember a line. He listened to the Cape wind sand-blasting the cottage and he felt what seemed to him to be the tenor of Claire's new life—obsessiveness and enclosure. A Dickinson line popped to mind, into this context of wind and sand and used-up feelings. He quoted: " '*Anecdotes of air in dungeons.*' "

Claire caught on instantly. She smiled with a shade of the old playfulness—the young Claire who had said, "Let's walk the beach," a beach thirty miles long—and she topped Abbott with another Dickinson line: " '*Through what transports of patience I reached the stolid bliss.*' "

Abbott looked unseeingly at the random movement of cars in the parking lot.

He looked at Avery. The baby, perched in his car seat, contentedly nuzzled what was left of his second cookie. Child neglect! The child's teeth would grow in rotten. Abbott leaned over and with his handkerchief wiped the cookie spittle off Avery's chin. He spat on the cloth—mothers do this, what the hell—and dabbed Avery's hands. Then he took a second cookie for himself. Another hundred-and-fifty calories, total now three hundred. He'd skip lunch altogether. Or else cheat a little: sneak a few spoonfuls of Avery's babyfood to keep body and soul together until dinner.

"I won't bore you with this much longer. Your mother's next. I guess, to her, it was like a long-expected death in the family: no surprise but still a shock. How dare her parents 'split,' acting like the young!

"I told her: 'Look at it this way. All your life you work for something, without result, but the work itself becomes your salvation. Your sour bread turns sweet—something like that.

"She gave me that squint of hers, through her specs, and she voiced her all-purpose evaluation of things. 'Bullshit!' She qualified it a little: 'That is pollyanna bullshit!'

"I played philosopher and told her about Sisyphus. I said, 'He works up a defiant joy as he rolls that stone back up the hill, every day, through eternity.'

" 'Camus!' she said. 'Adolescent crap. Haven't you read anybody since the nineteen-fifties?'

"You must remember, Avery, that this all occurred before you were born, when your mother was even more of a know-it-all than she is now. Your arrival has helped. I told her that if Claire wanted to recapture adolescence, more power to her.

"To this, Heath said, 'You always make excuses for people. Really, you think you can brush off a crisis with a one-liner or else you say nothing at all.'

"Well, she drove up to the Cape to see Claire for herself. On return, she briefed me. She said Claire seemed to be happy and 'I sort of half-understand the high she's talking about. You wouldn't understand, being a man.'

"Somehow, I kept my temper. I told her sexism had nothing to do with Claire's breakaway. At this, Heath flared her nostrils and tipped her head to one side, eyes closed—instant nap. This look usually means that she and I have reached some topic way beyond my ken.

"I asked her what Claire was inventing. 'She talked about inventing something,' I said. Heath said, 'Who knows? Mother talks starry-eyed but it usually boils down to something practical. Don't you know her at all? There were plenty of warnings, you know. You died on her, and she didn't want to go on sitting by your coffin.' After this, a look of apology suffused my daughter's sweet face, and she said, 'Sorry, Daddy, but that's the truth. She gave lots of signals.' I told her, truthfully—at that time—that I could remember none. She said, 'If there's anything I've learned from you two, anything at all in my life, it's the wisdom of having a great big fat mouth.' The new civility, in other words. Hi, friend, let's be honest and insult each other. Let's be brutal when there should be tact. I digress; the briefing went on. She said Claire might invent something new in pottery—she wanted her kiln moved up there. 'Mother *does* have talent, you know.' And she and some friends were thinking of opening a craft shop in P'town. Claire's friends—as Heath named them, I quickly closed doors in my head to bar any appearance there of those arty-farty people; forgive me. Heath said they planned to name the shop 'Wild Geese.' Saying this, she cocked an eye—and practically her fists—ready to defend 'Wild Geese' from any putdown by me. Then Heath thought for a moment, finger on her lip—like this: dainty. In one instant, a switch, you see, a switch in modes from wise-ass collegian to domesticated young girl, being chirrupy. She said, 'Oh, and Mother's doing some new things in quilting. A really beautiful thing, simple design but really striking; it's like a textile painting. She says quilting is going to be very big in a few years.'

"That's just ducky, I thought. I said, 'So my wife left me for a quilting bee.'

"For the first time, she laughed. She said, 'The whole thing's a stupid cliché. Mother runs off to Cape Cod for her art, and you rattle around here and mope. But one thing does worry me. Did you know she was having trouble with a front tooth?' I knew. It was an old root-canal job. She said, 'Well, she had it out. And she's not bothering to replace it.' I said, 'When money's short, the teeth go first. Ask the old farmers.' And she said, 'Daddy, I don't *give* a shit about the old farmers. Does she have hospitalization and all that?' This was insulting. I said, 'Did you think I would cancel her coverage?' She said no. 'You're not a bastard,' she said. 'Actually, you let people walk all over you in your kindness.'

"Kindness? This word stopped me. I wasn't kind. Kindness requires presence. I've told you about my delinquencies with your mother. Never there, in mind, during her infancy, nor later on, in her time of Kotex and tears, as Claire once phrased it. In our society, fathers tend to get sidelined. Look at your own. Myself, I was present in a few roles. Chauffeur, mainly, driving her to those lessons and meets. One memory stands out; I told you about it. She climbed into the car after a lesson, dragging her cello case through snow on the curb, and she said, 'Oh, I'm so *sick* of it!' Sick of what? The cello? Snow? She stunk at the cello, and it had been a long winter.

"She said, 'Mother wants me to be talented, but I'm not, and I'm not *going* to be.' "

Eureka!

Remembering those words, Abbott slapped his hands on the steering wheel of the car, startling Avery. Those words had eluded all his past tries at recall. He was improving in his assignments—in the journey inward and back, as hard in its way as any journey forward.

"You're next. Enter Avery. Trumpets! Cellos. No, make that liquid and wind. You joined our happy circle, *in ovo.* Claire panicked, at first. I've told you about our dialogue on the phone, lines right out of a made-for-TV movie. She told me I didn't care about Heath. She said, 'Will you just once, for God's sake, take a stand!' "

Abbott went silent. Avery was restless, crooning in a tone of mild complaint. That tone, and also a mother's sense of timing and body language, told Abbott that the infant needed a diaper change. Had they been sitting here in the shopping center through a whole cycle of digestion? Abbott lifted Avery out of his seat, took him around front and lay him on the hood of the car for the changing. To hell with the young mothers in the parking lot. Let 'em look.

At home, Abbott plunked Avery in the highchair and prepared lunch. After two cookies from a delinquent caretaker, Avery probably wouldn't eat much real food, but Abbott mixed some vegetables in the blender. He added liver, which Avery detested. Perhaps the blend would camouflage the liver and fool the child into accepting some protein. But no; the baby didn't even bother to spit; the first spoonful dribbled out of the front of his mouth. And Abbott, slow of reflex, failed to pull the bowl away in time to prevent Avery's hand from plunging into it.

Ah, what the hell. Abbott understood. Food is fun to touch, like anything else. If Face offers it, why not take it in hand? Why not lather your highchair with your beets?

The chair and the floor around it were encrusted with food from previous meals.

What the hell. On impulse and in mild exasperation, Abbott dunked his own hand into the bowl. It felt like warm mush, a bit gritty, oozing between his fingers. He closed his eyes and saw an image of gold kernels in brown mush. A miracle of retrieval occurred. He was seven or eight years old. He was standing in a sunny pasture with junipers. He had been running but now he stood still, aghast. Slowly, he wriggled the toes of his right foot. He had stepped, barefoot, through the outer crust of a cowflop into its hot interior, which was releasing its steam and its sweet stench, now, to the morning.

A disgusting delight! And he might have gone to his grave without ever reliving this earthy moment, if not for Avery. Burden or not, the kid was surely a mood lifter. Like some whimsical vandal, spray-painting a jalopy, an old chassis named Abbott, sunk hubcap-deep.

Abbott rinsed his fingers at the kitchen tap. "One more loose end to the story. After you were born, Claire offered to help. She wrote to me. She said, 'I know when I'm beaten, and I was the last to find out about the arrangements. I'll take time out and help you, if you want.' She said, 'It's not fair of them to put the whole burden on you.' She didn't know I'd put it on myself.

"Well, my first impulse was to say, 'Hurry, hurry.' Because Claire knew all the practicalities, you see. Having been a mother, she knew what clothes to buy, the shots for distemper, and so forth. And what little ailments not to panic over, the way Heath and I panicked over your cradle cap.

"On the other hand—oh, we editorialists are good at 'on the other hand'—if Claire came home, she'd be compromising her so-called freedom. What I mean is, I wondered if the letter was a signal that she'd had enough of garret life up on the Cape.

"On the third hand, Claire had always been candid.

"So I resolved all this doubt with a phone call. 'Do you

or do you not want to come home?' Like asking a coy candidate to get off the pot and say whether he's going to run.

" 'No!' she said. 'But if you're overwhelmed, please call on me.'

"Lovely woman, my wife. I decided right then and there that I didn't want a divorce.

"On the other hand, I didn't want her help any longer even though I was overwhelmed.

"I seemed to be taking a stand."

That night, Abbott, having chattered to Avery most of the day, tried to omit story hour at cribside. But the creature of habit tossed and whimpered until Abbott assumed the customary position, resting his elbows on the crib rail. Talked out, he made nonsense noise—"Blab bloop whoopity-whoop whinnyway doodle-dee-do"—varying the tonalities and the syllables more or less like speech. Avery was content with this; he lay still and his eyes grew groggy. And Abbott, after subduing his overview of himself as a babbling idiot—or as a purveyor of some higher truth—found a hypnotic calm in his nonsense, and another release of memory as his voice diminished to a whisper. A memory not simply of people's words and a few signpost gestures, but of full sensation, like the recollection of the pasture, and of the farmhouse weeks ago.

Although the scene was dark, he knew instantly where he was. On a porch, on a street of woodframe tenements with porches tiered on their fronts, families sitting out on them in the dark. In the tiny front yards, laurel bushes shone like hammered silver in the light of passing cars. Crickets sang in gardens—Victory Gardens?—in the small back yards, and hens rustled in their sleep in little coops there. What year was this? Had Hitler invaded Poland yet? The boy observing this scene would not have known. Seated on the porch, he was half listening to two low voices in the dark. The scene had much human presence, although the mood of the boy—or of the man reliving the boy—was a kind of despair mixed with restlessness, like a bereavement. The man and the woman were trying to recall some day in their lives, the date of some small event, something that had occurred in a countryside from which they had moved. Outlined in the shadows, the woman swayed slowly in a porch rocker, her face upturned. The man, in a sleeveless undershirt and a long-billed cap, sat facing the street, hunched forward with his elbows on the rail of the porch. The sag of his posture contrasted somehow with a blitheness in the woman's voice. Shc said the event they remembered had happened in May—"the dogwoods were out." The man grumbled no, July, the shop where he worked had been closed for summer shutdown. As the two talked on in their sparse, soft batting of the breeze, neither looked at the other. And neither, the boy knew, was listening to the other. Their voices were parallel monologues, the woman's now sounding mildly needful to fix that date in their lives, a date grown fateful in the little world of this moment. The boy wanted to help them, to bring them to a mutual discovery, but he couldn't remember. What boy ever knows what the day is?

The boy—no, the man reliving thc boy—closed his eyes against tears.

10

BULLETIN.

News from Earl, that stranger, so shocking that Abbott went dumbstruck on the phone. Earl said he'd been mugged, hurt.

"Abbott, are you there?"

Abbott recovered his voice. "Where are you?"

"Home. Now listen to me."

"How bad is it?"

"I said listen to me!"—testy now, as if Abbott were a young rewrite man who'd muddle up a leg reporter's facts. And Abbott pictured Earl's face at such times: pinched like that of a little crone about to spit.

Earl said he had double vision from a blow on the head. "I can't see well enough to drive. Therefore, I want you to come over here and drive me to the hospital. Got that? Abbott?" Abbott was silent. "Must I ask you to repeat after me?"

"God almighty," Abbott said. "A concussion."

"Don't diagnose; just get your ass over here."

Earl hung up. His call had interrupted Avery's bedtime. Though tired, the child would have to be bundled along on the mercy mission. He grubbed at his eyes as Abbott dressed him in a heavy sleeper for the outdoors. On the drive over to the apartment he grew wobbly-headed in his baby seat.

Carrying him, Abbott rushed into the building and banged on Earl's door. Earl responded from within—"Medic! Medic!" Entering, Abbott noticed the lock had not been forced.

Earl lounged in the easychair, one leg over the arm. Abbott felt a twinge of pride in his fallen-away crony, who affected a style for this occasion. A man wounded but insouciant, a bloodstained cigarette sticking up at a jaunty, Rooseveltian angle from a fat lip. Abbott tipped Earl's head back for a closer look at that lip—it would need a stitch or two, yes. Earl grunted and brushed Abbott's hand away. He squinted one eye at Avery. "I see you brought your dog along."

"Where's yours?" Earl was alone. No Sharon there. And no excited neighbors, no cop taking notes.

The room had been ransacked. There was a central, shocking vacancy where the TV set had been. Earl's books littered the floor; every one must have been skimmed for cash. Abbott wagged his head over the thoroughness of the job. "Did they miss anything?"

"Not 'they,' " Earl said. "He. One kid got it all. My VCR, my tape recorder. My .38—he'll fence *that* fast. My goddamn binoculars I stole in Korea. Even my typewriter. How's this for a head: HE LOOTED AT HIS LEISURE?"

Earl continued his story on the drive to the hospital emergency room. "I left work early so I caught the punk by surprise. He was carting my stuff to a van. He told me he was Sharon's boyfriend and he was robbing me blind to teach an old fart like me not to mess around with young girls." Earl laughed hard, a laugh quickly terminating in a yelp of pain. He pressed a handkerchief to his swollen lip. "And he dared me to call the cops. He'd tell them I committed statutory rape." Earl laughed again, but hollowly, with less of a mouth stretch. "Well, I closed on him. What else would a red-blooded, two-fisted old fart do? I figured he'd be easy: a skinny longhair, looked like a druggie. He took a karate stance, that silly pose, you know, arms up like fucking candelabra branches." Earl demonstrated, thrusting out elbows and upright forearms. "I figured, shit, trick this sucker with the old right feint. His right guard'll come down. Then throw a left hook, a doubled-up hook, pow-pow"—Earl threw two punches toward the windshield, snorting—"to head and body, and then a right uppercut. But . . ." Earl dabbed with the handkerchief. "Abbott, I learned something. My reflexes. They're gone."

"It happens," Abbott said.

For the first time, Earl looked and sounded disconsolate. "Gone! Shot! I've got to get in better shape. I saw the openings but couldn't get to 'em, and then I stayed down; I didn't want the lad to have to face a murder charge." Earl gripped Abbott's shoulder. "You've got to do me one more favor."

Abbott nodded. "I'll call while they're sewing you up. They'll want the serial number of the gun. And an inventory."

"Inventory?" Earl stared, his head cocked because of his double vision. "Abbott, I'm beginning to think your reflexes are shot."

"You'll need an inventory. You know how it works. Inflate the values."

"Abbott, you're not listening! The kid practically handed me the phone."

All right, now Abbott understood. Earl would face no charges if the boy blabbed, but word of his involvement with a minor would leak out in this small city, probably via a *Call* police reporter, and reach Denham. And Denham, for all his reverence for old pros, brooked no semi-public scandals.

"I don't care if I get canned," Earl said, "but I want it to happen *my* way." He leaned close to the car's instrument panel and peered, cockeyed, at the clock. "I want you to call Sharon. She's due home about now. When she finds the place wrecked, she'll have a shit fit."

Abbott blinked. "You questioned my reflexes. Now I question yours. She probably set you up."

"Maybe." Earl was old enough not to show surprise or even sadness. He cranked down the car window and spat a jet of blood into the street. "If so," he added, wiping his mouth with the bloody handkerchief and then releasing that, too, into the dark, "then *c'est la vie* —I came out way ahead in trade. But she's innocent until proven guilty."

Abbott emitted a mild Bronx cheer. "Do yourself a favor. Stop playing with these dead-end kids."

"Don't get stuffy. I've never had so much fun in my life."

"May I point out that you were clobbered and robbed?"

"I'll heal, and possessions are a prison. I'm learning things, Abigail."

At the hospital, Abbott waited out Earl's examination. Between calls to the apartment—unanswered—he paced the corridor to calm Avery, irritable from being kept awake. Avery squirmed and whined. He clutched Abbott's collar and small fistfuls of Abbott's cheek.

Earl reappeared in a wheelchair pushed by an aide. They'd bandaged his cut and dressed him in a hospital johnny. "No sweat," he said; his eyes would uncross. "But my goddamn blood pressure's way up and they want me to stay the night. Did you call Sharon?"

"No answer. But I'm sure your assailant has filled her in."

"You've got to go back there and explain."

"Absurd! They're probably splitting the loot."

Earl reddened, and his narrow chest puffed up under his johnny. "Look, the young lady might—just might—feel some loyalty to me. Will you please go back there and ease her mind?"

Okay, okay. To prevent a stroke, Abbott would grant this final favor. He would deliver an absurd message, from victim to perpetrator, while at the same time lugging an infant who'd begun to squall over its upset routine.

It was the squalling that, later, proved to be a password into the apartment. Upon Abbott's return, the door was locked. No one responded to his knocks. But as Avery continued to cry, the door opened on its chain and Abbott saw a sliver of face and a large wet eye circled with smeared makeup, raccoon-like.

"Oh my God," Sharon said. "Wes!" She hustled him into the room and slammed the door, replacing the chain. "Am I glad to see *you*." She had been crying. Now her fear had the look of anguished wonder as she bent, hands on knees, to touch noses with Avery. "And you, too, sweetie. Oh, you are a honeybunch! Yes, you *are*!"

Avery stopped crying. He responded with a cold infant gaze to the cootchy-cooing. Oh, the infant wasn't fooled, thought Abbott, who himself felt tonight the armor of indignation against commonplace charms. Tonight, no gooseflesh or prickling of his hair simply because a young female stood close. After all, here was a suspect, possible accessory to robbery and assault, describable as a white female in her teens, with a thistle-fleece, silvery streak in her hair, and houri eye makeup smeared by tears into a semblance of an outlaw's black mask; said subject wearing a white T-shirt bearing the words "SAVE KILLIAN'S POINT."

What in hell was Killian's Point?

Abbott, pacing the floor with Avery in his arms, described the evening's events. Sharon listened, crumpled in the easychair. Tears ran, but the girl's mouth remained hard set. At last she said, "Sonofabitch."

"You know the boy, then?"

"He's crazy; poor Earl shouldn't have fought him. Can I see Earl?"

"Tomorrow. He's all right."

"He might need me."

In his mind, Abbott saw, and quickly dismissed, an image of Earl lifting his johnny in welcome. "Save it for tomorrow. This boy, who is he?"

"Do you have to know?" She looked up at Abbott from a reproachful angle of face. "I don't know his last name."

"I won't tell the police. It's off the record."

"Frito," she said. After this revelation, she mimed a hard swallow and then swatted herself lightly on the mouth, as if for spilling a secret.

"All right," Abbott said, "*what* is . . . Frito?"

"I told you! He's this guy I know."

"He told Earl he's your boyfriend."

She glared. "That's a bunch of shit. He follows us around, that's all."

"Who's 'us'?"

"Me and Regina and Pam. He's crazy."

"How did Frito get a key?"

The girl shrugged. "Maybe he stole mine and had one made. He might come back. Would you stay here tonight?"

Abbott persisted. "How could he get hold of your key?"

"We live there!" She scowled over Abbott's ignorance. "I mean, I live there when I'm not here. I room with Dee and Rae. This happened before."

He motioned to her to go on.

"A guy Angela was going out with—his place got robbed. We thought Frito did it, but nobody knew for sure. Now we know, and we'll tell his goddamn probation officer."

Where did all these children—these Dees, Raes, Sharons, and whatnot—live? In a jail? A halfway house?

In sudden irrelevance, the girl said, "He'll never go to sleep if you bounce him around like that."

She was referring, Abbott realized after a moment, to Avery, squirming again as Abbott paced the floor, high-stepping over the strewn books. "This man"—Abbott kicked books aside and pushed on with the interrogation—"Regina's friend—"

"Angela's."

"—did he report the theft?"

"No, he didn't want to get us all in trouble."

"Was he older? Like Earl?"

"Yeah, he was older." Sharon snuffled; the waterworks had resumed. "So what?"

"You like older men."

"So? Young guys you meet are just bums."

Now Abbott saw a pattern, or at least a bizarre possibility. It appeared that the young thief called Frito, stalker of Sharon and her friends, had discovered an arrest-proof form of burglary among dirty old men. In that case, Sharon might be innocent, her story too strange not to be true. So, chalk one up for Earl, even though Earl, in his dotage, had lowered himself into a hellhole of the young.

Abbott felt a wave of pity for the girl. Slumped there, a pigeon-toed huddle of defeat. As he studied her, he was reminded of something. This situation—this face-off between them—had a parallel swimming into awareness. What was it? Her eyes were shut, and her brow clenched tight to wall out further questions from him.

The parallel came clear; himself and Denham. Of course! The girl was himself, using the same evasions, more or less: fadeouts; playing dumb; non sequiturs; an air of exhaustion; a sulk with eyes shut and head bowed to the side like that of some arrow-riddled martyr on a cross. As Abbott pondered this ugly picture of himself, the martyr's face lifted with a smile of appeal. She had sensed the letup in the third degree. She was quick, he supposed, at spotting mood shifts—a keenness one derives from a rough childhood. He knew the feeling.

What feeling? Why should he know it? Again, he found himself caught in a double take. Why should he have assumed so readily that he'd had a rough childhood? He'd never thought much about it. Nothing's more tiresome than a man who tells you about a rough childhood.

The girl spoke. Her comment seemed shockingly apt. "You need a pacifier."

The referents fell into place. Abbott said, "I had one. He spit it out on the hospital floor."

"Well, you've got to do *something*. He's overtired."

Abbott hitched the baby higher on his chest and went on pacing. He decided to end his grilling of the girl. He underscored the pointlessness of it with a final, inane question. "What's Killian's Point?"

"What?"

"What it says on your T-shirt." Could be anything, he supposed; place, proviso, penis . . .

Sharon tucked her face down to look, making a small double chin. Charming, Abbott thought. She pulled her T-shirt down flat against her breasts in order to read the print upside down. Dark areolas peeped at him through the fabric. His genitals twinged.

"Oh, I don't know. I borrowed this from Dee. She goes to meetings. On the environment and all."

Under what roof on Earth did such things as probation officers and environmental concern coexist? Never mind, he wouldn't ask. He wanted to know nothing more about Earl's doxie. Curiosity's a killer; takes a whole lifetime to squelch it. Anyway, further talk was impossible. Avery's elfin fingernails had embedded themselves in the flesh of Abbott's neck, already raw as if from dozens of tiny razor cuts, and the baby was kicking Abbott's ribs and crying the hardest of all cries, a strangulated sound like breathless laughter. As Abbott loosened the pincers in his neck, he heard Sharon's voice rise above Avery's—"Oh, for God's sake, give him to me!"—full of exasperation. Gladly, he surrendered Avery to the girl. She cuddled the infant to her and began pacing.

Abbott eased himself down on the sofa. He lit a cigarette, his 11 P.M. smoke at only—he checked his watch—10:35, but surely he deserved a bonus smoke for this hard night. After several blissful drags he watched the girl glide back and forth with the sobbing Avery.

"It won't work," Abbott said. "I'll have to take him for a long drive."

The girl glanced over from her cradling and crooning. "It'll work. You'll see."

"Well, anyhow you're a softer perch."

Abbott froze. That last remark, sexually playful—had he, Abbott, uttered that? "What I mean is, women are better at pacing babies to sleep. My daughter can do it."

This qualifier didn't help. Abbott glanced at Sharon and saw a flirty wrinkling of her nose.

Dear God in heaven. Help, somebody. Anybody. Avery.

No use calling on Avery. His sobs diminished, and the only sound now was husky breathing as the infant gazed up at the new Face, the new presence that enveloped him. Abbott could not read his expression, a mixture of fear and fascination. That look passed without transition into sleep.

"See, I told you," the girl said. "Now come here."

She led him to Earl's bedroom. She placed Avery on the far side of the bed and spread the cover over him. On the near side she placed one of the bureau drawers that had been dumped on the floor in the theft. "So he won't roll off," she explained.

Could Avery roll? Abbott didn't know, despite his close observations of the infant, and he felt remiss. He followed the girl back to the front room. "You must be a mother," he said.

She laughed. "Are you out of your mind?"

So much for that.

She went into the kitchen and opened the cabinets. "You want a drink of Earl's booze? Maybe Frito missed a bottle, I don't know . . . no, he got every damn one of them. You hungry?"

Abbott, back on the sofa, fingering his tired eyes, heard the refrigerator door open. His hostess called, "You want a sandwich? Roast beef? I stole some from the bowling alley."

Bowling alley? Oh, never mind. "Nothing, thanks," Abbott called.

The refrigerator door closed. A few minutes later, Abbott felt the sofa heave. A weight settled on his thigh. The girl lay full length, her head pillowed on his thigh, and was looking up at him. "Please stay."

A violent shiver went up his spine and into his hairline. His belly and scrotum tightened.

She said, "I'm really afraid he might come back. You can sleep in there with Avery. I'll sleep out here."

"Why would he come back?"

"Who knows? He's crazy." Her eyes were soft, dazed; no playfulness in them now.

"Try to sleep," he said.

"I will."

He hadn't meant atop him, but she rolled sideways and snuggled up like a little girl, her head in his lap, facing away from him. Her breathing slowed, suggesting sleep.

Abbott reflected on this strange night. Here he sat, babysitting an imp who weeks ago had offered to babysit Avery. As the minutes passed, he monitored his physical state. The storm was abating—the flood of saliva, as from a tart taste, and the billows of gooseflesh over his flanks. The storm yielded to an erection—yes, up and holding steady—and a vestigial ache of the kind known by the crude term "lover's nuts" back in high school days.

Ah, the old high school days. Source of life's most vivid memories, some nostalgists say. He felt an impulse to place his hand on Sharon's ribs just below the armpit and inch it forward for a 1940s-style cheap feel, the kind you stole when sitting with your arm around a girl in a moviehouse, or in a car as you steered one-handed with the necker's knob on the wheel. But this was so puerile a whim that Abbott's hand moved at once to compensate with a gesture more humane; before his mind could stay it, the hand stroked Sharon's hair. It halted as he heard a murmur of appreciation. "That's nice."

"Go to sleep," he said.

"I will"—an obedient whisper.

She slept, or seemed to.

To keep his movements to a minimum, he lit his midnight cigarette one-handed in a way he recalled from those high school days. Kids called it "Hollywood style." With his thumb he bent one match outward, closed the book and rubbed the match across the flint. He accomplished this without scorching his thumb or igniting the whole book. Unlike Earl's, his reflexes were sharp. Bring Frito on.

And what of Frito? Well, if a young psychopath burst in, women and children would be saved first, boosted out the bedroom window; and then he, Abbott, would ram furniture at the bastard to get him off his feet, after which he'd apply a headlock and bellow like a bull, praying that Earl's neighbors would get involved enough to help scare the kid away. He'd pray, also, for a minor injury, even a mild heart attack, say, that would guarantee a leisurely retirement on disability. Hadn't Earl expressed such a wish? The idea was so alluring that Abbott fantasized a little—a trip to Mount Katahdin—*come on, Frito, you sonofabitch*—before falling asleep.

When he awoke, he saw pre-dawn light through the front-room windows. Sharon lay curled up at the end of the sofa. He listened for the stir and fuss of an awakening infant, and then realized that the early hour had given him a reprieve; Avery would not awaken and start making demands until after they were home, back to their routine. An enjoyable day beckoned. He'd call in sick again. They'd take their regular long hike, Avery riding in the stroller.

Abbott stood up and went to the bedroom. He ached from sit-up sleep, but the pain was the celebratory kind that follows a good workout, the kind of soreness that you joke about as you stretch. He gathered Avery in the crook of an arm. He pulled the cover off Earl's bed and dragged it into the front room and spread it over the sleeping Sharon. He took a last look at her. Last night had been peculiar, and he had played some unaccustomed roles, all flowing from his life with Avery. Comforter, for example. Protector. Even, you might say, father. But no, let's not overdo.

11

Heath sat on the living-room couch with Avery in her lap. For her benefit, he had staged the Con Game, the eye-glowing welcome and wholehearted hug, but Mother's visit today would have to be short. A pileup of work at the university would prevent her from spending the whole weekend at home.

"I wanted a word with you about the babysitter problem," she told Abbott. "It worries me."

"Worries me, too," Abbott said, although Heath's showdown tone worried him more at the moment. He settled deeper into his armchair. "Did I tell you about the one with too many men friends?"

"I don't want to hear it again, Daddy." She pressed Avery against her breast and nestled her face into the hollow of his shoulder, sniffing deep of his scent. "M-m-m-m-m, *Sweetheart*." She looked up sharply at Abbott. "We've got to stop putting this kid through a human chain of caretakers. That's really unhealthy."

"They're all unqualified," Abbott said, "one after another. Should I stay home?"

"Wish *I* could," she said. "Sometimes. I know it's not *your* fault." Heath nuzzled Avery's neck and both of them squealed with the pleasure of it. Delightful to watch, Abbott thought, this affection, but the voice resumed. She looked up and said, "If you expose a baby to a lot of people that way, he can get indifferent to people, or scared of them, or go any whichway. There's no telling. That's an observed fact in the literature."

Ah, so. The Book had spoken, in a tone airy and hurried, as if only a bore would ask for details or express dissent. "Do you think," she went on, "that maybe you're being just a little bit too . . . *fussy*, with these women?"

"Day care's a disgrace," Abbott said.

"Everybody knows that, Daddy; I'm not criticizing *you*. But maybe you're being too much of a perfectionist."

"Did I tell you about the one who propped him in front of daytime TV?"

"I'm trying to be serious."

"I *am* serious." Heath's look of youthful impatience, he thought, was more ugly than endearing.

"I was talking to Dhandipani about this," she said. "He agrees. We should try to settle on one person."

Abbott thought of Dr. Dhandipani, the pediatrician. A stark professional smile and an accent often hard to fathom. "What does he know about American children?"

"What?" Heath's face jerked up from Avery's neck.

"I said—"

"Yes, I heard what you said. You're joking, right? They're the same in Iran. Two arms, two legs . . ."

"Pakistan."

"Wherever."

"I think. His government paid for his education. Why isn't he taking care of his own people instead of fattening off the American middle class?"

Heath's eyes closed hard, and the hand that had been stroking Avery's back froze. "Oh my God," she said. "A bigot. Turning into an old bigot."

Was he? No, not at all. *Hey, Dhandipani, welcome aboard.* The issue was this: On Avery's behalf, a little paranoia was a healthy thing. Avery had to be protected, sometimes even from his own mother.

. . .

The orbits continue. Face comes and goes.

Once flat, barely a mask, Face is now rounded in contour. It has grown details someday to be known by me as "eyes," "ears"—tufts of gray hair in the ears. I know the recurring Face in its uniqueness, and grow wary of some of the others, the guises.

Space-time has widened. I sleep much less. The claw machine of my hands grows more efficient. More prizes float by, offering themselves to be grasped, mouthed, waved, banged, stared at. And, once more, grasped, mouthed, waved, banged, stared at.

And, once more . . .

More orbits, more practice.

All of me remains a mystery, but things recur, and there are symmetries.

Recurrences, symmetry—a hand on one side, a hand on the other. Toes on one side, toes on the other.

A wall on one side, a wall on the other.

Rock! Wall, left; wall, right.

On my back, my familiar plane, I rock myself from side to side. The motion is new, exciting—a thrill ride as in Face's arms.

So, faster! Laughter! Wall on the left, wall on the right, and between them a blurred glimpse of ceiling—a white space that I have gazed at for months, lately in boredom.

More practice.

Faster!

I am teetering . . .

Amazing! I have rolled over from supine to prone; all of me has rearranged itself. I see a new wall, neither the one to the left nor the one to the right. Against this new wall I see abstractions that someday I will learn to label "lamp" and "chair." And I see Face! The wondrous flopover has summoned Face, who is rising from the chair with a happy din of encouragement. Rising, Face drops some white shapes that drift down to the floor.

Crinkly, fascinating paper. I watch; a big flake lands almost within reach.

More orbits, more practice. More showers.

Each time, there's a gap between me and the nearest flake, a gap which I finally perceive as a gap to be closed. Grunts, cries—vast commotions occur inside me. I am feeling the imperative of millions of years of life.

Toes shove against the rug for leverage. The flake moves no closer. My chin digs into the rug, grappling for a hold. No closer. My head sways, puffing, dribbling. Arms paddle vainly against dead weight. My belly tightens and thrusts for propulsion.

More orbits, more practice.

Suddenly the flake inches closer. I have hooked myself forward on an elbow. Now the other elbow drags the tensed body. The flake is closer. Grunts, cries—a great weariness but my curiosity is irresistible.

Elbow and belly . . . grunt, whimper.

Elbow and belly . . . grunt, whimper.

The flake is in reach.

Gotcha!

Now grasp it, taste it, crinkle it, scrutinize its new shape.

Do it again: crinkle, study, taste.

Do it all over again. The combinations seem endless.

But this strained pose, up on elbows, limits the handplay of the investigation. Vaguely I recall a better position—a feeling-picture of recumbent, arm-waving ease—and, in time, I remember the way to live it.

Flopover!

So rock now. Over to one side, over to the other. Faster! Teeter . . .

That's better. Now pass the pasty wad from hand to hand. Wave it back and forth. Exhaust it.

For now, the paper has surrendered its meanings. It is lifeless. But beyond it—flopover again, back to prone—beyond it and now within reach is the living, ever-moving, ever-surprising Face.

"Am I right?" Abbott asked. "I prattle on about life inside your head. I impute intentions to you. We'll never really know, will we?"

Abbott gripped Avery's hands and helped him up, over the knees, over the paunch, up Mount Abbott. They played the Filler Game, a new one in the growing repertoire. Avery tugged at Abbott's lower lip and out of Face's mouth rolled a filler in robot-like monotone.

"If a frog's mouth is held open too long, it will suffocate."

Avery gurgled with pleasure and tugged again, enthralled by the link between tug and voice, this oddest of Face's many voices.

"Albert Einstein was three years old before he could talk."

The tugging ceased; Avery's fickle attention turned to Abbott's necktie.

"Bored? I don't blame you." Abbott did the lip-tugging himself, and intoned: "Despite folklore, the owl is a stupid bird whereas the screaming loon is smart.

"Oh, I got a million of 'em. The old newspaperman, you see. The old dilettante who reaches the level of wisdom where fillers eclipse the front page."

Avery chewed on the necktie as if it were his bonnet strap. Abbott yanked it away, then relented as the baby groped for it, squawking. What the hell, it was sanitary. No tomato sauce on it. Anyway, who wears paisley anymore these days? "Eddie teases me about my line of ties." Mentioning Eddie, Abbott thought about that young assistant hard at work and wondered why he himself was home, playing with an infant in midafternoon when he should have been at work like any other man—or any woman, these days.

"There's a pension in sight, you know. Got to reach it. Elbow and belly . . . grunt, whimper. Elbow and belly . . ."

Denham flashed to mind. That deadpan, dapper look-alike, saying, "Good afternoon, Wes, how are things at home?" in a voice that sought no reply.

"He and the Mrs. are back. He's writing travelogue for my pages. Not a word about 'funny pieces,' but maybe he's only giving me time. Rope to hang myself."

Abbott wrenched his necktie away; it was blotched with saliva. He carried the protesting infant over to the spare tire on the living-room floor and settled him in the pillow-lined hole. Avery wailed but calmed down instantly as Abbott offered his wristwatch as a plaything. Distraction—that's the trick; distract, don't fight. Avery stared at the watch. He gnawed on the band. After a while he began slapping the watch on the sidewall of the tire.

Abbott got his notebook from the desk and scribbled some observations.

Entry

Lesson: To drop and retrieve. (More practice of A.'s recent discovery of gravity.)

A. leans over side of tire. Watch slips from his fingers, accidentally. A. transfixed. Appears awed by this phenomenon of the drop, still unfamiliar. Long and sober deliberation. Suddenly, pounces to pick up the watch. Holds it out. Drops it. Awe. Pounces, picks it up again. Drops.

Many repetitions . . .

Abbott dated this note and interlined it with a rough guess at time intervals. He placed it on a growing stack of similar notes on his desk. He leafed through it, this unscientific record of a child's development and a man's idle fascination with it.

He found a printout of an Associated Press story about the baby black market. It indicated that an item like Avery, white and healthy, would bring twelve thousand dollars. "I'd say they're selling you short."

He had printed out this story in a mood of cheerful morbidity; now, with the joke spent (a poor joke, at that), he balled up the paper and threw it toward the wastebasket several yards away. A hook shot, falling short.

The shot caught Avery's notice. He bellowed and watched for another exciting move by Face.

"I should bring you up to date on the others."

Little to tell, though, that hadn't already been reported at cribside. Lew was still in Maine. His Appalachian hike had been interrupted near trail's end by a bout with the flu. Heath had taken time from her studies to drive up and cheer him, but had not taken Avery along, although Abbott had suggested this. Abbott sighed, "Will they ever get together? I mean, as a legal unit?" Only one thing seemed certain: He'd find it hard to part company with this bothersome child when the time came.

"And it'll come. I've been collecting horror stories about grandfather-raised tots. Over at Head Start they had a four-year-old who could read—actually *read*—but was never toilet-trained. Can you believe that?"

Well, Avery was neither literate nor housebroken yet, but he could crawl. Which posed an immediate task: baby-proofing the house. From where Abbott sat in his chair, he saw wall sockets that could electrocute the child; tangled lamp cords that could strangle him; plates of leftovers the child might eat; a deadfall of stairs; dirty laundry that might tumble down in an asphyxiating heap.

He'd take a day off to detoxify the place. No, two days. Two days of housework, a chore made bearable by transcendence over it, the feat of changing his scrungy home into a safe and festive place.

Hell, take the rest of the week off. Three days not only for cleaning but for extra games and hikes. Avery had learned to move; now Abbott himself would move a little more.

12

"Woman for you," Eddie said. He reached across the desk, handing Abbott the receiver of their shared telephone. "Sounds young."

Heath, no doubt, calling to cancel another weekend home because of the pressure at school. Abbott spoke at once into the phone. "The hell with it! You come home and get some rest." She had burdened herself not only with extra courses to speed her degree but also practical courses to land a job.

Silence. He supposed that Heath, unused to outbursts from him, was readying a putdown, a profane one. Then he heard, in a voice too thin and piping to be Heath's: "It's only me, Wes."

He spun sideways in his chair to insulate the call from Eddie. He hunched his right shoulder around the phone and plugged his left ear with an index finger. Eddie, alerted by these moves, ceased typing at his VDT and watched Abbott with undisguised interest. Eddie had the manners of a good reporter.

So sorry to bother you at work, Sharon said. Blah blah. An important message. Would have called you at home but couldn't find you in the book.

Thank God, Abbott thought, for his unlisted number. He had obtained it long ago over Claire's objections when his community involvement ceased.

"I can't talk over the phone," Sharon said. "Can I come to your office?"

Abbott lied, "I'm on deadline." He shot a glance at Eddie and jammed his eyes shut as Eddie grinned. Abbott pictured the thistle flower waggling into the newsroom, wearing a T-shirt with something like BULLSHIT printed on it. Colleagues who already shied from him would thenceforth watch from distant doorways.

"Can I come over to your house tonight?" she asked.

What, with Frito trailing to case the joint? Besides, what would the neighbors say?

"Huh? Wes? Where do you live?"

"I won't be there. I'm on assignment." This time he didn't bother to glance at Eddie for a reaction to his lie; a snicker was audible.

Sharon suggested a downtown meeting place. "The Green. I'm there now. Pick me up in your car."

Hunkydory. Witnesses would assume that Wesley C. Abbott, editor of the editorial page and victim of family problems, was leching after hitchhikers.

On the other hand, he hadn't recognized many faces downtown in years. The world had changed. His colleagues, most of them, were new. So were his neighbors, and they rarely spoke, even on the level of news-sports-weather. Wake up, he told himself.

"Five minutes," he said, and hung up.

Eddie said, "Who's the chick? You've got a groupie?"

"Personnel. Some screwup with my benefits."

Eddie's leer widened. This young assistant, this Type A go-getter, no doubt knew the telephone voice of the secretary in Personnel, and maybe of every secretary in the city.

"It was my masseuse," Abbott said, getting his coat. "I'm driving over to the parlor."

"Try the Businessman's Special," Eddie said. "I'm told it includes a prostate rub."

Eddie could be forgiven his nastiness. Abbott's three days off for housecleaning had cost Eddie two nights of work.

. . .

He felt a lightness of step and tremors of anticipation as he walked out to his car. He thought of the horses in old New England mills, hitched to the grindstones, plodding in tight circles all their lives in the darkness of basements. True plodders. Well, this plodder had perked up as if handed a sugar cube.

Nonsense. This was life, not a movie. And this errand a nuisance, not a tryst. Driving downtown, he wondered what Earl's girl did for a living. Waitress? Possibly. Not that he cared. Maybe a salesgirl. In a five-and-dime. Did five-and-dimes still exist, in some modern form, an avatar? She might be a beautician; those kids were known to doll themselves up gaudily. Or a carhop, perhaps.

Ah, wake up, he told himself. Carhops were extinct.

He spotted the girl kibitzing among checker-playing retirees on the stone benches along the edge of the Green. She waved, then stepped off the curb and flagged down his car like a bold sidewalk hooker. Abbott shrank down in the seat.

Today's T-shirt advertised a FUN RUN roadrace. Presumably, the shirt was on loan from a roommate—Dee? Pat? Peg?—who ran races.

She slid into the car and nestled too close to him. "Hi"—breathlessly. "How you doing?"

"Just dandy," Abbott said. "What's the trouble?"

"You never said good-bye that night at Earl's place." She pouted.

"You were asleep. Now why did you call me?"

She backed off, looking not hurt but sly, recalculating the risks of teasing him. "Drive someplace and I'll tell you."

As he drove away from downtown, she fumbled with the dials of the car radio. "It's broken," he told her. "A tube blew and I never replaced it."

"Aw. I thought we might have some music."

"That's not music, what the stations play."

She smirked. A knowing look, sign that he was behaving predictably. "I suppose you like classical."

"A little Mozart's all right, but mostly I prefer silence."

"Don't you listen to the news? For God's sake, that's your business."

"There's too much so-called news."

She sighed in disbelief. "How did a guy like you ever get to be a reporter?"

Good question. He'd often posed it himself. "I fell into it. In the Army. I was an artilleryman, and I became a news writer to get out of cleaning the guns. Played a little politics. Earl did the same thing—traded in his M-1 for a typewriter."

Why, he wondered, had he blabbered so much?

For several blocks, the girl was quiet. At a red light, Abbott glanced over and saw a startling change of manner. She sat with spine stiff, bust inflated, and a face thoroughly sour, the eyes fishy and the mouth drooped at the corners. Then, an oblique glance and the quivering start of a smile revealed to Abbott that she was mimicking him. Dear Lord, did he look so much like a stuffed shirt?

He glanced away and up at the light. "How about a Dairy Queen? I'm buying."

"Hey, yeah!" She dropped the pose. "I haven't had one of those since I was a kid."

Abbott drove to the Dairy Queen on the commercial strip near his home. Entering the parking lot, he looked around warily. With his luck, he might find himself parked between a white Lincoln, Denham's, and a van driven by a skinny longhair, Frito.

He inquired about Frito and received one of the girl's roundabout explanations. "We went over there. We thought we could get some of Earl's stuff back, especially that gun. But Clyde thinks he split for Florida. He broke probation."

Abbott blew out his lips in a long breath of relief. He recalled that, back in Army days, stateside, many young AWOLs fled to Florida and invariably were caught there.

He went into the Dairy Queen and returned with their

orders. Sharon had asked for an ice bar called a Mr. Misty Kiss. So commonplace was his imagination—no big surprise—that he could not watch the girl as she licked and sucked the bar. He crossed his legs and concentrated on his strawberry sundae. This would ruin his thousand-calorie-a-day diet, but surely he deserved a bonus on a day of rude interruptions.

She asked about Avery. "Did you get rid of that baby-sitter?"

"Which one? I've lost count."

"The one you and Earl made fun of. That was funny."

"Yes. Her foster kids were being assigned to tend the babies. Hardly qualified, you know. I walked in unannounced, like an inspector. Ever smell a room with a dozen unchanged diapers?"

"God! That's awful."

"We've hired a new woman. She lives way over on . . ." Abbott paused. "Do you know the city? Are you from here?"

"This dump? Are you kidding? You from here?"

"I grew up in dumpier places east of here. Now what's your beef?"

"You and Earl have a lot of fun together, right? In your own weird way. You're good together."

"We were a team, yes."

"You two go way back, right?"

"We grew up in this state and met in Korea. After the war, he went to New York and we lost touch for years, but then he came home. I got him his job."

"You're his best buddy, right?"

"I was."

"What do you mean 'was'? You don't just quit on a friend."

Abbott smiled. Scratch a lowlife and you'll find a sentimental moralist, every time. "Are you leading up to some point?"

"He came home feeling like a loser, right?"

"Not at first."

Sharon kneeled on the seat and turned full-face toward Abbott for the revelation. "Earl's very, very depressed. He's sick and he needs help, bad."

So that was it. Earl's tiresome decline. What would have been called, in Victorian times, his "degeneration."

"He's going to lose his job," Sharon said.

"He wants to."

"And he's drinking like a fish. Don't smile! He really is; he's stoned out of his mind half the time."

"I wouldn't worry about it."

The girl clutched Abbott's sleeve. "How can you say that? Booze is even worse than smack!"

Abbott looked away, suppressing another smile. How could this brat, streetwise or not, ever understand a seasoned old cynic like Earl?

With his spoon Abbott stirred the pink dregs of his sundae and tried to phrase in his mind an explanation that might help her understand. How should it go? Well, he could say: Sharon, some people look around and they deduce that life is a pretty raw deal. They say it's not kind, not humane, not just, not even intelligible—all things that humans yearn for. So, their response to it is somber, which—given the evidence as they see it—is appropriate, right? Even mentally healthy, you might say. So, don't call Earl "depressed," as if he's suffering from some curable condition at variance with the facts. Give him some dignity.

Yes, Sharon might grasp a speech like this. On the other hand, the girl had a point or two. Licking his spoon, Abbott enumerated them: (1) Earl, according to *Call* rumors, was indeed drinking more than he could hide; and (2), judging from Sharon, his game of re-creating lost girlfriends was not being played with the kind of style that might justify it as a way of life, as you might justify, say, skydiving, or philately, or, for that matter, opening a junkshop called "Wild Geese."

Sharon had been watching him, studying his face through

these ruminations. "What are you thinking?"

"Would you like another Mr. Misty?"

Her harem-girl eyes darkened. "You think I'm an idiot, don't you?"

"No." Ah, she was sharp. "But you don't understand Earl."

"No? Well, I'll tell you something. I don't know how you think it was with us, but it wasn't . . ." She searched for the word, and delivered it with savage parody: "*lovey-dovey*. All Earl did with me, I mean mostly all, was . . ."

"Go on," Abbott said as she hesitated. "I think I can take it."

". . . cry. He cries about wasting his life and all that, and I just don't want to hear that shit. I've got my own problems."

A shocker. Then again, no, merely a confirmation of buried suspicions. The re-created girlfriend was less sex toy than crying towel. Abbott pictured Earl blubbering on her breast, confounding her with his despair. What would Earl say if accused of this? Combatively: "Sure, I spill my guts to the kid, so what? It's good for you. Good for them, too."

"I don't date him anymore," Sharon said. "He went for Charisse because she's beautiful. But she's crazy herself. You're the only one who can help him get his head together."

Abbott asked, "Why did you . . . date . . . him in the first place?" Polite version of the basic question: Why a duffer thrice your age?

"Because he's funny. And cool. He sees through all the shit, you know? You're the same way, but you're more together than he is. Will you talk to him?" As she pleaded, Sharon's hand landed on his thigh, tinglingly close to the crotch. An unintended move, perhaps, but the hand lingered as she watched him.

Abbott lifted the hand, placed it on the seat between them and patted it. Uncle Abbott. He lied: "Don't you worry, I'll talk to him."

"Thanks." She stroked Abbott's sleeve. "I knew you would. I'll never understand why your wife walked out on a nice guy like you."

"Earl told you, hmm?"

"Couldn't you get along?"

Nosy, this child, but Abbott's words spilled out as if she were Avery. "There was nothing to get along for, anymore. It happens."

"Will you see a counselor?"

"What for? That's a word game, like Scrabble. Ever play Scrabble?"

"Oh, yeah." Sharon laughed with a roll of her eyes over some private joke. "All those games."

Earl had called her a schizophrenic. Maybe she had logged much game time in the wards.

The sugar-cube lunch was over. Abbott drove back downtown. She gave him an address that he recognized as a street in the Upper Green area, a neighborhood of Victorian mansions once occupied by the city's mill families, the Denhams among them. Now these old places with their gingerbread and turrets housed funeral parlors, realty and social-service offices, and many apartments. Sharon directed him to a mansion once owned, he believed, by the Trowbridge estate, long gone South to a cheaper labor market for its textiles. The house displayed no business signs. A volleyball net had been rigged up in the side yard.

"Today was fun," Sharon said. "Let's do it again, real soon." She poked him on the chest, a mock challenge. "Next time, *I'm* buying." Her hand withdrew, then shot out again. Abbott took it, conditioned to the ritual of the handshake, but he felt no reciprocal pumping. The girl simply wanted to hold his hand. Sometimes life is stunningly simple. And this instant held two simple options: (1) release the hand, or (2) squeeze it and yank her back into the car and drive off somewhere. His home? No, too many memories there. Out near the highway was a HoJo. That might do. Farther out, and more in keeping with Earl's kind of fantasy, was one of those two-hour-stay, gel-bed motels with mirrored ceilings—mirrors, Abbott thought, to multiply his wrinkles and Sharon's babyfat.

He released the hand.

She watched him a moment longer, expectantly, for the setting of a date.

Sorry, child. No next time. But as she went up the sidewalk, Abbott dug notes from his side pocket, found a blank surface of newsprint to write on, and jotted down the house number.

"Feel better now?" Eddie asked. "How was the parlor game?"

"Very refreshing," Abbott said. He did, in fact, feel refreshed.

He looked up Sharon's house number in the city directory. An institutional owner was listed: Genesis Inc. Some kind of cult? The only other source at hand was the living Eddie, young reporter about town. Abbott inquired.

"That's a group home," Eddie said.

"You mean a halfway house?"

"Oh, no. No badasses there." Eddie leaned back from the keyboard of his VDT and removed a soda straw from his mouth. "Kids. Referrals from the state and the courts. Why do you ask?"

"I was writing about the mansion. For the tricentennial. Do these kids run wild?"

"They're supposed to go out and find jobs, be free—it's part of the re-entry. I did a feature; didn't you read it?" Eddie looked offended.

Abbott tapped his brow. "Memory's going, you know. All the strokes I've been having."

"We can do without the sick jokes. That feature ran op-ed, for Christ's sake. You okayed it."

"This place," Abbott went on, "do they treat schizophrenics?"

"I told you, no badasses and no feebs. Why all these questions?"

"I was thinking of signing myself in."

"Not amusing." Eddie turned back to his keyboard, but on afterthought he topped Abbott's line. "Before you go, sign over your job to me."

"I'll will it to you," Abbott said, and looked away in guilt. Eddie still seemed to think that a deal had been made to advance him, that Abbott was planning a surprise move. Fat chance. But Eddie might, indeed, soon inherit the job. Abbott's work these days showed nothing but mastery of the minimal effort.

Quickly, he proofed the next day's editorials.

In the top spot was a tirade requested by Denham against a proposed state income tax. Two, a tribute to a retiring foreman of public works, a good fellow who had plowed Abbott's driveway on the sly last winter. Next, a scolding of the Soviets, on general principles. Last, a nature lyric—finches in the hawthorn trees.

To fill another column of space on the page, Abbott compressed some crackpot letters to the editor. Then he trotted out the longwinded piece he had written for the tricentennial. This story, illustrated with some space-waster photos, filled the rest of the page. The photos, solicited from readers, showed men in aprons posing outside turn-of-the-century shops.

Abbott sized the pictures, wrote headlines and captions, and sketched a layout for the compositors. There: his day's work. Surely, it would win a Pulitzer. Surely, Walter Lippmann would have been proud.

Abbott left the facing page, the op-ed, to Eddie. There, amid the regular columnists—Buckley, Erma, *et al.*—Eddie would play up his own bylined material, to be clipped by him later for his job-hunt portfolio.

As Abbott prepared to leave for home, Eddie asked, "Will I see you tomorrow—I hope?"

Abbott dug notes from his coat pocket and riffled through them for his schedule. Eddie waited, smirking with pipe in mouth, tapping his fingers impatiently, through the minute or so that Abbott needed to find his schedule in the clump of newsprint.

Tomorrow would be busy. The schedule listed food shopping (don't forget carrots for vitamin A), clothes shopping (a buy on baby undershirts, nickel apiece, at the consignment shop), laundry, an interview with a prospective babysitter who lived nearby, and an extension of the daily hike with Avery from two-and-a-half miles to two-and-three-quarters miles. Abbott said, "Maybe in the afternoon. Or I'll work at night, at home."

"What'll I tell the Man if he calls? Or if he shows his face in here?"

Abbott's stomach tightened.

Eddie said, "He called twice when you were cleaning house. Just checking. No messages."

Eddie, however, had a message of his own, unspoken but plain: no more coverups. That was understandable. "If he calls," Abbott said, "call me at home right away. Would you do that?"

Eddie nodded. "You're living dangerously."

A flattering thought.

With the long day done and Avery in bed, Abbott undressed for his date with Sharon. A Sharon of fantasy, behind the bathroom door. But the spark of libido that had burned throughout the evening glimmered out now. How pathetic, he thought, for a man of his age to depend on masturbation for a sex life. He'd come full circle, so to speak. A long, long trail of pecker tracks down memory lane, barely traceable in the middle but dense at both ends. Where had it all begun? Some forgotten spurt. On some floor of his boyhood.

Yes, a basement floor.

The basement of Charlie Mather's duplex. In the housing project. Strawberry Hills, named for the farm it had supplanted.

Another miracle of retrieval. Abbott saw Charlie's face,

and then Roland Dumont, Beebe—*Hiya, Beebe!*—and others, all with knickers down around their ankles. But no, not knickers; long pants. They were growing up.

Lord, where were these boys now? Old cops and firemen, some of them. Theirs was the last generation before the coining of "teenager"—a new class born of disposable income and leisure time. Maybe one had prospered and could give Abbott a job, should worse come to worst. Abbott saw himself entering a suite of offices and saying to an old chum now dignified and spiffy: "Say, remember the old circle-jerks?"

Today, Charlie finished first in the race of churning fists. As the semen dribbled, he threw back his head and caterwauled. A low-class reaction. It was Roland, next, who expressed a style, one almost inimitable. Roland the tough, who back in grade school could piss the highest above the urinals. Now, as Roland finished, he looked down at the blur of his hand and the wheeling spurts with a haze of belittlement in his eyes and a sneer on his lips.

"Cool" had not yet been coined. But what could be cooler than to scorn one's own orgasm, right in the midst of it? And what could better express the stoicism these boys would need to prevail?

Ah, the old neighborhood. No wonder Abbott had forgotten it. The drone of the warplane plant, spewing blue-collar wealth. Every able body working a double shift. V-8 engines plunked on dining-room tables for repair. Native WASPs and the Mainers and the Canucks playing musical beds. Kids running wild, their parents leaving half-dollars on kitchen tables for meals in greasy spoons. But rules existed. Discipline was a hazel switch for toddlers, and a flat-out punch in the jaw if you sassed somebody or screwed up. LOOSE LIPS SINK SHIPS. If you were a girl too promiscuous, you could expect reform school, no "group home." A simpler, slower time. Currier & Ives.

Still, there had been pockets of softness in that gritty place, and in the earlier ones. The scene changed: Abbott, younger now, watched a stranger on the back porch of the family flat in the milltown. Hitler had not yet invaded Poland. Abbott watched the man without fear, for others had come to the porch on other days, all to beg food. They were hoboes from the freightyard. Hunched there on the steps, the man wolfed a fried egg sandwich that Abbott's mother had cooked for him and handed out the screen door. Abbott realized only now—decades later, seated on a toilet—that the Abbott house must have been marked in the hoboes' secret code as a place of handouts.

His mother. He tried to remember her face from those years. An assignment.

Close the eyes. Concentrate, but not too hard. Clear the mind like a stage and let the image appear, fuzzy, as if seen through a screen door.

Nothing, only shadows. Then tension, as subtle as a feeling of being watched: a warning from some part of the mind that an image—unpleasant and contradictory—is shaping up as a result of your brainstorming. Abbott canceled the assignment. Just as well. Down that particular path of memory lay grief.

Almost midnight. Close the lid, go to sleep.

13

Vivid growth occurred now. He was zesty, always alert. He needed more toys but nothing special, nothing educational, so-called; anything will do if the world is new.

Like pots and pans. Abbott emptied the kitchen cabinets. "Clang, bang, good sounds for you." And plastic bottles. "Look! Plastic spoons." They were Dairy Queen spoons, Abbot's collection dating years back. He dumped them into a bowl for such games as put-in-put-out.

Next, Abbott offered food cans from the cupboard. Avery could pick the labels off. "All yours. We'll take potluck, opening cans for meals."

Living room next: There were doors that swung and books whose pages swung like doors and could be ripped. Abbott scanned the shelf and dumped most of the books on the floor.

He looked around for other toyland possibilities, and noticed the fat wooden legs of his furniture, so matronly and magisterial. Inspiration struck. Avery liked to trace with his fingertips the outlines of things, like Abbott's lips; therefore, Abbott would paste bright daisy decals on those legs, and the infant could trace the petals while crawling from piece to piece. Claire wouldn't mind such a zany desecration of their stolid front room and their few antiques; anyway, Claire had turned her back on this house.

Closet, next, the Fibber McGee storehouse. It yielded

an old coat, a good piece of Harris tweed to titillate the sense of touch, and many old shoes—good chewables, after a cleaning. Also, a bagful of spools that Claire had saved for some art project; Abbott would string them together to make a perfect toy. Digging deeper, he found a sort of bladder, blue and white. He looked at it and then at Avery—gawking from his playpen—with astonishment. "For God's sake, a beach ball! We old Yankees never throw *anything* away." Abbott took belly breaths of his improved wind and inflated the ball. It rolled big and bouncy into the clutter on the floor.

Among all these treasures there were some no-no's. The shoelaces, which could strangle the child, and boxes of buttons. Abbott also uncovered, way back, a pair of small reinforced cardboard cartons, and placed them high on a shelf.

Now he lifted Avery out of the playpen and into the greater playpen of the house. The child could scuttle around and transform all this novelty into the familiar. And then get bored. "Get disillusioned," Abbott said. "I think it's the principle of learning. Going along, getting older, you learn that less and less do you share in a world you once felt as whole."

But never mind such gloomy pronouncements. For now, Avery's world was a toy. He could handle it, bang it, poke it, push and pull, put-in-put-out, drop, bite, scratch, rub, pat, roll, fondle, pick, twiddle, squeeze, maul . . .

A babyfat dance of verbs.

"The other day," Abbott began aloud—and paused, startled by the rasp of his voice in the silent bedroom. He cleared his throat and continued in a whisper lest Avery awaken in the first tremulous minutes of sleep following newstime.

"It was the other day. I forgot to tell you about it. Forty years vanished—poof!"—Abbott snapped his fingers soundlessly—"just like that."

It was a stranger in the street, an old fellow wearing a long-billed cap. He was barrel-chested; his arms swung wide as he walked. He gave the impression of a rooster strutting with its wings half extended. Abbott, pushing Avery in the stroller, spotted the man's approach from half a block away. He had what used to be called a peasant build: long trunk, short legs, bandy legs in chino pants that were baggy, the crotch low-hanging. They were also high-water, exposing working-man white socks. One hand held a gallon jug of milk, a purchase from the 7-Eleven store on the corner.

Then the face came into view: stern, the lower lip a pout and the brow knotted, as if the man were pondering bad news in the solitary aura that one maintains amid a drift of faces.

Instantly, Abbott receded through time: a child again, tensed in a quandary: Should he speak? A spoken greeting might get him noticed, put him on the spot. Unbeknownst, the child might have erred recently. He might have been unmannerly—one never knew. Or he might have forgotten to take out the ashes or to clean the chicken coop. A spoken greeting could trigger retribution: a dizzying swat on the head, a ringing in the ears. Therefore, best be silent. Be cautious. Nod, that's all. Let your being contract to a simple nod of recognition, brusque, eyes flicking away. Don't look up at the man; rather, absorb his presence. Stand sullen in a storm of mixed feelings.

But, at a distance of six or seven paces the irate face softened. The brow lifted, the creases forming arches over quizzical eyes, banjo eyes. A sociable old gent, looking with friendly curiosity at the unusual sight before him: a middle-aged man in a business suit pushing a baby in a stroller. The old gent said, "How do?" and clicked his tongue at Avery. Abbott replied, "Afternoon," and passed on.

Abbott leaned over the crib rail. "Until the old boy smiled," he whispered, "he was almost a dead ringer for your great-grandfather."

Dead, indeed. Dead for years, Abbott's father, but still on hand, a disintegrated skeleton in the closet. He occupied one of the two cartons that Abbott had put out of Avery's reach—a carton full of bone chips, also containing a metal ID tag from a crematorium. In the other carton, similarly disposed, was Avery's great grandmother.

"As I told you, we old Yankees never throw *anything* away."

14

Joy. In a world full of tired perceptions, it was a joy to watch the creature sitting there with a purity of gaze and a throatiness of breath, playing in awe with some little thing as if it were the key to the universe.

The thing, at that moment, was a snap-button block, one from a set that Heath had brought home from some child lab at the university. The blocks were too advanced for Avery's age and hand strength. Abbott went into the kitchen and returned with some small empty candy tins. Light, round, and shallow, easy for Avery's stiff and fumbling fingers to place and let go of, to stack.

As Avery watched him, Abbott piled one . . . two . . . three . . . and then—cuff!—knocked the pile down.

He did it again. And again.

One, two, three, cuff. Avery looked intrigued, not babbling now.

One, two, three, cuff.

One, two, three, cuff.

One, two, three, cuff. " 'Through what transports of patience . . .' "

One, two, three, cuff.

The infant smiled!

One, two, three, cuff.

One, two, three, cuff.

Avery laughed! Laughter on the tenth repetition.

One, two, three, cuff.

Avery squealed and flapped his arms.

Abbott understood now. He understood on the eleventh repetition—the baby had fixed a pattern.

How obvious! Avery had added this thrilling event to the little deck of pictures in his forebrain. He had made a bit of sense out of all the clutter Abbott had given him, which, of itself, was both too much and too little.

Now Abbott assumed the infant would try the trick himself, that he would imitate.

"Go ahead," Abbott said. "Try it. Take the tins."

No?

Avery scooted off.

"Good work. Keep me guessing."

Entry 143

On and on it goes, the Abbott and Avery show. Have I ever been happier?

A. has reached another landmark: "object permanence," some jargon term from Heath. It means out of sight but still in mind. Now, when I wrestle the phone cord away, A. knows it doesn't simply vanish into eternity. He scrambles behind me for it, hollering.

He has constructed space, a fixity. By fiddling with things he has brought the new into the known. He is inventing laws. He is developing goal-corrected systems. He knows that different routes through the house lead to the same places. I follow him, upright or on all fours, bruising my kneecaps.

Entry 144

Recapitulation of vocabulary:

"Blublublub bubub, ah ah ah. Ah yeh ah yeh. Innhinn. Ackack. Pthuhft ffss pft. Bvem, bvam. Ohsee, ohsee. Aay, aay. Ba ba ba . . ."

A most enlightening series of statements. A language of pleasure rather than conquest. Emotional, not theoretical. Happily regressive.

I nag A. to express himself. How I hate to do this! But it's inevitable—sooner or later, I tell him, one must try to mean. It's our duty, I tell him; take it from a moralizing old New Englander.

He can use lip consonants and even the tongue-tippers. I've heard my own inflections. I've heard the weary march of my declarative sentences in his singsong.

We tried his name. I said, "Aay-verr-eeee."

A. said, "Ba ba ba ba . . ."

Okay, I said, I'd go with that. "Ba ba ba ba ba ba."

He said, "Ba ba ba bab bab app app abb app . . ."

"Try Ab-bott."

"Bapp bapp . . ."

Bapp! I'd go with that.

My name is Bapp.

Almost midnight. Abbott turned off the living-room lamp and lay down on the carpet, clearing a place for himself amid the makeshift toys. It was time for an assignment, another field report from the Impossible I. Abbott stretched out, a forearm over his closed eyes. Haltingly, sometimes in a whisper but mostly in silent thought, the Impossible I filed its dispatch.

More time, more orbits.

I continue to expand.

Once there was only the floor plane, along which I dragged myself: elbow and belly, grunt, whimper; elbow and belly.

Now I rise, scampering on hands and knees, breathless. And I rise higher—ascending planes are revealed to me. Up, up, onto the feel and color of the presence I will come to know as "sofa," up onto the sofa's arm, up onto its back. Up, up, on the "stairs," one panting step at a time.

But I forget. I forget the planes are behind me, that I

have climbed them. I fall—vertigo; everything implodes with pain. Face looms; Face gathers me up and restores the presences. Face plunks its hugeness behind me as a backdrop as once again I climb the stairs. Then Face guides my legs, extending one leg down, then the other.

More orbits, more practice. I'll remember.

Long-seen presences beckon to me from everywhere, most of them accessible now, but Face gets in the way. How can a part of me get in my own way? I hear Face's baffling "no" in the vicinity of the "stove" and by the "phone."

I approach the phone. "Hands off! No!" I freeze, staring at Face. "No, no." I inch again toward the phone, or I point at it and waggle my hand in frustration. "No-o!" I inch away, or Face lifts me away and gives me a not-phone. I rage at this perversity. Face envelops me and croons, "Avery, Avery."

What is "Avery"?

I hear this sound more than all the others that emanate from Face. Maybe I am beginning to feel what it means.

"Avery," I think, is what I do.

And what of "Bapp"? I make this sound over and over because it pleases and activates Face. "Bapp" is what Face does.

Move by move, I remember the Avery/Bapp doings—the game with candy tins, the hide and seek—these and innumerable others in all their detail; myself descending the stairs with Bapp's help, myself skirting the "no" zones. I remember and replay, and now "models" in my "mind" guide us, show instantly where we are, what to do.

And with almost every orbit come new actions that extend or revise my models.

Look! Look what I've done! I must call Bapp's attention to it.

Bapp! Aay! I was kneeling in my crib, irritable, sleepless, unlulled by your ongoing bedtime story. I was tugging hard on the crib rail when my body suddenly arose from the force of my arms and—*failed to sit.* My shaky legs hold me up.

Bapp! I stand.

Abbott sat at the old Underwood in his study. Would the typing awaken the child? No, the clackery of late-night editorials had never awakened him before.

Acting on an old fear in the quiet, Abbott went into the bedroom to ensure that Avery was still breathing. Yes; the little rib cage rose and fell under Abbott's palm. On his return through the darkened living room Abbott stepped carefully through the clutter of playthings, and he noticed the shine of reflected light on the decals, that raffish redecoration of his furniture. For better or worse, his life was changing, and he'd best take note of it before it slipped his mind. Bapp had been born—a new Abbott, an Abbott with revived creatureliness, thanks to Avery. The mind is a homeless wanderer, but one's creatureliness feels its way into a niche—a place, task, whatever. There, Abbott was unfolding, feeling a new solidity for his limbs to brace against. New coordinates.

In all of this, there was a hint of a "funny piece," a little story with a bare-bones plot and a wobbly climax. As a story, it was surely an exclusive, Abbott's own; he had done all the digging. Further, it had an old-hat but viable premise: Valuable things can happen between two people. Abbott could allow that he'd grown a little wiser and stronger. In the terms of pop psychology, he was more in touch with himself.

So there. Wasn't that a tidy resolution?

It stunk. It reeked of half-truth. The story was unfinished, like all stories, and Bapp the alter-ego was eavesdropping at the holes in this story, waiting for the story to be told. Waiting, mainly, for action. How, after all, did Bapp differ from Abbott, the repressed drab still sitting in Bapp's skin, a necktie on at 12:30 A.M. and a chronic mutter on his lips, chronic dread in his heart? Consider the past: so ordinary on the face of it, yet so opaque. Certain inactions of his needed explaining, a laying to rest.

There were secrets, as well, in the ever-changing, ever-surprising Avery. The latest was so shocking that Abbott had put off thinking about it: Avery's sudden fear of his mother, the real one.

The fear had spoiled Heath's last visit home, a quick trip to say hello—hi, I still exist. The loving but absentee lifegiver.

When she reached out for the customary hug, Avery turned away from her and tried to bury his face in Abbott's armpit. Stunned, the two adults gaped at each other, and Heath paled. "My God," she said, "what's wrong?" Arms still extended, she half-smiled to conceal hurt. Abbott thrust Avery toward her, but the baby squealed and thrashed arms and legs to regain the safety of Abbott's chest.

"My God, don't *dangle* him," Heath scolded. "Has he been sick?"

No. Abbott had no explanation for this bad show. He saw a glint of blinked-back tears behind Heath's glasses. Hurt underscored fatigue in her face: pouchiness under the eyes and a hollowing of weight loss in her broad shoulders under the college jersey.

Why hadn't Avery played the Con Game? He'd always played it for his mother—for anyone, after some initial wariness lately. The latest babysitter, Mrs. Persio, had called him "bashful," a stupid remark, Abbott had thought. Mrs. Persio had said, "It's just a stage they go through."

Abbott shrugged and told Heath: "It must be a stage he's going through."

"Well, I hope so." She removed her glasses and lightly dabbed her eyes. "I thought for a minute I needed a new deodorant."

Laughing off injury. Heath, however, was no comedienne; rather, her style of coping was to use aggressive shows of logic. "It does make sense. At this age they form strong attachments, sometimes only one. And you're the person he sees most, right?"

"That's right."

"Well, he'll get over it."

Heath nodded in agreement with herself and sat down across the room, keeping her distance from the child still huddled in Abbott's arms. After a while he loosened his grip and consented to be placed on the floor. Slowly he crept out a few feet, not quite midway between the adults, and looked from face to face. He seemed to be comparing them.

"Watch," Heath said in a stage whisper. "He'll warm up to me now."

Avery wore a frown, underlip out and brow puckered, as if Abbott had sneaked a spoonful of liver into a peach dessert.

Waiting for his next move, the adults talked. Heath noticed the daisy decals on the furniture legs. "My God, Daddy, you're really letting your hair down."

"Less of a fuddy-duddy, hm?"

"You said that; I didn't. Actually, I sort of like the new look."

At that moment the hot-water kettle whistled in the kitchen. Abbott went out to make coffee for himself and Heath. Presently, he heard a squall of terror and a scrabbling of hands and knees as the baby crawled out into the hall to find him.

Abbott scooped the sobbing infant off the floor and returned to the living room. Heath was slumped on the toy-strewn carpet. "I blew it," she said. "When you left, he started to whimper, so I went over to him."

"He'll come around, honey," Abbott said. "Give him a chance." The "honey" had leaped into speech from the forgotten time when Heath was not much older than her son.

"If I'd stayed still"—Heath's voice broke, rising in pitch—"he wouldn't have panicked."

Abbott clenched his teeth and quashed an urge to murder Avery with a bear hug.

"I'm just not around enough," she said. "I'm a stranger."

"For God's sake, don't start feeling guilty."

"That's easy for you to say." She knuckled her eyes. "You're not a mother."

Though this remark was funny as well as touching, and though Heath looked sweetly defenseless there on the floor, Abbott did not smile to himself. He reached out a hand to help her up and she ignored it. She stared up at him unseeingly. Could it be that, only now, she'd plugged into the reality of her motherhood? Impossible, Abbott thought. After all, this sensible and strong-minded girl had given birth—gut knowledge, to say the least, forever denied to men—and she knew that independence from her would dawn by tiny degrees. Yet Abbott remembered something Claire had said: "You know only what you know," and it's an awakening.

Later, leaving, Heath blew a kiss at her son from a distance of about ten feet as he clung to Abbott's neck. "See you, sweetie," she said. "Soon this will all be forgotten. Grandpa's babysitting days will be over, and you'll be with me."

That night at cribside Abbott harangued the infant for its bad manners. A chewing-out in the soft, soothing tones of a bedtime story or of newstime.

"Couldn't you have said 'mama' or something? That young woman is working her butt off for you. She longs to come home more often, but she can't spare the time and I can't spare the money. All this so she can support you."

Avery cooed in a rhythm faintly imitative of Abbott's voice. Inappropriately, Abbott was tempted to start a game, one of the morning favorites. He'd back up a few steps and then rush the crib, a looming menace with play face and play voice, growling "Aaaarrgh, *gotcha*" and clutch Avery's arms. Avery would shriek and convulse with giggles. But a game now would overexcite the infant; he'd want repetitions and wouldn't sleep.

Besides, at this moment was there not a serious topic on the agenda? Faces. The Faces you do not trust.

"It's all my fault, probably. Maybe she was right about the babysitters, a whole goddamn convoy of ships in the night."

He tried to remember them all. Mrs. Persio held the job now, and so far had not sinned. She'd replaced Mrs. Kowal, whose sins were two: (1) propping Avery in front of daytime television and (2) living too far away. Prior to her was the co-op, that chaotic scene of young liberal parents who blabbed about love and nurture as if they had organized not for practical child care but for group therapy. And, before that, there was Heaphy's military school. Abbott could not remember, offhand, any of the earlier caretakers.

Avery slept, thumb in mouth. Abbott adjusted the covers under the baby's chin.

He thought about the drift of faces in the streets during their daily hikes, that sea continuously parted by Avery's stroller. Faces drifting up, glancing left or right on the approach—instinctive signals for passing so bodies won't bump. Human apparitions. What were they walking away from, or walking toward, or off? Sometimes you felt like buttonholing one of those passersby and asking, "What's your story? For that matter, what's mine?" You felt like exchanging names, as at an accident scene, even though there was rarely a collision, rarely anything reportable, never any visible loss of life in these passings. Ah, the nothingness, the utter strangeness of everyday life. Did mothers ever feel this? Loneliness was part of it, and mothers get lonely. Abbott asked himself: Am I lonely? Hell, yes; why deny it? He missed Claire, even though their life together had been barren; why deny that any longer? And he missed Earl.

15

Though headed nowhere, Earl at least stayed in motion. This time, he'd managed to get himself fired.

"Fired or told to quit," Eddie said, filling Abbott in. "It's not clear which. The girls in Denham's office are stonewalling."

Abbott, reporting to work after a day's absence, was late on this story—a major in-house event. These were rare at the *Call*, and Eddie had confronted him with the news even before Abbott had time to sit. Eddie, chief gossip, was so excited that his cigarette substitute of the hour—a plastic coffee stirrer—remained in his hand instead of his mouth. He twiddled one end as if dusting ashes.

"You should have called me," Abbott said.

"I said I'd call if Denham was hunting for you. I'm not your goddamn correspondent when you're goofing off."

"All right, I've been scooped. What happened?"

"Quit or canned." Eddie thrust his face at Abbott across their shared desktop. "And I'll tell you this: It couldn't have happened to a nicer guy."

"Just tell me what happened," Abbott said wearily.

"I know he's a buddy of yours—"

"Was," Abbott broke in.

"—but he's also a miserable little prick who needs a shrink."

Poor Earl. Everybody was prescribing for him.

Eddie said that Earl had blown a story. "The murder-suicide."

"What murder-suicide?"

Eddie looked at Abbott in sorrowing wonder. "Here, read your own paper." He tossed over the morning *Call*, folded to the city page. "Notice the second-day lead on the story. That's because the first day we didn't have *one goddamn word*."

Abbott glanced down at what might have been the hundredth or two hundredth KILLS WIFE, SELF headline of his career. Eddie had bracketed the story with angry slashes of red grease pencil. The victims' names were unfamiliar. "Calm down," Abbott said. "What happened?"

"I *am* calm! I think this is funny! It's pure *Call*. Do you know the new girl on the copydesk?"

"No."

"Figures. To bring you up to date, her name's Ann, she's been here over a month, and she came from the *Patriot-Ledger*. Ever hear of that?"

"I've heard of that," Abbott snapped. "Go on."

"It happens to be a *good* paper. Well, Ann was on the late shift when Earl did his act. It was just before deadline for the Final, and she heard about this murder-suicide on the scanner. At first the cops thought it was a double murder."

Eddie leaned back in his chair. His crossed right leg jiggled at such a rapid pace that Abbott wondered how many miles that leg would log, in an hour, say, if a pedometer were strapped to it.

"So Ann did her job. She found out from the cop shop that the couple were white, they were middle-class—we *had* to have a few grafs, at least a bulletin with IDs. So she called Earl at home; he'd already sneaked out for the night. She figured he's the copy chief—he's got the clout to hold the page and assign a reporter. But all he did was chew her out for waking him up. She told me he sounded drunk rather than sleepy. He's been hitting the sauce pretty hard, right?"

"Go on with the story," Abbott said.

"You're not going to tell me, are you?" Eddie sighted down the coffee stirrer, pointing it at Abbott like a dart. "All right. He told Ann he didn't give a shit if every married couple in the city blew each other away. He didn't want to be bothered with a 'domestic.' A 'domestic,' for Christ's sake; calling a murder-suicide a 'domestic' like some burned-out old cop. Ann couldn't believe it; she freaked out; she froze; and the page went off the floor without a word. Then Ann covered her ass. She filed a report about Earl's great show of professionalism, and Denham got it the next day. Denham and Earl had it out over the phone, but nobody's talking."

Sadly, Abbott wagged his head. "Denham never would have noticed, by himself."

"Yeah, but that's not the point." Eddie slapped his jiggling knee. "Leaderless or not, this is a newspaper. We report news. We don't brush it off."

"I thought you found this funny," Abbott said.

"It's too much. We're a shitty paper, but we've been good at one thing, spot news, and Earl knows it. For Christ's sake, he's the one who set the standard."

"Then allow him this one lapse."

"He's been lapsing for a year."

Ah, how pitiless are the young.

Eddie straightened, alarmed, as Abbott got up, buttoned his jacket and headed for the door. "Hey, you just got here! There's a ton of work to do."

Abbott said he would return after a quick assignment. "I'm covering a sort of domestic."

Abbott knocked on Earl's door. After the answering shout—"Get lost!"—Abbott entered a gloom of drawn drapes, a stale stench of cigarette smoke. Earl lay curled on the couch in his underwear. He looked stringy and fit, even boyish, in the tentlike boxer shorts, but his face squinched like Mr. Magoo's as he rose up on one elbow to sight the intruder.

"How's your stomach?" Abbott said.

"Just fine. What the hell are *you* doing here?"

"I came over for a game of chess."

"Oh. And to shoot the shit, I suppose."

"That's right. The good old days." Abbott planted himself in the armchair. With a long sniff of aggravation, Earl sat up. He lifted a bottle from the coffee table, checking the level of sherry. "I'd offer you a drink but there's just enough for hair of the dog. Got to think today. I was trying to think when you barged in."

"Think about this: Was MacArthur right or wrong?"

"Abbott, give me a break." Earl uncorked the bottle and sipped. He licked his lips.

"I mean it. We never settled that one."

Earl sagged, smirked, rolled his eyes—the air of a captive listener, but one wryly unflappable. "Wrong," he said. "The emperor was wrong. We're no empire; we're kind. Fuckups but kind. Like you."

"I'm flattered, but I don't see the connection with the Yalu River."

"This is a movie, Abbott, right?"

"A movie?"

"This is the scene where the hero sobers up his drunken pal, am I right? Heaves him into the shower." Earl narrowed one bloodshot, bleary eye. "You lay a hand on me and I'll be compelled to make some very decisive moves."

Mockingly, Abbott raised his guard. "The way you handled the karate kid."

Earl sipped more sherry and again licked his lips—a victim, Abbott presumed, of post-binge dehydration.

Abbott said, "What was Adlai's best speech?"

This time, nostalgia suffused Earl's face, like a cloud settling over the wryness. "When he scolded the Legionnaires. In New York."

"Right. Principles are easier to fight for than live up to. I covered that speech. At my own expense, of course."

Perhaps the old magic could be restored. Maybe Earl could be sparked into one of their routines, the two of them topping each other's remembrances or epigrams like performers of a Durante softshoe. Was there any better medicine for the despair that ailed Earl? Abbott said, "What was Faulkner's best novel?"

Earl, however, had closed his eyes in lost patience. "Abbott, you're making it stink."

"In what round of the rubber match did Tony Zale knock out—"

"Third."

"Sixth."

"Third! He did it with body shots." Earl sprang up with arms pumping to demonstrate, but at once he clutched his head and lowered himself to the couch. The pain left him breathless; he spoke between ragged inhalations. "To this day . . . old Rocky . . . grabs his gut . . . when you ask him . . . about that fight. I interviewed him. And not at my own expense."

Abbott extended his hand. "Ten bucks on round six."

"You're on."

They shook hands. "I'll need the money," Earl said. "I'm out of a job, you know. I have the feeling you've heard." He rose to his feet again, slowly—"I need some goddamn tomato juice"—but his sortie toward the kitchen failed. He listed to the right, staggered, and caught himself by flathanding the wall. "Sonofabitch!" Jack-knifed, he shuffled back to the couch. Abbott, unasked, got up and fetched a glass of juice for this incapacitated ex-friend. As Earl gulped, Abbott looked around at the apartment, which had not been tidied up since the robbery. The books, magazines, and papers on the floor had been kicked into windrows to make space for footpaths. The place was as disordered as Abbott's toy-strewn living room. "Wouldn't your girlfriend help you clean up?"

"My dog, you mean? The old one ran away; I got a new one." Earl brightened. "You want to see her picture?" In bumpkin voice: "Hey, friend, you wanna see a pitcher of my girl?" With a hint of the old monkeylike agility, Earl squiggled down to the end of the couch, leaned over and pawed around on the floor, found his pants in the clutter, took out his wallet and extracted a Polaroid photo. "Here. Eat your heart out. Her name's Charisse. Like in Cyd Charisse, the dancer of our era."

Abbott braced himself for one of Earl's shocker gags. He opened his eyes on a naked girl, pretty of face and manic of smile, seated on a couch, spread legged. The setting—a room with a poster of some singer on the wall, mike in hand—was unfamiliar. Abbott handed the snapshot back. "Charming. You should submit it to *Hustler*."

"Nah. It's only swinger-mag quality."

"How about a gynecological journal?"

"You're being a wiseguy, Abbott, and I don't need that." Earl kissed the photo and expressed endearments as he put it away. "Bye, baby. I've got to think today, so I don't want any women around." He squinted at Abbott. "That includes you, Mary."

Abbott harrumphed. "Surely there must be some cooking or ironing I can do. Or your windows."

"You're a wiseguy, but the fact is, I'm kind of dizzy this morning."

And the fact was that Abbott found himself back in the kitchen, cooking a breakfast. What are ex-friends for? He had promised Sharon to try to "help" Earl, and despite Sharon's inconsequence, he was a man of his word. He scrambled eggs and doused them with ketchup, Earl's favorite dish from New York days, and served it at the coffee table.

Earl's fork hand trembled as he wolfed the food. "Two more favors, then you can go."

The favors were to continue playing fetch—to find Earl's glasses on the bedroom floor and to bring in the piled-up periodicals from the hall. Earl tossed aside the *Globe*, the

Times, the *Monitor*, saving, of all unlikely things, the day's *Call*. He opened it to the classifieds and spread it on the table. He read job titles aloud. " 'Exercise specialist.' Now there's one for *me*, huh? You got a pen?"

Abbott handed over his pen and Earl circled several ads. "What's a 'crisis worker'?"

"I don't understand what you're doing," Abbott said.

"Ever see Johnny Carson's bit on funny jobs? Not bad."

"Were you fired? Is it final?"

"Maybe I'll drive a cab. Old losers drive cabs."

Abbott reached down and picked a red-jacketed book off the floor. Eric Partridge's *Usage and Abusage*, the 1957 edition. Some of the entries had been underlined with red ink by Earl in a long-ago, dedicated time. "You've got a field and you're damn near an expert in it."

"Some field—copyediting. A grade-school teacher correcting the work of illiterates, especially from the Ivy League."

"It's a living. At your age, who'll hire you for anything else?"

"I've got friends, you know."

"We've all got friends. They might find makework but they'll be uneasy about it."

Earl continued reading. "Here's one for you. 'Centerless grinder.' " He circled the item with a flourish.

"Why throw your life away?"

At this question, Earl looked up sharply, his lips forming Abbott's words as if they—and their source—were incomprehensible. "Life"—he tossed the pen down—"is a throwaway by its very nature. People would trade their lives for one grand gesture."

"Romantic crap."

"No, hard fact. But you don't understand. Go pet your dog."

Earl lit a cigarette, which triggered a coughing fit. Hands on knees, he gasped like an asthmatic. Abbott moved to slap his back but Earl fended him off with a furious nod "no," and slowly recovered his voice between wheezes.

"Until something comes along . . . I might be . . . a short-order cook . . . old fantasy of mine . . . like your garbage-man . . . dream."

This reminder evoked for Abbott a vision of the sanitation men on their weekly rounds below his office window, tossing GI cans around like beach balls, even in winter when the cans were laden with ice.

All right, score one for Earl in the evocation of good, if not grand, gestures. Abbott went to the kitchen and returned with mugs of coffee. Earl, feeling better, wind regained, sat back and described his short-order fantasy.

"Okay, it's noisy. And it's hot. You're juggling the orders like a fucking octopus. Dozens of orders on the fire, every second a deadline, and people yelling. In a way, you're like a slotman putting out a paper, the good old-fashioned kind with hard news in it, something solid. Get the picture? There's beauty in physical work."

"Great beauty." Abbott closed his eyes. He was young again, working a loading dock. He was stacking hundred-pound bags of spring fertilizer—lime, fishmeal—in farmers' stake-body trucks backed up to the dock. A mud of sweat and lime dust coated his body and dripped from his hair. When he paused for breath, chill April breezes cooled him with the suddenness of a dive into lake water.

He sighed over this memory. He described it to Earl, who said, "Beautiful, yes! A bear hustling hundred-pound fish."

"Well said."

"In a stream of its own sweat."

"That's good, Earl." Now they were clicking—the vaudeville pair matching images. Abbott said, "A wrestler pinning all comers."

"Stacking them up—yes! In rhythm."

"You're all rhythm and revery in such work."

"You're tranced in its movements."

"There's repose deep within it."

"That's *good*, Abbott. A wholeness at the center and

you're happy in it." Earl's voice turned whispery with wonder. "A way of life."

"In the deepest strain," Abbott said, "when the sweat is flowing and the body is all rhythm and revery, you enter this repose. A peace. No matter how hard you're hustling."

"Ah, Jesus, yes." Earl smacked fist into palm, exultant. "Home."

The heart of routine, Abbott thought. Most days, however, were less rhapsodic. Days when fatigue pressed down like hands on your shoulders, buckling your knees, or days so blinding hot that the world looked charred beyond your dripping lashes, like a photographic negative. He wouldn't recount those days, though, and spoil the vaudeville act. Earl needed it, this taking of bows and twisting of balloons.

Predictably, Earl now spoiled it. He missed several cues, and his eyes, grown clearer after food and talk, ranged over Abbott. "You're more a physical type than I am. You could still drive truck or something if you hadn't gone to seed."

"Beg your pardon?"

"Look at that gut."

Abbott looked down at his middle, at the bunched front of his loose-fitting pants.

"It's a fucking shame," Earl said.

Such criticism from a scrawny man in underwear, drunk, disgraced, and—yes—"depressed," was easy to handle; but even so, Abbott felt slighted that no one but Heath had noticed his weight loss of more than twenty pounds. Well, his doctor, too, would notice, and be impressed; an appointment was forthcoming.

"And that tie!" Earl reared back. "*Blotched.* What did you do, blow your nose on it?"

Abbott held out his tie, the paisley one Avery had gummed.

"Once you were a sharp dresser," Earl said. "Like Denham. In fact, it can be said without too much distortion of the truth that you were a fairly presentable guy. But now, el slobbo. El slobbo supremo."

"Sorry, coach."

"Shape up. Do some push-ups. I'm going to do push-ups and sit-ups and maybe even run a little. The exercise specialist. I haven't been in shape since Korea."

"Earl, that was a long time ago."

"Hey, you and I fought a fucking war, don't forget it. Horror and risk—when a person is most alive."

Abbott gave a spare-me-the-details shake of the head.

Then, with unexpected warmth, Earl leaned far forward and plunked a fist on Abbott's knee. "Anyway, think of our luck. All these years we could have been moldering over there. Instead of moldering here."

This moment, Abbott thought, might be the last fraternal one of today's encounter, the right time for a pitch. He said, "Call Denham."

Earl shrank away. "Fuh-uck *him*."

"Call him. Talk to him. You're the model old pro; he might take you back."

This made sense, and Abbott tried to spell it out. Denham was stodgy, yes; he thoughtlessly flaunted privilege, yes; he shunned smalltalk, and would shake your hand only by the numbers at holiday time; but in spite of all this the man exuded a yearning that you be his friend and reinforce his fantasies. "Lonely and complex," Abbott said. "Aren't we all."

Earl wasn't buying. "Fucking dabbler," he said. "I called him, I told him I was sick of the same old shit, and he said—I quote—'Maybe it would be best for the *Call* and you to have a new beginning.' A real newsman would have told me to drag my ass. By the way, convey my apologies to what's-her-name. I gave her a bad time."

"Ann."

"Whoever."

"Were you fired or not?"

"I dunno. Goddamn shyster ambiguity. But it doesn't matter; I'm through. And it doesn't matter what I do now.

You don't understand that. A point is reached where you just jump into the ocean, willy-nilly. A man should do this every ten years to see if he's got any wits and balls left."

"Call him. Talk to him."

"See what I mean? You don't understand. I'm off on a 'new beginning,' as he said. I've got the guts to do it all the way and do it alone."

Abbott heard echoes of Claire in this declaration. Something about "brains and discipline" and solitude.

And he did understand. He could understand Earl's motive, if not condone the crazy actions. He could grasp the joy one must feel in a breakaway. A sniff of burning bridges, sweet as woodsmoke. Moments rich with possibilities, and without rules, you to make them. You, in your fifties, with good years left and most of the dues-paying behind you, the strongest hungers mercifully eased.

He thought of his own life: the circuit down Irene, up Eleanor, across Patricia (always the same route—why?), the drumming of his fingers on the steering wheel at interminable red lights. Someday, perhaps, he'd buck the traffic. He'd let Bapp do the driving. He'd disappear through the opening like air or water, some unencumbered strength that could capture new form for itself from open ground. FOOD, FUEL, SHELTER—those common highway signs would convey new meaning. SHELTER, something found anew with the skin; FOOD, something relearned with the tongue; FUEL, whatever ignited the spirit. And with sticks from this fire he would scratch landmark arrows radiating from himself. He'd cry: Look, my new map! My reinvented wheel! World, stand aside!

Romantic crap. He was Abbott, defender of routine, the discoverable wholeness at the heart of it. He had no further advice for Earl.

Alert now, and steady enough to have crossed the room unaided to the telephone, Earl began dialing for interviews.

16

Within a month Earl had disappeared. Phone calls to the apartment went unanswered. A knock on the door prompted no welcoming insult.

"You don't just quit on a friend," Sharon had said, and of course she was right. What kind of man was he, Abbott wondered, to need ethical pointers from such a source.

He looked up the super at the building, who said Earl had broken his lease and sold his furniture. The museum of so many years, that scene so life-giving to Abbott, was closed, and there was no forwarding address.

Trace him, Abbott thought. You were a reporter once, no great shakes but passable; you know how. The Motor Vehicle Department, for instance; maybe Personnel. Sharon could help, via her network of Pams and Kims and Debs and Dees and Raes, though he'd best avoid contact with her.

A hard look at motive: Was he truly concerned for Earl or just lusting after Earl's ex-wench?

Ah, the hell with all these on-the-other-hands, which strangle one. He'd let Bapp do the dialing.

He found Sharon's number in his notes and called during Eddie's coffee break. A girl answered, and relayed Sharon's name with a scream, giving the impression that Genesis was a dormitory with a payphone in the hall. Weren't counseling clinics quiet, like hospitals? Abbott heard muffled voices and, in a moment, the girl returned. "Sharon's working. You want her number, lover?"

Was the place a clinic, dorm, or whorehouse? Abbott dialed the new number and reached Sharon on an extension.

"Wes! Hey, how you doing?"

He stated his business, a quick missing-persons report. He added, "Maybe your friend, what's her name, Charmaine—"

"Charisse."

"—maybe she can help."

"She's no friend of mine. Listen, I want to see you."

Abbott hunched himself around the phone. Eddie might return at any moment to eavesdrop.

"I'll buy you a Dairy Queen," she said. "It's my turn, remember?"

"I'll have to take a raincheck," he said, adding for aloofness: "young lady."

"Raincheck, my ass. I want to say good-bye to you." She added that she was leaving "this crummy town."

The news saddened him and he wondered why. The inconsequential kid was moving on through life's revolving door—so what? Given his years, he should be well-trained for good-byes. "Congratulations! Where are you going?"

"I'll tell you when I see you." She set a time for a rendezvous at the downtown Green. "I'll find out about Earl."

Tit for tat. Abbott hung up, suppressing feelings too mixed to sort out, some of them suspiciously like joy. He concentrated on a fact: a background noise he'd heard over the phone. Intermittent thunder, like heavy machinery in a factory. She worked in a factory. Yes. As an assembler, probably, one in a row of women at a bench, all wearing bandanas to protect their hair from grit. And, to judge from the telephone privilege, she might be a chief assembler.

Elementary, my dear Watson.

Today she had gussied up: instead of a lettered T-shirt, a blouse, and instead of jeans, a jean skirt.

She slid into the car, jostling him with her elbow in

greeting as he stared straight ahead at the traffic, busying himself with the gear shift. He said, "Where are you going?"

"Huh? Wherever *you're* going, doll."

"I mean your getaway. Leaving town."

"Oh. Denver." She tossed it off as though naming a street down the block.

"*Den*-ver. A long way." His mind pictured office towers, metropolitan sprawl. "May I ask why there?"

"I don't know. The mountains, I guess."

"I see." Snow-capped Rockies appeared over the sprawl. "Strange. I've been thinking of mountains myself."

"I'm kidding. Regina's aunt lives there. We can live with her until we get on our feet, get jobs and stuff. Here"—she handed him a slip of paper. "This is all I could find out. He worked at some diner for a while; now he works at this place, nights."

During a pause at a red light, Abbott looked at the note. It said ABC Typography Co. A suburban address.

"It's weird," she said. "See, Charisse doesn't live with the group any more. She lives in an apartment with this older woman, her lover. You know what I mean?"

He felt the girl eyeing him. Damn these people—Sharon, Earl, Eddie, Heath—who considered him so unworldly. "I've heard of such goings-on."

"Okay, well, these two bi's moved Earl in with them. Weird."

"Outrageous."

"I mean, you wonder what they *do*, for God's sake, the three of them. I'm pretty broadminded, but that's too weird for *my* blood. Where's the closeness, you know?" The girl shivered as from a chill and nestled against Abbott's side, which swarmed with gooseflesh at this contact. "Don't tell Earl I told you. Poor Earl, they must need him to pay the bills. Hey, stop here!"

It was a shopping center. After Abbott parked, the girl caressed his knee—"Don't go away"—and scampered to a liquor store. She returned with a bottle of Lancers. "Fancy enough for you? I just *love* the bottle, the shape of it."

Touched, Abbott said, "You shouldn't have."

"I told you I was buying. Drink up." The bottle was uncorked. "I got the guy in there to open it for me."

"This is illegal," Abbott said. "You're underage."

"Wes, just take a drink, okay?"

After glancing around for witnesses and spotting none, Abbott said, "Cheers," and hurriedly sipped. He handed the bottle back to Sharon, who slugged from it, licked her lips with a whinny of pleasure, and passed it back to him as they drove on.

"This wine won't go with Dairy Queens," she said. "Let's have a picnic. Some quiet spot."

Yes, why not? He suggested stopping for deli sandwiches.

"Who needs food?" She jostled him.

Abbott took another sip and wondered about himself. This gaffer imbibing at red lights (also illegal) with a chippie at his side—was this the newcomer Bapp, the alter idem? No. Act your age.

"What are you doing to do in Denver?"

"I told you. Regina's aunt—"

"I mean your future. You know what you should do?"

Her hand cupped his knee. "What should I do?"

"Take up child care."

He glanced over. She had wrinkled her nose in astonishment. "I'm serious," he said.

Quick, quick, a spiel, a pep talk. Act your age and be a mentor; make this final meeting count. "You know practical things about kids, and child care is going to be a big field. Think of all the single mothers nowadays. And working couples. I've dug up statistics on this; I've written about it."

Indeed. He recalled a memo that Denham had appended to an editorial: *Wes: Soften this one. I find it a bit much for you to call single mothers the "new American family."*

"Listen, when you get to Denver," Abbott said, "do

whatever you have to do. Work in a factory, but go to school nights. Some community college will do. A degree in child care; I think they call it early childhood training. You'll get a job with a future."

Sharon smirked. "You know what those people get paid?"

The voice of reality. Yes, he knew. Then he slapped the steering wheel with both hands, for inspiration had struck. "Computers!"

She responded to his excitement, if not the word. She watched him as attentively as a schoolgirl, lips parted to smile or to frown at his cue.

"Programming," he said.

"Programming?"

"Programming, Sharon. Do you read the classifieds?"

She grinned. "Charisse took out a classified in a swinger magazine."

"I'm talking about *job* classifieds!"

"Oh." She clamped her teeth over her lower lip.

"Read them," Abbott said. "There are dozens and dozens of jobs every day in programming. It's the field of the future. As they say, get in on the ground floor."

He glanced over. She was watching him aslant, searching his face as if for some signal while pursuing thoughts at the edge of her mind.

Abbott said, "My daughter is going into programming. Right now she's finishing up college, but on weekends she goes to computer school. Which is why we rarely see her anymore. She wants a good job for Avery's sake, you see."

Sharon nodded. Her expression continued to deepen. The playfulness had given way to a soft-eyed look in which she seemed to be absorbing his person as much as his advice. As he talked on, she gazed at his mouth, seemingly fascinated by its workings, the mechanics rather than the meaning of his speech; and her head bobbed—"yes" bobs—oddly out of sync with his words.

"Stick it out," he said. "Work in the factory days, and

go to programmer school at night. You've got the determination, don't you? Of course you do. If you study hard and really pay attention—*really pay attention*, Sharon—you can finish in a year, so my daughter tells me. Then you get a job with good pay and a future. Do you hear me?"

"I hear you, Wes."

"Good pay and a future."

"Good pay and a future," dreamily.

"The field of the future," he concluded.

"Field of the future."

Why these worshipful echoes? Was she high on the wine? No, just naturally vague, he supposed. He turned and saw shining eyes fixed on his mouth, and for the first time he wondered if this baby really had the smarts to write programs. Such meticulous thought—could he himself do it? Hell, no; it had taken him months to master his relatively simple VDT at work, much to Eddie's amusement. And now he'd given fatuous advice to a troubled kid.

What did she want from him, anyway? With that look of adoration she seemed to see a father, mentor, lover, all in one. That mooncalf face showed the symptoms of romantic love, the old con to be blamed not on biology but on the mind's own sweet misuses of itself.

He had driven onto the highway. Now he turned off at a rest area for interstate travelers. Here, he'd spend his final few minutes with Sharon in an effort to snuff the romance and talk sensibly.

The rest area was crowded with parked cars, which faced a woods with a large picnic grove. Yet Abbott saw no people at the picnic tables. He recalled now that this area had notoriety as a cruising ground for homosexuals; the *Call* every year or so worked up an "exposé" about it. The drivers of those parked cars were deep in the woods, stalking one another with eyes as hungry as Sharon's.

O kinky day! First, the news that Earl had moved in with a couple of bivalves or whatever, and now a visit to a gay haven. But anyway, here there would be no embarrassing recognitions. No local closet gay of any repute would risk using a place so close to home.

As he parked at the end of the row of cars, Abbott saw one person nearby, an athletic-looking young man in a black, bikini-style swimsuit. The young man lay sunning himself in a portable lawn chair, on a grass strip facing the woods. He half-rose, removing his sunglasses, as Abbott parked, then sank back. Waiting for someone. He wore radio headphones.

Already, Sharon had sized up the place. She chuckled softly as though the woods had ears. With a tilt of her head she indicated the young man. "We won't have to worry about him."

Maybe Sharon, after all, had programmer smarts—or at least good intuition. She added, "We'll be safe here."

Safe for what? All Abbott wanted to do was talk. He would air an emergent truth: that he was an insubstantial sort of man, neither whole nor wise, unadorable, for sure, and unqualified to give her any advice. Inept on all counts. No wonder Earl had ended up blubbering in the girl's lap.

She took hold of Abbott's hand. He looked down, seeing his dark, slightly spotted paw in the grip of two pale hands, one wearing what looked like a high school ring. Abruptly, the paw become airborne. She was raising his arm over her head. She ducked under it and looped it tight around her right shoulder, snuggling against him, and flattened his captive hand on something spongy—dear Lord, her right breast. He turned to a face upraised for a kiss, which whispered: "It's okay. We're safe."

He twisted his face away.

"Loosen up," she whispered, lips on his cheek. "We're cool."

"Sharon—"

"Nobody *cares.*" The armhold eased. "Don't be afraid. Look!"

He looked, then shut his eyes in disbelief. She had hiked her skirt hip-high and was removing her panties with a shimmying motion. Next, a heavy weight rolled onto his lap. She was straddling him, her back against the steering wheel. A hand fumbled at his belt. "No one can see us. *Put it in.*"

Abbott opened his eyes in a cloud of her hair and shouted her name into it, spitting strands. At once, a hand cupped his lower face and she commanded: "Shush!" Leaning back, she followed the direction of his eyes to the young man out on the grass strip, who appeared to be watching them. Abbott imagined the scene through that witness's eyes: a gaffer and a girl, heads framed in a car window, bobbing nose to nose. Sharon hissed, "He doesn't *care,*" and as though to prove this point, she waved at the youth. A tiny wave, barely a wriggle of fingertips in front of Abbott's nose, but loaded with information. "Hi," it said, and "Yes, we're fucking," it said, and "We're cool" and "We're all friends here but we'd appreciate a little privacy." The sunglasses obscured the young man's look, but Abbott saw a smile —somewhat disdainful, he thought—and a lazy wave like Sharon's, a lifting of fingertips on the arm of the lawn chair. An OK sign, after which the youth spoke two words, not loud, though to Abbott they seemed to echo through the parking area: "Right on."

With that, the witness looked away, removing his headphones and lifting himself slightly in the chair as though, agreeably, he'd keep a casual lookout for the lovers.

Oh no, not like this, Abbott thought. Abstinence must end, but not here in a parking lot, with a deluded child, the two of them performing to a kind of peanut gallery. Somehow Sharon had opened his pants. With both hands beneath her, she was guiding his sex. He thwarted the angle of entry by thrusting himself upright, bumping his head on the car roof. With each thrust, she fell back against the steering wheel. "Damn it! Help me." She handled him roughly.

He gripped her by the buttocks and, in one grunting heave, lifted her clear of him and swung her over to the passenger seat, dropping a scramble of legs. His mind, from some unruffled height, noted the feat of strength: an arm-curl executed without leverage. He lacked testosterone, maybe, but had plenty of adrenaline.

Now, quickly, he'd have to invent some excuse lest this child feel spurned. Disturbed kids lack self-esteem, don't they? Sharon seemed an exception, but never mind that; quick, quick, zip up and give an excuse. What do women say to stop rapists? They plead menstruation and the like. Abbott gasped, "Medical."

Sharon, still in a heap on the passenger seat, gaped at him.

"Medical problem."

Her expression—the dropped jaw, the wrinkled nose—could be read either as sympathy or as skepticism. She disentangled an arm. She reached over and with thumb and forefinger traced the outline of his sex through his pants. "You mean here? You're kidding."

He cuffed the hand away; orgasm seemed imminent, the premature spouting of a teen. There had been no time during their tussle to monitor those feelings. "Heart," Abbott said. "It's my heart."

She went wide-eyed. He had not meant to frighten her.

"No, no, I'm okay. I have to take it easy. The strain. Can't do much." He groped for more restatements of this idea as she stared. What a day—from stupid advice to a stupid lie.

She lunged across the seat. Her face plunged into his lap, rooting. As one hand tugged to reopen his pants, she turned face up for an instant to flutter her tongue at him. She whispered, "You won't even have to *move*!"

Dear God, no; he gripped her shoulders. "Sharon, off! Off!"

"Let me, please!"

"Off!"

Her voice came up muffled.

Surely, the adrenaline and his will power would give out. But her weight gave first, and he shoved her across the seat and pinned her against the passenger-side door. "Let's talk," he said. "We've got to talk."

She went limp; only his grip under her arms kept her from slumping. "Are you all right" A foolish question, he thought, in light of that lolling head and that face stuporous with heat. She growled, "Give me your hand."

All right, good, she'd settle for hand-holding. But no, she put a double grip on his wrist and jammed the hand into place between her legs. Her thighs began squeezing down on it. Now he understood. All right, it was the very least he could do for her: lend a hand. As she bucked, body ingesting his fingers, he glanced out at the young man in the lawn chair. He'd turned away, headphones back on. Thank heaven for the indifferent world, dead to Sharon's loudening squeals in the quiet. These soon peaked; she gave a final spasm; she became, in her word, cool. After a long breathing spell she opened her eyes, looking dreamily at Abbott and said, "Wow," as though he were a giant among lovers. A truly charitable girl.

Abbott handed her the wine bottle. She took a long drink. He took a longer one, then started the car and backed out of the parking space. He paused at the exit to the highway while the girl shimmied her panties back on and tucked in her blouse.

"Do you really have heart trouble?"

"Yes," he said. Then, "No." No more lies. "A slight condition."

"I've known guys with bad hearts. They can do things."

"Look, I'm sorry about this."

"Hey"—a good-humored poke on the arm—"who started it? I got you all hot and bothered, didn't I?"

"Oh, you certainly did, Sharon."

"You okay now?" Her hand darted over.

"Sharon, let go."

"You want me to do this? As we drive along?"

"Let go!"

She let go, just in time. Wesley J. Abbott could not have returned to his office stained like a boy home from a date.

She sighed with compassion for him. "The iron man. Who are you saving it for? I know, your wife."

Wrong. But why, indeed, was he "saving it"? In any case, already it was gone—for the present—and so was the vestigial aching in the scrotal zone. Age has its blessings.

"Don't take it personally," he said.

"Oh, I don't. I know you: You're just an old-fashioned guy."

Wrong again.

"But I like that," she added. "I just wish I had one more week to work on you."

Abbott ignored this, and the accompanying pinch she applied to his nerves just above the kneecap. "What I told you before," he said, "about programming—forget it. I don't know a damn thing about it."

She shrugged. "People who go to those schools, a lot of them never get hired."

"Is that true?"

"They learn on old computers, so companies don't want them. Tell your daughter."

"I will."

"Now I've got some advice for *you*," she said, and he glanced over in surprise. "Take good care of Avery. Where is he now?"

"With his new babysitter. Who he detests, by the way."

"Who he what?"

"He doesn't like his new babysitter."

"What's wrong with her?"

"Nothing. She's very nice, the best yet."

"Well, take good care of him. Because little kids, you know, they never have a chance."

Her eyes were solemn, fixed on the road ahead.

He asked, "Do you speak from experience?"

She didn't reply. And he didn't press; it was rather late in the game to act like a caring adult and ask who Sharon really was.

He parked the car one door away from the Genesis house for the leave-taking. She retrieved the Lancers bottle from the car floor and waved it, faking goggle-eyed drunkenness. "Something to remember you by."

He sank into the seat, looking around for observers.

"No, seriously, I'm really glad I knew you, Wes."

He braced himself for a good-bye kiss on the cheek from her, but felt only a pinch. She had tweaked his cheek like a mother.

Around midnight, Abbott checked the sleeping Avery. There were signs of life: dribble on the pillow, and, from time to time, mouth-smacking noises. Abbott closed the bedroom door and went to the living room. He turned out the lamp and stretched himself on the floor.

Immediately he got up, feeling foolish. He needed no act-it-out ritual to reach Bapp, his second self. Bapp was no infant, to be fantasized. Although embryonic in action, Bapp had a full growth of brain and a command of English. He could be approached via a simple interview, something as simple as a question-and-answer format.

Abbott sat back in his armchair and lit his midnight cigarette. After the first few drags had sharpened his mind, he proceeded with the assignment. It would be like a game of chess with oneself.

Q. Are you there?

A.

Q. All right, I'll be specific. What you are, so far, is what I feel first. My first, best instincts. Is that true?

A. It'll do for starters.

Q. All right. Then tell me about today. Why didn't I go hog-wild with the girl? She's no more impaired than I am, for Christ's sake, maybe less. Why didn't I bring her home here and hump to beat the band? Am I a silly old prude?

A. No.

Q. Thanks. Am I an "old-fashioned guy," as she said?

A. Partly.

Q. I suppose. I cheated on Claire twice—two conventions. The *Call* was too cheap to send me on any others. Two hotel whores, wham-bam-thank-you-ma'am, and too soused to remember details. Are you still listening?

A. Good show, Wesley.

Q. Don't be snide. About today, why did I "save it"? It wasn't a matter of morality. So, why?

A. Try taste.

Q. Taste?

A. Good taste.

Q. Are you saying that you—I—we—are a person of good taste?

A. I try.

Q. Consolation prize. What other traits might I expect as you—I—grow up?

A. Decency.

Q. Decency? Another booby prize.

A. No, it is not.

Agreed. It is not.

17

Avery's aversion to strangers grew worse. He shied from his new babysitter, Mrs. Pease, despite her warmth and her credentials—her B.A. in elementary education, whatever that was worth—and he cowered from his mother on her rare visits. With Abbott, he continued to play the Con Game, giving pure welcomes that turned bad days into good, but otherwise he had become what Mrs. Pease described as the "careful observer type," soberly watching everything after initial timidity.

At the moment, Avery clung, face hidden against Abbott's chest, in a city park that lay at the midpoint of their daily two and three-quarter-mile hike. Abbott had stopped to rest on the park bench.

"I understand," he consoled. He stroked Avery's head. "You're spooked here." A strange place, a never-never land where Bapp had unaccountably stopped the stroller.

"Well, it's called Forestview Park, if that's any help. Whoever named it that should be fired for banality, don't you think? Even the *Call* would fire somebody for such a name.

"Nice spot, though. You'd like it. If you looked at it."

They were seated on a wide, elm-lined path. Nearby was a play area with swings, slides, and a big sandbox in which toddlers played, plunked apart, mutually oblivious.

"Look, Avery. Your peers."

On benches around the sandbox, young mothers chatted in groups.

"And there are mine. I speak their language now."

Avery writhed. He slid down to Abbott's lap and craned his neck around to look at the scene.

"Good work!" Abbott patted the child's back. "I knew you'd come around. Check out the crowd."

Abbott watched several young fathers among the women. "They don't say much—notice? Avoid each other's eyes. Self-conscious, as I used to be. But no longer.

"Good work!" Again, Avery had moved. He turned full front and sat beside Abbott on the bench.

"I could saunter right over there and say, 'Good afternoon, ladies, let's have a little talk about nutrition or something.' I'd say . . . oh, I'd say, 'Always include a green vegetable with your starch and protein. ' Or I'd leer. I'd say, 'Let's practice CPR.' "

An exaggeration, of course. Best to be prudent, as always. It was a nice neighborhood. Well-patrolled. "They'd kick out any old lechers."

Yes, and they'd kick out any pedophiles, or barbaric teens, or muggers, derelicts, eccentrics, characters, originals—they would ensure a bland middle-class peace in this enclave. It was for young children. More power to them.

"Good boy!" Avery had slid to the ground. He stood, clinging to Abbott's leg. "All you needed was time."

Abbott took out his notebook and jotted the particulars of an *Entry*, including the date and a guess at the time Avery had taken for his re-entry. The little sociopath had climbed down from chest, to lap, to bench, to ground, now to play.

"Sit down. Here in front of me. Look for toys."

Sand!

A patch of sand, a little pool of speckled white gold in the sunshine through the elms. A similar patch had glowed under Abbott's truck-tire swing at the ancient farmhouse.

"Look: This is sand."

Abbott crouched down beside Avery.

"*This* . . . sand.

"This . . . *sand.* Flows through my fingers.

"Give me your hand. Open it. Let the sand flow through your fingers."

Sifting sand.

As Avery played, Abbott lounged. He stretched out his legs, spread his arms along the back of the bench and tilted his face to the sun. Assignment time on a dreamy afternoon. He gave voice in his mind to the Impossible I, that fictional identity growing less and less improbable with the passage of time.

Sand. A new thing. I must be wary of it.

Once I stretched myself toward all things, hungrily. Now, though almost all things have moved within my reach, I am cautious. I don't comprehend this change, but, according to Bapp—let Bapp be pleased—I live it. I live the sense of these words without understanding them.

The new thing. New things have their secret lives, their independence outside the models I've built in my mind. I watch it from a distance. I don't move. I check on the whereabouts of Bapp the protector.

Does the new thing move, make any sound?

Approach it slowly. Back up. Point at the thing and catch Bapp's eye, get his okay. Go forward again. The thing has not moved, has made no sound. Pause now. Stare at it. Wait.

It is still. Go forward again.

The new thing offers itself to me in an unfamiliar place. It matches none of my pictures. I retrieve them in my mind, searching for a resemblance.

"This," Bapp says, "this . . . *sand.*"

Then, "Water. Sand. Sand. Water."

Water!

I know water, and it is safe. Bapp has stood me at the thing I will someday know as "faucet," which creates water. A wondrous stuff that playfully won't let itself be held.

It falls away between my fingers.

But this new stuff that Bapp trickles in my palm is "sand."

Is sand water?

I search my pictures. Water is see-through and cannot be held; sand is white and can be mashed in my fist.

Now Bapp opens my fist and pours more sand. And in my pictures of sand and water the discrepancies recede and a likeness comes forth: Sand, like water, runs away between my fingers.

Sand is familiar. I know water, now know sand.

I explore.

"Am I reading you right? Or am I screwing up again?

"We'll never know, will we? You won't remember this moment, and I'm bound to forget it."

It was midafternoon, time now to wheel Avery home for a nap. As Abbott lifted the child, Avery cried and windmilled his arms, wanting to take the sand with him. His body heaved at the restraints of the stroller, but soon he calmed down, lulled by the ride and by Abbott's low-voiced grumbling.

Almost a mile and a half to go. "Why do we bother anymore?"

Abbott updated news that he'd reported the night before as a bulletin at cribside. "New top on the story. Reaction from me."

Despite everything—new regimen, second childhood—the glitch in the EKG had worsened. "I should have known, really. Tamper with an old car—grind its valves, say—and it craps out on you."

A need for bypass surgery was not yet indicated, the doctor had said, but he upped the daily Inderal dose and said to rest the chest muscles.

"I hate to harp on this, even to you, but I was flabbergasted. I said, 'I've cut down to five smokes a day.' Instead of patting me on the head, he sniffed as though I reeked of the weed. 'Cut *altogether*,' he said. I said, 'I've lost over twenty pounds.' He said, 'Good man'—pat, pat—'but now freeze that upper body.'

"In other words, no more lifting for a while. Hike, but don't lift. This to a man who once made his living that way. No more bouncing you around. Or lifting young girls in heat—as if I'd ever get another chance."

Abbott glanced around for people in earshot. None. He resumed muttering to Avery, whose bonneted head he could see down front as they moved along the sidewalk.

"Sorry. I know. One quarter of the world's population hungry or being shot at, and here I am—pampered American bitching and moaning. My health is still intact. Or is it? I need a second opinion. I asked him, 'How about shoveling snow?' He said don't do it. I said, 'What if I have to change a tire?' Sad shake of the head. 'Raking leaves?' 'Better not.' I said I have to mow my lawn; needs a sickle. He said, 'Hire a boy.'

"Hire a boy! He should see our lawn, right? No neighborhood kid will cut grass for less than a fortune. I might as well hire the doctor. Or wait for you to grow up and become my yardbird. But you'll be gone. You'll be gone very soon."

This was the gist of another story to be updated, but for now Abbott went silent. A woman approached on the sidewalk, pushing a baby carriage toward the park. She gave Avery a long onceover, then raised doubtful eyes to Abbott. In passing, she did not smile even though Abbott executed his courtly hat-tipping gesture. Ten paces farther on, he said, "We failed inspection," and he stopped the stroller and stepped around front to see why. A dirty face: Avery's earlier tears had dried, smeared with dirt from his hands. Abbott knelt down and dabbed with his handkerchief, dampening it with saliva. "Got to keep you spiffy, or they'll arrest me. Your mother and Lew will have to bail you out of the pound. Remember Lew?"

Lew, at last, was home from Maine, recovered from the flu. He had taken an inordinately long time for his convalescence, which hinted a possible change of heart about being a father, or maybe just some heavy thinking about it. By phone, Heath and he had arranged a meeting at Abbott's house for a talk on everyone's future.

Abbott wheeled on. "I assume they'll get married now. Who knows?—some domestic equivalent. And they'll pluck you out of my hands. I'll be screaming as I wave bye-bye. You'll scream, too. They're so half-baked; will they treat you with proper respect?"

Abbott lowered the stroller off a curb and proceeded across a side street. As he neared the opposite curb, a car horn sounded, so close to him that his senses registered the brief toot as a blast of wind. He bellied forward as though stung or savagely goosed, and in one long stride, a flying giant step, he reached the curb, braked the stroller and shoved it up and over to safety. As he spun around, the offending car slid by, several youths in it, one of them grinning out the passenger-side window. That insolent face called: "Watch it, pops!" Abbott raised a fist and saw a ritual response: The youth flashed a middle finger. Tiresome, so tiresome. With a ritual shriek of rubber the car jerked into traffic on the main street.

Hand on his chest, Abbott recovered his breath. He checked Avery for fright. None: Sleepy-eyed, the baby chewed on his bonnet strap and began to kick as if to get the stroller moving again, to get the Abbott and Avery show back on the road.

Abbott checked the intersection. It had a stop sign; he'd had the right of way. He had not endangered his grandson with his preoccupied behavior.

"Punks!" he said. "To hell with them."

On a wave of bitter feeling, he added, "To hell with everybody."

He crouched down beside Avery. "Let's take off. Leave no trace."

A crazy thought but, hell, worth savoring, like his FOOD-FUEL-SHELTER fantasy. Never, he thought, or at least not in many years had he acted in a way that might be described as lucid-simple and crazy-right. Yet others around him were having their adventures. Count 'em: romanticism on the Cape; a sexual spree in the city; sweat on the trail; play-acting behind a desk and junkets around the globe; a Greyhound bus to Denver.

"First, I'll quit! Say, 'Shove the pension!' "

Sure. Given a moment of sovereign nerve, he might even throw the ultimate tantrum—pretend madness. Fake a swing at poor Denham, say, or expose himself in the newsroom . . . yes, hang a moon right there in the hubbub of first-edition deadline. He'd be committed for a while but end up drawing his benefits, maybe even his whole pension, granted out of horrified sympathy. Poor old guy, they'd say, old Wesley C. finally went bananas.

Abbott got up from his crouch at Avery's side and pushed on toward home.

"We'd be free. Off we'd go, in this stroller. Shall we plan the itinerary? I'll buy you a lemon Coke—there's an old soda fountain I know of in Woodstock, Vermont. And a sundae bar in Bar Harbor—exotic flavors to treat you to. We'll buy a box of Jax and feed the seagulls in Acadia, on the cliffs. They eat right out of your hand. You'll get used to them; you won't be afraid. We'll go climbing in the White Mountains. To hell with my arteries.

"Then we'll come home. We'll sell the house. Who needs such an ark? And such a lawn? We'll buy something plain from the twenties or thirties, like the millhouse where my parents lived once. Remember? I told you about it. I sat there wishing they were happier, there in the dark. On the porch. That porch had a wooden balustrade. Painted white. It faced a sidewalk where neighbors strolled in the evenings. Out back, we'll have a henhouse for eggs. And a big garden to subsist on. Shake a hundred pounds of potatoes out of it every fall. Tomatoes to can, sweet corn—I know gardening; I was a fieldhand, you know. Fast with a hoe. I'll teach you how to garden and how to read.

I'll teach you good manners, true civility. Taste. A decent life. I'll tell you about Adlai and Faulkner—people of my time—and people of your time, too; I'm better informed than anybody thinks. We'll welcome visitors—your mother, of course; your father. And Claire, if she's agreeable, and Lew's people. We'll sit on the porch, evenings, and talk, you and I, and invent new games. We'll fly, though deadweight. And we'll be unique, though routine."

Home again.

He remembered a ditty his mother used to sing, "Home again, home again, jiggedy jig," and bobbed Avery to its rhythm as he lowered him into the playpen. The child would sleep for a while, allowing Abbott a nap of his own on the living-room couch before the energy demands of dinnertime.

But today, dreams riddled Abbott's sleep. An old girlfriend paid a visit, head and torso riding up like a ship's figurehead—Jeannine again, groan-provoking in her sweet-sixteen loveliness (partly out of the dream he mouthed greetings to her), and other faces, other places: a patch of sand, today's or yesteryear's, and now a dusty interior stacked high with bags of lime and fishmeal. Mundane, this scene—the warehouse where he'd worked long ago—but now it dissolved into a records room, the stacked bags metamorphosed into metal file drawers, gray, tiered ceiling-high. Abbott rummaged through the drawers under a ticking fluorescent light. The tone was urgency; he was a young reporter again, no great shakes but passable, on assignment, tracing something through public records. Tracing himself, maybe—in dreams is it yourself you weep for?—or maybe Jeannine, or maybe the woman at whose bedside he now sat, keeping a vigil in a white room. The woman, his mother, slept, half-raised on pillows. No, she pretended to sleep, like a child, eyes too tightly squeezed and her body held rigid under the spread. He heard, out in the hall, the rattle of a cart, and an aide's boisterous greeting to someone. Did the aides have a cruel nickname for his mother, as they did for other patients? Some aide had put a red ribbon in his mother's white hair.

He spoke to her. The closed lids squeezed tighter, like those of a child in a snit, snubbing him. She had confused him with some old antagonist, maybe from way back in girlhood.

Wait. Now she knew him. It was another hour or another day, and the eyes opened, pale blue, tired but not at all faded below the domed, shapely, Yankee brow.

He said, "Did they give you a rubdown?"

The eyes held him in drowsy rumination. She licked her lips and worked one side of her mouth, the unparalyzed side.

"Hmmm?" He spoke louder. "Did they give you a rubdown today?"

He watched the small repertoire of her movements. Tremors, fidgets, a continuous twiddling of thumb and forefinger, rolling bits of thread plucked from the blanket. He noticed a speedup in these disarrayed movements, an agitation that usually signaled anger and resolve. Now it came: The motions united in a testy air of command. She tried to rise, and the hand lifted off the bedspread, fingertips rubbing with a dry rustle just short of a snap. This meant she wanted to communicate. Because she could not bear the sound of her stroke-slurred speech, she communicated only by writing.

"You want your pad?"

She nodded, an ague of nods. He handed her the pad and pencil from the nightstand and steadied her by the shoulders as she wrote, in a surprisingly neat script: "Im tired of it."

Abbott's editor's eye supplied the missing apostrophe in the "Im," and he wondered what, specifically, she was tired of.

"Tired of rubdowns? You need 'em. They stop bedsores."

He had misunderstood. So said the eyes, which now shifted through a range of emotion. First, defiance, the look of a dare. Next, weary amusement, along with pity for him, for the shortcomings of this moment that he, too, sensed: his kneejerk logic and his clumsiness of feeling. Last, he saw a strangely dissolute, drunken look. For some reason, this scared him.

"You're tired," he said. "You want to sleep?" He got up to draw the shades, but paused, held again by the changeling eyes. They narrowed in what looked like contempt before glazing over with boredom. To forestall another loss of recognition, he reached out and placed his hand on her ankle. He gripped it. Her foot was exposed. The toenails, he noticed, needed clipping. He told her he would bawl out the aides for neglect. He played for a laugh. "They're going to need pruning shears for the job, Ma!"

There was no reaction to this forlorn joke except a further drooping of the eyelids. He must be patient, he told himself, must not get exasperated with her, must stop yawning in her face and stalking out for smoke breaks every fifteen minutes. What in hell was she tired of? He tried to recall their earlier, one-sided conversations of this day. A few hours ago—or perhaps yesterday, so diffuse was this vigil—he had called her attention to some birds at the feeder outside her window. Two chickadees, alternately alighting for sunflower seeds. Even to see starlings fight is an event for the bedridden. And all her life this woman had scraped up seed for birds, just as she had rustled up fried-egg sandwiches for hoboes from the freightyard.

But, no, her note had not referred to songbirds. As realization swept in at last, Abbot marveled at the slowness of his mind. Life itself was the "it" in his mother's note. The dissolute look he'd seen was a come-on to death. No surprise, considering her illness and her hatred of dependency. Still, his glimpse of her despair left him panicky and at the same time blank, both empty of feeling and seething with it. He looked down at his hands in hopes they would fumble toward hers, but in this instant he was equally a semiparalytic. The eyes had closed, and her breathing had become rhythmic, deepening into a snore. Her petulance with him was sliding into a nap. She looked peacefully glutted, as after a heavy meal, drifting into a companionable stupor. This time, the sleep was not make-believe.

Is there any argument against being "tired of it"? Abbott, half awake, mused in the fadeout of this waking dream. He thought of Avery, awake now and whining in the playpen. Curiosity is the starting point, the force so vivid in that child. All things are new to you; you make them known. Then you try to make what is known to you new. You rotate, you recycle, and along the way you tire; suddenly you're old in mid-step, you're breathless on a flight of stairs. His mother had been a prime recycler. It was only she, in that farmhouse, who knew that each day should not be like the last, another sullenness. It was only she who knew what came next on the kitchen calendar, what excuse to celebrate a little, lest every day of a hardworking life be an animal sameness. She was an admonition, not simply "woman's touch" but a demand to the raggies to get that friggin' V-8 engine off the dining-room table and make way for a day's candlelit cupcake as well as its Spam or slumgullion. In those drab rooms, smelling of dryrot and dogshit, she placed bouquets in washed-out peanut butter jars. Out in the yard, amid the cordwood and the jalopies and the NITE CRAWLERS sign, she planted bulbs—tulips for spring, dahlias for fall. Flowers for a modest frame house, gray for lack of paint, with a blank mailbox at roadside. It was she who painted a family name on that box, THE ABBOTTS, in her script.

Avery's whining subsided. As Abbott knew, the child would amuse himself a while longer in the playpen, babbling to himself and sampling the makeshift toys there. The next cycle of demands would be louder, but meantime, Abbott was reprieved for further revery in the comfort of a slow wakeup. He resettled himself on the couch, closed his eyes and breathed deeply as his mother had breathed, long swells of the rib cage. Another assignment upcoming—perhaps the last. He had reached all the way back. On this dreamy day, the faces were rising readily, and they throbbed with a depth of life he had never imagined. Once they were makeshifts, mere rough likenesses he had modeled on the run, but now they were perfected in detail, as in a gallery of portraits whose subjects, long gone, are the more deeply seen. They bequeathed regrets. Hopefully, they would bequeath some directions.

A new scene: another bedside, another form of script. No, not script, a rough resemblance. A zigzag green line reminiscent of the old Palmer Method of penmanship that he had learned in grade school: peak and trough, peak and trough, like a child's crude drawing of blades of grass, wind-bent. It was heart's penmanship: the signal on a wall-mounted monitor screen relaying a patient's heartbeat. Abbott lowered his eyes to the patient.

Dread.

His own heartbeat jiggled, just as the signal on the wall jiggled whenever the patient shifted position in bed. And Abbott felt, in his hands, a tension just short of trembling. If he had to speak now, speak a longish sentence, he would gasp, just as the patient himself gasped in the moments of fear he couldn't conceal, when nurses awakened him for vital-sign checks and his eyes darted in terror and his teeth clattered on the thermometer.

At those times, Abbott—in his imagination—restored the old man, fixed him up cosmetically. Put his long-billed cap on. Perched a Lucky Strike on the thick and brooding underlip. Placed a mug of coffee or a bottle of Hull's in the blunt hands to animate them. Trimmed the hair, which was piled like wood shavings on the nape of the neck. Restored ruddiness to the face, which, below the creased brow, seemed to have frozen long ago in some solitary perusal of bad news.

Abbott took a deep breath to steady his voice. Briskly,

"You'll be up and around in no time."

"Shit."

The one-word, all-purpose reply. It sounded faintly nasal because of the oxygen tube in the man's nose. Otherwise the voice was whispery, a soughing exhalation.

A while later—an hour, or a day—Abbott tried again to act the comforter. "You'll be up and at 'em soon."

"Shit."

"They're asking for you down at the shop. They called."

Silence.

Abbott gulped air and said, "They won't lay you off. Not you."

No? Of course they would lay him off, if he survived, a man with a heart worn out by overtime. Abbott's well-meant lie merited not even a "shit," only a glare of disgust over such toadying. The man whispered, "Where's your mother?", rasping the words as if to say: Scram, you fuckin' ninny, and send my sensible wife in here.

The wife—who was to outlast this man by less than a year—had taken her knitting elsewhere for a break in the vigil. The old man turned away from Abbott and glowered at the ceiling. Abbott stared at the monitor screen.

In the blur of days, the two pairs of eyes were constrained to meet now and then; betweentimes, the ceiling and the screen were their resting places. Abbott sat mesmerized by the green signal. He visualized it as a message trying to learn to write itself. A short obituary—very short—for the failed farmer and used-up machinist who lay in the bed. The likelihood of death prompted a bleak sense of release, of elation, which in turn caused stealthiness, a hunch of guilt as Abbott marked time in the bedside chair.

Why, youngest of the three sons, was he here alone? Dana and Keith knew what counted. They came down from Maine on the day of the funeral in a brand new pickup with their logo on its doors—ABBOTT TREE FARM. During the vigil, those sons the old man grudgingly admired were no-shows, while the nonentity stuck close.

In the hospital room, the two pairs of eyes left ceiling and screen and chanced to meet. Abbott saw recognition, the momentary openness and neutrality of it, harden as usual into judgment.

A judgment never specified. Had Abbott done too little with his life or too much? A year in college, a buck sergeant's stripes—did the old man envy such accomplishments or did he demean them? He'd never said. BUTTON IT UP. LOOSE LIPS SINK SHIPS. Though over the years he'd said enough. Of Wesley's chosen work: "It don't pay shit." Of Wesley's wife: "Goddamn snip, and ugly to boot."

What, Abbott wondered, did he want from this troglodyte? A sign of respect? A kind word? Surely you don't need such strokes if you're over thirty and you've modestly "made it" in your own eyes. Or do you? What do you need from a dying sire who can't understand you and who never had the opportunity to understand himself?

Waste, all a waste.

The painful glances grew less frequent. The old man increasingly lost touch. Now, when his eyes scanned the room and landed on his son, they registered a long span of surprise before the annoyance.

"Who's writin' the fuckin' paper?" he whispered one day. "Why are you here?"

Off the poise of a deep breath, Abbott offered: "Just dropped by. See how you're doing."

"Shit. Don't waste your time, Bunce."

Bunce—a childhood nickname, forgotten, like Abbott's own "honey" for Heath. In this daydream and on its sidelines, Abbott blinked tears.

The old man whispered: "Go back to work."

Work. His only word ever of advice.

Detaching from the dream, Abbott looked once more at the old man and at the woman knitting at his bedside and thought about their differences. Custom had held them together, its barren devotions. If his mother's way of life was to embellish, then his father's was to routinize. Habit, not hope, lives a life, is its help and real blessing. Surliness aside, was the old man wrong? Harsh slogans underlay his kind of cool, or cold. NEVER BE BEHOLDEN. PAY AS YOU GO. He was a grown-up version of those stoic playmates who trained for the future by sneering at their orgasms.

Surely, the Greeks had a word for it. Ataraxy?

Think about this, Abbott told himself. Dismiss the grief revived by these dreams, and their reminders of the bones in the closet, and take refuge in the abstractions here.

Think of old Marcus Aurelius. A workhorse always out on the road, patching a broken-down empire for some crazy heir. Old Marcus, classical workaholic, in a bind, pounding sand, neither moaning nor crowing about it, just doodling to himself in his journal as he waited for death.

Think of old Solon: "No mortal is happy"—a slogan preferable, by far, to such modern ones as "enthusiasm for living." Spare us such pious optimism and massive denial. Call off the happiness police. All things hold out promises they can't keep, and by the time you wise up, it's all over and half your fault.

Bracing, this line of thought. Perhaps he should write something, a piece of pseudophilosophical whimsy for op-ed, sort of like an Ellen Goodman column in style. Denham would no doubt misunderstand and nix it. (*MEMO: Wes: Are you saying we should all be sourpusses?*) Ah hell, he'd write it anyway. First, he'd discuss it with someone because of the great gaps in his self-education. He'd discuss it with his daughter. Why not? She had majored in anthropology, had she not? He had never talked enough with his daughter. Summon her, he told his wandering mind. Summon Heath . . .

Wait. Later. Right now someone was calling him out of his slumber. Not his parents, certainly, and not Heath. The voice was odd, thin, shrill, chanting something like "Aay bapp aay bapp aay bapp aay bapp."

Abbott opened his eyes on an infant in a playpen, a

male child waving his arms to be lifted, standing spread-legged, his mite of a penis erect. A sodden diaper had slid down around his knees.

"Good evening, Avery." Once more Avery had welcomed him back to the world. A gift deserving wry thanks.

18

Abbott kept a grip on Avery to allay the child's stage fright. Displayed in Abbott's arms, Avery welcomed the guests for the conference. He allowed himself to be cuddled briefly by his mother, and he endured without tears his father's vigorous greeting. He watched in awe as Lew performed a finger-snapping jig, like a warmup exercise, shouting, "Hey, pal, how you *doing*!" Lew had not seen his son since the trail-side meeting with Abbott. Avery's lower lip began to tremble only when Lew reached out uncertainly as though to take the child. "He's gotten so big!"

Abbott, pulling Avery back, said, "Three times heavier and nine inches taller than at birth."

"You're kidding me!" Lew's hands continued to hover as Avery turned away from him and wrapped his arms around Abbott's neck.

"And six teeth," Abbott said.

"Fantastic!"

"He's had a very easy time, teething."

"Great." The hands stopped hovering and fell to Lew's sides.

"And I think he'll be an early walker." Abbott volunteered all this information on a surge of camaraderie toward Lew; the boy looked so genial, strong, and young. He had regained weight and was growing a new *bandito* mustache. "On top of that, he never gets sick any more," Abbott said.

He disengaged one hand from Avery and rapped a knuckle on the living-room table—knock on wood for luck.

Lew frowned a little at Avery's cowering back. "Any words yet? Mommy? Daddy?"

How can there be words, Abbott thought, for entities that don't exist? "We're working on it," he said, and then excused himself and Avery; the hour was past the baby's bedtime, he explained; he had kept him up for this command performance for the parents.

Talking Avery to sleep took longer than usual because of jumping-jack nervousness over the strangers in the house. Abbott, leaning over the crib rail, held the infant down and mumbled old news that trailed off into nonsense syllables before Avery at last slept. When Abbott returned to the living room, he found the conference already in progress, the two strangers seated on the floor, cross-legged in their jeans, dusting their cigarettes into an ashtray between them.

Déjà vu. That floor, that busy stage with its smelly carpet. There, Abbott recalled, he had performed his first fetal, and Avery had chased a snowflake of paper, and those two youngsters had quarreled months ago. Abbott eased himself into his armchair as into his old role—a resource to be thumbed by these kids for a stray fact, or for comic relief—examples of obsolescence or the unlived life.

Tonight, though, he found himself at once hearing grievances, like a marriage counselor.

"Lew says the hike was a waste," Heath said, "but look at him: He *glows*." She spoke with pride and no little affection.

Lew shrugged. "What can I tell you? It's a sidewalk out there. I didn't see Bambi once."

"Cute," said Heath. "What did you learn about yourself? What private meaning? Share it with us."

"I like soft places to sit. Now how about the first weekend in October?" In an aside to Abbott: "Wedding plans. She's putting me off."

Abbott nodded with a heaviness of head that he hoped

would look sagelike. He cupped his hands in front of his lower face to hide its workings—at this instant, a grimace over his daughter's obvious fatigue. Those raw-boned shoulders in the college jersey, those dark-pouched eyes roving defensively from face to face. Where was the husky girl who had won trophies in the butterfly, and where was the erstwhile go-to-hell spirit?

"Two months," she said, "and I'll have my working papers. So why rush? You could've stopped at Seabrook on the way home."

"I stopped at Colby to see my brother," Lew said, then, in a double take: "What? Where did you say?"

"Seabrook."

Lew gaped. In response, Heath added testily: "You know, the nuclear plant."

Lew, still gaping, said, "I wanted to get home to you. And the baby."

"I know, but there's a lot of action up there now. Hadn't you heard?"

"All I've been reading is job ads."

"You said last year you wanted to protest nukes, for Avery's sake."

Silence fell. Flustered, Heath said, "You could have stopped by. That's all I meant."

Lew, cross-legged, tilted his upper body toward Heath and studied her face from a low angle. He waved his fingers inches from her eyes. "Sweetie. Hi. Look at me. I'm home now. I just walked my ass off on the basis of plans we made."

Heath removed her glasses and busied herself breathing on the lenses and wiping them—a series of prim movements. "I only meant there's still time for things."

"The instant protester," Lew said with irony. "Getting trampled by the reporters. Right, Wes?"

Abbott acknowledged there might be a media circus at Seabrook. "There are those of us in the business," he said, "who miss the nineteen-sixties. Present company excluded." This remark failed to ease the tension over his daughter's strange drift.

"The last week in September," Lew persisted. "We can set up housekeeping at Noz's until we can afford our own place."

Noz, Abbott presumed, was a friend of theirs at the university. What kind of person, he wondered, would answer to the name "Noz," and should Avery be in such company?

Lew added, "We'll get Avery off Wes's back."

"Oh, Daddy doesn't mind."

Abbott, startled, thought he had heard jealous pique in her voice.

"I'll watch Avery days," Lew went on, "and get a night job."

"Why?" Heath asked.

"Why what?"

"Why get a job when you don't have to yet? Right, Daddy?"

Abbott blinked. Her face showed pressure, befuddlement. What on earth did she want him to say? As he hemmed and hawed, she rephrased the question: "Why should anybody join the goddamn rat race when there's still time?"

"Time for what?" Lew had again tilted his upper body toward Heath, and he ogled up at her, slack-jawed. He looked demented in his puzzlement.

Heath opened her hands in an appeal for understanding. "Listen, you walked the trail. That was good. Good, but private. Now you have a chance to do something . . . oh, I don't know . . . public. I mean, not self-serving, and not self-searching . . ."

Lew cried, "What *is* this shit?"

"Last year you talked about a long canoe trip, remember? You could make a cause out of it. You wanted to canoe down the Intercoastal Waterway."

*Intra*coastal, thought Abbott. A correction, a small point of editorial accuracy to cling to as he rode out his shock over Heath's suggestion. Another brush-off of Lew, in the form of another test for a half-assed Hercules.

Yet why be surprised? Abbott recalled that his assignments—his recollections of their earlier talks—had all pointed to such an outcome: a Lew hellbent on conventional life and a Heath with cold feet.

Lew smacked himself on the brow. "I don't believe this."

Heath pleaded, "Listen to me!"

Lew sagged. He hung his head and groaned to the carpet. "You're stalling. You're *still* stalling."

"I'm not!" Her splayed hands danced around. Looking anguished, she grabbed the sleeve of Lew's field jacket and shook him. "You don't get my point."

"You're telling me to get lost again. That's your fucking point."

"I'm not! I'm telling you to do something for the environment. Something that'll enrich us as a couple. We've both got to *grow*, and there's still time."

Lew, rocking from the tugs on his sleeve, gave a shriek of laughter and repeated her word, wonderingly. "*Grow!* Wes, did you ever hear such bullshit?"

Abbott raised his eyes to the ceiling.

"Paddle up shit's creek," Lew said. "That's what she's telling me. And run up a flag for the whales."

"I wasn't thinking that," said Heath, "but is it really so silly? Is it so silly to raise consciousness a little?"

"Wait a minute." Lew closed his eyes and spread his arms, a signal for calm and sign of an impending brainstorm. Slowly the hands descended as if subduing the dispute, downsizing it, patting it away. "Okay, I think I know where you're coming from. These things—you really want to do them yourself, right? I mean, it's *vicarious*. You want to go play, but with me leading the way."

"Well, sure," she said, "I'd love to. But first I've got to get a job and get settled with Avery."

"After we're married, you can do these things," Lew

said. "You can go up with the Greenpeace people. You can paint the baby seals red—any fucking game you want, and I'll go with you. We'll even bring Avery."

Heath scoffed. "Sure. In a little parka. On a little sled."

"The point is, we'll do these things together. As a family."

Heath, stone-faced, turned to Abbott. Her expression reminded him of Claire's wooden Indian pose of the past. She said, "All right, Daddy, how many whales were slaughtered last year? And I'm not being silly."

Abbott executed a reach-and-riffle of memory through past editorials on the ecosphere.

"Come on," she prodded, "how many?"

"Twenty-three thousand, I think. But if you're serious, Lew ought to run up a flag for the sea turtles. They're down to half a million."

"I told you this isn't a joke," she said.

"No joke about the turtles," Abbott said. "It's a damn shame."

"Daddy, bug off, okay? Lew, you could collect pledges for every mile and donate the money for lobbying or something. You could talk to groups along the waterway."

"Sure," Lew said. "To the cheering millions on the docks."

Abbott, matching Lew's mockery in his mind, composed an Earl-style lead on the unlikely story: "DATELINE—A young canoeist surfaced here today to make waves for whales." Only upon hearing Lew's hysterical laugh and seeing Heath's glare did Abbott realize that he had muttered these words aloud, as if Avery were his audience.

"Daddy, will you shut up! Both of you!"

Beyond her shout, Abbott heard—or telepathized—a distant sound: sighs and tossings, a message reaching him via maternal empathy. He excused himself from the shouting match and went down the hall to Avery's bedroom. He saw that cigarette smoke from the hard-puffing pair had drifted in and beclouded the room, and Avery was stirring. If he awakened, only a night ride would put him back to sleep.

Damn that pair! Abbott opened a window and waved his arms to fan fresh air toward the crib. Why hadn't they quit smoking, like so many young people today? Like Eddie? Heath had quit during her last months of pregnancy, but now was puffing up a storm again, as was Lew, their cheeks working like Avery's on a pacifier, both of them destroying fine young lungs. Okay, their privilege, but they had also given Abbott a nicotine fit: He quivered inside for a good, pungent unfiltered Camel, or a stinkbomb Gauloise. Even a hand-rolled Bugler. Inconsiderate bastards!

Did they really care about Avery? Yes, as an abstraction. And that was forgivable, in light of their absences. Don't, however, make excuses for them, he thought. Or for himself. For himself, this night was a repeat of the past, a night of playing the onlooker who cranks out quips and updates but rarely takes part, rarely feels the grief as the toll rises.

The ongoing debate reached him through the closed door.

"You're afraid of your mother!"

"Bullshit!"

"You're afraid of close relationships!"

"Bullshit! You're afraid of your family!"

"My family doesn't even *talk* to me any more!"

Enough. The voices were rising, and Avery would surely awaken in terror. Abbott strode back to the living room. Entering, he found himself lurching out of character, telling the pair to shut up. "That's a human in there"—he pointed toward the bedroom—"not a goddamn toy."

They looked up at him blankly, without recognition. Understandable: They faced, not the Abbott of old, but the new, reconditioned, revitalized self that had tagged itself Bapp. Abbott himself watched this persona with surprise and approval as it chewed the pair out.

First Lew, who blinked as though slapped.

"Start acting like a father," Bapp said. "Either that, or back out."

Next, Heath.

"If you talk Lew into another stunt, you'll lose all pride in him. And he'll lose it in himself."

Heath responded with a show of fists and a scream. "Who the hell are you to talk about pride?"

That did it. Bapp blew up. He told the pair to get out of the house—and to get off the pot. "Don't come back until you make a decision about Avery!"

Abbott paused for breath. Bapp had propelled him to the hilltops of adrenaline, where life is heady—and yet peaceful; voices reach you there as only a faint, inconsequential buzz.

The buzz was Lew, finger-jabbing at Heath, making some ultimatum of his own. He sputtered about getting a job and saving money, and he imposed some deadline for agreement on a date. "If you cop out again, I'll sue you for custody. I mean that! I'll go to Family Service and get a lawyer!"

In the hilltops, Abbott dismissed this tantrum bluff. How can a boy sue for custody on the basis of nothing more than a paternity statement?

The door slammed. Lew was gone. Suddenly, Abbott felt very tired, back down to sea level. It appeared that his interference had only split the hotheaded pair even more. He looked down at a cigarette that Lew had left smoldering in the ashtray. He wanted to pick it up and drag deep, then lie down on the carpet and fantasize about the Intracoastal Waterway.

Fog.

Cranes.

Crabs. Blue crabs.

Wait. Something loomed in his peripheral sight.

Heath, still there.

Heath, now against his chest, the spot occupied so often of late by her fearful child. She was crying, eyes hazed red.

She had stretched the neck of her college jersey to her wet cheek. Abbott's arms snapped shut around her, by reflex, as if she were little again and might fall.

"It isn't Lew," she said. "It isn't Mother. So many things can go wrong . . ."

Abbott stood silent, holding on. No reassurance was possible about anything, except to be there, be present.

A father, being present.

19

If the event had occurred in a smaller place in a bygone time, it would have been news. A social note.

"Avery Abbott of Irene Street marked his first birthday today. Many happy returns, Avery! The birthday boy's mother and his maternal grandfather were guests at the gala. It was held in a booth at Mr. Pizza on the strip."

So much for village flavor. The honoree's father and maternal grandmother didn't show. There was no extended family with age-mates for Avery to cringe from or to poke and prod. He cried as if abandoned when Abbott left the booth to shoot a picture of mother and child with Mother's Instamatic.

"Reminds me of wire photos," Abbott said after his return to the booth had restored calm. "Babies being held by politicians or popes. The kids scream and everybody thinks it's cute."

"So?" said Heath.

"It's cruel. It's unintended cruelty."

"Daddy, you sound like some kind of mother hen."

"I'm just saying it's ignorant bad manners."

"Pampering my kid. *My* kid, remember?" This rebuke, though, was good-natured; Heath's manner had softened since the row several weeks ago at Abbott's house.

She took the spoon from Abbott and tried to take over the feeding of birthday cake to her son. Avery went wide-eyed and ducked his face away.

"Damn!" she said. "It used to hurt me when he did that; now I just get mad." She rubbernecked at Avery, her features pinched like those of a little girl showing spite. "I'll *bop* you." She recoiled as Avery leaned toward Abbott with a holler of fright. "Oh, sweetie, I was *kidding*." She clutched Abbott's sleeve. "Make him stop."

Abbott placed the slice of cake on the highchair tray, and the sobs ceased instantly, on a catch of breath. Avery proceeded to pulp the cake and eat it off his hands.

Heath shielded her eyes from the mess. "I've got a lot to learn, don't I? Yet, when he was only two weeks old, I taught you all you knew."

Abbott put a slice of cake on Heath's plate. "Here, seconds. You're too thin."

Obediently, she took a forkful. "Do you know how important a child's first year is?"

"I've had an inkling."

"It's crucial, and I've missed almost all of it. His first year has been so weird." Reflecting on this, she reached out and touched Abbott's sleeve. "I mean, I know you've done your best."

Abbott waved his fingers in acceptance of this compliment—or was it an insult?

"Now it's up to Lew and me," she said. "I guess."

The on-again-off-again pair had reconciled, somewhat. Heath stroked the nose of a large teddy bear sprawled on the booth table. It was Lew's gift to his son.

"He really wanted to be here today, but he had to work. Gung ho, as usual."

Through a relative Lew had found temporary work at a construction site. Abbott pictured the young worthy in hard hat, striding the high iron—or, rather, picking up nails on the ground. At any rate, Lew had dropped his silly threat to sue for custody, and, in return, Heath had agreed to consider, not marriage, but what she called an "economic and parenting arrangement." She smiled to herself. "The latest is, he's telling me I've got a postpartum depression; it just happened to hit late. I wonder which of his sisters told him that."

Was such a thing possible? Abbott decided not to invite ridicule by asking. He said, "He's got some growing up to do, but he can do it without canoeing up Mount Everest."

"Daddy, you're laughing at me."

"How about if he swims to Spain?"

"Go ahead. Rub it in. When he's around, I can't think. He's too much." She joined her fingertips and rested her chin on them. Her gaze at Abbott turned wistful, then emptied out halfway to his eyes. She looked—what was that slang term?—spaced out. Spacey, sad, suggestible; for a moment, a young woman without much sense of herself but willing at least, and at last, to let it show. "Maybe what I'm really afraid of is a stupid goddamn sexist marriage."

"Does Lew want that?"

"Who can tell? He's never thought about it. I'd go on Welfare first."

Abbott assured her that she would never need Welfare so long as he had a job. There was no need to add that his job was in jeopardy.

"I'd be a single parent," she said.

"That's pretty tough."

"So I've heard."

"Officially, they don't exist, but there's a growing crowd. Would it annoy you to hear the figures?"

She reached out and squeezed his arm, and her eyes glistened with a yearning, it seemed, to placate him, to be absolved for all their past friction. "You don't annoy me. It kills me to hear you say things like that."

A warm moment. Heaven help us, yes, a sunrise in the woods. Abbott broke eye contact. He hitched himself forward in the booth and ran a hand through his hair. What does the etiquette of such a moment call for? Well, time permitting, you sit back and talk. He asked her about school.

"Oh, I'm so *sick* of it."

"It's almost over."

"Liberal arts. That's a buzzword so professors can think their tiny little worlds are important."

"That's too cynical."

"Oh, I know. I don't care a hell of a lot about learning COBOL, either."

"Who's he?"

"Skip it." She sliced a piece of cake and put it on his plate. "Forget the diet. You look wasted."

He ate a forkful.

"Now the figures," she said. "Tell me how much company I'll have in the poorhouse."

Abbott patted his lips with a napkin and with the other hand reached out to right Avery, who had tipped himself off balance in the highchair in a try to reach the table. Avery was getting bored. It was Avery who controlled the time.

"Eighteen million, last I heard. Single mothers."

"Wow!"

"A new class of poor. And many of them are very young, children with children. Not as savvy as you are."

"Thanks for the pep talk."

A pep talk, precisely. By day, pep talks and playing cupid; by night, fantasies about kidnapping Avery. The days won out; a stifling good sense prevailed.

Again, Avery teetered toward the table edge. He seemed to be trying to reach the handful of lollipops that Mr. Pizza had provided for the fête. Abbott moved them out of sight behind the gifts and put another slice of cake on Avery's tray.

Heath's eyes bugged. "Another sugar fix?"

But the baby, as Abbott knew, hungered no longer. He played a two-fisted game of mash the cake, accompanying this with a deep-throated growl, a new sound he had discovered and was testing at various volumes.

Heath wagged her head. "I don't think I'll let him pig

out like that. When I take over."

Abbott asked about Claire, whose birthday gift lay on the booth table, folds of blue fabric with rockinghorse designs, blue for boy. The long-awaited crib quilt.

"She doesn't take long beach walks any more. Gets out of breath." Heath fingered the fabric. "She really wanted to be here today. Something came up."

It occurred to Abbott that he had not seen his wife in over a year. "I should drive up and say hello. Buy something in her shop."

Heath didn't reply.

"Would she give me a discount?"

"Don't go up there."

"What?"

"Not right now." Heath lowered her eyes and went on stroking the quilt.

"Are you trying to tell me something?"

"I'm not supposed to, but I will."

Abbott's mind reeled, performing a quick scan of his feelings. Given Heath's darkness of look and her hesitation, the news had to be bad.

What did he fear most? All right, face it: Claire had found another man. Some crafter, maybe, some executive who had given it all up for a second life, as she had. But, strangely, Abbott's scan picked up no jealousy or hurt, only a neutral tone; call it peace. Surely this meant his marriage had died, for no truer test of feeling exists than this ambush test of the gut. His life with Claire rolled by in a few vague images. He remembered their rare dinners out, two bottles of wine followed by sex that was old-shoe but agreeable—agreeable at least to him. Familiarity. Sloughing dance of a fond old boot in its chosen tidal flat . . .

"Earth to Daddy! Earth to Daddy!"

He looked at Heath. She asked, "What are you thinking?"

He opened his hands. "Well . . . more power to her."

"What?"

"I wish her well. I guess this means we'll have to hire a lawyer."

Heath had tilted her head inquisitively; now she cried, "Oh, for God's sake," and began a long drawn-out tittering laugh that brought tears to her eyes. People at adjoining booths glanced over. Abbott put on a good-sport smile, and his eyes groveled for a hiding place until she lowered her voice. "You're thinking that Mother's found romance. Aren't you?"

Abbott grunted.

"Romance up on old Cape Cod."

"Like a movie," Abbott allowed.

"In the first place, Mother's over fifty." Heath raised a hand to forestall any protest. "Okay, okay, biologically possible, I know. Even psychologically. But in the second place, Mother would have to be the sort of person who cares about how she looks, and she never gave a shit."

"You're exaggerating."

"It's true now. She never replaced that front tooth." Heath jabbed a forefinger at her lower jaw, then pulled down her underlip. "And now she's lost two on one side"—Heath sucked in one cheek—"like thish. All shunk in." These enactments ended now, to Abbott's relief. "And she wears her hair in a bandana all the time. You know what she really looks like? She looks like some big, beefy, tough old middle-aged peasant artisan, sort of like Picasso when he was old. And that"—Heath shrugged, round-eyed with insight—"that is what Mother really is. An artisan, I mean. It's what she should have become, from the beginning. Actually, in a way, it's wonderful. She's found herself."

"Then what's the big problem?"

Heath sobered. She leaned forward in the booth to mouth the terrible word. "Money."

This time, Abbott's scan of his feelings signaled a red alert—an abdominal clutch and cold panic. He was a young GI again, diarrheic in the troopship. A dead marriage is one thing but money's another, life or death, when you're getting old.

"Wild Geese flopped," Heath said.

He gaped.

"Her shop, Daddy. The name of her shop."

"Of course."

"She owes back rent and taxes and other stuff. Not a whole lot but . . . money."

As Heath enumerated Claire's debts—money, indeed—Abbott recovered his breath. He searched for consolations or humor in this new crisis, this new twist in the soap opera. Meanwhile, Avery struggled to climb out from under the highchair tray, and his singsong of crankiness was rising in pitch. Abbott's hand shot out to yank the baby upright.

"She wants to reopen," Heath said, "in Orleans, I think. She doesn't want you to know all this because you'll think her adventure failed. Your opinion still means a lot to her, believe it or not."

"I understand."

"I knew you would. She's teaching and doing the craft circuit, but that's barely enough to live on."

"I have some money." A lie. He was broke. He couldn't borrow any more. He'd had to take out a loan not only for tuition but for babysitting expenses. He couldn't very well sell the Wellfleet cottage out from under Claire; it was half hers. Should he sell the house? He'd fancied such a move. The notion triggered another inner scan, which detected no tug of sentiment toward the costly old ark. Sell it, then, and split the take with Claire. Cut roots; make a clean break with everything.

He rubbed Avery's back in the slow, circular motion that sometimes calmed the baby down.

"She went into it like a child," Heath said. "No marketing study or anything."

"Marketing study? For a junkshop?"

"Not a junkshop, Daddy, a *craft* shop, and yes, a marketing study. It's a tough world out there."

"I've noticed that."

"The problem was location. Commercial Street—all that P'town schlock. She was stuck in with a bunch of T-shirt shops, so nobody came. She tried, put out penny candy and stuff, but nothing worked."

Penny candy! A delight from the past to cling to and dwell on in this crisis. Licorice sticks, jujubes. Abbott asked, "Did she have root-beer barrels?"

For a moment Heath stared at him, then tolerance—perhaps for the wandering minds of the aging—allowed her to proceed. "When Mother first went up there, I approved. It was personal growth. But she was conned in a way. I mean, sometimes we 'sisters' do a number on each other. The magazines are full of stories about women who turn their hobbies into big successes in the real world. It's a crock."

Abbott shrugged. "All I know is, one good thing has happened." His search for consolations had turned one up. "You two 'sisters' seem to get along better now."

"Oh, we do." Heath beamed. "We really do. I've made peace with the past."

Abbott smiled over hearing this claim from a twenty-two-year-old.

"It was never a big thing," she said, "really; I mean it wasn't the kind of problem a person would need counseling for. It's just that I was stuck inside Mother's kiln. Being baked in there. Do you know what I mean? Being baked in Gifted Child mold. But now we joke about it. We have positive interaction now."

Abbott winced over this jargon but welcomed the news. No further assignments would be needed to divine Heath's motives on this score. She had been Momma's Girl, snatched up by Claire—hands off!—in an unrewarding life. Under pressure in that kiln, Heath had chewed parental love notes into spitballs.

She clasped Abbott's hand on the table. "Do you like Lew?"

This non sequitur startled him, and he answered honestly. "I don't know. He reminds me of myself about thirty years ago." Yes, the lusty bullworking boy, the piss-and-vinegar kid. Yet Claire had characterized him back then as a wallflower.

"Tell me what you were like"—Heath's hand tightened on his, and her voice softened—"thirty years ago."

"Memory falsifies," Abbott said. A reply too pontifical, and Heath fluttered her lips in a mild razzberry. "Come on."

"I really don't know. I never thought much about it."

"Were you fearless?"

Fearless? Abbott smiled.

"Lew is. Two summers ago we went to Quebec and lived off the land. All summer."

Gone all summer? "I don't think I ever noticed," Abbott said.

"I was glad you didn't. Mother did; I told her I had a resort job. But we lived off the land. We shoplifted for food and stole gas. Lew siphoned it."

"Maybe I shouldn't be hearing this," Abbott said.

"In Montreal we panhandled. Did pretty well, too." Heath laughed. "Couple of Irish immigrants down on our luck—that was Lew's pitch. They're not too crazy about Yanks up there. You should hear Lew's brogue."

"Tell me one thing," Abbott said. "Did you have a tent?"

"Sure. We camped. Why?"

Someday he'd tell her about the famous Cape Cod hike, in detail. They'd swap stories.

She squeezed his hand. "I want to know what you were like."

"I really can't say. I'll have to get back to you on that."

"Oh, come on, Daddy. Don't fink out on me now. This has been fun."

"I wish I could remember."

"Talk about it."

Yes, he'd talk—talk himself blue in the face—but not

now. He slid out to the edge of the booth, slapped one knee and sighed a conversation-ending "W-e-l-l . . ." There'd be time later for the heart-to-hearts he'd never had with Heath and for a mutual solving of the world's problems. For now, Avery came first, and Avery had called time. The cake-smeared child would have to be swabbed down quickly; he'd reached flashpoint anger and soon would be a screaming embarrassment in the restaurant. Abbott dipped a wad of napkins into his water glass to begin the cleanup.

He also swept the lollipops into his coat pocket. Young Eddie could use them as cigarette substitutes.

20

Hearing Eddie's voice on the phone, Abbott felt that an event of D-Day magnitude had commenced (all proportions kept) and there would be no turning back. He checked his watch: 2046 hours. The house silent, Avery in bed.

"He wants you first thing," Eddie said. "He's going to have your ass for breakfast."

Abbott closed his eyes to face the possibilities. At worst, he'd be fired. He'd be out in the cold with Earl, whom he'd lacked the heart to look up.

"I almost shit when he walked in," Eddie said. "I thought he was still in China or wherever."

"So did I."

Perhaps a choice would be offered. He, Abbott, might hear: "Come back to work, quit, or go on psychiatric disability." Fair enough. He'd have fired himself months ago for goldbricking and insubordination. In the past, he himself, after handwringing, had fired people for less.

"I tried to cover," Eddie said. "I gave him the family emergency line."

"I appreciate that."

"But he asked me for how long and I had to tell him you were out all week. What else could I say?"

Nothing. The excuse of family problems would cut it no longer. Comp time; sick time; vacation; leave, paid and unpaid—all gone, all IOUs cashed in, and many time cards falsified. Despite all this, no columns written. A recent memo had noted in acid terms that samples were a tad overdue.

"Hello," Eddie said. "Hel-lo!"

"I'm still here. I haven't had a heart attack."

"Save the sick jokes for tomorrow."

"Did he mention samples?"

"What samples?"

"Something I was supposed to do for him."

"Do what?" Eddie, always the tenacious reporter, even as the bearer of bad news. "I do everything there is to do in this office, as you know."

True, Eddie was there even now, ink-staining his shirt at 2048 hours of this fateful night. He said, "I finished all the tricentennial crap. The follow-up."

"That's good, Eddie. We're safe for another three hundred years."

"I'm greatly relieved. Now what's this about 'samples'?"

"Nothing. Did you get the editorials I mailed?"

"Two editorials in one week. A great help."

Angry, but you couldn't blame him. Abbott said, "Eddie, I appreciate this call."

"It's part of a deal. Remember?"

"I remember."

"Though I think I'm on the short end."

Abbott pondered this: the exchange of his know-how for Eddie's labor over the months. Yes, Eddie had been shorted.

But, having griped, the young man sounded mollified. "I don't think you'll be canned. Demoted, maybe, I don't know. Drop in here first and I'll bring you up to date. So you won't look completely stupid when you go in."

"Eddie," Abbot said, "quit!" Whatever its source of energy, this outburst went on. "Listen to me. You're only thirty years old!"

Sounding bewildered, Eddie said, "Thirty-one."

"That's even worse! Get out of there before you turn fifty overnight, the way I did!"

"I know what you mean," Eddie said, after a pause.

"No you don't! Don't wait. Don't wait for me to get fired, and don't wait for me to retire. Don't wait for me to drop dead." Strange: He was spouting like a disappointed father. "Join the real world. Make your move; do *anything*, just get out of there. Take a year off and walk the Appalachian Trail."

"That's the *real* world?"

"Sail a canoe down the Intracoastal Waterway."

"Christ! What's *your* real world these days?"

This offhand, innocent query was the kind that can draw the deepest of answers, if the answer leaps straight out. "Parenthood," Abbot said, and he stood stockstill amid the reverberations of this word. His mind seemed to have taken leave of thought and blundered into spirit, a radiance.

"You're pissed," Eddie said. "Get some sleep and don't worry. I'll brief you tomorrow." He hung up.

Phone still in hand, Abbott lowered himself into his chair.

Parenthood! It was true. A moment of truth, a sensation of perfect fit, of dazzling self-unison.

Parenthood. He hung up the phone. He put hand to brow and reviewed the evidence.

A parent, yes. He had been Avery's parent for a year, no mere investigative babysitter but a bona fide parent. Furthermore, his parenting had spread out beyond Avery. He had tried to act the mentor with that girl, Sharon. After fumbling with Sharon, he was learning to act the parent with Heath, his own daughter, for the first time in their lives. He had scolded Lew like a paterfamilias. Likewise he had just sputtered at Eddie.

As insights go, he thought, all this was shamefully obvious, as plain as the nose on one's face. But it must be remembered that one's nose is only a faint smudge, a transparent shadow in the visual field. Now you see it, now you don't, like your prejudices, or, for that matter, your motives.

Ah, parenthood. His trail, his waterway. His dream shop and his resurrected girlfriends. His big snowflake on the living-room floor. A parent, years late.

He got up and went into his study, where he had been writing an editorial when Eddie called. A piece on single male parents, running households. A count of 446,000, of which he was one, a warm body in that tally, at last fitting in, finding the right coordinates. Nurturing, protecting, providing . . .

Providing! A parent, especially an aging one, had better damn well keep his job.

Abbott typed.

At this hour, would the noise awaken Avery? It never had. If it did, the baby would rattle the doorway gate to the study, wanting to play with Bapp's clackety-clack toy. Long, quiet games would be needed to lull him back to sleep. Count the spoons or stack the tins. One . . . two . . . three . . . cuff! the pile down.

By 2200, after an hour of clackery, the child had not awakened. In that case, should his breathing be checked? Abbott told himself: no. He, Abbott, was supposed to be grown up now, and he wouldn't do that any more.

He rolled another sheet of paper into the Underwood. His random notes had taken the form of a do-don't list, advice to Heath on the care of the child she would soon reclaim.

> Don't let him play with television knobs. I should send you and Lew the bill.
>
> Don't worry about his diet. This week, nothing but hamburger for three days, but the intake balances out in the long run.
>
> The same for attention. He regulates his intake. He resists both overmothering and undermothering. It's best to let him lead, let him meander. Lately, he's been spending forty percent of his time—I've measured it—picking at cur-

tain threads and simply watching things, adding to his pictures, elaborating his models. The careful observer.

Keep things fairly predictable, not novel. Not too easy, not too hard. He's a living argument proving the need for a routine life. He's conservative and learns by little increments. I presume that by the time you read this, his scariness will be gone.

What else? Pages were piling up.

Praise his little feats—be a good straight-man for the performer. Maintain an aura of welcome. Foster the good self-image. In a word, practice good manners with him, human to human.

Bingo! Here was an idea for a column: a look at civility in the parent-child tie, which forces one to be a better person than one is.

The column wrote itself easily, flowing from his preconscious through his fingers to the paper. Then Abbott turned to the do-don't items, converting some of them into columns. These all sounded like a baby-care manual. Everything already had been said, by people far more qualified, but maybe he could say a few things slightly better. He switched to the lingo of the assignments.

Deep down where the models are being elaborated, there's an opportunity to plant a sense of . . . say, good weather. A benignity of sky as the model-maker goes about his work, building all those interconnections that become his life.

I'm thinking of Face—a good Face—as the benignity of that sky. Face: always there from the opening need to the closing cry. Good weather deep inside you, taken for granted as years go by but still orbiting invisibly there and giving you the power to be alone because you are not alone . . .

All right! This weather metaphor might serve as the gimmick for another column. Twiddling a pencil, Abbott sat back and waited for a flow of associations. As they came to mind, he scribbled. Later, glancing up at the window, he saw first light. In a few more hours he'd be presenting these samples to Denham. None, of course, fit the specs. The boss wanted "funny pieces." He wanted a comic strip featuring a curmudgeon with the cuddlies, something as sentimental as a diaper commercial. But these efforts might buy time.

21

His heart skittered and his mouth was parched as if he had chain-smoked a pack of cigarettes.

Rampant anxiety. But why? He was no screw-up facing some giant of the trade, like Benjamin Bradlee. Nor was he a ten-year-old facing a wrathful patriarch.

He left Denham's outer office and went to the water fountain in the hall. On his return, he exchanged another formal smile with the secretary, a new woman who had not recognized his name when he had announced himself for his appointment. *Call* turnover: a revolving door.

He waited by the window, steadying himself against dizziness with a grip on the sill. He gazed down at the street. Where were the huskies today? Wrong hour, wrong day.

He sniffed at himself with amusement—too loudly. As the secretary's eyes lifted, he whipped out his handkerchief and pretended to blow his nose.

He had reconstructed by now the Abbott of thirty years ago. No hell-raising husky; rather, a *good* fieldhand, a *good* soldier, toeing the line, fearful of authority even if it was vested in a figure as mild, say, as a Denham. Another plain-as-your-nose insight. The self-knowledge was freeing, in a way, but also academic, for the anxiety had a life of its own. Soon he was summoned into the inner office with all the symptoms undiminished.

If he spoke, breathless, he'd sound chilly. In lieu of a

greeting, he marched across the carpet and thrust out his manila envelope full of sample columns. *Present arms*!

Denham, on his feet, was distributing sheets of paper from a stack in his hand to separate stacks arranged on the desktop. Without raising his eyes, and with only the faintest of smirks, he said, "Glad you could drop by, Wes."

He blinked at the manila envelope leveled at his chest.

"Samples," Abbott gasped.

"Oh?" Denham looked blank. Then, after recollecting a moment, he said, " 'Grandfather Knows Best,' " and snatched the envelope in irritation. "It's been quite a while, hasn't it?"

Abbott gulped air and said, "Took time. Getting the feel of it." His voice quavered but did not crack; short phrases were manageable. He risked a complete sentence. "I tried a lot of different angles."

"Are they funny?"

Abbott reached back to rub his locked neck muscles.

"I said, are they funny?" Denham rustled the envelope. "I want a *dynamite* column and I know you can do it."

Dynamite? Abbott noticed rolled sleeves, a loosened tie; Denham was functioning at least partly in the Old Pro mode. Abbott said, "I think they'll knock your socks off."

"I hope so." Denham lay the envelope on the corner of his desk, distastefully.

Abbott cleared his throat. "How was China?"

There was a pause ominously long, and the boss's mouth arced downward at the corners. It was the look he wore in reaction to possible scorn, to jokes of which he might be the butt. He said, "Mrs. Denham and I were in New Zealand."

Abbott smiled. If you've goofed irretrievably, by many miles, what can you do but smile? You wear the dashed grin of a joke-teller who forgets the punch line.

But Denham himself chortled. Apparently, the gaffe had fallen within the limits that he could endure from the nut case that he presumed Abbott to be.

"Next time," Denham said, "we'd better send you a postcard."

Abbott gave this dryness the good laugh it merited.

"Your assistant made the same mistake. I straightened him out." Denham looked away and gave a self-prompting snap of the fingers; he was trying, Abbott realized, to remember Eddie's name. Abbott realized at the same time that Eddie, though "straightened out," had neglected to "straighten out" Abbott in the 7:30 A.M. briefing. Thanks, Eddie.

"Your assistant"—the effort of memory had failed—"told me you took the week off."

Abbott licked his dry lips. "Emergency at home."

"I'm sorry to hear it." This response, flat, confirmed that official sympathy had ended. Denham added at once: "I need a favor from you, soonest."

He continued to lay out the papers in his hand—they were typed letters—in stacks, as if he were dealing a game of cards. "Sit *down*, Wes. Relax."

Abbott sat. He had been standing at rigid parade rest.

"Did you hear about my appointment?"

Luckily, yes. Eddie hadn't skipped this news, that the boss had been named by the governor to chair some citizens' commission charged with pondering the future of the state, or something. Let Eddie be forgiven his little stab in the back.

Abbott said, "Congratulations. That's an honor."

Denham remained deadpan, but his cheeks colored a little. "An *awful* chore. I've got to draw up an agenda for the first meeting." He swept his hand over the stacks of letters. "That's why I want you to do me a favor."

Abbott leaned forward, relieved at this strange twist in the showdown.

"Mrs. Denham and I were booked for a little confab. I think UPI is sponsoring it. Now we can't go, what with this chore. I want you to go in our place."

Denham ceased dealing and eyed Abbott for a reaction. Abbott found himself voiceless again.

"Well?"

For the moment, Abbott could not reply, not even a croak.

"Consult your crowded appointment book, Wes"—the tone was downright nasty—"and tell me if you can see your way to going. You'll be going to San Francisco."

Abbott stared at the knot of Denham's tie. He strained to remain poker-faced. San Francisco! The Golden Gate! He has not seen that gorgeous skyline since Truman's time.

"It's a symposium," Denham said. "A weekend shindig on the First Amendment. Nothing important, but I want the *Call* to be represented there, among the small independents."

The last words had the ring of a policy statement. Abbott found his voice in a near shout: "Good idea!"

"I thought you'd think so."

"We should keep in touch with the other independents."

"Exactly. That's what I do, even if my staff never knows where I am." Denham gave a chiding smile; Abbott responded with a snigger and briefly hung his head.

"There aren't many of us left," Denham added. "No surprise, considering the costs."

"We've got to hang in there," said Abbott.

"The chains come around all the time. They say we're stagnant, have nowhere to go. They don't know what it means to be a tradition."

"They're only in it for the money," Abbott said.

"I'll never sell."

Almost any chain would improve the *Call*, Abbott thought, but partly by demoting, or dumping, himself. He nodded faster to hurry the boss through this digression.

"You'll have to drop everything," Denham said. "Fly out Friday."

Fly! Abbott's muscles stirred. He was flying with the

kids on the swings at Forestview Park, pushed by the young mothers.

Denham dealt out the final card in his hand. He sat down, patting the stacks into orderliness. "All this is on the tab, of course. Check with Personnel before you go."

Blurred scenes unfolded in Abbott's mind. He saw an assembly of men applauding one another. Their business done, they adjourned to a bar of Tiffany decor, full of women, mature women adept at handling menopausal men. Overall, there was a sense of fellowship. A falling-down drunk would be led safely to his bed.

"Wes?"

Abbott looked up. Denham was leaning back in his chair, arms folded, a man who had presented an attractive deal and was politely awaiting slow-witted comprehension of it. Half a gift, half a bribe. Company-paid R&R to a garden spot three thousand miles away for a once-valued old hand now considered cuckoo. On his return the old hand would be obligated out of honor—still an important virture—to get back into harness and write funnies about his personal life. Perhaps Mrs. Denham, the shadow publisher, had suggested this junket. Perhaps, in response to Denham's grousing about the old hand, she had said, "The poor man. Mothers need a timeout."

Denham stood up, looking a bit deflated, resigned, as if he had expected a sign of gratitude but could forgive its absence, knowing Abbott. Such a moody, surly fellow, hunched there like an old farmer grumping at you.

Denham extended his hands and rubbed the palms together, a subdued sort of coach's gesture; rally, team, go-go-go. Go out of my office. Go have a good time. He said, "I won't need a report on this shindig, Wes. Just enjoy yourself." He was subtle enough not to wink.

Going out, Abbott lurched on stilts and his heart fluttered. Symptoms of agoraphobia, maybe, owing to his sheltered life of past months—rather, past years. But soon enough, his heart would drumroll into vigor. He'd walk nine feet tall in the adrenaline hills, way up where people's voices are indistinct.

Except for Avery's voice.

"Ite!" Avery demanded. He clung to Abbott's leg. "Ite! Ite!"

It was time for the light-switch game, the most exciting game of all now, and—by Avery's edict—an absolute must before bedtime.

"Ite! Ieeeeeet"—rising frenzy in the child as Abbott hoisted him onto his chest, on a level with the hall light switch. Avery's fingers fumbled to the switch and Abbott lay his own forefinger atop them, applying gentle pressure.

"Light on," Abbott intoned. After an interval for bug-eyed awe over the illumination, Abbott chanted, "Light off," and pressed again.

"Ieeeet"—in the dimness a cry of wonder over these contrasts of light and shadow in the world, and the power to effect them.

"Light on . . . Light off."

Tomorrow, Mrs. Pease, not Abbott, would be playing this game. That exemplary babysitter would be his stand-in. He had made the arrangements.

"Trust her," he told Avery. "I've briefed her on all the rules. Fifty repetitions of this, no fewer."

Avery squealed and gave a jiggle of annoyance over Abbott's voice. It had interrupted the rhythm and the spell of the game.

Abbott resumed the chant—"Light on . . . Light off"—and composed to himself an explanation for the child. Avery deserved the excuses due any human, literate or not. The child's keeper was about to waltz off on a spree at a time when the kid was fear-ridden without him. The first separation. Or—call a spade a spade—the first desertion, for it probably would feel like that to the little neurotic.

What can I tell you?

An explanation for oneself. Sum it up. Health. Job. Sanity. Sex.

He had realized how badly he needed a break. Another shallow insight. For months he had been yearning without knowing it to touch an adult—an adult for a change, a human whom he wouldn't have to feed and whose pants he wouldn't have to change. He had been yearning to *talk* to adults, even if all they voiced was shoptalk and bedroom groans, which would be the case at the convention.

Pondering all this, Abbott hesitated, and Avery squawked and squirmed over the skipped beat in the game.

"Light on . . . Light out."

Another squawk, this one over the careless substitution of "out" for "off." Abbott breathed deep to regain patience, and chanted on.

Mrs. Pease had been reporting on the child's behavior. He'd warmed up some, she had said. This very afternoon at the house, while Abbott was out for a quickie haircut, Avery had crept closer than usual to Mrs. Pease and showed her a spoon from the Dairy Queen collection. A good omen.

"Light on . . . Light off."

Abbott sagged. Surely, he'd reached the fiftieth repetition in the game. He knew this not by silent count but by the ache in his arm and chest muscles from Avery's weight. Despite doctor's orders, his chest had continued to serve as shelf and observation post—as crow's nest. Nothing else would do, anatomically, in the absence of a real mother's handy hip.

Bedtime now, another ordeal. He tightened his hug and hurried down the hall to the bedroom. Avery struggled, kneeing Abbott's ribs, and Abbott resolved to alter his nightly schedule, put a less thrilling game last. The baby was capturing control, as well as time.

Shrieking "Ite! Ite!," he scrambled up from the mattress.

"Down," Abbott bellowed. Tackle, takedown, and pin.

"Ieeeeeeeeet!"

Abbott reflected in some calm corner of his mind that someday the child would master the "l" sound in "light." One of the hardest to pronounce, according to Heath's research.

After a while Avery quit writhing and his sobs eased. Abbott withdrew his hand and leaned over the rail of the crib to talk him to sleep.

"Trust Mrs. Pease. She's going to stay with you. Right here, on home ground. She'll live here the days I'm gone. She didn't swoon today upon seeing the clutter we've made—we can trust her. She'll take you to the park every day. She's to follow all the routines, even the hikes. She thinks I'm a crazy fussbudget. Trust her."

What else to add?

"I gave her an extra fifty bucks. She'll earn it, you tyrant."

Avery lay still, breathing hoarsely.

What else?

"I have a joke. Think of wise old Socrates. He used to go to the Corybantic rites to let off steam. Likewise, this lowly grunt must go get drunk and get laid.

"Funny?"

No, not very funny. Not funny at all.

22

"They've ruined that gorgeous skyline," Abbott said. "All those new buildings."

He couldn't picture it now, though, that cityscape. It and the events that had occurred there already were fading, only an hour after homecoming.

"Fun," he said. "I wore Denham's name tag."

Because of the last-minute switch, no tag had been printed for himself, he explained. The mislabeling had startled some of the boss's friends from the Midwest.

"They liked my speech. A Free Press/Fair Trial number. We applauded one another's speeches, us ol' boys."

Abbott closed his eyes to retrieve a sense of the fellowship but all he found in the dark behind his lids was a sharpened awareness of hangover pain. His eyes burned, hot spots in a generalized ache. His fingers quivered, though less from boozing than from fatigue.

"Do you want to hear about the clowning around? Not much to tell. The Southerners are best at it."

He couldn't recall, by now, the woman who had broken his long sexual drought, though the expense would linger for a while as another deficit in the household account.

"It was worth it. Blessed relief. On the other hand, lust begets lust. You'll learn."

Abbott got up and shuffled, hand on head, to the kitchen. He returned with last year's Christmas bottle of sherry and resumed his position on the living-room carpet, where he had dumped his luggage an hour ago amid the strewn toys. He sat with his back against the wall, elbows on knees. He took a long swig from the bottle and licked the sweetness off his lips. "Hair of the dog. Earl's trick." He shuddered as the warmth spread. "Listen, one shouldn't drink alone. Would you like some apple juice?" Louder: "Avery! Apple juice?"

Avery sat a few feet away on the carpet, his head bowed in dejection. He was motionless. He had not welcomed Abbott home. He had not looked at Abbott or reacted to the smalltalk. He sat slope-shouldered, naked except for diaper and rubber pants. A jug-shaped body, fat little jug, sealed, with no label.

"Ball," Abbott said. In announcer's cry: "Play-y-y ball!" He extended a foot and kicked the beach ball in Avery's direction. It nudged the infant's shoulder and rolled away into the litter.

"Look! Filler game." Crouching forward, looming above the child, Abbott projected his lower lip. "Go ahead—tug it. No? I'll do it myself." He tugged and a filler rolled out, a long one, in which his tired voice trailed off several times in its spoof on Avery's immobility.

"The record for inert life . . . is held by lupine seeds, which sprouted in warm water . . . after ten thousand years in the frozen tundra.

"Avery, sprout! I can't last that long."

Despite all these antics, there was no break in Avery's indifference, not even a flick of the eyes. Abbott touched the baby's arm; the flesh twitched.

"Should I act like a clod and snap my fingers in your face?" No, he wouldn't do that. Nor would he toggle Avery's dab-of-putty nose.

He took another drink of sherry, swishing it like mouthwash. Already, the sherry had calmed his jitters—or befogged them—and created a flush of what felt like energy.

Ersatz, no doubt, but energy just the same, even mental energy, a surprising onset of it. He took another swallow and then reflected on Mrs. Pease's babysitting report, which she had presented before going home.

"Avery missed you," she had said. The child had cried, wouldn't play, wouldn't eat. He had rocked in his crib, losing himself in what sounded to Abbott like the rhythm of womb return.

But she minimized these symptoms. "It's only a stage. You'll get the silent treatment for a while; it's his way of punishing you for going away."

Punishment? Silent treatment? These words didn't fit. Abbott looked at Avery's bowed head and the old-man curve of his spine; here was a case of anguish, not tactics. Abbott felt like placing his hand on that hung head in some occult effort to intuit the pain.

He stretched out on his back next to the child, to rest. Assignment position. Yes, why not do an assignment while waiting for Avery to come around? Another fetal—one more raid on the imagination. A final bit of error-prone fancy and guesswork on what made Avery tick. But this time he'd try a switch. Bapp, not the Impossible I, would do the monologue. Bapp would try to guess the infant's feelings and transpose them into his own adult world, disrupting that world with absence. Abbott draped a forearm over his eyes and began mumbling, slowly, as the associations flowed.

I have returned from a toot to find Avery gone.

I crouch behind the closet door, playfully to pounce. But no one swings it open to discover me there.

I push a stroller long distances. It's empty. I talk aloud to a strapped-in absence. Passersby stare.

On the floor of the living room I stack tins. I pile them: one . . . two . . . three . . . and then *cuff*—knock the pile down. I do this over and over to restore Avery with magic.

But no one materializes to watch me, to squeal and flap his hands, possibly to imitate.

Heath and Lew are gone. Another mystery. The phone never rings.

Claire is gone. The forearm of Cape Cod has eroded into the sea. I find Claire's hard-won art floating like pulp off Monomoy.

Earl is gone, presumably murdered. Our museum was sacked by young vandals.

Strangers inhabit the *Call.* A Denham lookalike ignores my nod of greeting. A young man I knew as Eddie sits at my desk, sucking on a pipe, and gives me a runaround as if I were a member of the public. He seems not to hear my reasonable questions as to what has happened, what has gone wrong.

I scream to be recognized. I shove the young man; I swing a wild punch at the Denham lookalike. Security guards pin my arms, apply a hammerlock. They bum's-rush me down to the street. They think I'm a harmless crank.

I am alone in the street. Where are my parents?

Interesting.

I mean, why should I think of my parents?

Anyway, they're long gone, long dead. All my people are gone, and most of the landmarks.

I return to my closet and crouch behind the door, playfully to pounce, to restore my world with magic. But now the closet changes. It becomes the gray file room where I searched the drawers for some ID in a dream. The space changes again—this time it's a room of metallic white, like a morgue. And the tiers of drawers, ceiling high, hold corpses instead of records.

I undress. It is time for the ultimate fetal. The dance of verbs, stilled, will be tagged with my name and filed away in one of these shallow drawers.

It slides shut, and the dark and isolation are terrifying. I feel vertigo, as if I lay on a slanting ledge. Air currents and gradations of tone in the dark suggest presences. I hear noises, feel uprushings, smell breath, smoke. I can't explain any of this, can't cope. Did I cause all these changes to happen? Without memory, like some crazed drunk in a blackout, did I wreck my world? Or did my world, angry over my failures, strip itself to punish me? I have been abandoned, and there's no recourse of action or mind.

Wait. There's one escape—within. I huddle, hug myself and rock. Horror to the left, horror to the right, all giving way to a calm rhythm within, a blur of peace, of apathy. Of liquid and wind . . .

Abbott sat up and took another sip from the bottle. "How'm I doing? Is that how it feels?"

Avery's floorward gaze remained fixed.

"Listen, do you want me to shut up? Should I stop bending your ear?

"I'll answer that: no. What you're used to is a flapping jaw, so that's what you'll get. Familiarity. I've got to restore it.

"Bapp. Remember him? The co-designer of your world. Your 'permanent object,' as your mother would say.

"Well, this Bapp double-crossed you.

"I see that now. All these months here you mapped out your world; you fashioned your models of where things are, of what they do. Including you and me and all our actions.

"Then I disappeared, yanked the thread.

"Oh, no harm done. It's 'only a stage,' as they say.

"Through me, you had built up trust and many expectations. I betrayed them. A politician's kiss.

"Listen, let's go on with this. It's an indictment. Silly, but it does make sense. I put the lie to all the signals we had invented. I brushed off all that rapport. I stamped INVALID on the pictures in your memory.

"Hell, you'll get over it, like a bruise from falling. But

that's not the point. The point is, I was Face, Bapp, part of you and the benignity of your sky. That sky went out like a light.

"I caused your terrain to become haunted. I wrecked your cosmology. For such a crime, grown-ups normally slaughter one another.

"Feel any pain? Tough it out. I'm not apologizing. I'm not crazy. I'm not apologizing to a one-year-old. People have to leave each other; they have to die on each other in the most unmannerly ways.

"May I sit closer to you?

"Thanks."

This time, Avery didn't flinch, and Abbott sensed from the tilt of the child's head that he was listening. Perhaps Avery couldn't believe in Abbott's reappearance; in which case, Abbott was right: He'd have to re-create himself with his yakking and routine moves.

"First, another snort of sherry. It's working wonders.

"Do you want some apple juice?

"*Juice?*

"You haven't eaten, you know, Mrs. Pease said. The food was great in San Francisco. Anybody will tell you that.

"Aha! Caughtcha. You peeked. I think. Peekaboo?

"All right, forget it. I have a theory. A quack speculation. Professor Abbott, lying here beside you and speculating.

"The villain of this piece may be life itself. I mean the natural growth of your mind. Question: what's the prime motive? Answer: to resolve uncertainty. But at your age, there's no way. That little brain has to keep playing catch-up, and I think it must trip on itself as it grows. So, it gets scared. It wants protection.

"I've made observations over in the park. The morning before I left we were talking with Jolene, remember? That young mother in tight cutoffs—that's a detail you wouldn't notice. Her daughter, Trudy, shoved you. Trudy shoved you aside and punched me on the leg for stealing Jolene's attention.

"Next, Trudy climbed into Jolene's lap and nipped her right on the throat, leaving a love bite there. Jolene clouted her, *whack*, and carried her some distance away. She sat her down in the grass and told her to stay put. It was this banishment, not the blow, that got to Trudy. Only then did she cry."

Abbott rolled to his side, rose on an elbow and took a sip from the bottle. "I'd better eat or I'll get soused all over again. And you've got to eat, too; you fasted.

"Avery, are you hungry?

"Hamburger. Ham-bur-ger.

"Forget it, I'll go on. Back to the park. There are two parks. The mothers and I see safe, middle-class Forestview. The kids feel someplace primeval through their genes. They're little monkeys and, for them, the park is full of leopards. They want parents close by.

"Funny. We seem to be in a hell of a fix. For you, there's a leopard out on the lawn. And for me, there are skeletons in the closet."

Abbott opened the closet and looked high on the shelf. Seeing the cartons, he felt disbelief, as if part of his mind had expected that the passage of time, all by itself, would have removed these two coffins and their contents from his life. He carried them to the living-room table one at a time, although each was not much bigger or heavier than a large can of pipe tobacco. He moved carefully as if something horribly comic might happen, like a skeletal rattle, should he jostle them. His hands trembled, not from fatigue or his hangover so much as from a flare-up of emotion over these remains. After so many years, why? He backed away from the table and sat down on the carpet beside Avery.

"Meet your great-grandparents. Their ashes. Bones, actually. 'Ashes' is a euphemism. Little fragments, with rainbow colors in them. And a gold filling, in your great-grandfather's box. Metal ID tags.

"Morbid, huh, this little cemetery?"

Avery had not looked up. Sitting slump-shouldered, lumpish, he continued to stare at the floor.

"Macabre. Claire thought so. You see, Claire had some legitimate complaints. Did I ever tell you?

"First, a belt of Harveys . . .

"I think I'll have to phone for our dinner. I wouldn't dare drive. Are you hungry? How about a pizza? Pizza to go! This day won't go down in your history as a nutritional plus.

"All right, Claire's gripes. As the years went by, she got spooked by the little graveyard in our closet. The cartons kept falling on the vacuum cleaner, I guess. She said, 'For God's sake, go spread them somewhere.' She said one day, 'Spread them in Wellfleet Harbor. It's a beautiful place; they would have loved it.'

"Not so; they weren't salt-water people. I did drive them up there to keep the peace. I waded out at low tide, one under each arm, but I couldn't bring myself to scatter them there among the oyster shells.

"They used to vacation at a lake near their home. That was the custom then in pre-superhighway days. My mother would drag my father there. She'd sit in a rocker on the old hotel verandah and jaw with people while the old gent fished alone. And while I sneaked around peeping through cracks in the women's bathhouse. My brothers, I presume, were at some beer joint up the road.

"Later I went back there—took those cartons—and found the hotel gone and the lake weedy—eutrophication. It was a pond with a few outboards churning it up.

"Another time I drove them to the Berkshires. But they hadn't been woods people. They were domestic—purely domestic, Depression-time, back-yard people. By then I owned my own back yard here on Irene Street. But I couldn't very well dump them out there among the bones of little Heath's pet hamsters.

"Okay, why was I making such a bizarre fuss? Who were these people, anyway, this dust?

"Well, I didn't know. That was part of the problem. I remembered the old man's open-handed right cross. Open hand for me, fist for my big brothers. And I remembered the lunches my mother packed me for school—thick, soggy tomato sandwiches; the seeds and mayo dribbled down my chin. I loved those sandwiches. Maybe I loved the right cross, too.

"Are you sure you're not hungry? We'll order a pizza. With hamburger."

Abbott could not be certain, but Avery seemed to have loosened up. There was less tension walling Abbott out.

"I'll go on. Blabbermouth will go on so you'll know I'm not just an apparition. And I do think we're getting somewhere, closer to some kind of truth. Something I've known all along but never knew I knew.

"Okay, they died about a year apart. After both had been shipped home from the crematorium, there was no root place to spread the ashes. Relatives were all scattered. We had no Ye Olde Family Burial Ground, and I'm not one to place urns around the house. The places where I'd grown up, the rural slum and the milltown, were gone, pretty much; they were engulfed by the postwar suburbs, and they had a new populace: people driving new cars and vacationing in places like Hawaii. We sold my parents' old duplex for a bundle. Smart move, but I should note for you that old Yankees are hard on their pasts. If the price is right, we'll sell you the Village Green. If you ever go looking for your roots, check the dumpster behind the Caldor shopping center.

"Anyway, in carting them from place to place, I seemed to be getting to know them a little, for the first time. I felt I owed something to that dust—an act of energy and imagination like, say, choosing a perfect gift for the living. The only gift now possible was the right grave, the right spot in the terrain. I wanted to do this one private thing right, do right by them.

"As you can see, they're still here. The right coordinates remain to be found—if I should live so long.

"How about sausage on the pizza? What do you say? Sausage and hamburger, both. Mozzarella. Spinach, for your green vegetable. All right, no hurry. Cheers.

"I remember standing at the door at my mother's funeral. I was shaking hands with the people saying good-bye after the service. An odd sensation: It seemed that my past was fleeing episode by episode as the faces filed by, leaving me a blur. A blur of selves only half remembered. Unassimilable. A quick widening of the mind, the mind betraying itself.

"In other words, who was I? And who were the dead? We had known each other only gut-wise, in the roots of our feelings. We depended on nudges, hints—and blows. No language for intimacy, and, God knows, no banquets of advice. Tough, grim people, long on guts but short on inner lives.

"I think I'm discovering my legacy. Better late than never, wouldn't you say? It's quite clear. There's more of her than of him in me. A lot more, the embellisher who did her best in a time when good feelings were hard work—heavy lifting. But all these years, I've lived his way. I dressed myself in his skin, and I even invented a myth to go along with it. The old stoic. The sage of non-feeling. Since more days are bad than good, glaze them all with routine. Double shifts at your lathe, so to speak. Lose yourself and your fears in a hard job of work. Make that your repose. There's repose in the heart of the hardest work. Your 'stolid bliss.'

"I can't say he was wrong. 'People should communicate'—that's the bromide—but, hell, they communicate too much; the din never abates. Does it matter that I never said good-bye to him, or he to me? Hell, no, the old bastard. Did it matter that my mother didn't know me at the end? Not really. Did it matter that Claire and I broke up? That was a blessing. Does it matter that I lack the guts to call an old friend who's gone bonkers?

"Does it matter that I've never reached anyone at all?

"Okay, yes. There are times when it counts, and this is one of them. I must talk, talk, talk so you'll know I'm real."

Abbott arose, and, weaving just a little in his steps, returned the cartons one by one to the closet shelf. "The visit is over. Wave bye-bye." He resumed his place on the floor beside Avery, and displayed his hands, which were trembling again despite his numbed nerves. "Look at Bapp's funny meathooks, how they shake.

"Do you trust me yet?"

Abbott extended one hand and loosely gripped Avery's arm. The flesh did not shudder, but Abbott quickly let go, thinking: Easy, go easy. And keep talking.

"Mourning. How obvious! I should have guessed right away today. I went away, died on you, leaving you to begin over. Or to postpone beginning over, and to mourn. Maybe I'm still mourning, too.

"Well, stop it. Stop hanging your head.

"Look—"

With a grunt, Abbott rolled over onto his hands and knees. He crept about in the litter of makeshift playthings on the floor, searching for the small tins that he used with Avery in the stack-and-count game. He found several.

"See these? Familiar, aren't they? How many times have you seen me stack these? And you've never imitated me.

"*Tins.*

"Shall we try again? Why not? Then I'll phone for our dinner. They're going to deliver a pizza with a dozen toppings. I don't know about you, but I'm going to eat.

"First, let's work. A job of work, my old man's way. Focus yourself on the hour, not the day; the detail, not the plan—there *is* no plan; the locale, not the route, for there *is* no route. Trust what's at hand, your tiny area of competence. There are worse ways to live.

"*Tins.*

"*This* . . . tin.

"This . . . *tin.*

"I pile one . . . two . . three, and then . . . cuff!—knock the pile down.

"Watch now. I'll do it again. And again. A hundred repetitions. A thousand, if need be. Repetition is the key. Before you know it, it's all over and done with.

"One . . . two . . . three . . . cuff!

"One . . . two . . ."

Eyes on the game, Abbott sensed movement beside him, a springing followed by pressure against his leg. Avery clung to him and cried.

Abbott found that he too wept, or, more accurately, that his bloodshot eyes were seeping.

23

A wedding!

Heath hadn't used that word, precisely, but what else could the good news be? Over the phone she had said, "Lew and I have a big announcement for you. It's a surprise." Her voice almost rang the bells with its cheerfulness.

"Let me guess," Abbott said.

"I'm not telling. We're going to make it a celebration, telling you. Can you come down tomorrow?"

"You're going to take a canoe trip."

"Fun-ny, Daddy. No, we're going skydiving. Can you come down? We don't have a car right now."

"You're going to set a date."

"I said it's a surprise. But you'll be happy to hear it." She dictated an address, a street in the university town. "That's Noz's apartment."

So! Once more, the on-again-off-again couple were living with their friend named Noz. How big was that apartment, anyway? Big enough, it seemed, for the growth of serious intentions at last.

On the drive the next day, a Sunday, Abbott reflected that he was to be the father of a bride, a party-giver. Okay, he loved a party as much as any man—damn the cost. For cash, he'd push his plan to sell the house and split the take with

Claire. He'd write to her soon. He'd throw a big blowout at a reception hall, a catered affair with an open bar and a band. Two bands. Two bars. A blast for everyone: Lew's big family—said by Lew to enjoy a party—and *Call* staffers, former babysitters; what the hell, everyone.

He awoke from this fantasy, startled. "You'd think I was the happy couple," he observed to Avery, strapped beside him. There were serious problems to think about.

One: Their offspring notwithstanding, Heath and Lew were too young for marriage. Claire would agree.

Then again, of all life's gambles, marriage is the chanciest, the least rational at any time.

Two: He barely knew the bridegroom-to-be. Big, energetic, genial, the boy was a tonic to have around, sort of like an overgrown Avery at Avery's very best, but his prospects seemed vague.

Then again, given life's strangeness and its vicissitudes, such doubts lacked weight. To play a managerial parent at this stage would be absurd.

Therefore, dismiss all fears of parental delinquency and focus on the detail, not the plan, for there *is* no plan. And the detail, in this case, was a wedding—no less, no more—soon to be announced for some agreeable, distant time, probably after Heath found a job and the couple were settled in their own place.

Abbott found Noz's place in a campus fringe area, a low-rent neighborhood of boxy three- and four-story tenements, porches tiered on their fronts. Evocative: He remembered the milltown street of his boyhood. He recalled tiny but well-kept lawns with laurel bushes and privet hedges. Here the lawns were dirt, rutted by student parking. Some of the houses, like Noz's, lacked front doors; hallways stood exposed, a few heaped with black plastic trash bags.

"Students. They're the worst kind of tenant, you know," he told Avery. "The most irresponsible."

He mounted the stairs. Avery, tensing in this unfamiliar scene, felt like one hundred pounds of feedbag against his chest, but Abbott's wind held up, even unto the third-floor landing. No puffing, no dizziness or heart skitters. Hell, despite doctor's orders, he could climb a mountain. A modest one.

Lew clumped down from the fourth floor to greet them. As Abbott watched, a familiar pattern unfolded. Lew, shouting, "Hi, fella!," bore down on Avery, who hid his face and clung to Abbott in panic, as if the baby had been submerged, suddenly, up to his neck in water. Rebuffed, Lew diverted his energies to Abbott, talking with those extended hands. It occurred to Abbott once more that, as a father, Lew would need some coaching.

But anyway, the boy looked good: lithe, deeply tanned from construction work. Abbott said he'd heard that Lew was keeping commendably busy.

"Oh, I love it," Lew said. "Working my ass off, but I love it." He said he planned to take some courses, nights. "Get an M.S. and go into the business end; I don't know."

Heath met them on the fourth-floor landing. Another pattern repeated itself. Heath reached out for Avery; Avery clutched Abbott; Heath backed off, exasperated. "Hi, you little brat," she said, sweet-voiced.

Heath looked good. With her marathon year of study ending, she had regained some weight and some color in her cheeks.

"Welcome to our humble abode, Daddy, and I do mean humble. We'll give you the House Beautiful tour."

As the couple led the way, Abbott's reportorial eye spotted details. A grease-encrusted stove and worn linoleum, dirty, though less dirty than in his own kitchen. He saw roaches—no doubt a fixture of this old house—scrambling on a stick of oleo that had been left out on the counter by the sink.

The living room had a few deck chairs and a stereo set. Innumerable record albums were stacked along the baseboard of one wall. Abbott gaped at a Claire watercolor, a seascape, that had been hung at an absurdly low level of view, its bottom edge about a foot off the floor. Following his gaze, Lew laughed and said, "Off-the-wall neighbors." He lifted the painting to reveal a hole in the plasterboard, kicked through from the apartment on the other side, presumably by some drunken grad student or crazed voyeur.

The back bedroom had two mattresses, on one of which lay a life form under a blanket, tousled head of hair exposed. "Noz," Lew explained in a whisper. "He works nights." Lew closed the door gently, and the tour party moved back to the living room.

"It's kind of crowded here," Lew said, "but we save on rent. More money to spend on Avery."

"And on saving for our own home," Heath said. She eyed Abbott. "I know what you're thinking, Daddy."

Thinking? Abbott took stock to find what he was thinking. He was thinking it was high time for the joyous wedding announcement.

Heath said, "This place is a rathole but we'll be out of here before Avery's much older."

Poverty? That didn't bother him at all. Hadn't he ever told Heath about the Depression? In future, he'd be a codger most loquacious. And, right now, he'd be a busybody and force release of the good news. He buttonholed Lew. "My sources tell me your family's going to have a big party, after all."

Lew said, "Party?" A blank.

"I'm looking forward to it," Abbott said, "even though I'll be picking up the check."

Lew broke his usually relentless eye contact. He consulted visually with Heath. She also looked puzzled, but then she seemed to guess Abbott's drift, and she drew herself up in a stance of self-ownership: one foot slightly forward, arms folded high across her bust, spine straight. She looked at Abbott as a teacher looks at a troublemaker, and said, "What we've got here is an economic and parenting setup. It'll do for now."

"Yeah," Lew affirmed. "We're setting up housekeeping, as a family, you know, to see how it goes." Lew elbowed Abbott, a hard nudge that rocked Abbott on his feet, causing him to hitch the baby higher on his chest. In a mock aside behind his hand, Lew added, "She's afraid that some night there'll be dishes and wash—all that domestic shit, you know—and I'll walk out and go play racquetball."

Only Lew laughed at this household joke. Abbott lowered his head in rage at himself. Stupid, stupid—once again he'd jumped to conclusions. No wedding plans. But what, then, was the big news? These two kids had been shacking up "as a family" on and off for several years.

Dear God in heaven, was the girl pregnant again? Mother or not, he could never handle two.

Heath had stepped out into the kitchen. She returned with a bottle of red wine and three tumblers. She passed out drinks and proposed a toast: "To Daddy's liberation!"

Now he knew.

In a stupor, he saw, way down at the end of his free arm, the three tumblers clunking together.

Heath said, "Your babysitting days are over, Daddy."

And Lew said, "You're a free man now."

The wine sloshed around in Abbott's mouth, behind his reflexive smile, tasteless.

Lew said, "We're getting Avery out of your hair—today. I know a guy with a pickup, and he's waiting for my call. We'll go load up the kid's stuff."

Take Avery's stuff?

"I'll do the work," Lew added. "You just supervise when we get there."

Heath said, "We're going to put the crib over against the wall, where the records are. We'll turn this into a family room, sort of. Wish us luck."

Take Avery's crib? Put it here?

Heath said, "We've been pretty selfish. We talked it over and decided it was time to start thinking of *you*."

As in a dream, Abbott watched the couple go into action without waiting for his response. "We'll have him all settled by tonight," Lew said as he paged through a directory by the phone. Heath began carrying record albums from one wall over to the other.

Abbott stood open-mouth, waiting for words. He tightened his grip on Avery. All along he had assumed that he and Avery would have more time together, many orbits before the transfer of custody.

Words came—"Avery's not ready"—but no one seemed to hear. Louder: "Avery's not ready," and, again, silence from everywhere, overwhelming—from Heath and Lew, from the offstage Noz, from whoever lived on the other side of the hole in the wall.

Abbott touched Heath's arm as she paced back and forth, carrying records. He said, "Avery's not ready."

She smiled in passing, a twist of her mouth that seemed to say: Oh you're cute but please don't bother me now.

Abbott turned to Lew, who was dialing the phone, and said, "Avery's not ready."

"Come on, Wes." Lew didn't look up. "That's not one of your best jokes."

Joke?

Of course! He was joshing them, they thought. He was Abbott, known to them as a card, a joker, and it was a joke to think that the feelings of a baby should have any weight.

Abbott said, "It's the truth! He's in a scary stage."

No one looked. Abbott sputtered: "It's the wrong time for a switch. We can't change horses, you know, in midstream."

This fumblemouthed cliché arrested the two. They looked mystified, those youngsters who had expected only gratitude from him. Heath stopped carrying records. Lew finished dialing. He stood there with the expectant, oddly vulnerable look of a caller waiting for a connection. His look did not change as he put the phone down.

Abbott inhaled deep. It was time for a spiel; it was a time when talk counts. He began a speech as Avery's champion and constituency of one. He told the parents he appreciated their concern, they were decent people, but Avery came first. And Avery wasn't old enough yet, he said, to cope with a long separation from him. Even short ones, he said, like bathroom breaks, could set Avery whimpering now, after the San Francisco junket. He reminded Heath of what she already knew or had read—that Avery needed a predictable routine and someone steady to count on. He told them how he could no longer hire Mrs. Pease, a good babysitter, because Avery grew antsy at the sight of her, anticipating another disappearing act by Abbott. Avery saw her as treacherous, just as the sight of his doctor prompted fears of a shot. "I drop him off at the new place and he screams. I stand behind the door and the screaming goes on—or he goes catatonic. It's heartbreaking, and some days I can't handle it. I go back in and get him and bring him home. I know I sound like an old maid, but he's got to stay with me a little longer. Just a little."

There. A convincing speech, he thought, although the audience looked pained and pitying. Those faces seemed to reflect a conspiracy—an agreement possibly reached before today that his care of their child had become something worrisome.

"Come on, Wes," Lew said. "Sit down. Take a load off."

"I'm serious."

"Let the kid crawl on the floor."

What, down on that filthy floor, in this roach farm? Abbott said, "Right now he wants to be held."

"There comes a time, you know, when you've got to let 'em know who's boss."

"I wish it were that simple."

"That's our natural kid," Lew went on, "and we're the natural parents. We'll get used to each other." Lew followed this up with a stern look at Avery, a by-the-book fatherly admonition: "We'd *better*."

"I know what you're talking about, Daddy," Heath said.

"It's called 'stranger anxiety,' but I wouldn't worry about it." She had tossed off the term glibly, with an air of anticipatory boredom should anyone be so gauche as to ask for the meaning.

"No, it's called grief," Abbott said. "Nothing less."

"Oh, shit, Daddy, you're making a big deal out of a little thing. He's gotten better; he's more used to me now."

True, but only guardedly, and after an initial distance, in a familiar place, in Abbott's presence.

"Watch." She reached out and chucked Avery under the chin. "Hiya, sweetie, you wanna come live with your mommy? You want a normal life?"

Avery looked disgruntled, but he did not cringe, even when Heath bent forward for a quick nuzzling of noses.

"Hey, look at that," Lew said. "Damn near a smile!"

Abbott looked down, craning his neck, to check the expression: no, not a smile, merely a mouth agape.

Heath straightened up. "The truth is, Daddy, you've spoiled him a little." She clutched Abbott's sleeve and looked into his face. "You'll miss him, won't you?" Her eyes moistened. "We knew you would." Across the room, Lew dropped his gaze, equally rueful. "We're sorry about that," she said, "but we thought you'd be glad, mostly. We want you to come see him whenever you can."

"Right!" Lew brightened. "We'll always need a baby-sitter."

"And after we get a car," Heath said, "I'll drive up a lot for visits. We'll try to make it easier for both of you." Heath paused, then shook Abbott's sleeve. "Tell you what: Next weekend we'll come up for a visit in the pickup." She turned to Lew. "Can we borrow it then, hon? Sunday?"

"Hell, yes," Lew said. "I'll just *take* it."

"Good. Then everything's settled." Heath moved her hand from Abbott's sleeve to Avery's shoulder. This time, Abbott felt—or thought he felt—a tightening of the child's hold on him, and Abbott responded with a reassuring pressure of his own. Heath, face against Avery's cheek, crooned, "Welcome home."

Ah, no use. No more talk, Abbott thought. These people couldn't possibly know what he knew of their son after a year of closeness. The coordinates today felt all wrong for a stand on Avery's behalf—yet right: This apartment was an arena, and these innocent kids, sad to say, were his adversaries. The issue was trivial—yet vital: a question of pain, another bereavement for Avery, another "no harm done" lesson in withdrawal, another small death, one not even necessary because time alone, a small measure of time, could avert it. And how many more little deaths lay ahead? Abbott looked at the kids, who had resumed their work in embarrassment over the sorrow they believed he felt. Lew dialed the phone and Heath carried records, both sneaking peeks at him. This pair was no model for care-giver stability, even month to month. Think on this; assemble the evidence. Look at the divorce rate, and these parents weren't even married and might never be. Avery might become a shuttlecock or the ball in a three-cornered catch.

Abbott reached a decision. An inner cheer arose from his Bapp persona. "Not yet," he said. "I'll let you know when. I'll be in touch."

He backed toward the kitchen door. His stand was taking the form of a flight. Deep down in the mind, wherever paranoia conjures its images, he was alerted to expect a lunge and a tug-of-war over Avery's flesh. As he moved away, Heath's upper arms seemed to quiver once, as if straining against the weight of the albums in her hands to take possession. Abbott continued to back away, watching for moves. The pair stood frozen. Lew had the phone in his hand, at his side; in the silence Abbott thought he heard the crackle of a voice on the line. Now the pair disappeared from Abbott's sight in segments, their images cut step by step from the legs up as he backed down the stairs. When he reached the first-floor landing he saw their faces reappear up above, looking down at him over the railing. Neither spoke. In their eyes he had undergone three metamorphoses: jokester, Nervous Nellie, and now kidnapper.

He drove home. No cars gave chase, squealing their tires. No leopards sprang from the curb. But tomorrow, he thought, the forces of paranoia would regroup, and they would storm the nursery door.

24

In a crisis, count on habit. Habit awakens you, buttons you up. It gets Avery dressed. It makes the sick call to work and hangs out a thick skin against Eddie's anger. It reactivates the current routines—moves the spoon from breakfast bowl to Avery's mouth, over and over, with power-shovel hum rising to crescendo: "MmmmmmmmmmmmmMMM." One after another, a long trajectory with a rollover of the payload onto the tongue, or, failing that, onto the chin. One of these days Avery would learn to wield the spoon himself.

"MmmmmmmmmmMMM.

"*This* . . . spoon.

"This . . . *spoon.*

"Spoooooon—beautiful word, isn't it?"

Avery matched the long "oooo" sound.

The doorbell rang.

Abbott jumped up and peered out through the kitchen curtains. He saw a pickup truck in the driveway. Sooner than expected, the parents had invaded. Well, once again—and again and again, if need be, orbit after orbit—he'd tell them why they couldn't have their kid for a while.

He opened the front door. Lew stood there, alone. Apparently, Lew had stolen time from work; he wore a tool belt and a sleeveless undershirt, the kind nowadays called a tank top. This getup, along with his physique, the tan, and the mustache, gave Lew the look of a he-man in a beer ad.

Only a hard hat was missing; Abbott presumed Lew had left one on the seat of the truck. Abbott said, "You're looking fit this morning."

"Sure. You going to invite me in?"

Abbott stood his ground in the doorway. It was his Thermopylae, you might say, and Lew the first Persian intruder, grim, glaring over Abbott's head in search of Avery.

He said, "Where's my son?"

"At the babysitter's," Abbott lied. "Where's Heath?"

"A job interview. Listen, I don't get this." Lew raised his hands, flustered, half entreating.

"I'll explain again," Abbott said.

"All at once," Lew went on, "you come to. You start kicking ass. You tell Heath and me we're not thinking enough about Avery—and you were right. But now you *steal* the kid. That's what it is. Child stealing. A crime, for Christ's sake. You're acting crazy."

"I know it looks that way," Abbott said. He closed his eyes. "I'll explain again."

"No, I don't want to hear that shit. Neither does Heath."

"Does Heath know you're here?"

"Yeah, she knows. Now go in there and bring him out. I know he's in there."

"You'll have him when he's ready," Abbott said.

"Bull*shit*. He's our natural son, and we've got a Constitutional right to him."

Abbott puzzled for a second over this odd legal notion, then, Samson-style, he braced his hands against the sides of the doorframe. Paranoia had emerged, evoking apt images and questions; for example: Did this kid, like Earl's opponent of some months ago, know karate?

Lew hunched one shoulder like a football player about to lunge across the line. "I'm coming in," he said. "My kid and I are going home."

"You'll terrorize him," Abbott said.

"I don't give a shit if he screams all the way. He's going

home." Lew reached out a hand, which hovered midway to Abbott's shirtfront. "Now *move*, Wes. *Please*."

Quickly, Abbott inventoried his arsenal. Nothing. Words, only words, to sling at this young Goliath. Well, why not? Abbot let fly with the first zany combination that popped to mind. "Your father's mustache!"

Pow! Direct hit.

In surprise, Abbott surveyed the damage. The hulked shoulder had turned defensive in its function; Lew had tucked his chin behind it. To cause such a recoil, Abbott supposed, he must have appeared startlingly bold to the boy—or startlingly close to breakdown. The hand near Abbott's shirtfront had crumpled, the fingers curling palmward into a half-fist, like the spider curl of Avery's hands way back when the child was only weeks old. Abbott looked beyond the faltering hand to Lew's face. The lips moved, repeating Abbott's words, it seemed, in silent stupefaction.

"It's an old phrase," Abbott said. "From before your time. It'll come back."

Lew tried once more—"I'm coming in"—but the thrust of his impulse had been broken. The half-fist fell to Lew's side. He wagged his head with an unreadable scowl—pity, Abbott presumed, and impotence. If you're young and strong, would you shove a raving elder?

Lew turned and waded away through the high grass of the lawn, his head ducked as if bees were buzzing around it. Before getting into the truck, he looked back and called: "I hate to ruin your reputation, Wes, but you give me no choice!"

Did that mean a complaint to the police? Ah, never mind. As Lew drove off, Abbott felt himself flying. He could feel himself above himself, dancing in himself; a transcendence; Zarathustra on the mountain.

No, stop it. Grow up. As victories go, this was a cheapie. Lew, a gentle, middle-class boy, hadn't been up to bopping a crazy coot. Fatherly feelings, however, no matter how undeveloped, would not allow Lew to leave his son in such a coot's hands. He'd be back, maybe with a few luckless cops scratching their heads over the law in this case. What charge would apply? Kidnapping? Certainly not. Child-stealing? Maybe custodial interference, if Heath signed a complaint.

Family law: as fuzzy as the modern family.

Abbott returned to the kitchen, where Avery was scribbling in the cereal puddles on the highchair tray.

"We'd do well to take off for a while," Abbott said. "Disappear until hot heads cool down."

He poured himself a cup of coffee and sat down at the kitchen table to think. He recalled that, weeks ago in Forestview, he'd daydreamed of an escapade with Avery. Yes, an itinerary of treats, including a Coke at a restored 1950s soda fountain.

Well, why not?

"I'll buy you a lemon Coke. In Woodstock, Vermont. And we'll have to buy it with a credit card."

Insane! But why the hell not? Let Bappian laughter prevail.

Let's pack, quick! We're under siege. Look out the window, that ugly mob in the street. Those cruisers, sirens on and the dome lights spinning. Cops, bearing warrants. All the applicable blanks have question marks.

Here comes the next wave: lawyers waving subpoenas. Next, social service bureaucrats. They're pointing unsharpened pencils at us.

Denham's out there, too. Poor Denham; I'll have to write him a note before we leave, test his patience once more and pray that I'll have a job upon return. He's out there in his Lincoln. He's climbing on top of it. He's unfurling an enormous memo, like a banner. *WES: You took San Francisco bribe, now deliver. I want funny columns on old fart being mother surrogate.*

Next, an unmarked van. It's disgorging white-suited bruisers. They're armed with hypos and a straitjacket for me.

And do you see the leopards, Avery? Their tawny, spotted backs are sliding through the high grass of the lawn. Some of them, brazen, are out in the street with the hominids. They wait on their haunches like house cats, licking their claws.

We've got to move fast.

Look: This is a nail. Add this to your vocabulary.

This . . . nail.

This . . . *nail.*

You hand me these nails and I'll hammer up two-by-fours across the doorway.

There!

Now take this water-soaked diaper. If they lob tear gas in here, breathe through it. We've got to pack our survival kit and slip out of here. We'll outsmart them all.

Thermos and brown-bag lunch for two.

Check.

Pampers.

Check.

Premoistened wipes.

Check.

Inderal for heart rhythm.

Check. In fact, I'd better pop one right now amid all this stress. An Isordil, too.

Now down to the basement. The front door's being rammed and I hear windows shattering.

We'll swat our way through the concrete down here and tunnel into the back yard with your pail and shovel. We'll tunnel through the moldering graves, these shallow drawers full of the smothered impulses of my past. We'll break into the storm sewer over on Eleanor Street, lift the grating and climb out.

Okay, up the ladder after me. You can climb. We practiced, remember?

Now the grating. Back straight, lift with the legs. It budges! I can still lift!

We're home free.

. . .

Ah, it was no laughing matter. Abbott sat at the kitchen table, chin in hand, as his coffee cooled. At this juncture in the soap opera he needed somebody to talk with over his coffee, someone sympathetic. Which narrowed the field to one, probably. Himself.

So be it. Kind of man that he was, he needed a rationale for what he proposed to do. A child snatch. Why?

Earl had warned him long ago he'd "exploit" the child. Made sense. A fogey getting over-attached, treating the child like a royal pet, a little mutt you groom and talk to, and whose fawning you can't live without. A neurotic mutual dependency. Had that happened?

No. He, Abbott, merely wanted to avert some pain. The pain could be averted by prolonging the child's stay with the one human he trusted until such foolish loyalty was outgrown. Beyond that, any creature that feels pain has rights. Hell, all sentient life has good grounds for revolt, life being what it is.

Ah, can it. He'd better get moving. Even now, Lew might be talking to a desk sergeant, bewildering the man.

"Let's pack, quick," Abbott told Avery.

And don't forget, he told himself, to pack those cartons.

Parents. Check.

This would be their last trip.

25

Before the getaway, one quick stop. There might be a chance—maybe, just maybe—of finding one sympathetic listener besides himself. From his files Abbott dug out the note with Earl's job number. He called; a receptionist told him that yes, sir, Earl Bushnell still worked there; Mr. Bushnell was on the night shift; call late.

Abbott spent the rest of the day at Forestview with Avery, and, after dinner at McDonald's, he dropped the sleeping child off at the home of Mrs. Orsini, the latest babysitter. Avery deigned to tolerate this woman for short intervals without Abbott, so long as she kept her distance. After Abbott's visit to the ABC Typography Co., he and Avery would stay at the HoJo and leave early in the morning on their route of treats.

That is, unless Earl—at one time no total stranger to good sense—could talk him out of the trip.

Night had fallen by the time Abbott found the type shop. It was housed in a squat, cement-block building, one of many on unmarked roads in a treeless industrial park in the suburbs.

The front door was locked. Abbott rang the bell. Through the glass he saw a figure, backlit, enter the darkened front office from the shop area. Earl, no doubt about it. Wiry little guy; even if Earl lived to be 100 and his springy step became a hobble, he'd still look boyish in silhouette.

He yanked the door open with both hands. "I'll be god-damned!"

On this visit, no comic greeting; no cry of "Dear Abby!" or "Mary Worth!" Earl, for once, seemed glad for company. Maybe he, too, wanted a sympathetic listener. Looking him over as they shook hands, Abbott saw some cosmetic changes: tonsure dyed black, and, in place of the loosened necktie of *Call* days, a gold chain around the neck. Best not to mention this faddish touch, Abbott thought; at least his old pal had no earring on.

Earl led the way to the lunchroom, a space with two picnic tables. He took a brown paper bag from a refrigerator and pulled out a six-pack of Michelob. "Since I'm the whole night shift, no one knows I tip a few. Sharpens your eye for copy." He handed Abbott a can and opened one for himself. "How did you find me?"

The name eluded Abbott. "Celeste . . . ? She went West."

"Sharon!" Earl lifted his can in salute. "The dog who ran away."

"To better things, I hope."

"She'll marry some duffer—some hale and hearty guy—and have kids, like Lolita. The old ways will live on through Sharon."

A sage prediction. Abbott, raising his beer in the toast, remembered Sharon clearly now, her brassy face and her admonition to him to take good care of Avery. All things considered, a decent young woman. "I remember you called her a schizophrenic."

"That was her favorite joke. Didn't she tell you?"

"We didn't talk much."

"Too much action, huh?" Earl jerked his hand, loose-wristed. "Well, she was admitted to a state hospital once. The shrink on duty tagged her as a paranoid skitz after a thirty-second interview. Rubber-stamp city."

"That's sad. What was her real problem?"

"Incest. Every hooker's story. Why are we talking

about *her*? What's new with you?"

"I'm playing catch-up. Was she a hooker?"

"I see you're well-informed as always, Abbott. No, a countergirl in the bowling alley, the one at the mall. I met her there."

"You're not serious."

"About what?"

"You met her there? You bowled?"

"What's wrong with bowling? Have you become a snob, Abbott?"

"No! No! How did we get into this?"

Earl reached over and patted Abbott's arm, calming a rattled man. "The doctor told me to bowl for the arthritis in my knees. A few strings every day before work. Got that?"

"I see." A mystery solved. Abbott recalled Sharon's mentioning a bowling alley. He also remembered a phone call in which he mistook pin thunder for factory noise. Reality: How banal it is, as well as strange. There, in that bowling alley, a strange meeting occurred. A troubled man who was trying to re-create in his life the heat and poignancy of old girlfriends met a troubled young girl who was looking for a father figure or a father in the flesh.

"Can I fill you in on anything else in your life?" Earl asked.

Abbott looked around at the lunchroom. The vending machines were posted with gripe notes from shortchanged users. The wall above a garbage can was spattered from lunch scraps that had been thrown high of the mark. Abbott asked, "How do you like it here?"

"Dayside it was better. I worked with a bunch of young girls."

"You must have been in your glory."

"Nah. They're all plain and introverted. And they make the minimum wage like me."

"How are you living?"

"On savings. What you see before you is a lowly proofreader." Earl delivered himself of a long, quavery burp, and he opened another can of beer. Abbott declined another, sensing reluctance in the offer. Earl apparently needed his buzz.

"I tried the cab company, but they've got a waiting list. Before that I cooked: short-order. The all-night diner, they know me there and they let me sub. Ah, it was fun, Abbott, just like I told you. People yelling, especially in Zoo Hour after the bars close, and dozens of things on the fire at once. I thought, 'Holy shit, I'm a juggler on deadline, I'm back in the fucking newsroom.' But my legs couldn't take it. I've got to get back in shape." Earl lifted his Michelob. "I'm working on it."

"Maybe," Abbott said, "you should get your job back."

"Hey!" Earl's palm shot up like a traffic cop's. "Don't start that. Did you come here out of the blue to tell me that?"

"Not really."

"Then what's new?" In the absence of an immediate reply, Earl added, "That's what I figured: same old shit. Still have your dog?"

Dejectedly, Abbott gazed at the notes on the soft-drink machine.

"I still have mine," Earl said. "Both of them." He whistled loudly as if to summon them.

In red grease pencil, a note on the machine said: "THIS PIECE OF JUNK OWES ME 50¢. RUTHIE."

Earl hadn't changed. Not at all, and Abbott knew now that he couldn't air any news. Earl wouldn't understand the issues of the forthcoming escapade, given his crudity of mind this year. He'd only trot out one of his tiresome analogies, like: "Dogs get attached, too, so what? Stop acting like Aunt Nellie." Something like that.

"Listen, I don't know why you're here," Earl said, "but there's something I want to show you. Step into my office."

Earl's "office" turned out to be a desk in the proofroom, equipped with a reading stand and a fluorescent lamp—one of a dozen wooden desks arranged in two rows in the room, giving it the appearance of a classroom. Earl pulled a manila envelope marked DON'T TOUCH from a drawer and extracted what looked like tissue paper. "I call this 'The Naked Majorette.' " He sat down. Head tipped back, he began reading through his bifocals, his voice slow and declamatory.

"This brass band—
it's a foul mouth
full of popcorn.
And pitchmen snarl
amid their pitches;
the clowns preen
like grand marshals.
Life in the cages
is all sores, and
even little children
demand a refund.
O let us hear it
for a new feeling:
this show remade,
brought back alive.
I fling my baton;
with hop and skip
I shuck my spangles.
And now what?
What do I say?
I'm being followed . . ."

What do you say upon learning that an old friend is writing poetry to himself, misery verse? The etiquette of the moment seemed to call for a good capsule review. As Earl finished his piece—something about the prophetic majorette being gang-raped by the spectators—Abbott said, "I like the half-rhymes."

"I knew you would." Earl lowered his eyes and reddened a little. "They're subtle. I knew you'd see that."

He opened another beer and returned an empty to the brown paper bag. "See, you've got to stay creative. At the *Call* I could rewrite everybody's stories—did, too; fuck 'em—but here I can't change copy, only correct the typos. So I go to the john and write verse, spread the toilet paper on my knee. It's a coarse grade, your pen doesn't poke through."

Abbott, seated at a desk across from Earl's, slapped his hand hard on the wooden top. "All right. I'm going to say it again: Go see Denham and get your job back."

Earl's features knotted together. He seemed to have stopped breathing.

"Officially," Abbott said, "you haven't been fired."

"Who *cares?*" Earl rolled his eyes for deliverance from nagging. "You still don't understand. You sit there in fucking judgment."

Abbott forced a laugh. "From where I sit, it looks like good duty. A job where you can swill beer and write poetry."

"It's costing me. I'll tell you about my boss; don't go away." Earl excused himself for a run to the bathroom. The beer was catching up. In Earl's absence, Abbott remembered something. Like those vending machines out in the lunchroom, he was in debt; he had lost a bet with Earl in the last of their antiquarians' disputes. He took out his wallet and handed over a ten-dollar bill when Earl returned.

"Zale by a knockout in the third. I swallowed my pride and looked it up in a record book."

Uncharacteristically, Earl accepted the money without crowing. "I'll need it," he said. "I'm a short-timer." In a rush of words and dramatizations, he sketched his boss, someone named Daphne, chief, apparently, of the proofreaders. "About my age. Bouffant blonde hair piled yea high—like this—the old-fashioned way, a beehive. And glasses with goddamn rhinestone frames, on a black cord. She reminds me of a teacher I had in grade school. Big but lightfooted, always up on tippytoe"—Earl fluttered a hand at the ceiling—"scratching on the blackboard. Like the words

I was supposed to copy fifty times. *Don't chew gum* or *don't pick nose* or whatever."

"Or up on tippytoe blowing a note on the pitch pipe."

"That's *good*, Abbott. You haven't lost it. Well, last week I was writing a pretty good poem, one I may send to the *New Yorker*. You'll see it when it's done. Anyway, when I came out of the john, she chewed me out. She said, 'Hey, Earl, you were in there so long I thought you were having the *curse*.' Well, the whole proofroom laughed, this whole goddamn all-female shop. But I shot her down. I said, 'Hey, Daphne, sometimes you're in there so long I think you're having the *change*.' "

"A delightful workplace," Abbott said.

"The next day I was switched to nights. I should write a headline: POWER FIGHT IN THE PITS."

Earl opened another beer. "She's job-scared, you see. I'm a better reader, a rival. Also, male, so she's doubly scared. We're supposed to read five galleys an hour—that's too fast. Sweatshop pace. The U.N. is a client, so we do population tables, and we do technical manuals. So all of us leave typos, but only mine are being counted. Get the picture? I'll be canned in a week or two."

"And then what?"

"Who knows?" Earl snickered. "Skid row. I'll be sleeping in the railroad station."

"Too many muggers. Try the abandoned Pizza Hut."

"No, the dumpster at the 7-Eleven."

Abbott exchanged a startled glance with Earl. Suddenly, they had a number going, a duel of lines as in their routines of the old days, the Abbott and Earl show, more stimulating, in its way, than the Abbott and Avery show. Earl leaned back in his chair. Abbott stood up and began pacing. He said, "A boxcar."

"A cardboard carton," said Earl.

"Somebody's parked car."

"A kid's tree house."

"The riverbank."

"Your front porch."

"A pay toilet at the bus station."

"Ouch! That's *good*, Abbott. But take this: a bag-lady booth at the all-night diner."

"Got me!" Abbott clutched his chest and faked a stagger. "But better yet, a clothing bin at the mall. Salvation Army or Goodwill—take your pick of accommodations."

Earl dangled his head. "Nice shot." He fired back: "Snug under the highway overpass. With all the kamikazes crashing down below you, into the abutments."

"You win." Abbott sat down at a desk, no longer amused. He remembered the acquaintance of theirs who had turned "kamikaze" in the past year.

"Cheer up," Earl said. "I've got my family to fall back on. Bet you thought the nuclear family had disappeared." With an eager wiggle, Earl reached back and dug out his wallet. Abbott readied himself for more black humor. Earl handed over a Polaroid photo, saying in gee-whiz voice, "Say, buddy, you wanna see a pitcher of my family?"

Abbott saw two women, side by side, naked, their backs to the camera. One young and the other in midlife, judging from the two sets of buttocks, one firm, one doughy. Both women were bent forward as if to touch their toes, and were looking back at the lens from between their legs. Pendant breasts flanked each upside-down smile. Beyond the two was a stand of trees.

Abbott returned the photo. "An interesting composition."

"Don't be snide. That's Charisse on the right; she plays daughter in the family game. The heavy one's Leah; she's mamma. Used to be a go-go dancer in Boston—notice the 38s?"

"Couldn't miss them. Where's Daddy?"

"Who do you think took the fucking picture? I took this on Family Fitness Day, outdoors. It's a game, but it's also dead serious. I'll tell you about it; don't go away."

Earl left on another bathroom run. In his absence, Ab-

bott expunged the images from his mind—God *damn* Earl and his pornography—and leafed through the stack of proofs on the desk, Earl's night's work, somehow to be read on the strength of a snootful of beer. It was U.N. Security Council correspondence. Galley after galley of complaints from the Palestinians about Israeli land policies. The Mideast—an echo of a world hotspot here in this bleak room late at night, occupied only by two has-beens exploring the ends of lines. As Earl returned, Abbott restacked the copy and looked up, resigned to hear Earl's story about the *ménage à trois*. Who else in the world would listen?

Earl fumbled in the paper bag for another Michelob, but all had been consumed. With a sigh, he stashed the bag under his desk. "Every morning I have to sneak these empties past Daphne. Forget to bring 'em out to my car before she comes in." Earl slumped forward on the desk. He rested his chin on an outstretched arm and stared at the wall, his face losing all expression except for an abstracted sourness. "What were we talking about?"

"I get the feeling you want to tell me about the so-called family game."

"You'd never believe it. They're very inventive people. I'm not a shy man, but there are things I can't even tell *you*, and we go way back. Things get . . ."

Abbott suggested: "Crazy?"

"Don't get stuffy on me."

"How about 'sick'?"

"Don't get bourgeois."

"How about 'too much'?"

"All right. When Charisse wears diapers . . . but I don't want to get into it. I'll tell you the good parts. In the morning I go home to royal treatment. Big breakfast—scrambled eggs, Philadelphia scrapple, whatever I want, served to me in bed. Other goodies, too. I'm off Harveys and into nose candy. Do you know what I'm saying?"

Yes, Abbott knew the slang for cocaine or whatever, and was dismayed only to hear the trendy "into," no less, used unself-consciously by this one-time master of English.

"Not to mention other good things to eat. All this because I'm Man of the House—it's part of the game, you see. I bring home the bacon. Not much—I'm ashamed to show my paycheck—but there's still some bacon in the bank."

"Don't your playmates work?"

"Leah does, part time. Charisse can't hold a job even though she's a beautiful girl—wouldn't have to lift a finger. Leah's your everyday cashier. By day a cashier, by night a ringmaster. Leah and Charisse have something going between them, and I've got something going with the pair. I won't paint you a picture but it's fantastic."

"Must be tiring."

Earl's face, under the fluorescent lamp, showed a hollowing of the eye sockets that Abbott hadn't noticed earlier. Still looking away, morose, with his chin propped on his arm outstretched on the desk, Earl said, "Frankly, it wipes me out. But they prefer me to some young stud who might come between them. That would worry Leah. Do you get my meaning?"

"Got it," Abbott said. "Crazy, sick, and too much."

Earl's eyes sharpened. "I knew you wouldn't dig it. I should've kept my mouth shut."

" 'Dig?' What I 'dig' is, these people don't take you seriously. A paycheck and a plaything."

"I thought you might say that. You're too cynical, Abbott."

"I 'dig' that you should do what you do best. See Denham. Or I'll see him for you." A rash offer. How, Abbott wondered, could he plead Earl's case if he lacked the gumption to plead his own?

Earl tensed himself to rise. He splayed his fingers on the desk and lifted himself in the chair, but then slumped back, a man too weary to bother with a display of anger. His chest flattened again on the desktop, and his outstretched hand flopped over from palm to back, a fish flop, a dispirited gesture that seemed to say: "What's the use?"

He said, "You'll never understand. Look at me. I'm fifty-six years old. I thought I'd done it all, seen it all. Had a marriage, fought a fucking war, worked forty years, some of it in big jobs. But I was wrong. I'm learning new things. You think these women and I are just lonely kooks and we deserve each other. Well, we're part of a world that's growing, and you'd be amazed. Suburbanites. Bigwigs!"

"Are you happy?" This seemed the only relevant question.

"You mean could I die happy, right now?" Earl scowled at the wall. Then he cocked his head, cheek on his extended arm, to study Abbott's face. Abbott gazed back, thinking that, already, Earl looked dead, given his pallor under the lamp and the droop of his upper body on the desk, spread there as if for an autopsy, an opening of the spine. Abbott felt a surge of sorrow, which in turn stirred the Bappian nursing yen. He felt an impulse to step over behind Earl and massage his neck as would a fighter's corner man, that stringy neck that he'd often wanted to wring. But Earl probably would mistake this tenderness for a late-in-life homosexual pass, and he'd go crazy for sure.

Earl's eyes were slitted, burning at Abbott as he continued to ponder whether he could, in this moment, die happy. His outstretched hand did another flipflop, this time from back to palm, smacking the desk for emphasis. He declared: "Fucking A right!"

Abbott shrugged, said good night, and turned to go. He heard: "Wait, do me a favor," and he spun around, relieved at this hint of a reversal. All the old pal had to do was ask.

Earl held out the bag of empties. "Take these out to your car, will you, and ditch 'em somewhere."

26

A sniff of burning bridges, sweet as woodsmoke. As Earl might say, this was the part of the corny movie where the music swells and there's a long shot of a car on a highway. Surely, this escapade wasn't one of your Great Moments in History, but it might qualify for a low rating on a scale of the bizarre. A grandfather traveling aimlessly on credit through New England with his stolen grandchild and the dust of his own parents. A saga of four generations, one of them absent and no doubt frantic.

"I never heard of nothing like that," the clerk said. A woman, elderly, plump, she eyed Abbott from behind the cash register of what appeared to be the only drugstore in Woodstock's downtown. The store was wholly modern; it had no 1950s-style soda fountain.

"It was here, ma'am," Abbott said. "Ten, fifteen years ago."

She looked affronted. "I've lived here all my life and I never seen nothing like that."

"Are you sure? It had the old spigots, for syrup." Abbott reached out and enacted a pulling of levers. In his eagerness, boyish, he bunched his lips and imitated the noise of seltzer, the fizz in a glass.

The woman tensed, and Abbott pictured in his mind a store camera, the kind you see on counters, recording transactions "for your own protection." He smiled tightly. She did not smile back. He appealed: "We've come a long way for a Coke."

Such unfriendliness! Such Yankee ice in this tourist town! The little woman with her white curls and pale blue eyes looked past Abbott to Avery, who was ensconced in the aluminum-and-canvas carrier on Abbott's back. Was Avery dirty? Slobbering on his sunsuit? You could never tell what he was doing back there.

The woman turned away to another customer after craning her neck a moment longer, as if to memorize Abbott's face for a police lineup.

He left the store, shaken. He'd suffered paranoia over a little old lady; now cut that out! He'd experienced self-loss over a minor lapse of memory. Perhaps the soda fountain was up in Bar Harbor, a place he knew a little better—good old Bah Hahbah. It had attractions surpassing a lemon Coke. It had—ten, fifteen years ago—an ice-cream parlor with butcher-block tables and exotic flavors. And it had Acadia National Park—certainly Acadia hadn't vanished—where he and Avery could visit the sea cliffs and feed a box of Jax to the gulls.

Very well then, they'd leave for Maine within the hour.

First, though, a break, a little picnic. Abbott bought some deli cheesecake, breathtakingly expensive, and a small bottle of Lancers, and strolled to a bench on the Woodstock Green. He unharnessed himself partway from the carrier straps, wriggling Avery around to the side to be lifted free. No easy trick, this; a contortionist's feat. He should write a "funny piece" about mastering this contraption and how, so far, he'd avoided strangling himself or spilling the baby.

But no, don't think of columns. Not today. Denham hadn't liked the batch of samples delivered before the escapade. In a memo he'd called them bland.

Think, instead, of the fine weather, this lovely Green, the commodious inn nearby, and, all around town, the restored Federal architecture, his favorite style. A style of brick and white wood, smallish, finely proportioned and clean. A long walk would be enjoyable—he might never again see this town—but not with Avery on his back or even in the stroller, unappreciative. The child had finished his cheesecake half and was crawling off the tarpaulin on which Abbott had placed him on the grass. Avery wouldn't be interested in a tour talk.

In truth, talk had been losing its magic. The child wanted more of it these days. He was distractingly imitative in his babble, as if at last he wanted his own say and would drown Abbott out; and he wanted to explore; he wanted to hunt for edibles in the grass of the Green; he wanted to practice walking in his tilted, careening way. He wanted to stay awake for hours, even in the car. He wanted constant attention over the miles; he exhausted playthings; he ripped up magazines.

The picnic over, Abbott stopped to buy some cheap magazines on the way out of town. He left Avery in the car, strapped into his safety seat. Let the kid squall. In the drugstore, Abbott watched the clerk's face as she counted out his change. The little old lady didn't appear to recognize him, even though only an hour had passed since their encounter. Maybe she'd forgotten him. Perhaps the soda fountain had slipped just as easily out of her memory.

Bar Harbor, thank heaven, had the downtown ice-cream parlor he remembered. He ordered pistachio for himself and Avery—a flavor not so exotic, but a good grade of ice cream with plenty of nuts. He complimented the young manager behind the counter.

Back at the motel, he changed Avery out of his splotched outfit, washed it and hung it out to dry, and dressed the child in a sailor suit. Spiffy. They went to a supermarket for a box of Jax and then drove out to the cliffs near Otter Point for their appointment with the seagulls.

This was like a business trip.

. . .

Anticipation beats reality; an early lesson continuously re-taught. It was no surprise, really, that the gulls terrified the kid. The only surprise to Abbott was that he—Abbott the empath—had thought even for an instant that Avery might be thrilled.

A misjudgment, the kind that showed him to be foolish, an old fool who thinks he can mind-read and who gabbles to strangers as though he were a young reporter again.

Harsh cries filled the air, and blurred wings materialized at arm's length as Abbott held out Jax to the scavengers. Now and then their bills scraped his fingertips or left them wet from God knows what, gulped from the sea.

Meanwhile, Avery huddled against Abbott's chest, his face buried and his body quaking with suppressed sobs. He dared not cry. No human had ever scared him as much.

Abbott dumped the rest of the junk food down the cliff, creating a fluttery mealtime of short duration.

All right, Avery could shun birds, if he wished, but not people. Exposure to crowds might be good therapy for the little misanthrope. In the evening, Abbott carried him into the thick of the tourist promenade in downtown Bar Harbor. He left the back carrier in the motel, for Avery had been tiring of its confines and had developed a habit of pulling at the hair on Abbott's nape. Now, Abbott carried the child on his shoulders, and, finally sore from that, he invented a new game.

"Let's call it . . . inch-walk."

Holding Avery's hands from above, and with the white baby shoes perched atop his scuffed gunboats, Abbott did the walking for both of them. He stooped along at the edge of the crowd in a slow waddle.

Anticipation beats reality, yes, but it's also true that a disastrous trip can be redeemed by one good moment, a freebie out of the blue, a plenitude. Avery, of course, would remember nothing, but Abbott knew that he himself would never forget this night despite worry, loneliness, and fatigue. He shivered with sudden happiness. The game had something to do with it, the insouciance, moving in tandem with the child at a child's pace through these streets and their sensations. He heard chamber music from the craft shops, commingled with the crowd noises. Incense warred in his nose with the aroma of fried food. The tourists, many of them, were middle-aged. He saw women wearing white cardigans over ice-cream-colored dresses, as Claire used to wear. Some wore corsages, as if this night were Easter.

It was late by the time Abbott had inch-walked back to the motel. Though exhausted, he would have to sit for a while on the edge of the bed, ready to intercept as Avery, too keyed up to sleep, scurried around the room and tried to climb the furniture.

How about a "funny piece"? Travels with Baby.

Another day, another picnic. In the afternoon, Abbott packed the cooler with baby food, cracked lobster, and a bottle of chablis, and drove to the Acadia cliffs. He found a secluded picnic table. Today he'd brought along his typewriter to catch up on the transcription of his entries, his file of shorthand notes on Avery's behavior.

No; his intention, obvious even to him as he carried the typewriter to the table, was to outwit himself into starting some real work. The entries were no longer the observations of a man fascinated by an emergent mind; rather, they had become perverted: They were ticklers for possible columns.

He recalled Denham's memo. A long one, in which the boss said, "If I wanted a bland column on baby care, I'd buy one from a syndicate." He had, however, liked the piece comparing a child's well-being to good weather. "Not funny but heartwarming. Keep trying."

Oh yes, he'd keep trying. Abbott had given this pledge in a return note, dropped into the office mail on getaway day. Meanwhile, he'd added, the *Call* would have to indulge him one more open-ended absence, hopefully the last in his year and a half of family difficulties. He'd spare the publisher the personal details. He'd keep submitting samples by mail in his free time and return ASAP. (Denham might like the snappy, wire-service "ASAP.")

Maybe, when he returned, he'd still have a job. Maybe not.

At once, before he could talk himself out of it, he began batting out a column. It was about his mastery of Avery's back carrier. His mind cut off the flow of self-ridicule at about the 700-word mark, and he read what he had written.

Not bad, if you liked this sort of thing. It might be mildly amusing to some mothers, he supposed, and even to some men, ex-GIs, for example, who'd tussled with the straps and buckles of a full pack.

Flushed with this success, Abbott skipped the polishing for later and grabbed fresh paper for another column. Idea: teaching Baby to type. Why not? Often, Avery had wanted to play with the clackety-clack toy. A column could be faked.

Abbott typed, winging it.

It's time for a story conference.

Toddle on over here. Climb into my lap and type.

Go ahead, poke.

No, with the fingers, not the fists!

I'll untangle these keys . . .

Now type.

No action? Your fingerbones are Popsicle sticks; you need hands like mine, like post-hole diggers, to get action out of this old Underwood. It dates way back to the 1960 political conventions, the 1955 floods. My heyday. Now flatten your fingers against mine like little splints and I'll do the poking.

Type us a b. Type us an r.

Type us . . .

Too many consonants, like a bad Scrabble hand. We need vowels.

Give us an a.

Give us your name, A v e r y.

Give us my name, A b b o t t.

Give us—upper-case—H O O R A Y T E A M.

Hooray for the story-writing team!

You're my preliterate co-author. We're collaborators . . .

All right, enough already. Abbott yanked the paper out of the machine. This material was horseshit. It was cutesy, self-conscious. He glanced over at the "collaborator." The baby lay on his tarpaulin on the ground, snoring open-mouthed, worn out by a long morning of inch-wading in tidepools.

Abbott's maternal eye spotted a tinge of sunburn on the fat shoulders. He went over and dragged the tarpaulin, Avery on it, into the shade. He returned and scanned the aborted column once more before crumpling the paper and pitching it into a fireplace.

Should there be an update, he wondered, in the personal "funny piece," his and Avery's real story? There had been some much-needed action, a little; now the flaccid tension was gathering toward a twang. Wryly, Abbott went on musing about this. By now the character Supergramps knows in his ramshackle heart that he cannot keep the child who has revitalized him, though at some level he wants to. He knows the story must go on, get itself told, or half-told, like all stories; he feels the deadline pressure. He must prepare himself for the grave of the child's absence. The final item on the parental do-don't list: detach. Given his age, Gramps should be a near-master in the wisdom of detaching from people. Yet look at him: a grown man unable to bury his parents, whose remains lie on a shelf in a motel closet.

Abbott shouted at Avery to wake him up. The child

flinched. Abbott put the dustcover over the Underwood and opened the cooler. Time to eat. Maybe Avery would like to suck the meat out of a lobster claw. They could inch-walk down the rocks, flat as tables, terraced, and have their picnic by the seaweed where the rocks sloped below the tideline. There's no other way to eat lobster than to sit on an old dock—or cliffside rock, in this case—and toss the shells into the sea after you've sucked the sweetness out of them, the wind and salt on your face, your bare feet wet, your hands smelling fishy. Glorious!

But the kid still lay there. He was tired. Let him sleep.

Late in the day, Abbott returned to the motel. As he drove into the lot, he did a double take: That car over there, the one parked by the wing with his housekeeping unit, looked official. Even ominous. Yes sir, a state police cruiser. His heart underwent a painful displacement, cutting off breath. Later he would be able to congratulate himself on his speed; his reflexes were still sharp. His foot swung from brake to accelerator and, in one hard turn, with no telltale squeal of tires, he gunned out of the lot and headed back to Acadia. He slipped into the anonymity of a crowded parking lot at the Visitor Center. Only then did he think.

Paranoia again, and not the useful kind. Not the kind that's a fair index of reality. Even if Heath had signed a complaint, and even if a warrant (charging what?) had been issued, there would be no APB and interstate search in such a trivial case. He'd never be found, anyway, in light of his whimsical itinerary. The trooper had been tracing some other fugitive or, most likely, helping the locals solve a theft, probably of TV sets from rooms.

It was dark by the time Abbott got back to the motel. The cruiser was gone. There were no visible signs of a stakeout. The clerk at the front desk had no messages for him. His room was locked, as he'd left it. Apparently, it hadn't been rifled.

Next, he'd be looking behind the shower curtain. "Tired," he told Avery, who was himself half-asleep. "Going on nerves."

Too tired to make dinner, Abbott drove out to a McDonald's in Ellsworth. Avery, after eating some fries, fell asleep again, his head lolling on the highchair tray. Abbott carried him out and bundled him in the back seat of the car, then stepped to an outdoor phone booth.

The glass walls of the booth held his reflection, superimposed on a darkness awash with traffic, the headlights like phosphorescence. A busy roadside in the Maine coast night. As he dialed a number, he felt a sense of loneliness so grinding that he huddled over the phone and cupped his hand over his free ear. As the number rang, he jammed his eyes shut to rejoin the people to whom he was connected, no matter how poorly—by blood or whatever other excuse—and to fiercely relive being with them.

"My God, Daddy, where *are* you?"

"Bah Hahbah." An old family joke: mimicking the Mainers.

"Uh huh"—overagreeably, as if he'd said, "Down the street." It was no time for jokes. He said, "I want you to know Avery's safe and well."

"I never had any doubts. How come you're way up there?"

"Little break in the routine."

"Mm hmm. Why didn't you call?"

Good question. At some level he had wanted the escapade to be endless.

"We were getting worried," Heath said. "We thought you went up to Mother's, so we called her. Now she's a little worried, too."

"I'll get in touch."

"So what are you doing?"

What was he doing? What a rare joy it would be, if, when casually asked "What are you doing?," you could give an unambiguous account. He said, "We've been going on a lot of picnics."

"Oh. Good weather up there, huh?"

"Gorgeous."

"I envy you."

Enough of this pussyfooting. After further assurances and a few anecdotes about Avery—tanned, happy, enjoying the terrain—Abbott said, "We'll come home soon. Meantime, I don't want Lew calling the FBI. Tell him federal law doesn't apply."

"So *that's* it! Listen, he won't. I mean, he did—that morning—he went to the police, but they gave him a runaround. They told him I would have to get involved, and I won't. I wanted to hear from you first."

"Tell him not to write a letter to the President."

"Daddy, listen to me! He never told me he was going over to the house that morning. It was macho bullshit and he's sorry about it."

Sorry? "Any father would have done the same," Abbott said. "He's improving."

"He's got a lot to learn about kids, like they're not basketballs you slap out of somebody's hand. The police made him feel like an asshole."

"Let me talk to him. I'll console him."

"He's at class; he's going for a master's."

"Commendable," Abbott said. "He mentioned you had a job interview."

Heath was silent.

"How did it go?"

"Oh, I don't know," she said, "and I really don't much care. Isn't that crazy? All my hard work, to be a superwoman, and now I'd rather be a stay-at-home. I'd like to stay with Avery until he's three."

She seemed to be asking for permission. Abbott said, "Why not?"

"Well, women aren't thinking that way."

"I'm half a woman."

"Really? Would've fooled *me*."

"Surprised *me*, too. I'll tell you about it when we get home."

"When you get home"—her tone was bitter—"will there be visiting rights?"

Heart breaking, Abbott said, "Honey, we'll visit a lot. More than before."

"Bring him home. Now. It's normal, what he's going through." She gave a hurried lecture. "It's the anxieties, and they're normal. Anxiety over strangeness, and over separation from what they call the primary caretaker. The literature is full of it. But some of the latest studies say these fears don't even happen in a lot of cases."

"So far as Avery is concerned," Abbott said, "those studies are horseshit."

"I'm just telling you that there's mixed opinion in the field."

"Fuck the opinions of the field!" Bapp talking. Abbott heard: "Daddy . . . ?"—a voice-in-the-dark tone. Where had staid Daddy gone?

"Beg your pardon," Abbott said, "but I've learned some things on my own, and I'll stick with my story."

Silence for a while, palpable doubt over the line, then: "All right. After all these months I suppose you should know him better than anyone."

"Right. Grandfather knows best." Abbott cringed over this inadvertent use of the column title.

"It's so crazy," she said. "He bonded to the wrong person."

"True. Like a chick following a duck around."

"Are you trying to make a joke of all this?"

"Not at all."

"I don't know whether to laugh or cry. Mostly cry." She did sound close to tears. "I've missed his whole first year. I want him *back*, goddamn it."

"You'll *have* him," Abbott said, "as soon as he gives the word."

"How the hell can a baby 'give the word'?"

"We have our own way of talking. Any mother can tell you." Again Abbott cringed; that last was unintentionally cruel, a wisecrack gone awry. There was a horrible silence on the line, and then her voice, an octave lower in hurt: "I've tried to do my best. If you think I'm unfit . . ."

Oh Jesus, no. Hurriedly, Abbott explained his meaning. She loved Avery, was brave to have had him, and had worked hard on his behalf. But she hadn't been on hand through all the repetitions, the contexts day by day, all the orbits—she had missed out on the intimacy needed to see the extraordinary changes in the ordinary little creature that Avery was. "The scariness will change as fast. Babies are quick-change artists. He'll mature."

Abbott eased his grip on the telephone and crossed his fingers for luck.

"Well, I do know one thing in this whole mess," she said. "You do love Avery. I was never quite sure."

Love? "Call it good manners," he said. "I'm just being civil."

"Okay, Daddy"—a sigh of tolerance—"whatever you say. *I'd* sure hate to complicate things."

Was that a subtle putdown? No doubt. But never mind; he probably deserved it. He ended the call with a promise to return as soon as possible. ASAP.

On the drive back to the motel, Avery stirred awake as Abbott nodded at the wheel. Apparently, their highs and lows of energy would never coincide. Alertness would be needed over the next few hours to save the child from spills off the flimsy furniture. Between rescues, Abbott would force his numb mind to dictate a letter to Claire. He'd broach the idea of selling their house, careful not to hint that he knew she needed money. A careful letter: diplomatic, sentimental where required, about their home of twenty-odd years. A sad letter, but—like Claire herself—ultimately hardheaded.

Yes, keep it up. Soon he'd be a near master in the wisdom of detaching.

Why rush it?

In the morning, inch-walking Avery back from the letterdrop, Abbott lifted his eyes to Cadillac Mountain, a sunlit hump overlooking the Atlantic. Beautiful day. There was no need to go home at once. Let 'em all stew in their sweat back there.

Only one errand remained: disposal of the old folks. Abbott immediately put that out of his mind. But with fair weather continuing and the credit limit not yet reached, why not live out a few more of the reveries that had led to this willy-nilly trip? One of those was hiking a mountain. That daydream predated Avery.

So, go for it. Cadillac was pretty to look at, but, at only 1,530 feet—according to the park guidebook—it would be kid stuff to climb.

Head west, then, to the respectable White Mountains of New Hampshire. Why not?

They'd leave within the hour.

No, they'd leave after a couple of hours in the crowded laundromat.

Whimsical, but not crazy.

Mount Washington, the granddaddy of the range at 6,288 feet, was an all-day climb. At his age and with his arteries, he'd never make it despite all his exercise in past months with Avery.

No matter. He'd never been a man to aim for the top. Routine, not height, was still his key. He'd keep his mountain modest.

Look back. Look at this trip. No trailblazing wingding; rather, a circuit of tourist spots. And look back at his career. He'd settled without any pangs at all into facelessness, a state somewhat redeemed by Face. Nor did it bother him that the only achievement of his later years might be nothing more than saving one small human from a little bit of anguish, only to have that human grow into higher forms of anguish, naturally.

Therefore, all things considered, why should he feel despair today? He was despairing on the side of a middling mountain when he should have been happy.

Mount Chocurua, elevation 3,475. Middling but dramatic, perhaps the only bald peak in the national forest. He'd spotted it while driving in from Conway. It had its own Indian legends, according to the pamphlets in the Information Center. He'd even considered carrying the old folks up to the bold granite summit; but, no, that would be too showy a gravestone for the unpretentious couple.

For himself and Avery, a good moment no doubt waited up top, the consummation of a mini-adventure, last and best of their trip. The trip needed all the excuses it could get. But Abbott knew now, gasping at trailside, that he couldn't hike any farther. The steepness of the trail had winded him, put stitches in his side and in his chest, and rubberized his legs. After a mile or so of level ground, the trail had inclined sharply, becoming less a path than an erosion cut, or dry stream bed, rocky and uneven. He was climbing uneven stairs, and by midafternoon, in the fourth hour of a trek billed for six hours, he had lost track of the flights. At intervals he rested against trees at trailside to huff and puff. His pedometer, adjusted to a normal stride, was inaccurate for this kind of hiking. His trail map gave no indication of his progress. Other hikers, passing him, were equally uninformed, but they were blithe about it. Not him. If he survived this trek, he'd gripe to the rangers about the lack of signs; he'd write something, damn it, in scant hope of embarrassing the government. He looked for the summit and saw only the forest canopy. He looked for a sign of higher elevation—maybe fewer maples, more firs—but the woods presented a blank face. Meanwhile, Avery, in the carrier on Abbott's back, jabbered and whined in boredom. He tossed himself, his weight yanking back on Abbott's shoulders.

Abbott counted off thirty steps and paused for another rest, embracing a tree trunk. After sucking in air, he freed one arm and swigged from his canteen, spat, and poured water on his head. He'd go on. He would endure his puffing, the burn of it, and his cotton mouth and his jellied legs, even the weight in his chest. Pressure on the breastbone, like a heavy foot, is a signal you should not ignore, but he'd damn well ignore it. He'd climb this mountain, for whatever meaning it had for him. He lurched ahead another twenty-five steps, grunting out the numbers. Then, as he toddled sideways to a tree and embraced it, he felt two new sources of pain, unendurable last straws. In the same instant, Avery pulled hard on his nape hair and a woodfly stung him on the cheek.

No energy remained—none to swat the fly; none to reach back blindly and strangle Avery, thumbs against the little bastard's windpipe.

Abbott slid down to his knees. He worked each leg out in front of him, each thigh still trembling uncontrollably, and sat himself down, splat, on the moss, his back to the tree. Here, let it end. No more up, no more down. Stay here, and let time and the weather claim him.

You can't, though, succumb to despair and its joys on a busy trail, not unless you're certifiably mad. Lew was right. Northeastern trails are sidewalks. Eyes closed, Abbott heard youthful voices approaching, which hushed suddenly as if out of respect for a grandpa's nap. He heard pauses in the footfalls, indicating that quick observations were being made for signs of life. His heaving chest should suffice. Avery remained still in the presence of these strangers. Abbott heard a low-voiced greeting—"Hiya, kiddo"—addressed, no doubt, to Avery, and he imagined Avery's response: somber eyes, face set to cry. The footfalls went away.

Abbott opened his eyes and looked uptrail through a

blur of sweat on his lashes. He blinked. More people were coming down. A couple, middle-aged. They wore shorts and big maroon backpacks. The man appeared to be in fine fettle—so said his downhill swagger and the tilt of his grin. Surveying Abbott, he gestured with his forearms as if to boost him, and said, "Great view up there."

Sonofabitch.

The woman, keener-eyed, spotted Avery, who was wedged in his carrier between the tree trunk and Abbott's back. The woman said, "Are you two guys all right?"

Abbott, still panting, could not speak. He nodded. The woman backed off, looking unconvinced. As the couple went on down the trail, she looked back once or twice.

Abbott decided to head downtrail before another inspection party showed up. There would be no privacy up here in which to die. He'd have to do it some other time.

His legs had knotted up during his rest. He swung around to face the tree, hugged it and shimmied up with his arms, raising himself to a genuflection, one knee and one foot. He turned and threw his center of gravity up and forward. His legs held him, caught his lolling weight and stabilized it. There. He could walk; he'd learned all over again. He could manage the descent without too comic a wobbliness. He paused for a quick systems check. Respiration: returning to normal. Pressure in chest: easing. Heartbeat: palpitant, but that was almost Standard Operating Procedure.

A babble of voices approached from below. A file of girls came into view, youngsters wearing Scout blouses. Abbott stood aside; the kids were moving fast and chatting obliviously; maybe they had climbed Mount Washington in the morning and were tapering off now on Chocurua.

Their leader followed, a woman in her thirties in an Army fatigue shirt and shorts. She wore clodhopper hiking boots disproportionate to the slimness of her legs. Her elbows pumped, and she puffed, though not with exhaustion but like a weightlifter in a workout. In passing, she smiled at Abbott and wiped hair off her brow. "Hi. I hope you and the little fella left us some blueberries."

Blueberries?

Of course.

On the mental screen where all events unfold in perfection, Abbott saw himself and Avery on the summit, huddled in the lee of a windswept rock, gorging on delicious wild blueberries.

He told the woman: "We left them all for you."

The last stop, a step down in elevation to the Berkshires of Massachusetts. The town of Stockbridge, which he and Claire had visited on long Sunday drives for antiquing and art shows in the years of family peace. Déjà vu: Sunday again, and the late-afternoon music rang out from the Children's Chimes Tower on its lawn by the Congregational church. Some tourists sat around near the base of the tower, that stone campanile built at the bequest of a Yankee notable; the old Yankees hadn't been *all* bad. In the street, empty of traffic, several schoolgirls rode by on horses, at a walk. All the elements of the scene—the chimes, the listeners, the tower, maidens on horseback, and the cemetery across the street with its solemn white pines—all these combined to make a fairy tale of the moment. Abbott laughed outright over its charm—and over an inspiration.

He pushed Avery's stroller across the road and into the cemetery. The child was quiet, wonderstruck over the tunes in the air. The cemetery was deserted except for a few boys on bicycles, circling a headstone. Seeing Abbott, they pedaled off.

"A tour talk," Abbott said to Avery. "You're going to get one whether you want it or not. Over that way"—he pointed west—"is Alice's Restaurant. The Last Mohican is there, getting drunk. That church behind us"—he jerked his thumb—"Jonathan Edwards is preaching there. He's saying our souls will be dropped into hellfire like spiders.

Meanwhile, there's a kid somewhere around here named Field; he's dreaming up an invention. It's the transatlantic cable. At the same time, book fairs are under way. Melville and Hawthorne are running them. Also, it's Election Day. The village burghers are voting. Believe it or not, some of them are voting for Andrew Jackson. And Rockwell's at work over there in his studio—Main Street, I think—painting the locals for his posters. And right here, in this graveyard, a funeral's about to be conducted. Two humble heirs of the Puritans are about to be laid to rest. Welcome to the rites."

Avery had not responded with any copycat babble; he remained transfixed by the music, eyeballing for its source.

Abbott braked the stroller and pushed it over the curb onto the turf. He had reached an older part of the cemetery, farthest from the campanile. Here, weathered stones were arranged in large circles on family plots. A pine and some bushes stood between the last family circle and an open field beyond. The greenery provided some concealment for the impropriety of the rites.

"I'm sure there's an ordinance against this. They'll take me for a graverobber. First I rob the cradle, then the grave." He winced over this joke. "Sorry."

Joking would be no further help. His hands trembled as he removed the two cartons from the back of the stroller, and he knew that his voice would crack if he continued jabbering to Avery. His lower lip quivered as well as his hands, and his eyes flooded. *Damn* these emotions. He bit the insides of his cheeks. Be methodical now. He set the cartons on the ground. He removed from the stroller a foldable trenching tool, an inheritance from GI days. He had transferred this tool, along with the cartons, from the trunk of his car. Quickly, he scraped a shallow trench in the ground cover of pine needles. He opened the cartons and poured the contents into the trench. With quick strokes, he covered the grave and tamped it. He closed the cartons and put them in the stroller for disposal later. He stowed the trenching tool. He grabbed the stroller bar and hurriedly pushed Avery back over the grass to the road.

"I suppose"—hoarseness, but his voice did not break; he cleared his throat—"I suppose there should be words now, hm?" Yes, there should. Jabber away; it counted. "We can dispense with prayers. They were said the first time around. How about some adolescent questions? How about 'What to do?' 'How to live?' "

Abbott halted at the entrance to the cemetery, across the street from the small crowd of listeners idling on the campanile lawn. He parked the stroller under a pine and sat down in the grass next to Avery to wait out the concert. Afterward, he would find accommodations for the night. One more stopover before going home. Final night of the lark.

"I'd live here," he said, with a sweep of his arm, "if there was any work. I'd retire here, in all this afterglow. You could grope around in it, grope toward growing old. Find out what that means: to grow old. Gracefully, I mean."

He nudged Avery with his elbow. "Help me out, co-author." Still spellbound, the child did not react.

"Let me say exactly what I think I'm saying, lest I miss my own point. Growing old. We need a metaphor. An old inn, say, no Red Lion or hotspot, just some lived-in place; it would still be open in the off season. Too maudlin for you? Try this, then: some small invention. It's not impossible, you know. Or a small farm, say, a small farm in oneself, not yet sold or foreclosed."

The music ceased. Abbott, lost in thought, would not have noticed but for a change in Avery's expression. The child looked surprised, and he ogled the air as if the vanished tunes, the program of "old favorites," had left visible traces. The air held a vibrant quiet after the plangency of the chimes. As the tourists left, every *chunk* of a car door's closing, every catch of a starter motor, was distinct; and Abbott heard, in the background, the sound of more distant traffic, perhaps from the turnpike, like a long wave perpetually breaking. In minutes, all the tourists were gone. The quality of the moment was fading, hardly stirring, late afternoon, with traffic remotely awash at its edges.

They'd leave for home immediately. No more whims or symbolic play. Time was flying; and before one can grow old, one must grow up.

27

Okay, off my knee. Go explore now.

I'm your base camp in these wilds of Forestview.

You waddle out a few steps at a time. You pause, glance back at me.

Yes, I'm here. *Present and accounted for, sir*!

Five yards, ten yards . . .

Yes, I'm still here, on our favorite bench.

See me wave? What's new, way out there on the grass?

Ah, the tree. You point out the sapling. You look back at me for reassurance.

Yes, it's safe. No leopards in it.

See me nod? Do I confuse you with all these gestures?

Feel the tree. Make it sway, the way I showed you yesterday.

Good! See me applaud? I'm your cheerleader.

And I'm your chronicler, making these shorthand entries. You squawk when you see me writing instead of watching.

Take me for granted. I'm here and won't move away while you explore.

Take me for granted, like this good weather, the benign sky.

I'm smiling, see? A death's-head grin. Biology's biggest con.

Damn! Here comes an intruder.

A jogger. Laboring along. My age, white shorts, jiggly paunch. He's going to jog right by you out there.

Friend, hear me via telepathy. Please, please, disregard that kid. Don't play uncle. If you reach down and pat that head, you'll cause a scare. You'll undo days of work.

Friend, my thanks!

Only a smile, a puff of what looked like greetings. Away you go, propelling that gut like mine.

Hang in there, Avery!

Sat down hard, froze; now you wheel in a semi-crouch, watching the jogger go.

Yes, I'm looking at you. See me? Look, I smile.

You're rollicking back, fast gait. You balance with your arms as an aerialist uses a pole.

You fall—routine *ouch*—scramble up. Continue.

Someday you won't need these quick returns to camp. To my lap. You won't need these recurrent contacts in the flesh.

Someday a phone call will do. Or a letter. Ultimately, a photo. A photo in an album.

What now? You've paused. No full-scale retreat, after all.

You bend down, spread-eagled. Stagger a little. You've found something in the grass.

You're bringing it to me.

This means you've forgotten that jogger already. Assimilated him. Great!

Welcome home, to my knee. That was a good outing. The best yet.

"Dis?" Avery held out his hand.

"Let me see," Abbott said. "Open your fingers."

"Dis?"

"Filter. Butt end. Some of the young mothers smoke too much."

"Dis?"

"And I tell them so, too."

"So too."

"No. Filter. Fil-ter."

"It-ter."

"Filter."

"Itter."

"Filter. I shouldn't let you handle it, really."

"Itter."

"But, between you and me, if you happen to find one with a dry butt attached, of respectable length, I might be shameless enough to smoke it."

"Itter."

"Right. Now listen: Don't *eat* the thing."

"Itter."

"May I have it, please? Thanks. I'll keep it here on the bench beside me. *Mine.*"

Abbott expected a fight over this confiscation, but Avery looked less wronged than intrigued. He gazed at the filter, then at Abbott, and toddled away, moving in short bursts, scanning the grass. By afternoon, a collection of filters had accumulated on the bench beside Abbott.

Entry 1,126

Each afternoon I nudge you through a receiving line of young mothers. The plan is to saturate you with kind faces while in my presence, the multiplicity of Face. Over and over you hobnob with Alice, Jolene, Seretha, *et al.*, who are park regulars, like me. We're kindred spirits. And we're an information exchange. We sit on the benches by the sandbox, and discuss such issues as the relative merits of Total and Lucky Charms cereals, and the prices of kids' clothes at the Penny Saver.

I wonder, typing this, if you'll ever be idle enough, or curious enough about the blank space of your early years, to read these notes, this closet comedy of ours that I'll leave behind as part of Abbott's Collected Papers. Do you, even now, have enough brain power for adult remembrance of any of this, even as only an inkling?

Take the tour with me once more:

Meet Alice. She has a daughter, Courtenay, four years older than you—a Methuselah!—over on the swings. And here's Jolene, wearing cutoffs. The little girl clutching Jolene's lovely thigh is her daughter Trudy, the terror whom you know. Be on guard for Trudy's sneak overhand right. Next, meet Paulette. Her son Robert is only three months old—that golden age!—sleeping in the carriage under the netting. And here's Seretha, your favorite. Seretha is the wife of a foreign student, and her accent has captivated you. You willingly stay with Seretha while I put in appearances at work.

Yesterday, you stayed with Seretha for more than three hours. When I returned, you had a big greeting for me, an imploring arm reach. You held on for a fairly long while. But during my absence you didn't cry or go cataleptic, Seretha said.

I think we're getting somewhere.

Entry 1,127

Today, you tugged my hand, holding us back, as we were walking to the receiving line. You wanted to watch the action in the sandbox. You rubbernecked at those exciting creatures, a little bigger than you, in their parallel play and random scuffles. That's the first arena, and you aren't ready for it yet. Among us mothers, you can count on being cared for—love, as they say, which is never enough. In the arena you need respect. Take it from Grandpa.

28

Grandpa's voice shook. Denham raised one hand to cut off the stammering and said, "Just tell me this: Are you going to stay put for a while?"

Abbott nodded.

"If I happen to call you tomorrow, next week, next month, are the chances a little better that you'll be there?"

This chewing-out dragged on, reprieving Abbott from the need to speak. Earlier, while waiting in the outer office, he had tried to prepare himself for this showdown. Deep-breathing exercises, dashes to the water cooler to allay dryness of mouth, a dash to the john as a result of the dashes to the water cooler. All in vain. Old anxiety reactions—was that the right jargon?—die hard, even when you face nothing more than a Denham.

Denham riffled through the sample columns on his desk. "You're getting the hang of it, anyway. This one about straps and buckles is funny, I think. Hang of it—no pun intended." He smiled, then looked up, askance, as in a failure of recognition. He seemed to be trying to visualize the Abbott he knew—that fellow hunched there like an old yokel—squiring a baby around on his back in public. For whatever reason, the yokel today had a mouthful of pebbles. He gasped the kind of quip for which he had a reputation as house wit: "Squaw. With a papoose."

Denham chortled without smiling. He held up another

column. "This travel piece is funny, too, I think, though we shouldn't call a motel room a death trap for children. Not by the name of the chain."

The critique went on, column by column. It extended Abbott's breather, giving him time to reventilate as he bobbed his head in yes-nods. There was a major truth to remember: Today, talking counted; he must display, in Heath's words, a "great big fat mouth." He'd prove that schizophrenics like himself could function very well in the real world, sly about it.

". . . a good column," Denham was saying. "You're no Erma Bombeck, but between the two of us we're cooking up a nice little feature for younger readers."

"Forty percent," Abbott said, eavesdropping on his own voice. It did not quaver.

"Forty percent what?"

"The number of elderly"—still no quaver—"in the city. Our readership. You asked me once."

"Oh, I know, I know. That's the problem. Our readership is dying off."

"There's another problem." Abbott breathed deep; the timbre of his voice had stabilized. As Denham looked over with a fraternal smile—his first in this faceoff—Abbott put down his only bargaining chip. "Speaking of old folks, I'm thinking about retiring."

In good Yankee fashion, Denham showed no surprise, only a tic-like flutter of one eye. This was followed, for a second or two, by his characteristic look of hurt, the downcurved mouth, and then by a pokerface. He waited for an explanation.

Burnout, malaise, identity pangs, and a longing for change—Abbott blended all these pop symptoms into a spiel that sounded convincing, at least to him. Denham listened, hands folded and shoulders squared. At last he said, "You've really thought about this?"

"At great length."

"A man your age, Wes—*our* age, I should say—has a lot

of good years left. You should be raring to go, still."

"That's just the point."

"How would you live?"

"I'd do some freelancing."

"Have any contacts?"

"A few," Abbott lied, and looked away from eyes crinkled with skepticism—or with concern over his mental state. Though a dilettante in the trade, Denham had been around more than long enough to know that "freelancer" means jobless journalist. Denham said, "What about your pension?"

The bottom-line query, cutting through the crap. Abbott shrugged to indicate that, for a greater good, the pension could be sacrificed. Denham had picked up a pencil and a yellow legal pad and was jotting figures and dates. He said, "You won't lose it, you know, if you work part time."

Bingo!

Abbott feigned surprise. "Is that company policy?"

"No, and I don't like it, but it can be arranged. Retirement is no step to take lightly, Wes."

Abbott ducked his head and sighed, portraying a man torn between options. "Your offer does change the picture."

"Early retirement can send a man to hell in a handbasket. I've seen it happen, Wes. It can be a dilly of a mistake in times like these."

"I'll have to consider your offer."

"I know you've had problems. I understand there were some difficulties at the police station."

"A misunderstanding," Abbott said, not surprised that Denham knew. He volunteered no facts.

"Just ease up for a while," Denham said. "The rules can bend. I'll bend them."

"Thanks. I'd feel able to stay on if I could cut my duties."

"You'd do the column?"

For a change of pace, Abbott spoke frankly. "There

are single parents out there who don't know what they're doing, and maybe I can reach a few of them."

"Fine and dandy"—Denham's voice thickened—"but I want that column to be funny. Let's keep something in mind: I've been pushing you for a year to use your best talent."

"The function of a good editor," Abbott said.

"I try. I try with all my staff. I know how to work with creative people, Wes."

"Thanks. By the way, I'll use a pseudonym."

"No problem. We'll dream up something catchy."

"And I want to write some stories. Series. I'm kind of old to go nosing around but it doesn't embarrass me any more."

"You're only as old as you feel."

"True. I'll go on working with Eddie on the pages, but I want our positions to be switched. Eddie can take over."

Denham reared back slightly at this curveball. "Say again?"

"I want Eddie to take over my pages. And my title." Abbott gave these words the tone of non-negotiable demand.

"Eddie's only a greenhorn."

"I've trained him. We work well together."

"He's only . . . what? Thirty?"

"Thirty-one. When I was his age, my editors wouldn't let me cover the city council. Nowadays, thirty-year-olds cover the world. They run foreign bureaus. For God's sake, they topple presidents."

"My God, yes." Denham joined with Abbott in a slow wag of heads over the enormous changes they had witnessed together in their years in the trade.

"Also, Eddie won't cost you much."

Another bottom-line point. Denham tightened his lips over it in thought before talking on in Personnel lingo. "Has he shown initiative?"

"Oh, hell, yes. He fairly bursts with it."

"Leadership potential?"

"Yep. He'll write what you tell him, too."

"No sentimental liberal, hey?" Denham's smirk invited Abbott to join in a collegial chuckle at himself. Abbott declined, going deadpan, but on second thought he succumbed. "Ah, you've got me there. But, no, Eddie's no McGrory. No Buckley, either. Very flexible viewpoint."

"If he's all that good," Denham said, "we'll lose him. We're only a training ground, you know, except the old hands like us."

"If he quits, I'll fill in until you find a new hand."

"You would? Full time?"

"You have my word on it."

Denham wrote something on his legal pad. Abbott, trained by oldtime hot-type work to read upside down, saw "See Eddie." The boss said, "This might be agreeable to me so long as you're there, keeping an eye on things. What's your new title going to be?"

"I've outgrown titles."

Denham didn't smile over such drollery; no man ever escapes titles. He twiddled his pencil. "We'll have to cook up something. It's a brand new position." He rapped the pencil on the pad. "I've got it!"

" 'Associate Editor'?"

"*Dull*, Wes. I'm surprised at you. Try this for size: 'Editor of the Editorial Page, Emeritus.' "

Abbott was silent.

"Well?"

"It has a nice ring to it," Abbott said.

"Needless to say"—Denham spoke without raising his eyes from the pad, on which new figures were accumulating—"all this involves a cut in pay. We'll have to talk about it."

"At your convenience."

Fight tomorrow's battles tomorrow. And tomorrow, Abbott thought, he would lose, outmatched by Denham the lawyer amid the mirrors and smoke of company benefits.

But for today, rejoice. With little resistance, he'd gained the prime objective: the positioning of Eddie for a good move. Abbott closed his eyes for a moment's rest, a microsleep, proportionally equivalent to one of Napoleon's catnaps on the battlefield, or, better, one of Edison's naps in the lab of invention.

"One more thing," he said. "I'd like to put in a word on behalf of one of the old pros here. A former old pro."

He spoke Earl's name and watched closely for the reaction. He saw perplexity, that look of a man who suspects he has been insulted and can't fathom why. Abbott said, "I'm sure you're tired of hearing about us staffers with our problems, but Earl's an old pro and I think he'd like to come back."

Translation: Earl has nowhere else to go, and perhaps can be persuaded.

"You've been in touch?" Denham asked.

"Close touch," Abbott said. "In your shoes, I'd take another chance on him. If I may speak so boldly."

"I do like *Call* staffers to be squeaky clean."

"I realize that's company policy."

Denham leaned back, hands behind his head, face solemn and then wistful. "He came to us from New York."

"That's right, the big time. He was an assistant M.E. on the old *World-Telegram*."

"Which folded in . . ."

"I think '63."

Evocation of the old *Telly*. This, usually, preceded the boss's Lou Grant act, and Abbott waited now for the removal of the coat, the loosening of the necktie. But why wait? Beat the Great Editor to the punch. Abbott extended his forearms. He gazed down at them as though, under tweed and white Oxford cloth, there were emblems of an adventurous past, like blurred tattoos. "The *Telly* was a good paper," he said, head bowed in this memorial. "Not great, but good."

Denham had made no move to perform. "Earl never came to see me," he said. "He's off the payroll but still on our insurance, lucky for him."

"Lucky?"

"It'll pay his hospital bills. Some of them."

Abbott's head jerked up in un-Yankee-like shock.

"Didn't you know?" To his credit, Denham didn't gloat. He reported that Earl was a patient at a mental health center. "The police picked him up downtown, drunk as a lord. In the *morning*. They called us. Apparently, he has no other people." Dryly, Denham added, "We've had a lot of contact lately with the police."

Abbott ignored this. "Was he hurt?"

"Nothing serious. He'd fallen on his face."

Abbott heaved a long breath, recalling the damage once done to that face by some kid named . . . some punk nicknamed after a potato chip. Abbott said, "I saw him only two weeks ago. I had no idea."

"The diagnosis is depression."

"I don't believe it. You can't believe those bastards."

Denham, startled, said, "You can't?"

"They'll tell you anything."

"Well, better look him up. Update your story, so to speak."

A zinger, that last, but Abbott supposed he deserved it. "I'll see him. I'll see him today."

Denham opened a desk drawer. He took out a memo slip and copied a room number from some other papers—the hospital bills, perhaps. He handed the slip to Abbott. "If he straightens himself out, I'll talk with him. You can tell him I'm still waiting."

"He'll be glad to hear it, I'm sure."

The drawer closed, and Denham rose to his feet to end the interview. Abbott looked up at him with a sense of revelation. At last, after years of fatheadedness, a glimpse of humanity. Thinking this, Abbott became aware of a return gaze as searching as his own, and he made a final assumption, a final effort to read a grown mind. Denham, he thought, was thinking: At last, after years of withdrawal, some clumsy spunk.

29

Entries

Today you gathered more filters and piled them beside me on the bench. Your distance from me increases daily as you crawl away in the grass, combing it for "itters." Our movements compose a sort of yo-yo—I'm the finger—with a lengthening string. It's our umbilical cord.

This afternoon I moved, jerking the yo-yo. Without warning I sauntered from our favorite bench to one some yards away. You looked up, as if preternaturally warned, and stayed rooted until I was seated on the new bench, writing in my notebook. Then you hurried over and leaned against my knee for a while before wandering back to the grass. There, you re-established the former distance between us, between the protector and the protected. Your feel for yardage is acute. From now on, I'll change benches every few hours.

You have discovered the tot slide beyond the swings. When no other kids are using it, you climb on the ladder—backward. Why? Why must you evoke your grandfather's bad style? I refer to my backward flight down the stairs when I stole you.

You have learned to say "juice," though the "j" sounds French, as in "Jacques."

❧

Rainy day. We did our hike in the enclosed mall—long looping laps through the crowd until the pedometer said two-and-three-quarters miles.

❧

Today you fell from the slide ladder. I was talking with Seretha when it happened. I turned and saw you craning your head from prone position, calling upon the universe for sympathy. You were able to rise, still hollering—no lost wind or apparent fractures. Seretha and I went on talking, as indifferent as the stars. A couple of smart mothers. Soon you were climbing again—still backward.

❧

This afternoon we inch-walked over to the soccer field during a game. We mingled up close with the loudest fans, those like Red Sox fans. See Face scream. See the friendly leopards.

❧

Saw Earl again today while you stayed with Seretha. The Band-Aids are off, but he still can't update his story. His eyes glaze over, and he rambles. I catch key words like "dog" and "money" and, of course, the profanities, but the rest is garbled. He has drug-therapy cottonmouth, keeps tasting his tongue. Atropine? Are they electroshocking him? I don't know and won't ask. It pains me to see him lying there like an old bum, some down-and-outer with scabs on his face from falling on the sidewalk.

Today there was a fresh bouquet in the room. The old one—wilted now and relegated to the windowsill—was from the *Call* staff. I'd collected the money for it myself and passed around the get-well card. Even young Eddie, overjoyed these days as he updates his résumé, made a contribution and signed the card. The new bouquet, at bedside, was a gorgeous array of glads. I recognized the handwriting on the card, having seen it on many a memo. It said, "The Denhams."

Denham continues to surprise. How did he or his wife know that the gladiolus happens to be Earl's favorite cut flower? (Be reminded that Earl once had tastes.) Probably from a casual remark made years ago at a company outing at Denham's place, with its formal garden. Denham must be a mother hen like me, in a way. He wants to keep his flock together, his tiny flock of semi-talented misfits who come cheap and who have nowhere else to go.

❧

Rainy day. Mall again. For your information, two-and-three-quarters miles equals twelve loops. We strolled with Heath for company. In the afternoon you played in my bureau drawers, a game of dump-in-dump-out with Abbott's mismatched socks.

❧

Another day. A morning at the park, afternoon at work, now night at this typewriter, batting out these entries on life with grandfather. You're asleep in the crib, but I imagine we're collaborating here, in the study, that together we remember and think and type. Your mother has dreamed up an ingenious plan. A slow transition. She's spending time with us daily, and you and I are to spend time at the apartment, gradually conditioning you for a stayover in that place without me. Ingenious and sly, this plan, in that it's designed to condition me as well as you. Who does Heath think she's fooling? She's postponed her job hunt.

❧

Yesterday, for almost half a mile, you led the way home from the park as I pushed the empty stroller. This morning you yourself pushed the stroller part of the way over here. Your anticipation grows daily. Gobble breakfast, grab my hand, jabber—"Let's go, let's go" (pronounced less fluently than herein spelled).

❧

Your father was here Sunday to help me clean the house. I showed him how to swing a scythe and he chopped my lawn down to power-mower height and then mowed it for me. Inside, I cleared some of the clutter, throwing things out by armfuls into Lew's borrowed truck. Your place of reassurance is slowly disappearing, but so far you haven't noticed. The housekeeping hasn't traumatized you—or me. Even the living-room carpet is clean now, lest prospective home-buyers gag. I offered Claire half the take, but she settled for less than a third, along with the Wellfleet cottage. Fair enough. She'll have enough money to found a new "Wild Duck" or whatever, and I'll have enough for a cheap condo around here. I'll no longer be your "primary caretaker" but still the best babysitter within a day's drive. And I'll do what little I can to help bankroll your parents. My dwindled income will amount to a sort of small garden out back, from which I'll dispense a few tomatoes and other modest goodies. In time we'll get you out of that rathole apartment and onto some boring Irene Street.

❧

Another afternoon at the apartment. You played with everyone, including the rudely awakened Noz the night worker, groggy and tousle-haired, on the so-called "family room" floor. I spotted no roaches. Lew was conspicuously gentle, and you deigned to sit in his lap so long as I stayed in the room. Heath wanted to keep you overnight. "For Christ's sake," she hissed at me, "he's not afraid anymore." But I told her to trust meddling Grandpa a little longer. Maybe she's right, but my creatureliness tells me no.

❧

The jogger returns to Forestview. The man my age, with white shorts tucked under a jellybelly. You were squatting near the maple sapling when he jogged by, and this time the man broke stride. He reached down and stroked your hair. You looked up, puzzled, and watched him go. But no fright, no hurried toddle back to me. You glanced at me—a glance sufficed for security.

Friend, whoever you are, you're forgiven. Also, I noticed you can trundle that belly like mine a whole circuit of the park. Do you have your cardiologist's okay?

❧

The longest journey yet: over to the mothers' benches, where the "itter" pickings are best, and then all the way to the edge of the bicycle path, for a handful of gravel, before returning to camp.

❧

You stayed with your mother all day, at the house and the park, while I worked. You played in a wide circle around her, prattling to yourself as if she were me. A big welcome on my return, but briefer and less clingy than the last. I'm jealous.

❧

The yo-yo string continues to lengthen, and yesterday marked a reversal: You were the finger, causing me to move. You meandered toward the street, rather than in the direction of the hedge and the picnic grove. By the time I reached you, you were on the sidewalk, gazing at the traffic. I inch-walked you back.

Any day now it will happen. The yo-yo string will break.

❧

I write this with equal feelings of sorrow and success.

I was talking with Alice and Courtenay when—as if preternaturally warned—I looked around and saw that you had vanished. I called out. No mothers could see you near the street. You had been wandering near the hedge. I began walking fast toward the gap in the hedge where it opens into the picnic grove.

A stride, then a run, becoming a flat-out sprint, though I don't know why—surely, you were safe. On some level I probably wanted to die. Why not? My work was done, climaxed by this run. The first run in years: belly jouncing like the jogger's, pectorals flapping like breasts under my shirt. My pants slipped hipward and I tugged them up and held on; my thighs refused messages from the brain to flex faster. But, I remember telling myself at the same time to calm down and quit being so self-dramatic. Amid all this confusion of mind I reached the gap in the hedge and saw you a few yards away—safe, of course. You hadn't been trampled by berserk picnickers; you hadn't been run over by a mad bicyclist. Hunkered down, you were scraping through the leaf-litter on the ground.

When I gasped your name out of relief, you looked up at me in the manner of a bemused and snotty clerk, as though to say: Ye-es, may I help you?

❧

Tonight you're at the apartment. Here, at home, I listen for your breathing and do double takes in the silence. At last Mother Nature has done her work. A negligent old bitch, sometimes, but still the goddess of routine. And now I can quit writing these serendipitous notes for you, all this minutiae of a short-lived, odd-couple link. I'll probably throw them away in the housecleaning. It's time for this parent to detach, per the do-don't list. The parent disengages and begins over. You pick up pieces of the wreckage—anything—a clapboard, say, or an ice-cream stick. One splinter of something, fondled, can revive the touch; two, together, suggest a design. Soon you have a renewal project between your stiffening fingers.

No better place than here to dictate another paragraph

for the obituary, which is always on mental file.

". . . Abbott's legacy is marked not in monuments or in dramatic deeds but in the comforting effect he had on those who hardly knew he was influencing them, so subtle was his way."

30

So subtle?

It was not subtle to tote his chessboard, emblem of happier times, to Earl's bedside. As Abbott propped the board against the bedstand, Earl rose up on an elbow to squint.

"What's that for?"

"For a game, if you'd like."

"I see. End of the movie." Earl lay back and spoke to the ceiling. "This is the scenc where you ask me to play, and I say yes, meaning the old stumblebum is coming back to the land of the living."

"All I thought"—wearily, Abbott sat down on the edge of the bed—"was that you might be up to a game by now, if you're not too drugged."

"Play the music," Earl said. "Roll the fucking credits."

Still drugged—the eyes glazing over, the tongue tasting itself. Thorazine? Abbott wouldn't ask. He looked down at the heirloom board. Eight rows, eight squares to a row, eight times eight equals sixty-four squares of inlaid wood. A little math soothes the temperament, as Epicurus knew. It had been a long day of work at the *Call*, covering for Eddie, who was off on a job tryout, and of dickering with the house-buyer.

"Two geezers over their board game," Earl went on, his voice slurred but more animated than on the last of Abbott's visits. "You're backsliding."

Yes, Abbott conceded to himself that he'd backslid a bit. He must have been feeling that the old museum of their friendship could be restored, and made portable, and carried to this ward and folded around the two of them like a screen, walling out the clatter of carts and the shuffle of patients.

"A year ago," Abbott said, "I worked out a wrinkle of my own in the Sicilian Defense. I don't think you can beat it. If you want to try, fine. If not, the hell with it."

"Hey! So *huffy* today!" Earl raised himself off the pillow and glared, head wobbly, to keep Abbott in focus. "Where's the sweet old biddy I knew so well?"

Abbott heaved a long puff of irritation.

"What's happened?" Earl asked. "Something has happened."

"Nothing's happened."

"You lost your dog."

Credit Earl with perception, even under drugs. Caught by surprise, Abbott felt the full pain of his loss, as though it were the hour for the daily hike with Avery, or the lull in late afternoon when loneliness springs its ambushes. He felt himself reddening, and for a moment he couldn't meet Earl's eyes.

"Sorry about that." With a grip on Abbott's arm, Earl held himself in mid-sit-up position, his thin neck corded. "Man's best friend. Really, I'm sorry."

"Let's skip this scene," Abbott said.

Earl let go and fell back. He grabbed tissues from the bedstand and whisked at his eyes as if the sudden tears there were pesky gnats.

"You were a dog fancier yourself," Abbott said.

"My dogs abandoned me. I've been remembering. Before, I couldn't remember. They zapped my brains, you know. The shrinks."

"Everything will come back, I've heard."

"It will? Then I'll sue them."

"Are they talking to you, the shrinks?"

"Who needs it? I'm not depressed, just pissed off. Anyway, they don't talk, they just dispense dope. I'm tapering off so I can sign out of here."

"And then what?"

Earl's eyes went blank and he tasted his tongue. The eyes rekindled. "I remember we were talking. At the type shop. About places where you can hole up for a night."

"One of our best routines."

"All-time best. You mentioned the clothing bins at the mall. Where people throw old clothes. Well, I'll tell you something, a little info nugget for your tickler file. The Salvation Army bin has a sort of baffle in the opening, a sort of flange. You can climb in okay, but you have to be a fucking gymnast to climb out."

"A good travel tip," Abbott said.

"I took a header." Earl ran his hand over the fading bruises on his face.

"Now you can cancel your lease. Move in with me for a while."

Earl's eyes shed more bothersome tears, and he mauled them with tissue. "Abbott, you're high on something."

"I'm buying a small condo. You can do the cooking."

Earl blew his nose. He said, "You and I would never hit it off as roomies, pal."

Indeed, not. Earl's intensities would be harder to live with than an infant's colic.

Earl said, "I wouldn't want you gassing to me about the glorious past."

"I said for a while. Call it a sort of halfway house."

"Call it burnout bungalow."

Abbott nodded. "That's good, Earl. You haven't lost it."

Earl said, "Try this: You and I are a couple of old dogs with a new leash on life."

"That's not good."

"No, but it would make it as a *Call* headline."

"Are you telling me you'll see Denham?"

Earl glowered for a while, then glanced over at the windowsill, at the withered bouquet of glads there with the Denhams' name card. His reddened eyes swam back to Abbott. "I've got to tell you something."

"No more skid-row stories. They're painful."

"Skid row toughens you up. But no, it's not about that. It's about my sicko dogs. I wouldn't tell this to anybody else in the world." Earl raised himself on both elbows and looked around with pop-eyed suspicion, as if for eavesdroppers.

Abbott said, "I don't want to see any more photos from your wallet."

"I lost my wallet. Listen, do you remember about the family game? I told you, the game my tarts played."

"No more details. Tell it to the shrinks."

"Why waste a good story on them? I told the girls about our dog shtick, how an old friend and I had this running joke about our dogs, meaning people."

"Let's get back to Denham," Abbott said. "He's a man of noble patience. Or Yankee cunning. Take your pick."

"Abbott, I've got to tell you this story."

"Basically, he wants to be one of the boys. Captain of the team, without being laughed at."

"Will you let me finish, for Christ's sake?" Fresh tears welled in Earl's eyes.

All right; Abbott settled himself resignedly on the edge of the bed. Who else in the world would listen?

"O-*kay*." Earl paused for a deep breath to steady his voice, and went on. "The girls dropped the family game. From then on, it was all *dog* game. I won't go into detail. But I remind you these are creative people. Sniffing around on all fours. Burying the bone—"

Abbott raised a hand. "I get the picture."

"The whole range of pet behavior and owner psychology. Okay? Now. To make a weird story short, one night we were out drinking with some friends. When the bars closed, the girls said, 'Earl, tonight we're going to abandon the dog.' We drove out to the highway and they shooed me out of my car."

"Shooed you?" Abbott tried to picture, from Earl's descriptions, the matronly Leah and the fey and lovely Charisse waving pugnacious little Earl out of his car.

"I *had* to," Earl said. "I had to go along with it. I'd lost my job, and these fruitcakes were my meal ticket, not to mention my sex life. They drove off, and I knew I'd have to leg it all the way back to the apartment. Follow their scent, you might say. I knew how the game should go. There'd be a reunion, a new place in their hearts—and elsewhere—for old Fido. But when I got there, they were gone."

Earl paused. Abbott waited.

"Split. Flew the coop. The kennel. It's a furnished apartment; all their personal stuff was gone. So was my car. There'd been some talk about New Orleans and other places but I'd never listened."

Abbott gazed at the floor. A shocker, this story, but no surprise.

Earl snuffled—it was laughter, not weeping. "Maybe they joined Sharon in Denver."

"That's not fair to Sharon. They joined the corn chip in Miami."

"The who?"

"The punk who taught you karate."

"Oh, *him.* Yes, in just one year, you see, my foundlings and/or their associates have robbed me blind."

"Exploited you," Abbott said.

"And so I got drunk. But now I'm seeing some poetry in it. Poetic justice. Also, there's the poetry of an absolutely fresh start. How many men are so lucky?"

"Burnout bungalow is rent-free," Abbott said.

"Thanks."

"Did you report the car theft?"

"I said it vanished from the parking lot. Why make

trouble for those crazies? All in all, we broke even."

"Noblesse oblige. Now, what's next?"

"Did you ever read T.S. Eliot?"

"No. Yes. Years ago. I said, what's next?"

"Eliot says old men should explore their origins. Discover themselves, sort of. The problem is, you might discover a platitude come to life. Do you know what I'm saying? After fifty years, you find out your life confirms some goddamn cliché."

"I've had that experience," Abbott said. "But by our age, who cares?"

"Let me finish. At our age we don't learn anything; we're just reminded."

Abbott reserved comment on this opinion.

"When I was a kid," Earl went on, "there was a saying: 'If you have your health, you have everything.' Now I think there's more truth than idiocy in that."

"So? Will you return to your oar at the *Call*?"

Earl closed his eyes and tasted his tongue in disgust. He said, "I'm talking about truth. You're still slow, Abbott, you've always been slow; you're not listening to me."

Abbott listened.

"Health!" Earl peered around the room again, as if for spies, and added, "Do me the decency of not laughing."

Abbott, bewildered, continued to listen.

"For years and years I've talked about getting in shape. Now it's my truth and my future."

Where, Abbott wondered, was this odd speech leading?

"What you see before you"—Earl tugged at the neck of his hospital johnny—"is a fitness freak."

"The Senior Olympics," Abbott fired back. Surely, Earl had launched nothing more or less than a vaudeville routine.

Wrong. Earl cried, "You're *laughing*, you sonofabitch," and he grabbed fistfuls of sheet at his sides, jerking himself into a sit-up, his face bristling inches from Abbott's. "You mustn't laugh!"

Abbott clasped Earl's upper arms to smother any feeble

punches. "I'm sorry! Fitness is *fine*."

"Don't patronize me, and don't laugh. Not you. You're the only guy in the world I'd tell this to, because you're the only guy I've ever known who is . . . " Earl took a deep breath and expelled it quickly. ". . . of whom it can be said, 'He's a gentleman.' " Earl shook himself free of Abbott's grip and fell back. He grabbed more tissues from the bedstand and swiped his wet cheeks. "Goddamn waterworks. It's the drugs."

"I understand. And thanks for the compliment. Must have hurt."

Earl pointed a cautionary finger. "Now don't kiss my ass."

"I'd rather kick it. Denham's waiting, and there's nowhere else to go. At least not until you become a lightweight contender."

"You're laughing again, goddamn it."

"Not really."

"No choice. Health clubs cost money."

"Maybe I'll tag along," Abbott said.

"Only obsessives need apply." Earl kept his face averted, mopping it with the wet wad.

"I might join for part of the ride," Abbott said.

"All right, join."

"A limited membership."

"Suit yourself." Earl sobbed—or laughed. "I'll sign you up for the shot put, big fella."

"The high jump," Abbott said, and he thought of Chocurua.

Why not? After some workouts, he might be able to do that modest peak in a hop, skip, and jump. Without a baby on his back.

31

Claire looked good.

No, not really good. Admit it. He preferred the Claire of the old days, middle-class matron in something subdued: a pantsuit or else an ice-cream-colored dress along with a cardigan to ward off a chill. This new Claire matched Heath's description: She wore a smock like those sack dresses of twenty years ago, swelled out by her bulk, and had her hair in a bandana like some Gypsy grandmother. An arty sort of getup, he supposed. He noticed an indentation of the left cheek, a slight sag of the leathery face there, caused maybe by the loss of teeth Heath had mentioned.

"You look good," he said, after they'd politely embraced and found a bench in the mall lobby.

"So do you!" She seemed truly pleased by what she saw. "You've lost weight."

Abbott looked down at himself. "Not enough."

"A lot. And Heath told me you quit smoking." Claire waved a brown-paper filtertip in her hand. "Wish I could. How's the—?" As if the word "heart" were unsayable, she patted herself on the breastbone.

"Still ticking," he said. "At last report."

"Still on Inderal?"

"They upped the dose a little. How's your breathing?"

She reached into her handbag and removed two vials for his inspection. "I had to cut down on my walks."

"I'm sorry to hear that. Once you did the whole National Seashore, and dragged me along. Kicking and screaming."

She smiled. "You didn't exactly kick and scream."

He asked, "Remember when the rangers caught us?"

Her smile flagged a little, implying that she had not driven here today, all the way down from the Cape, to play a game of Memory Lane. Abbott looked down at the vials she had handed him, tipping his head back to read the labels through his bifocals. "Slophyllin . . . Prednisone."

"Still the man of words," she said. "Half the time I forget how they're pronounced. The Prednisone's supposed to have dangerous side effects."

"Like what?"

"It's too early to tell." Claire tittered—a mimicry of girlish excitement as though an adventure lay in store with her medicines. He thought: Well then, they'd have a fresh topic to talk about next time they met, a new vein in the mine of a shared past. The shared past of a couple their age; imagine it: so much junk down there: the empty vials and old IDs, the spines and tinsel of old Christmas trees—a heap one would like somehow to reconstitute as a cause for celebration rather than regrets.

They could have met, he supposed, in a livelier place. He had chosen the mall because their bank had its offices there, and the closing for their house sale was scheduled in a few minutes. At this hour of the morning, the lobby was a haunt for the old. In mid-afternoon it would teem with suburban wives, and later with school kids, so-called "mall rats" hanging out, but for now Abbott saw only the elderly on the benches amid the potted trees and the window displays. Watching this crowd, he thought of pigeons in a public square—some of them meek, some cheeky. Faces ranged in expression from benign to agonized. Nearby, a woman presumably in her eighties quarreled to herself in two voices, one cajoling and the other spitting mad.

He and Claire eavesdropped, having exhausted the subject of their drugs. Claire translated the quarrel in a whisper. "She's peeved at her daughter. Seems her daughter dumped her here hours ago and went shopping. Poor thing."

"Look over there." Abbott inclined his head toward a man making what used to be called goo-goo eyes at a flustered little lady pretending not to notice. "Watch. He'll flash."

Claire didn't laugh. "Be charitable," she said, and gave a look of resignation, lips compressed and eyes wide. "Who are we to poke fun?"

Who, indeed? Who are the aging to smirk at the aged, like a young couple in a love story, presuming a special deliverance? Abbott had noticed that his and Claire's whispers were overloud. He thought of young couples whose being together is so intense, so full of jumpy awarenesses of each other, that their speech has the quality of relieved shouting. Two solitaries rediscovering their tongues together.

He spotted a Friendly's off the lobby. "How about an ice-cream cone?"

"Oh, no thanks."

"My treat."

She patted her thighs. "Too many calories."

He thought of suggesting a quick walk through the mall, but his heart would break should Claire the erstwhile hiker begin to puff. He wiggled on the bench, shifting hams like an adolescent who can't sit still. He could turn to her like an adolescent of the 1950s, facing a sweetheart after the afflatus is over, and voice the line of that period: "I hope we can still be friends."

Precisely. There she sat, his wife whom he had not seen in a year, planted solidly there, thick legs apart, a jaunty plodder like himself, like himself an S-curve of hump and paunch, although in her case this shape was less ugly than endearing.

Bapp sprang up in him. No shirker of opportunities, that re-invention of self performed an act akin to walking a long beach or climbing half a mountain. It reached over and took hold of Claire's hand.

She looked down, blankly, and leaned away a little as if to distance herself from the clasp. Then she relaxed and gave a half-smile. Abbott glimpsed in that smile Claire's own self-invention: a skeptical calm, an immunity to soap operas, even their own. She had earned . . . what could you call it? No. Call it better weather inside, still a trifle cold. She appraised him as if this Abbott was not quite the Abbott she remembered, and perhaps no improvement. This Abbott talked a bit much, squirmed with nervous energy, and played grab-hand.

He looked down at her hand. Now that he held it, what should he do? How about swinging their joined hands the way young couples do? This way and that—idly twisting the handhold like a crank, as if tinkering with the silence, trying to get himself and Claire aloft again, contained in some topic that could overfly the sadness of their quiet.

Then again, he could simply give up. He could use the clasp as a chin rest, propping his face on it as he sat forward on the bench, glumly surveying the mall and its old folks. He'd brush his lips against the linked fingers, back and forth, brooding.

No. All things considered, he'd hold hands sedately. He positioned the clasp between their bodies and slightly out to the front, to show anyone who cared that two adults were sharing mild affection, nothing more, no funny stuff.

He said, "Will you open another 'Wild Duck'?"

"What?"

"Will you open another shop?"

" 'Wild *Geese.*' "

"Of course. Sorry."

"I don't know. Maybe a school instead. I'm doing pretty well teaching."

In letters, she had divulged the business setbacks of her first year alone. Abbott relayed something Heath had told him: "Quilts are *in* now, just as you predicted."

Claire brightened. "I've sold some at shows."

"Any breakthroughs?"

"What do you mean?"

"You said you might invent something up there. Techniques."

"Well, I'm painting on wood and tin."

"Huh?"

"It's an old colonial craft. I'm doing new things with it. It might get popular."

Deliberatively, Abbott echoed, "Painting on wood and tin," but he followed through with no questions, and Claire provided no more details. She said, "How are things at the paper?"

"Remember Eddie? My assistant?"

"No."

"He went to Philadelphia. The *Inquirer*."

"Oh. Does he like it?"

"Haven't heard. Denham's wife is going to take his job; she wants to join the working world. She'll be my boss—*and* my trainee."

"Is that good or bad?"

"It's nepotism. And double dealing."

Claire looked puzzled.

"Denham outsmarted me," Abbott said, "that's all. Let's talk about something else."

He felt pressure against his fingers in the handclasp. Claire had squeezed. She said, "Do you miss Avery?"

"No. Not really. I'm still the babysitter, you know."

Family news! Why hadn't he thought of it! The gimmick for further talk, and no doubt the big story of years to come. "I do miss him at times. I used to push him in the stroller on hikes. Now I hike alone, and sometimes I catch myself holding my hands out in front of me, like this"—in demonstrating, Abbott released Claire's hand—"like this, like a dog begging. It's as though I'm still holding the bar of a stroller." Abbott laughed.

Claire nodded, bemused, maybe recalling little losses of

her own during Heath's progress through childhood, the shedding of selves. She said, "You'll get over it."

"I know." He thought of recapturing the hand but it had slid out of sight. Let it go. He said, "I'm still his refuge against the world. That's what a grandparent is."

"You think so? I don't think grandparents should interfere."

Claire kept smiling, but her words had blazoned a readiness to argue this point. Abbott skirted it. "They're alone now, you know—the family. Did you ever meet Noz?"

Claire crimped her smile. "No, and I haven't seen that hovel they live in. I worry about that."

"It's safe. Maybe we can help."

"Maybe."

"This Noz is a professional student," he said, "but a nice fellow. Tends bar nights. He moved out of the apartment even though it was his. He said Avery made too much noise for a daytime sleeper. So the family is alone now. Man, woman, and child under one roof—a nuclear family. That's pretty rare. Only sixteen percent left, I think."

"Do you think our nuclear family will ever get married?"

"I don't know. They talk about it. Do you think we'll ever get divorced?"

"Do you want to?"

"Seems a lot of bother," Abbot said. "And expense."

"My feelings, exactly. I'm very busy."

Abbott heard a shout—someone had called his name. He looked up and saw his lawyer and the realty agent at the door of the bank, waving to him. "Time," he said, and stood up, grunting from an unexpected stiffness of the joints. He extended an arm to Claire, who gripped it with a sigh of thankfulness for the support.

The ritual of a closing—hopefully, it wouldn't take long. He and Claire would sign many documents passed around at the big table in the conference room. A ritual like a high-stakes game of cards in which you don't know the rules although the money in the pot is yours and many take a cut. At this stage of their lives, however, he and Claire—good dues payers—would get to keep most of the pot.

And then Claire would drive home to the Cape to paint on wood and tin. And he'd drive home to his condo to write a "Grandfather Knows Best."

They took seats in the bank board room. Abbott slouched, resting his chin on steepled fingers. He mused as the room filled slowly with the signatories: the bankers and the lawyers, the agents, the buyers.

And then, after batting out a column, he'd hike. Cling to your habits. One-and-a-half miles out, one-and-a-half back. At last he'd reached three miles, the limit long ago prescribed by the doctor. It was tiresome, but who knows what you'll find, even on the most humdrum route. Curiosity: the deepest of human mysteries. If another Cheryl ever appeared—Sharon, rather, her name was Sharon; if another ever appeared—older, preferably—he wouldn't hesitate, this time, to ask where she worked and to buy her a Dairy Queen.

More people took seats at the table. Abbott leaned over to Claire and introduced her to the buyers, a fortyish couple who talked of their remodeling plans. The bank's lawyer began to pass out the documents to be signed. In legalese, he muttered explanations. Abbott, pen in hand, set himself to write many repetitions of his name.

Yes, cling to your habits. But don't let them robotize you. Was that the simple lesson he had learned? Practice variations. A mile-and-a-half out, a mile-and-a-half back, but from different starting points, different parking spaces. And as you plug along, try to feel unique, though you know you're only pedestrian (pardon the pun), and try to feel light, though you know you drag tail.

How's that for a philosophy of life?

All right, forget it.

Somebody was mumbling his name. Claire's voice. "Wes!" She nudged him. His lawyer joined in—"Wes, wait"—reaching over to grab a document freshly signed.

Hell! He, Abbott, had signed on the wrong line. A hurried conference ensued, joined by more of the signatories. One of them, for some strange reason, talked in a whisper behind his hand like a lawyer huddling in court, perhaps suggesting Abbott's committal. A verdict was reached. Abbott's lawyer patted him on the back. Claire whispered, not unkindly: "Wake up." The signature could be X'd out and another written above. Carry on.

Had he learned anything? Pursue this. Get back to the hike.

It would diminish, of course. Segment by segment. Sometime later, people would barge into his room and shout that he was one hundred years old—older, with any luck. They'd prop him up on pillows for a photographer, and a *Call* reporter would ask him the secret of longevity. Something would be propped in his paws—a telegram of congratulations from President Whoever. With the last of his strength he'd choke out a scream, the final complaint against a fate that, by all gut standards, is cruel and unusual. He should get the figures on it and write something.

No. Be honest. Know Thyself. If able, he'd act responsibly. He'd make wise use of the power of the dying. He'd give his survivors a farewell they could live with.

Yes. These musings called for another paragraph or two for the obituary that is always on file.

". . . At the end, Abbott did not rage against the dying of the light. 'Why be a pain in the ass,' he remarked, 'and worsen some nurse's hard day?'

"He went civilly . . ."